THE UNBROKEN QUEEN

THE BONE THRONE

TERINA ADAMS

Edits by Parisa Zolfaghari

Cover design Jensen Adams

AUTHOR'S NOTE

Hi Dear Read,

Thanks heaps for giving The Unbroken Queen a try. I hope Tressya's and Tamas's journey is one you'll fall in love with.

The Bone Throne series is planned as a trilogy, so sit tight there's more to come.

You can sign up to my newsletter if you're keen to be the first to hear about new releases, and to receive bonus scenes and extra freebies.

CHAPTER
ONE

TRESSYA

"What does the princess desire?" Carlin asked, twirling a long lock of my hair around his finger.

Lying naked atop him, savoring the warm, sticky sweat of our bodies, I gazed out the barn window at a dark cloud churning across the sky. "I need to try harder. I need to be better."

"You're perfect already."

I exhaled. "What?" I glanced down at him, momentarily disoriented, then smiled. *Don't lose this moment.* "I desire the freedom to marry whom I choose." I trailed my finger down his chest. "I have my eye on a certain carver."

My answer could have been more profound, a litany of words to make him wish he'd never asked, but those were secrets I could never share.

If only I could. Secrecy was one of the six pillars. Secrecy, discretion, loyalty... The foundations of my life sometimes felt like tar. *Damn it, no.* Not now. Not with Carlin. I always strove to keep these two parts of my life separate.

Carlin quirked an eyebrow. "I challenge that man to a duel." He finally laughed. "The princess asks too much. Why not a grand palace or a priceless jewel stolen from a mighty dragon's lair deep within the mountains?"

Struggling to find my way back to our moment, I pressed my palms to his chest and pushed up to straddle him. "Let me see." I mimed counting on my fingers. "I already have a palace, a box full of jewels, and there's no such thing as dragons."

Carlin caught my wrists as he rose in one swift motion, flipping me onto my back. The straw I now lay on itched my bare skin, but I didn't care. I wasn't sure when Carlin had stopped being fun and became a necessity. He was a dangerous distraction at a time when I could afford none. Would there ever be a right time?

He rolled on top of me, using his lean, muscular body to cage me beneath him. I entwined my legs around his waist as he raised my arms over my head, anchoring each other in place.

Coppery streaks ran through his lush brown hair like a smithy's molten pour. In these stolen moments, I always tangled my fingers in it, as if holding onto a moment soon to fade.

I was never meant to love. In this one thing, I would be selfish.

"The princess must ask for something within my reach if she has any hope of receiving it," he said.

It didn't matter that the sky threatened to unleash fury; Carlin's presence brought light into the stubborn darkness inside me.

"Can I ask for you?" It was both jest and a solemn request from a place in my heart I kept locked away. Like distraction, it was a weakness I couldn't afford.

I wrapped my arms around his shoulders and matched his gaze, inhaling the scent of sex, sweat, and Carlin: the sweet seed oil he used to protect the delicate wood carvings he lovingly fashioned, pouring a small part of himself into each one.

"Why ask for something you already have?" he replied.

His silvery-gray eyes stared into mine, creating a sting of pain in my heart at the conviction they held. Dismantled by his earnest gaze, I shifted my attention to the laden clouds before I ruined our stolen moment.

I can't have you. A poor stable boy, his bloodline offered nothing. I was a princess and a disciple; there would never be an 'us' beyond the secret moments we stole. He deserved happiness, and I was holding him back. Two years older than my twenty-three, he was of an age to be married. It was cruel to keep him to myself.

Carlin was everything I'd never had until the day I met him. He was gentle, kind, thoughtful beyond measure, compassionate to those less fortunate, and fiercely loyal to those he loved. Carlin knew his heart, and he loved me.

Loyalty and discipline, two more tenets of the six pillars; my purpose, my duty.

Carlin released my arms and stretched himself alongside me. Though he stood at my height, he was a half body's width wider. Lean muscles built from hard work, skin browned from days outdoors, hair sprinkled with sun-kissed love, Carlin was no gentleman wearing fine coats and gloves. Rather, he was born into poverty and raised in the hamlet closest to Aldorr Castle.

I closed my eyes, feeling the warmth of his body, following his finger in my mind as it feathered down my throat, between my breasts, and along my stomach to circle my belly button while I listened to the distance flock of frog-mouths sing their mournful song as they sought shelter away from the threat of rain.

I heard the rustle of hay, then felt his lips brush across my bare shoulder. "I have but one love."

I smiled without opening my eyes. "Your dog?"

"Hmm... I was thinking of something a little less slobbery."

"Your shoes?"

He trailed his lips across my shoulder to my throat, a languid trail sending warm tingles to my nipples. "Cuddlier."

"Your blanket?"

"Exactly," he whispered onto the skin at my nape.

I playfully smacked his shoulder and pushed him away so I could look into his muscovite eyes. It was my turn to twirl loose strands of hair, the untamed threads covering his brow. His hair was like him, beautiful yet unruly.

But I could never say the words he longed to hear, no matter that they grew within that place locked in my heart.

His face grew solemn, and I wanted to wipe it away and bring back my Carlin, the one who made my heart smile.

"I know things will change," he said.

I trailed my finger across his forehead. "Not my title. Or the expectations."

"We've survived both this last year," he continued.

"For as long as it takes, we'll survive more," I whispered against his lips. We both knew we were doomed. We only had our kisses, bodies, and words—and the silent promises neither of us could keep.

"Your Highness," Radnisa called from outside the stable door.

Carlin pulled away from my desperate kiss. "How does she do it?"

How did she find us every time, regardless of our caution? I wouldn't tell him, and it wasn't a lie because half the time I asked the same question.

My lady-in-waiting disapproved of Carlin, disapproved of all my activities beyond my official duties. Her husband, Baron Ledredon, had the ear of my father, the king, and sat within his council. Even so, I trusted Radnisa would keep this secret because she had far too many secrets of her own.

"Shh," Carlin whispered, pressing a finger to my lips. "You're not here."

I gently pulled his finger away. "I can't escape my father nor the Sistern. Radnisa would not disturb me if it were neither."

With a sigh of surrender, Carlin rolled to the side and slid from between my legs, allowing the cool breeze to replace the warmth of his body. Already, I ached to be with him again; already I counted the days.

Carlin tried to shake the volumes of my dress straight

and plucked random strands of straw from between the stays while I slipped into my undergarments.

"Your Highness." Radnisa's voice was more insistent this time.

Carlin screwed up his face, mimicking her call, not bothering to hide his loathing. Though they rarely spoke, it was in the looks they exchanged their mutual disrespect for each other.

I giggled and kissed him to silence, then extracted myself from his greedy, grasping hands and moved toward the ladder. Carlin rushed to head me off, grabbing my waist and spinning me around, then proceeded to gather armfuls of my dress and tuck them into my undergarments, creating a billowing effect at my middle.

"I won't have you trip and break your royal neck." Then he seized my cheeks between his palms and kissed me as if he could force me to stay. And I felt the lure. For one precious moment, I tumbled into the fantasy that I could hide up here with him forever.

The fantasy didn't last. I pulled away from his kiss. "I have to go."

"I know," he whispered back.

I didn't look at him again. The moment was gone.

The ladder was an easy descent, even with my ridiculous skirts. At the bottom, I loosened everything from my undergarments and hastened to the stable door, straightening my clothes and hair as best I could. When I reached the doorway, I was once again Princess Tressya.

Radnisa's back was to me when I stepped outside. She glanced over her shoulder, her lips pinched tight, then slowly her gaze worked its way down from my face to the front of my dress, her lip curling in disdain. She was taller than me, her back straighter, her bearing more dignified, and her eyes sharper. And she was a snake.

"Your dress is not fit to be seen."

I glanced down, stroking the front of my skirt with no hope of smoothing it out.

"There's hay in your hair."

"Oh?" I ran my fingers through my hair, convinced I had rescued every strand, but found some speared through the elaborate braid behind my ear.

She heaved a sigh, seeming to grow even taller with her exhale. "You have no time to make yourself more presentable. The Mother Divine is here."

My hands froze midway through my hair. "What?"

"You have kept her waiting." Radnisa's cat-like eyes of watery green sliced across to me before she turned away, dismissing me with that one move. "She's most displeased."

"I'll head there now." I gathered my skirts, readying for my dash.

"Advisable." She scrutinized my crinkled dress one more time, and already I could see the Mother's displeasure through Radnisa's eyes.

I fled toward Aldorr Castle, leaving Radnisa behind to pick her way with more care across the sodden yards of the stables. The young goats galloped alongside their pens as I hurried past, scattering ducks and clucking chickens in a flurry of feathers. My shoes sunk into the sludge, as did my skirts, roughly gathered in my arms.

The gentle slope upward toward the church hampered

my pace as I ran across the lush green lawn. The bone-white marble of Aldorr Castle tinged a sickly light gray against the ominous clouds, threatening to loosen their load.

A guard stumbled out of his post in the brick wall as I fled past and dashed underneath Staffork Bridge in a flurry of mud-stained skirts. I was gasping for breath when I turned right at the cobbled courtyard, the small chapel, tucked close to the servants' quarters, now in sight.

When I finally reached the chapel doors, I took a moment to release my skirts and tidy myself, then covered my nose with my hands and inhaled deeply. The smell of Carlin remained deep within the tiny creases lining the skin on my palms. One inhale for fortitude. And one for me.

Once my breathing leveled, I pushed open the old wooden doors and entered the small, ill-used chapel. King Regnier built the chapel for his long-dead queen, or so everyone thought—I happened to know it was for another woman entirely. Now he had little time or patience for cleansing his soul. Everyone within his household shared his lack of faith with enthusiasm, so the cobwebs hung across the narthex like the massive chandeliers adorning the king's ballroom.

Mother Divine stood at the front, staring up at Goddess Eheia, whose piety and benevolence to the ostracized and poor saw her rejected by her cruel lover, Dadteus, God of hunters, fighters, and all things unjust. I suspected Father only kept Eheia in her place within this chapel to ease his guilty conscience.

The small arched window on the left drew in little light, shrouding the Mother in the chapel's gloom. Few ever bothered to light the candles. Dressed entirely in black, she formed a dark contrast to Eheia's marble white. Her appearance was not the only stark divide between the two women. Without looking away from Eheia, Mother Divine eased herself back into the front pew and awaited my arrival.

I came around to stand in front of the Mother, slipping to my knees at the last and leaning forward to kiss the emerald stone on her ring.

"Mother, I would've come earlier—"

"You still waste your time with that boy?"

I stayed on my knees, feeling the heat of her gaze as I stared at the worn stone floor. I didn't need to look to see the condescension she wore in her expression. Her eyes were like a hawk's, so dark at first glance they seemed black, and all-seeing.

"I take my tinctures nightly. There'll be no mistakes." Hearing the defense in my voice, I fisted my hands at my sides.

I heard the thunk of the church door closing. Radnisa had already arrived. She must have also rushed here, not wanting to miss a single punitive word the Mother said.

"Make sure of it. Nobody loves a bastard."

The word was like a slap to my face. With a sharp inhale, I pulled my shoulders back and lifted my head to meet her disapproving gaze. Dark-lined eyes, recessed deep under her brow, stared back at me, unblinking. Her elaborate headdress created more shadows across her face, hiding the myriad of creases chiseled from decades of disapproval and the strain of bearing the weight of Mother Divine to the Sistern of Silence.

The king acknowledged me as his daughter out of devotion to his lost love, my mother his mistress, and not out of compassion for me. It mattered little because the Mother rescued me from the disgraced life of a bastard child by accepting me into the Sistern, teaching me their practices and disciplines. An ice heart like the Mother's was needed to become an exemplar of the six pillars and master of soul voice.

I needed the six pillars, just as I needed the Mother's teachings, and the strength and power they gave me to survive the cruelty of my life. In the Sistern, I learned a great many things, but most importantly how to shield my heart.

I resisted the urge to glance over my shoulder, knowing Radnisa had positioned herself behind me. Judging from the rustle of her skirt, she had moved close.

"Of course, Mother. I'll never forget."

"Twenty-three years. It's time you fulfill your duty to the Sistern."

"I practice the disciplines every day, Mother. My duty lives in the front of my mind. As always. I'm a disciple before all else." I disappointed the Mother and myself every day I failed to achieve the disciplines to satisfaction.

I should've released Carlin long ago.

"As your mother would have you be." Her eyes narrowed, slitting like a cat. "Remember that." My birth mother was the perfect disciple—unlike me. That was the only piece of information about her the Mother shared.

Her gaze traveled over the top of me, meeting Radnisa's behind. The first prickles of tension coiled their way through my stomach and across my shoulders.

"King Regnier has made his decision. He signs his alliance as I speak. But I'll not have my plans ruined."

I stayed silent, wondering what she was talking about. As disciples, our purpose was to obey, never question or try to understand. I knew the Mother would reveal her reason for traveling to Aldorr Castle at her discretion, disclosing her intentions when she deemed necessary. Most of the time, she let little slip. It must have something to do with the king's eldest daughter, my half-sister, Edilene, because the Mother never interested herself with matters concerning men.

"I give my life to your service," I repeated, not for the first time and never for the last.

"Repeat the six pillars."

"Loyalty, discipline, courage, precision, secrecy, discretion."

"Loyalty."

"To the Mother Divine, then to one's sisters. Finally, to oneself."

"Discipline."

"Steadfast mind and fearless heart through rigorous training."

"Courage."

"Never waver from what must be done."

The chapel's creaking side door shattered the silence that followed. I held my breath, unclenching my palms to feel the clamminess of my sweat. The soft tread of slipped feet across the stone floor flurried an itch up my neck. I longed to look over my shoulder but held the Mother's gaze, as was expected of me.

All my attention remained on the newcomer and Radnisa behind me. Now there were two of them: one so close a single slice was all she needed, the other carrying more hatred in her veins than blood.

"Precision." The pillars were now forced into the recesses of my mind.

I struggled to wrench it forward. "Never miss," I whispered.

The rustling of fabric alerted me to Radnisa's attack. I caught the flurry of movement in my periphery, already raising my arm to defend. I dropped to my knees and swiveled, blocking her strike with my forearm, then knocking her blade sideways.

With her hold firm on the hilt, she countered with a fierce jab forward, but I was already on my feet and dancing to the side.

Her striking arm inhibited by her position next to me, I came in with my elbow, jabbing her hard on the back of her shoulder. Her weight caved forward and her grip loosened on the blade, sending it clattering to the stones.

Defeating Radnisa wasn't easy. She went with her fall, swiping the blade from the ground before I could reach it, and rolled to her feet. But I was already barreling toward her. I kicked her in the stomach, and my skirts flared, momentarily hindering my vision.

Still coming to her feet, the kick destroyed her balance. Radnisa went backward, losing the blade once more. I rushed for it, but another caught the blade mid-air.

Edilene swiped up in a small arc, catching me on the lower arm. I bit back my cry and danced out of her reach. But

Edilene was a vicious fighter when it came to me, and she charged forward with a flurry of strikes that I was powerless to avoid. She nicked the back of my jaw, a carefully placed cut that no one would see to teach me a lesson.

I jerked my head away from her next slice, evading another counter stab by arching my body away. Cutting off Edilene's advantage was the only way to defeat her, moving forward instead of backward, marrying the delicate balance between discipline, precision, and courage.

Escaping her jabs, I rushed toward the altar and swiped up the candelabra from its setting, its candles falling to the ground. She smirked at me as she crossed the blade from one hand to the other, her usual taunt.

"Really, sister? That's all you can do. No wonder your mother left you. You're pathetic."

My mother died birthing me. Hardly a choice, but I wouldn't bother to speak it.

I shook her words aside and concentrated on the task at hand. When she believed she'd won, the words flowed, and right now, Edilene smelled her victory. Speaking was a distraction, dividing my focus from my target, so my habit was silence. Instead, I watched her eyes, her shoulders, her chest—the details that signaled her next strike the moment she set the intention—ensuring I moved in opposition before she had even begun.

"I might just chop it into little pieces."

I tore at the hem of my skirts, dismantling the lace and undergarments, anything that hindered my movement. Miraculously, she patiently watched as I freed my legs.

Edilene was bold, overly so, for a good reason. She was

good. Better than me. Something she made sure I knew. Repeatedly. But I was determined, maybe more so than she. Too many times I'd proven myself unworthy in the Mother Divine's eyes, too many stings regardless of how shielded I thought my heart to be. I couldn't surrender.

Courage, discipline, precision. Of the six pillars, I held those three to my chest as tightly as I held my name, my title, my life.

"Or better still, I'll chop you into little pieces. How about your ear goes first?"

I matched her step for step as we circled each other. She was a caged lion, roar and jaws, bold and strong. I was a weasel, silent and adaptable, slippery and fast.

"Hmm," she crooned, dropping her sure-footed tread for a swagger. "You'll counter my right jab, move in low with a swift strike. But... if I were to wield two." She slipped a knife down her sleeve from under her cloak. "Then I'll be ready for your counter move."

Edilene was the one person who could sharpen my focus into a blade. By this stage, she had latched her focus onto me, giving me little of the valuable information I needed. Instead, I narrowed my concentration on her shoulders and chest, hoping to find a sign of which way she would strike. If she thought to strike with her left, it would begin with a twitch on the left side of her chest, echoing up into her shoulder before she moved her arm. Once I caught the subtle shift, my peripheral focus would drop to her legs in case she intended to follow through with a kick.

She read me as closely as I read her. The stark difference between us narrowed down to one thing: Edilene believed in her ability and worth far greater than me, to her benefit and detriment. Right now, I saw in her crystal-blue eyes a hatred foreign on such a beautiful face. Her hatred made her a dirty enemy. Though sometimes it made her desperate and foolish.

Today was different. There was something maniacal about her expression, an unsettling darkness behind her glare, twisting the solemnity on her face, the grace in her movements. There was no understanding Edilene's moods, and today she was sniffing my blood. When she stopped taunting, it was time to pay attention.

The first strike caught me off guard. She muffled her clues, but years of fighting against her meant there was little she could throw at me I wasn't ready to face.

I absorbed her strike, allowing her to get close before I swooped low and lashed out with my candelabra. Rather than blocking, I dove forward, aiming for her stomach, one fierce, fast jab before I dropped to the ground, feeling the swift shimmer of air overhead as she struck with the second blade.

Her furious cry and equally furious kick to my back followed as I rolled away. The impact sent me scrambling forward, tripping on the remaining hem of my skirts and tearing the last strips of fabric. Edilene arrived prepared, dressed in pantaloons, easily disguised under volumes of skirts she must have subtly discarded before entering the chapel. In short, Edilene came for this.

The fabric hindered my escape. My feet disappeared in a tangle of expensive lace, so I gave in and dropped into another roll, desperate to free my feet.

Edilene spared no time, striking me on the back of my elbow, one more streak of blood to smatter the pale green of my gown. I hissed through the sharp arrow of pain and came up in a semi-turn, with the candelabra, slamming it into her knee. She doubled back, her left leg buckling.

Already, I was on my feet, rushing forward, sending her blade clattering to the stone with a blow across her right arm. I came in too close, though, and Edilene's boot struck my side, sending a jolt of pain into my chest.

Gasping in shallow breaths through the pain, I struck again, using both hands to support the weight of the candelabra, now feeling like lead. I doubled my attack. As my desperation grew, I lost sight of the single most important pillar during a fight: *precision*. My strikes were wild, as frenzied as Edilene's had been at the start. She only needed to dodge until I burned myself out in my pain.

Instead, she continued to fight, perhaps sensing my end. In her fierce will to ground me out so thoroughly before the Mother, she became foolish, placing herself too close. I rewarded her mistake with a powerful blow of the candelabra to the back of her head.

Edilene lost her blades and her footing, tumbling forward to her knees. The edge of the candelabra was smeared with her blood, as was her silvery hair, now loosened from its elaborate knot.

I stepped forward, lifting the candelabra for my final strike. Nothing was ever decided until your opponent couldn't rise again; at least not so soon.

"*Aetherius*," Edilene shrieked.

The word punched through my heart, encasing my body

in a cast of stone. The candelabra remained poised in the air, but I was powerless to finish my strike.

"Your knees," Edilene snarled, clutching the back of her head while staggering to her feet. Her eyes, described by many suitors as jewels worth stealing, along with her heart, now flashed with a deathly fury.

"Get on your knees," she commanded.

Powerless, I succumbed. Though my mind screamed against its cage, my body was a victim to her demand.

Edilene used soul voice against me. In front of the Mother.

The candelabra clanked to the floor as I fell to my knees, already rerunning our fight through my mind, retracing every step I took, trying to determine other moves I could have made that would have silenced her before she uttered my soul word.

Loyalty, one of the greatest pillars, was for the Mother, but also the Sistern. It was forbidden to use another sister's soul word against her. In her rage, Edilene had broken the rule, hoping to reveal my biggest weakness: I had yet to master any defense against my soul word, that one undecipherable word that ruled my soul and rendered me powerless against the wielder of the word.

And while I could still speak, for now, I would not accuse her or look to the Mother for help. Pleading for the Mother's interference was a weakness I would never show.

Unsteady on her feet, she stumbled toward me, trailing blood as she came. On my knees before her, I was powerless to do anything more than accept the blow she gave to my left cheek.

"Enough," barked the Mother. "Bring her forth."

I had forgotten about Radnisa until she appeared beside me. Both she and Edilene clutched me under my arms and hauled me the short distance to the Mother, my feet dragging behind me. They shoved me into the Mother's lap, wrenching my arms out on either side of me at painful angles.

"You are of my making, but you're ill-prepared as you are," the Mother snapped down at me, her voice filled with the bitterness of tasting tart fruit. "Bare her chest."

It was Edilene's rough hands that tugged at my bodice, ripping the front garments right down to my chemise, pushing the fabric aside to expose the skin above my left breast.

I pressed my lips together, holding in my protests. Instead, I looked up into the Mother's dark eyes and refused to shift my gaze when I caught the glint of the blade in her hand.

"Prove to me your mother's sacrifice was not in vain."

And she slashed across the skin above my left breast with the small blade. I would not squeeze my eyes closed in reaction to the pain. Instead, I inhaled deeply. Neither would I look away. I held the Mother's eyes, my breathing growing faster as the flush of panic screamed at me to fight. Edilene tightened her hold on my arm, feeling the tension build in my muscles.

"Turn her face away," the Mother continued.

Edilene seized my chin and yanked my face toward her, forcing my eyes to meet the cold shards of her gaze. She didn't smile at my suffering, not even at the sudden burn, like a branding iron, spearing into my open wound that made me press my lips together hard enough to taste the iron of my blood. Instead, her fawn-like eyes narrowed into daggers, her features becoming the branding iron itself, marking me as her enemy until we were nothing more than aged bones in the ground.

A writhing, oily black mist clutched against my throat, scorching its wriggling filaments along my chin and down my neck, as if fighting against the Mother as she worked it down into my wound.

I inhaled but could no longer find the air to fill my lungs. The mist was suffocating, like hands at my throat.

I tried to steady the wild seizure threatening to blanket my head, but my fear was slowly winning.

Let courage become me.

As the agony splintered my mind, I couldn't control my focus enough to feel the words settle inside of me. The restraint of withholding my cry tore at my throat. Instead, I felt Edilene's fingers press against my skin as she held my head in place, digging her nails into my jaw.

Then, as suddenly as the attack began, it ended. Edilene and Radnisa released me, sending me backward onto my ass at the feet of the Mother, who glared down at me with merciless judgment.

I shuffled backward, glancing down at my bleeding wound with its blackened edges, seeping a watery gray fluid. The throb pounded through my head. I swallowed to settle the wild rage of my heart and peered up at the Mother, then flicked my eyes to Edilene and Radnisa standing on either side of the Mother.

"You think me without heart?"

"Never, Mother."

"Come here."

Head bowed as I kneeled before her, I held my breath at the first touch of her finger under my chin. She tilted my head up. "I have not spared you from the hardships of your life for good reason."

"There is no success without sacrifice and pain."

"As a woman that's especially true. Few woman have any power in this world, but with the six pillars as your shield none can touch you." She leaned down and placed her hand gently over my heart. "Always remember that."

"As a loathed bastard your life has known much suffering, but within the Sistern you're more than an illegitimate daughter."

"Every day I'm grateful for what you've given me."

"Your mother chose this life for you. It was her gift to you. The six pillars are mine."

"I hold it in my heart."

She glanced at my wound. "Now I have raised you above the rest of your sisters."

I faltered before replying. "Thank you, Mother." What had she done to me?

"Repeat the third pillar to me again."

"Courage. Never waver from what must be done."

She nodded. "We all must sacrifice ourselves for the might of the Sistern. Live by the six pillars and you'll succeed. Your duty to the Sistern has just begun. Go."

I burned to know what the Mother had put in me, but neither Edilene nor Radnisa would tell me, if they even knew. The three of us were not of the first order, those within the inner circle, the closest to the Mother Divine, and so the two of them would simply accept the Mother's actions as a necessity to further the Sistern's purpose.

I dragged my feet underneath me, getting caught in more of my tattered hem. The ragged edges of my torn skirts dusted the stone as I retreated down the church aisle.

"The first pillar, Tressya," the Mother called before I made it halfway.

I didn't look around as I replied. "Loyalty."

"The Sistern are you family."

"Always, Mother."

Outside, the gloom of early evening swallowed my disheveled appearance and my fear. I took a moment to stand outside the door and steady myself, the shuddering echo of my soul word still slowing my mind and body as if I was encased in bands of iron. I regretted my choice when Edilene appeared. It was too late, but I would not walk away. Instead, I looked over my shoulder at her.

She stepped in front of me, this time leaning down so I could see the bands of white slicing across the blue in her eyes, giving them the appearance of fractured glass. "You stole from me." She jabbed at her chest. "It was meant to be me. I will make sure you pay for this. That is my solemn vow."

Everything about me, who I was, my lowly status within the palace, including my possessions, was stolen from Edilene, according to her, even though our father held her in greater esteem.

She blocked my path for moments more, ensuring I understood how deep her venom ran before turning away.

I watched her leave, wondering what this destiny was that she wanted so badly. I rubbed around the wound on my chest, feeling it throb still.

Whatever the fate, it was now mine. For the Mother, and for my birth mother, I would fulfill my duty.

CHAPTER

TWO

TAMAS

THERE WERE STILL spaces within the feasting hall of Ironhelm
—vacancies that the clan heads should have filled. The
central fire roared, its flames licking the open cavity in the
roof and disappearing into the clear night sky. However,
nothing could dim the raucous noise driven by more than a
hundred men, drowning in a belly full of ale. My feasting hall
was the largest north of the Saiguaina River, and tonight, the
rousing company filled it to overflowing.

My gaze followed a young woman across the room as she
carried full tankards with both hands, sloshing ale with
every nimble sashay she made in trying to evade greedy
hands. Mesmerized by the delicate sway of her hips, I failed
to notice Garrat, my second-in-command, move in beside
me. He slunk down into the seat next to me and followed my
gaze to the young woman before us, now laughing with

Hedwreic, one of my best—powerful with an axe, strong with his fists, and loyal in his heart. If he won the lass tonight, he deserved her.

"Meechep's daughter. Hedwreic will lose a hand if Meechep weren't stuck in his bed tonight."

I huffed a laugh. "Then Hedwreic had better make the most of his night."

"She's a willing young thing. Rumor has it she'll do more than one man at a time."

I nodded, finding more interest in her with each revelation. "And you've come here to give me details of my next bed partner?"

"Nay, I'm here to tell you five of the largest clans have come tonight."

I eased back into my seat. I called it a seat, even when Garrat insisted I should think of it as a throne—something I wasn't prepared to do, not yet, not at Ironhelm. Perhaps the day would come when I called my seat my throne, but that day was not now.

"I see the lower mountain clans, but I don't see Kaldor."

"It appears he's not made the journey."

I wanted the allegiance of all the clans. Failing that, I wanted the best. Wildelm was the strongest clan on the southern side of the Draghunn Mountains, one I wanted on my side, but Kaldor was unyielding, volatile, and more often than not, untrustworthy. His ruthlessness made him a prime pick, though he would want more than promises of glory if I were to gain his alliance. And definitely more than a generous feast, shared tales, more ale, and more willing women than any man could handle in one night to lure him to my table. But I knew Kaldor's weaknesses. Perhaps I would have Garrat pay a visit to Ledbric Hall in person with more pleasing bribes.

For the moment, I couldn't offer promises of glory. My only offer was hope and possible death on a blood-scarred battlefield, if we even managed to cross the dividing river and traverse the wasteland known as the Ashenlands.

More worrying was the absence of the Huungardred; that I had not expected. Thaindrus was a good and loyal friend, a blood relative. A little distant, granted, but with the Huungardred, blood bonds were life bonds of servitude and loyalty. Beyond all others, I had expected him to be the first to arrive at Ironhelm.

"Send someone to Droshrar. I'm worried about my dear friend."

"I'll dispatch someone first thing tomorrow."

"Tonight. Tomorrow he won't know his ass from his horse's."

Garrat snorted a laugh, then leaned away to wave young Idrus over. The young lad had not long left his mother's skirts but was eager to prove his worth. He was fast and agile, despite lacking skill with a sword, and not so battle-weary to dismiss leaving his seat, abandoning the plump young woman to run a night errand for his liege.

Distracted once again by Meechep's daughter, agile in her steps to dodge a grope at her left breast, I had missed Aric's approach.

"Tamas Savant of the Razohan." He performed a mock bow with a great deal of effort, given he had downed nearly twice his weight in ale. I knew because I'd kept a keen eye on the clan leaders attending tonight, noting who partook of my generosity and who withheld.

"Aric Khildron, you are welcome at my feast." Aric, the clan head of Ebonthorn, had once shown great courage on the battlefield. His now rounded belly had blunted his skill with a sword, but, like all clan heads, his mood could change quicker than the wind. With advancing years, he had taken to mastering other talents, namely political artifice and the occasional poisoning. 'Tame' was not a word that sat comfortably on the shoulders of anyone sitting at my feasting tables tonight. That's why I needed them.

The Ebonthorn controlled the lands abutting the Draghunn Mountains to the east, stretching down to the river Lanrial—a vast expanse of fertile plains ensuring the clan's iron grip on grain trade.

"I hear you're expecting another littlun."

If rumors were to be believed, Aric had fathered more children than he had men in his service. His wife had reportedly stopped taking them in when the number reached twenty.

"A babe in their belly will keep them by your side."

I wouldn't ask what Arietta should do to keep him by her side.

"She insisted on coming, but the journey's too arduous for one so far along." He took another swig from his tankard. "So tell me, Tamas Savant, what brings us such a plentiful feast and fine ale?"

"You have just arrived, Aric, my friend. Let tonight be for feasting and fun. Tomorrow, we shall talk of more serious matters."

"Aye, I have a hankering for trivial pursuits tonight. No war talk when there is a belly to fill." He patted his generous girth and took more ale.

Of course, he would think my call to the clan heads would be for one goal, and he was right to assume so.

After wiping his mouth on his sleeve, Aric refocused on me. His brown eyes appraised me as best they could, considering I was perhaps nothing more than a blur of heads dancing before his vision. He stamped a foot atop the lip of the platform upon which my chair sat and leaned his arm across his thigh.

"Young Tamas of the Razohan..." He nodded his head as if he had already finished what he meant to say.

Elbow leaning on my armrest, I smiled behind my fingers as I rested my head in my palm, waiting to see if he could gather his wits to continue.

"The Ebonthorn will ride with you against King Henricus. That I swear on my father's bones."

It was fortunate the House of Tannard had already dared to make incursions into the northern realm, protected from the vile creatures roaming the Ashenlands by their foul wizards, the Creed of Salmun. I doubted the clans would welcome news of war against the south otherwise. Those here tonight were among those most affected by Henricus's incursions. I already knew I would have their allegiance.

"Your offer means a great deal to me."

"Your generosity to my clan..." He swayed on his feet as he half-spun, waving his arm as if to include the rest of the room in his speech. "To all the clans present here tonight and those yet to come. The courage and loyalty you've shown to all the northern peoples against the south will win you men and women willing to fight by your side."

While they all willingly swore allegiance, the northern clans' loyalty stayed within their pockets and rarely reached their hearts. As long as King Henricus claimed an enemy of the northern region, the clans were mine, but his coin shone brighter than gold in the ground. Northern clans knew how to survive in a land that refused to be tamed. They did so through cunning, tenacity, and true fealty to themselves alone; I was not so naive to believe I wouldn't find an enemy within my own home.

I rose from my seat and stepped down, bringing us to eye level, though I was a good head taller than the Ebonthorn clan leader, and embraced the older man. "A strong life to you and your people."

Aric clapped me on the back. "And a great victory to yours. For all our sakes."

Upon releasing Aric's embrace, I found Osmud waiting to the side of us. It was his solemn expression that caught me in place for seconds before I released Aric's arm. "There's more ale at your table."

"Now that's a feast." Aric laughed and staggered away.

Free of Aric, I gave Osmud my full attention. As youngsters, Osmud and Garrat had stepped out of the forest one day, ragged, thin, and close to death. Neither spoke and were thought to be mute for the first year of their new lives in Razohan. Back then, and as adults, they had no memory of their time before they found us, so it seemed their complete lineage would never be known. However, the Razohan know their own; the ancestral links to the Huungardred could never be hidden.

Osmud was sober, as I expected of my men during these times.

"The Nazeen is here," Osmud said.

"And you welcomed her inside?"

Romelda was not one for friendships or gaiety.

He did not respond to my snide remark. "She awaits you outside."

As I expected she would. "I don't suppose she shared her reason for ruining my night."

"Tamas," Osmud admonished me, something he could do as one of my closest. "Her presence here must be important."

"To inflict upon me more ill omens."

Osmud grabbed my wrist as I turned back to my seat. "To tell you the truth you refuse to hear."

"Truth according to the Nazeen. I'm growing tired of listening to the witches." I was growing tired of the nagging guilt she made me feel.

"As I'm sure Romelda grows tired of your bullheaded stupidity."

"Careful, brother, I may decide Loireen is more to my taste than I did the last time we met."

Loireen was Osmud's new flame. She had chased me with a vengeance, but after I declined her again and again, she focused on Osmud. He'd been smitten with her since he spilled his drink on her during a game of Gambits Quest.

"I'd like to see you try. You're long behind her."

I huffed a laugh, knowing he would be right. It had been

a long time since any woman caught my attention for more than one night, and I wasn't complaining. Neither were any of my men who benefited from the fallout.

"I'll see her. But only for a moment. I need to speak with the clan leaders."

"Your time for that is tomorrow."

"Tomorrow is for politics. Tonight is for reminding them all who still holds the greatest feasts." I leaned closer to Osmud, hinting at a secret. "Subtle persuasion at the bottom of a tankard."

And still his solemn expression remained. Osmud took the augury more seriously than I.

It's not that I claimed Romelda's inciting a fake; I believed every word. But I was not yet whom she foresaw me to be. Maybe I never would be. At twenty-seven I still felt unready. How many generations had come and gone? Yet Romelda proclaimed I was the one. She knew my history, what I had done, yet that did not dissuade her. "You think they'll listen to you now? Look around you, Tamas, they can't even stand on their own two feet."

I grunted, disliking that he was right, also disliking what the Nazeen was here to say; the same thing she said the last time she came to me. She spoke an uncomfortable truth that I feared was upon me already, even if in my heart I tried to refuse it.

Osmud patted my shoulder as I pushed past him and headed for the side entrance. A long, narrow corridor led into the castle proper, separating the grand hall from Ironhelm. It was the only entrance from the feasting hall into the castle, and tonight I'd stationed my men at every exit, and hidden throughout. It paid to be cautious without appearing to be cautious.

I pushed out into the night air, feeling the ice chill common when the winds turned toward us after sweeping off the Draghunn Mountains many leagues to the west. The skin on my face tightened to the bite after the warmth from the fire, and I wished the Nazeen would, for once, accept my hospitality and come inside. She always refused, saying Nazeen feared entrapment from the four walls of men.

Their magic was untamed magic, gathered from the very earth and air surrounding us, and should never be considered human-bound. The Nazeen lived wild, lonely lives, like some shy forest creatures. Even so, they were deeply respected and sometimes feared by the clans of the north, except the Razohan, who the Nazeen seemed to favor second to the Huungardred.

Romelda had her back to me as I left the warmth and rowdy merriment of the feasting hall and approached, pulling my fur-lined coat closer. She continued to dismiss my arrival, staring up at the moon, and I wondered what she read in the discoloration on its surface.

"I hear you've refused my hospitality," I said.

She didn't turn to face me but waited for me to join her. "How many have come?"

"Most of the clan heads from the lower regions. Some from the deep north," I replied. Surprising for this time of year as the roads were nearly impassable this late in the season.

"Thaindrus?" she inquired.

"Not to be seen," I said. "I've already sent a rider to

Droshrar."

"I fear his time grows near."

I could only nod, knowing she was right, not wanting to accept that inevitability. "This is why you have come to see me?"

There was silence when I expected her reply. As a man, my eyes weren't as strong in the moonlight as my blood relative, the Huungardred, but all I had for now was her profile as she continued to stare at the moon. Nazeen weren't augurs. They did not divine the future but had an eerie sense of knowing all the same. I was often uncomfortable during our silences, left wondering what unseen omens or spirits Romelda sought in the quiet.

Slowly, she turned to face me, and I thanked the night sky for shielding her expression. Romelda's eyes were the color of blood, unique to some of the Nazeen. Legend had it the blood-soaked eyes of a Nazeen signified true loyalty to the Bone Throne, marking her as a descendant of the witches who once fought against the sea invaders, the Levenians.

For their loyalty to the last king of the Bone Throne, King Ricaud, the Nazeen paid a price—the blood-soaked eyes, their curse. But not all the Nazeen took the oath. Romelda had taken the oath, she was a blooded, accepting her place in an unbroken bond to the true heir who would rise again one day.

I knew the tale. During the Levenian war, King Ricaud sent his only child, Princess Ammelle, into the far eastern demesne of Strathembrook. On King Ricaud's death, the Nazeen fled to the far north with Ammelle and buried her deep within Huungardred lands. Ammelle's granddaughter,

Sophila, began the Razohan line when she fell in love with the then Huungardred principle, Makyelus. As Razohan we were descendant of that line, and the blood-eyed Nazeen marked me as the heir to the Bone Throne. Romelda had sought confirmation of my destiny with the augurs and divined it in other magical ways only the Nazeen understood.

She came to me this night for the same reason she hunted me down when I was a boy, for the same reason she haunted my days in manhood and would continue to be my ghost long after I passed from this world if I failed. Over the years, with each successive visit, the conviction in her heart slowly broke me down.

She wanted me to reclaim my rightful place as heir to King Ricard's line. Which meant war with our powerful neighbors the House of Tannard, the current claimants to the Bone Throne.

"I ask you to travel with me."

I inwardly groaned. "Not the augur?"

Augurs' sight was beyond many, but this made them mad. Most of the time, their prophetic babble was nothing more than the wanderings of insanity.

She stepped toward me. "The time is fast approaching, Tamas. I want you to hear what he has to say."

"I don't need to hear it." Lately, I felt a quickening in my veins at any mention of the Bone Throne. Stirring thoughts kept me awake most nights. A relentless prowling took root in my legs. My hands itched to grip my sword. The Etherweave was now calling to me and no one else in my clan, proof I was the true heir.

"Many of the clan heads did not come. I need time to travel the northern lands. Speak with them."

"There is no time for—"

"You want me to destroy the House of Tannard. I can't do that without men when Henricus's legions are many. I can't hope to win against such a force without the united might of the north. And beside him march the Creed of Salmun. As I stand now, I offer my men, and any who fight with me, for the slaughter."

"No amount of men will help you win if Henricus or any of his sons claim the Etherweave and sit upon the Bone Throne."

I spun from her insistent tone and paced away, allowing movement to burn through my frustration. With my back to her, I continued to speak. "How can I take the fight to Henricus, if we can't penetrate beyond the Ashenlands to reach the south? We need more time to make sure the passage we make through the cursed lands will work. My people are strong, but unless we find a way to succeed against the wizards' beasts we'll fail before we even face Henricus's army."

"Appeal to Thaindrus."

I spun back to face her. "You said it yourself. Thaindrus is old. He can't pass out of the north and hope to live."

"He will send the Huungardred with you."

"This is not their war."

"This is everyone's war. If the House of Tannard sits upon the Bone Throne, no place within these lands will be beyond their reach."

I speared a hand through my hair. "I need more time."

"You have none. I have come to you these years to teach you, to warn you, and you have done nothing to prepare."

Damn. She would bring this up.

"And if you refuse to try, then you had better have one of your own chop off your head right now and hand it over."

Pacing now, I continued, "I invited all the clan heads here tonight for th—"

"You already have their allegiance. You're wasting your time."

"Kaldor has not come. Nor Macrillion from the Storm-forge clan. Two significant men."

"I say you are wasting the precious little time you have left."

I strode towards her. "What do you know of war?"

"More than you." She closed the remaining distance between us, craning her neck to look up at me.

"I took my place at the head of the Razohan by sword. Please tell me you remember that."

"And I bear the mark of the faithful, young Razohan. Or has that escaped your notice? I carry the memories of a millennium in my soul. Do not question my wisdom."

In my anger, I wanted to spit venomous words, but Romelda drained my strength.

A thousand years of exile, or so the legend said, was enough time to call this place our home, if not for the darker future Romelda wove. I would have turned my back on the south, content with what I had here in the north, but I was no longer a child. I could no longer ignore the truth in the Nazeen's words, could no longer ignore the calling...

Still, concerns dogged my decisions, filled me with questions and doubts. It was not my fate alone to take the Bone Throne. According to the Nazeen I was the sole heir of the north, but not the sole heir, capable of taking the Etherweave and claiming the Bone Throne. The heirs of the House of Tannard could also make a claim. The Bone Throne was as much their ancestral right as it was mine.

I could not make a mistake; I could not afford to lose. For if the House of Tannard succeeded in taking the Etherweave and claiming the Bone Throne, it would begin a war to annihilate us and claim power over the seven realms. I would give my life to avoid the former for the sake of the northerners, my people, but also for all within the seven realms.

I began pacing, trying to ease the anger surging through my body. If I didn't, the anger would erupt in words—words once spoken I would forever regret.

But Romelda punctured the silence. "Hear what the augur has to say."

I barely kept from rolling my eyes. "And have him lead me on a wild path?"

"The time is nearing, Tamas. The augur has foreseen it. The night shall be lit as day, and the Etherweave will rise. There mustn't be a single Tannard left in the south to claim it. It is time to destroy King Henricus's line and claim your rightful place on the Tarragonan throne, and then once you take the Etherweave in you will claim the Bone Throne. The power will be yours."

"And what if I prove to be as evil as the Levenians. Is it not true there is no greater power than the Etherweave and there is no greater corruptor than power? Who would stop me from inciting a war to claim control over all the seven realms?"

"It saddens me you have such little faith in yourself." Romelda moved toward me, bringing with her the faint odor of oily sap, the smoke of sage, and a millennium of blood-drenched promises and dark-spelled oaths. "Don't blame yourself for what you had to do to claim Ironhelm."

"Kill my father, you mean?"

"I saved your life young Razohan. Your father was not the rightful heir to the Bone Throne, no matter how much he wanted to be. He was ready to forfeit your life in hope he would take your place."

"Because one of your cursed augurs told him it could be done."

"He misinterpreted what he heard."

"That's not hard when they make no sense."

Romelda took a moment before replying. "I know you feel the Etherweave."

I heaved a sigh, expelling the air from my lungs, sinking forward with the release and into the fierce march of fate, feeling the swell of resistance seize my heart.

The Creed of Salmun had sworn an oath to protect the bloodline of the Levenians—King Henricus's bloodline—until the Etherweave rose again. I shared my bloodline with Henricus, but I was not of the Levenian line, which made me their greatest enemy.

If I could destroy the Levenian-Tannard bloodline for good, placing myself as the only descendant of King Ricaud capable of ascending to the Bone Throne, then the Creed of Salmun might choose to side with me. Then again, they might destroy me. But once the power of the Etherweave was within me, and I took my place on the Bone Throne, none could defeat me.

"I'm not interested in the Tarragonan throne."

"It's your heritage, but your choice if you chose not to sit on the Tarragonan throne. The only throne that matters is the one you will take when you're united with the Etherweave. But you must act swiftly, for rumors have reached me that Henricus is negotiating a bride for his eldest."

"I have greater concerns than the crown prince's love life."

"She will bear the next heir. Another heir, Tamas. More blood that must be spilled. And an innocent, too. It would be far better if you ensure the bride's womb is never filled. Far better if you ensure she never reaches Tarragona's shores."

"She's from across the sea? Henricus can't find a broodmare from his own stable?"

"What does it matter?" Romelda snapped. "He has set his sights on Merania, from the House of Whelin."

I ran my palms down my face. A plague to all the Nazeen had shared. Yes, Prince Juel must never plant his seed, but there was little I could do about that when greater challenges lay before me. Ensuring some damsel never reached Juel's bed was the least of my concerns, not when I had tasked myself with gathering a force mightier than Henricus's army.

"I will travel with you to the augur."

"Tomorrow."

"Tomorrow I take counsel with the clan heads."

"Tomorrow Henricus signs the treaty with Merania and

takes his bride. Tomorrow he lines up his armies to face the Ashenlands. Tomorrow he marches for the divide. Tomorrow is a day closer to the Etherweave rising."

Her voice grew louder with each pronouncement. "The Creed of Salmun has their own ways of knowing. They know the night of day draws near. Henricus cannot risk a surviving heir to the Bone Throne outside the House of Tannard. If you do not start the war on your terms, he will. He will come for your head, and all of the Razohan."

She seized my arm. "You must ensure it is you, and not the Tannard heirs, present when the Etherweave rises. Your first priority is destroying the House of Tannard. Once you have achieved that set your sight on hunting down the Etherweave. Find the Senjel Oracles, have them guide you to where the Etherweave lies. It's our only hope."

The Nazeen who fought the Levenians over a millennium ago had entombed the Etherweave, but then it was said the entombing rock was lost. In their desperation to flee north with Ammelle to prevent the entire bloodline of King Ricaud's from falling under the control of the Levenians, the Nazeen lost trace of the rock and the Etherweave. If we hoped to reach the Etherweave before it rose on the day of nights we needed the Senjel Oracles, a tome of prophecies divined by an augur after the great war when the Nazeen fled north, announcing the location of the Etherweave, amongst other things. The whereabouts of the Senjel Oracles wasn't known, but I would say the Creed of Salmun had an idea, which presented me with another headache: convincing the wizards to reveal its location.

CHAPTER
THREE

TRESSYA

"Your father has summoned you," Radnisa exclaimed, bursting into my bathing room. The water was already cold because I had spent more time staring out of my small window at the clouds than bathing myself.

These past three days, I had felt sluggish, dragging my body from bed long after the sun had risen. All I wanted to do was curl into a ball and sleep, which made completing my menial tasks challenging.

I was certain my lethargy had something to do with the wound and whatever infection the Mother had placed inside of me. Whatever she had placed upon me, I would endure. I had to. All who belonged to the Sisterhood offered sacrifice without question, and I was born into it. The Mother was my mother, and her word was my law.

This meant my question would forever remain unasked.

What the Mother had down to me, placing a mysterious misty black substance inside of me, seemed like magic, but the Sistern weren't magic wielders beyond soul voice, so how had the Mother managed to do what she did?

I dropped my soapy cloth. "Now?" I hadn't seen the king in four days and wasn't supposed to for another three days, according to his meticulous schedule.

"I know you're an imbecile, but it's time you stopped showing it. Stop gaping and gawking and do as I say." She threw a dry cloth at me without aim, so it landed in the soapy tub water.

Radnisa rolled her eyes as if it were my fault the cloth ended in the water, then spun on her heels and left. I eased slowly up from the tub, expecting a twinge from the ache in my side, only to find my bath had soothed the stiffness. I curled my toes on the cold wood floor and hurried to retrieve another dry cloth neatly folded on a stool.

Radnisa waited on my bed, arms folded across her chest, a rich deep red gown, more suited to a ball, spread beside her. Her shrewd eyes followed me across the floor. Avoiding her intense gaze, I headed for the pile of folded undergarments on the other side of the bed. Any minute, she would decide on the perfect remark, something disparaging, provocative, or penal, so I prepared myself by taking slow, methodical breaths and concentrating on dressing.

Once dressed, and with no sharp words forthcoming from Radnisa, I walked around to stand beside her and picked up the yards of silk, lace, and finery. I didn't bother to ask Radnisa why she had insisted on a gown so clearly unsuitable for an ordinary morning summons from my father instead of the many more appropriate daywear gowns available. Radnisa's ridiculous choice of dress likely had something to do with my father's mood, which was erratic at best.

The long gown cascaded down to the floor, accompanied by multiple layers of petticoats I struggled to navigate on my own. I fumbled through the layers as Radnisa rose from the bed and strode toward the door.

She yanked it open and stepped out. "You," she shouted moments later, while I continued gathering all the skirts.

A young girl, dressed in the beige apron of a house servant, entered the room, casting timid glances between Radnisa and me.

"Your Highness," she bowed to me, then startled when Radnisa slammed the door shut behind her.

"Tend to her," Radnisa barked.

The young girl glanced at Radnisa. "You... I'm..." Her words faltered, her round eyes flickering between us both.

"Blessed Mother, just do as I say," Radnisa snapped, pushing the girl toward me.

"You may lace me up." I smiled at her, attempting to ease her confusion as I pulled one sleeve of my dress over my shoulder. Lucia, my lady's maid, was usually the one to assist me with dressing. Radnisa would never offer a helping hand, and given the king's impromptu summons, she wasn't willing to wait for Lucia to arrive.

The servant girl hurried over while Radnisa marched behind, once again folding her arms across her chest. She slowed her pace, her eyes dropping to the ugly mark above my left breast. Three days had passed, and the wound no longer appeared angry. Nevertheless, it would likely fuel gossip and raise questions, so I pulled up the front of the dress to conceal it, then turned around, presenting my back to the girl.

"Tighter," Radnisa barked from behind. "Her waist must be thinner than my wrist."

The bones of the corset lodged into my ribs, pinching my skin. I pressed my lips together and took a deep breath, feeling the twinge from my wound as a reminder that I had to train harder. I'd reworked every move I'd made from the fight and saw my mistakes. Misjudging, mistiming, acting with impatience or fury, becoming overly confident, failing to study my opponent, these were lessons I had to learn to perfect my skill.

"That will do," Radnisa snapped. "Do you know anything about hair? Never mind. Of course, you don't. Go."

The girl responded to Radnisa's harsh remark with hurried footsteps, disappearing out of my room like a frightened mouse.

"Sit. I'll have to do it myself," Radnisa sighed.

I complied, knowing I would discover the reason for all this fuss once I was standing in front of the king. However, if I arrived forewarned, I could adjust my approach accordingly.

Asking direct questions would only invite Radnisa's venom, and I would gain nothing but a verbal lashing. Instead, I would have to be discreet.

"Is Edilene to meet with the king?" I eased down before my mirror.

I was rarely invited to the other side of the castle, the

places within Aldorr reserved for the king's legitimate children, so it wasn't uncommon for weeks to pass before I saw either of my half-siblings, and rumors never made their way this far into the west wing.

Radnisa dragged the brush through my hair, not bothering to ease out the knots. "Edilene is none of your concern."

I took that as a no.

There was no way he would know about Carlin. I stared at my reflection, seeing the pink in my cheeks fade with the growing pace of my heartbeat. We had been too careful. Was the dress an attempt to appease him or soften his anger upon learning that his daughter was no longer a suitable commodity for a strategic marriage?

The tight bodice restricted my calming breaths, but I was more interested in Radnisa's motivations for dressing me this way than in worrying about my inability to breathe.

"What about Prince Arnaud?"

"Care more about your own fate than that of his."

A yes, I was sure. He would preside with the king. And that was a sign she knew what fate I faced. It didn't sound promising.

Brushed free of knots, Radnisa yanked my hair into an elaborate knot reserved only for balls. She aimed to ensure I arrived before the king as visually pleasing as possible, despite my plainness. This could only mean the king was furious. She had never cared how my father treated me before, so why did she bother now? Unless it was under the Mother's directives?

In recent years, Arnaud stayed by the king's side during

all matters of grave concern to the kingdom, whether significant or, more often lately, otherwise. The king's age had slowed his judgment, but not his anger or resentment. What the king wanted to say had nothing to do with my lack of competence in my lessons or duties, which were regularly reported to the king. Arnaud didn't need to be present for such a discussion.

Curses, this was serious. I pressed my palms flat against the bureau, feeling the cold on my clammy palms, and stared at my trembling hands, then gazed into Radnisa's eyes through the mirror.

It made no sense that after all this time Radnisa would expose my secret. Her loyalty to the Mother ran as deep as mine. There was no purpose served in locking me under house arrest and subjecting me to a whipping for tarnishing my virtue with a commoner. Edilene's ties to the Sisterhood were equally strong, but her animosity toward me could run even deeper. Could it be she was the one who revealed Carlin and my secret? There was no other reason for my father to deviate from his usual schedule and arrange a meeting that required Arnaud's presence as well.

"When will the Mother depart?"

The temple of the Divine Order was located on a small, isolated island off the coast of Merania. The Sistern made sure to extend their influence far and wide across the nearby realms, wherever they deemed it important to exert control. However, no uninvited person ever journeyed to their island.

I hoped she would provide guidance and perhaps reprimand Edilene in the process.

"The Mother's movements hold no significance for you."

I swallowed hard, already caught in my father's trap. I would have to find my way out of it or hope the Mother had other plans for me beyond imprisonment.

Silence had always been my best defense. It allowed me to listen, learn, and strategize. So I swallowed the rest of my questions. I already knew things were dire for me.

"As unfortunate as your appearance may be, there is little more I can do for you," she declared, throwing down the hairbrush.

I stood, relieved to be free of her and her rough hands. "Am I to meet the king in his office?"

"The council hall."

The council hall. A public humiliation, then. This had to be at Arnaud's insistence. Yet why tarnish my virtue publicly, allowing rumors to spread far and wide across the kingdoms. The corset constricting my waist already made breathing difficult, but the horror welling within me suffocated me.

Remembering who I was with, I dipped my head so Radnisa couldn't read my expression in the mirror. Why give her any more pleasure than she had already derived from me so far? I focused on finding my calming breaths. Panic was a curse, but fear was a weapon. I would find a way out of this.

Stepping into the corridor, I was relieved to escape both my room and Radnisa. Two servant women slowed to curtsy as I passed, their eyes flicking to my chest before lowering their heads to stare at the ground. Unsurprisingly, news of my ugly wound had already traveled through the dim halls of Aldorr. Gossip within the castle spread faster than the king's favorite falcon. Many would feel sorry for me, believing the king or Arnaud responsible. Little did they realize neither man could deliver half the pain that any disciple of the Sistern could, both to my body and to my heart.

Once in the west wing, I passed courtiers strolling through the long hallways for exercise, the inclement weather keeping them indoors. Unlike the servants, those of noble birth made little effort to conceal their contempt. They feigned the slightest curtsey as I passed or didn't bother at all. I paid them no attention. Instead, I kept my eyes on the history of Merania's rulers displayed on the wall of the corridor—a line of grim-faced males painted in all their finery.

Father had commissioned his own portrait long ago, ensuring they captured him in his youthful splendor. Since then, the king added more, depicting the trappings of the family. Those paintings hung on the opposite wall. I would never find myself among them.

The council hall was on the other side of Aldorr, and by the time I arrived, I had grown accustomed to my fate.

At the entrance to the council hall, I paused to steady my nerves, leaving the palace guards to stare at me, then at each other, unsure of what to do. Whatever awaited me beyond these doors, I was strong enough to endure. Blessed be the Mother. I would get through this.

What if they hunted Carlin down? The thought stalled me steps from the doors. The guards, who'd leaped for the doorhandles, froze, staring at me like I'd lost my mind. I wouldn't put it past Arnaud to weave a false tale and turn Carlin into the villain, using rape as the perfect accusation, leading to a judgment severe enough for a beheading. Filled with a defense for Carlin, I strode forward, forcing the guards to scurry open the doors, and came to a sudden. The king sat regally on his throne, with Arnaud on his right side, but what had stopped me was the stranger seated uncomfortably in a high-backed chair just below the king.

The stranger's presence at the king's feet indicated his higher status among common folk. His jacket, made of fine cotton woven by skilled artisans, shone in the color of gold. It boasted winged shoulders, pickadils, and a ruff extending up to his chin.

Coming to stand before my father, I curtsied, attempting to display the grace that apparently eluded me.

"Your Majesty," I said, stumbling over my words as I tried to place the stranger in my punishment.

The stranger examined me with his close-set eyes.

"Stand straight. Let us see you," commanded my father, curling a finger at me.

I moved toward the foot of the dais, feeling the stranger's sharp beady eyes roaming over my body. I turned to look at him, questioning who he was to dare ogle me so brazenly in front of the king.

"She is only half as beautiful," he declared, his cropped beard disappearing beneath the fastenings of his ruff as he spoke. He raised an eyebrow as he met my unwavering gaze.

I was mistaken. His gaze wasn't lustful but assessing, and from the slight twitch of his upper lip, I would say he found me lacking. I found him repulsive, including his over-powering scent—an excessive application of the odent flower favored by the aristocracy—which suffocated the air.

"The agreement was for the eldest," he stated, dabbing

the corner of his nose with a handkerchief as if I emitted an unpleasant odor.

"She's spoken for," snapped Arnaud.

I tore my eyes away from the pompous man and directed my attention to Father. His expression remained as stony as ever. I lowered my head, shifting my gaze to the floor. Panic welled within me, breaching the tight control I had forced upon my emotions, and a whirlwind of unsettling possibilities raced through my mind.

"Forgive me, Your Majesty, I mean no disrespect, but the esteemed King Henricus is expecting me to return with the agreed-upon daughter..." He turned his gaze back to me. "Not an unsuitable substitute."

Blessed Mother, the implications behind his words constricted my throat.

"The king will have to be content with what I send. My eldest is no longer with us. She now belongs to King Rennard. She is Prince Guillenet's wife."

The clammy feel of my hands mirrored the sickening dread enveloping my heart, pulling it down like a wild animal ensnared in a trap. I straightened my posture, lifted my head, and fixed my gaze on the sniveling emissary, all the while counting the pounding beats of my heart.

This had nothing to do with Carlin.

"Sire," the emissary exclaimed, springing to his feet, and thrusting out his protruding belly for all to see. "If you had indeed signed a treaty with your eastern neighbor—"

"I did no such thing. The princess's disappearance was not my choice."

"Your Majesty, forgive my confusion, but what exactly are you saying?"

"The affairs of Merania are none of your concern," interjected my brother, his voice laced with indignation.

"Forgive me, Sire," the man bowed. "I must return with a justifiable reason for—" He gestured toward me. "This. She was not part of the agreement. The portrait sent was of your eldest. There is hardly any comparison to be made between the two."

His demeaning words failed to penetrate my skin. He was right. There was little resemblance between Edilene and me. In appearance, she was day, while I was night; she a dove, and I an eagle. The austerity of her beauty bestowed upon her the air of an untouchable queen, for that was her destined role under the guidance of her guardians within the king's household and under the strict tutelage of the Mother. While Father ensured I received an adequate education to mitigate the disgrace of my birth, a nobleman with an insignificant title was all I had thought father would bother to arrange for me.

"The daughter your king expects was forcefully taken from my household and compelled into marriage. There is no reason to retrieve her now."

Meaning King Rennard held enough power to jeopardize Merania's stability if he disputed the loss of his eldest daughter. Yet something didn't feel right. If Edilene had been taken, there would be whispers. The servants knew everything; their knowledge of my wound confirmed that. I would have heard something of Edilene being gone.

My eyes narrowed at the floor. I doubted Edilene's disappearance had anything to do with abduction and forced marriage. Rather, she had escaped in secret under the Mother's orders to clear the path for me. This was the destiny Edilene had accused me of stealing.

"Indeed, grave news, Your Majesty. You can trust in my discretion. King Henricus extends his sympathies."

His insincere platitudes faded into the background as my fate crystallized before my eyes.

I could imagine the king's fury at losing his prized daughter for a strategic alliance with the powerful Tarragonans. After all, he'd ensured her education covered the language and political dynamics of the region. I wasn't sure if a marriage to the Tarragonan prince was what he'd had in mind, but Edilene was the perfect daughter for such a union. Curiously, the Mother had ensured from a young age I, too, learned to speak fluent Tarragonanese. The Mother's intervention had thwarted Father's plans, yet he would never know who was truly responsible or why, as was the way of the Sistern.

Why send Edilene to marry the prince of a kingdom far less strategic than Tarragona? Why intervene in favor of me?

Blessed Mother, I didn't want this. I always knew Father would force a disagreeable marriage on me, but not so far away.

I swallowed the sinking realization of my duty—not to the king, but to the Mother, the only person to whom I pledged my allegiance. It mattered little what I thought; what truly mattered was what I did. I exhaled and held my head straight. For the Mother's will, I would endure. I had to.

Sensing his power to negotiate had waned, the emissary

shifted his attention to me, scrutinizing me from head to toes as he circled like I was livestock. His gaze dismissed my face but roamed every inch of my body.

Outwardly, I remained motionless. Inwardly, I directed my awareness toward him, activating the part of my mind honed through rigorous training and discipline by the Sistern. I delved into his essence while I listened to the sharp thuds of his boots circling me. I sought to gather the fragments of his soul, the parts of him that would assist me in understanding him, allowing me to mold those pieces into a very special word—his soul word.

Yet I was not Edilene, Radnisa, or any of the other disciples whose training came effortlessly. The soul voice remained beyond my grasp. I couldn't piece together his soul word. Nonetheless, I persisted in my practice.

By now, the emissary stood before me. Though short in stature, we locked eyes at the same level, neither of us flinching.

"It appears Crown Prince Juel receives second best," he remarked.

"Nevertheless, she is still a woman. A woman signifies a womb. That is all your king requires? Your crown prince need only plant his seed, then he is free to take his pleasure elsewhere if she's not to his liking," my father retorted.

My father's words held as much importance to me as he did, which was none. I touched the spot above my left breast where the ugly scar remained hidden. What were the Mother's intentions? Not for the first time, I yearned to ask her. There were many things I wished existed between us. My foolish childhood heart had wanted her to love me. A part of me was still that young girl, still hoping for her love, even though I knew it was impossible. But she had chosen me to marry the prince instead of Edilene. A prince. A match I had always thought beyond a bastard. And the heir to the Tarragona throne. I couldn't fail in this duty. Perhaps the Mother would view me more favorably.

"Malicious rumors claim she is a bastard."

I kept myself from recoiling at the word, but just barely. The word never failed to reverberate in my ears.

"A bastard will still breed. She carries my bloodline. What does it matter who the mother was?"

Making no progress, I withdrew my probing mind from within his soul and shifted the focus of my gaze, looking at the emissary with fresh eyes. Instead of directly at him, my gaze darted around him, searching for his death echo—the essence of his life on the precipice before it plunged into eternal slumber.

Even though the death arts of spiritseeing and spiritweaving, were hereditary traits passed through the House of Whelin, the talent had faded over the centuries. Spiritseeing was rare, spiritweaving rarer still. The last spiritweaver within the Whelin line died over four hundred years ago. Edilene inherited nothing of the Whelin ability. Both Arnaud and I saw death echoes, but neither of us had inherited the more powerful talents of spiritseeing and spiritweaving.

I didn't always see people's death echoes, though. It required concentration and a shift in my vision. Deep hues of burnt honey enveloped him, a man with many years left to live. More's the pity.

Father rose from his throne and descended the dais. He was a tall man, towering over the emissary, so his head reached the small knot in the king's throat.

He took great pride in his physique, maintaining fitness through regular sports, such as hunting and jousting. Arnaud, on the other hand, had grown lethargic, showing little regard for his own health, and rarely engaged in any physical activities.

"What is your response?" Father inquired, peering down at the man.

The emissary cast a brief glance at me. "King Henricus expects me to return with a bride. Your Majesty leaves me with little choice. She fulfills the requirements."

"A wise decision. The woman is educated, though not enough to pose a threat to a king. She is not dumb but knows when to hold her tongue. I believe your prince will find her compliant. Perhaps that will compensate for her lack of beauty and grace."

"Of course, Sire, her education was never in question." He dabbed at his nose with his kerchief, sneaking a lecherous gaze in my direction, openly ogling my chest for the first time. I thanked the Mother my bodice pressed my breasts flat, concealing them from his greedy eyes.

"Now we have our alliance, come," Father beckoned, gesturing for the man to follow behind him. "Let us engage in more pleasant pursuits. You may leave." With a casual flick of his hand, he dismissed me as an afterthought.

He half-turned to Arnaud. "Attend to the arrangements." Then, without even glancing at me, he strode away, the emissary scurrying after him.

CHAPTER

FOUR

TAMAS

THE CHILL FROZE NOT ONLY the air but also all sounds in the forest, amplifying the clomp of our horses' hooves into a thunderous echo. Dense fog clung to our cloaks, hiding our path. Fortunately, Romelda could tread this path on a moonless night, or we would have wandered lost through the undergrowth for days.

Augurs, those who communed with the unseen, preferred deep wilderness, far removed from human habitation. The wanderings of their minds drove them to a solitary, nomadic life. As the south was densely populated, augurs rarely ventured beyond the Ashenlands. At their worst, fits of paranoia sent them scampering to the distant regions of the north, where they would bury themselves away. As it was, we found ourselves far off the normal trails, tramping a path of our making.

This particular augur was one Romelda greatly favored, regularly tracking his random journeys. I once thought she acted out of emotion, not gain, but time showed me otherwise.

Garrat dozed beside me, having spent the night in the company of a handful of maidens, if I was to believe his story. On the other side of me, Osmud munched on some dried deer while droplets of moisture clung to the fur of his hood and hung like decoration around his face. We all rode huddled under our cloaks, breathing mist through our mouths, and choosing not to speak too much as the ice wind burned down into our lungs.

"Will we reach him by nightfall?" Osmud asked, still munching on his meat.

"Four days she promised. Today marks the fourth," I replied.

Although Garrat was no stranger to time in the saddle, he didn't much like our destination. All that travel to hear the crazy mumblings of the insane was his response to this journey. I had said nothing to counter his grumbling as I had thought the same.

Ahead, Romelda's horse whinnied. The sudden panicked sound rippled a quiver through my horse's flanks. He raised his head and chomped at his bit as Osmud's mount shied into his rump.

"Steady, girl," Osmud crooned, patting her withers. "There's nothing beyond this fog to fear but rodents."

All the same, he glanced into the bone-white mist. There was no hope of penetrating the veil to see what prowled close on our tail. Romelda's horse stomped on the spot, as

Osmud's horse attempted to slip from his hold, prancing sideways and squeezing my leg between their hot flanks.

The mist swirled around us. From disturbance or wind? It was hard to tell. Prickles itched across my back, and I tightened my hold on my reins. The horses sensed it first, but now the unease of being watched danced across my skin, and a yearning thrummed through my veins, a primal call thick in my head.

"Halt," I announced.

At the same moment, Romelda's mount reared, but she held her seat. I heard her mumbling and knew she was calling up some spell to make visible whatever was using the fog as its veil, or perhaps to bind it in place.

"Wait."

She looked over her shoulder, her mouth set in a line, the tension from holding back whatever incantation she had begun. I swear her red eyes glowed like an animal in the night.

I slid from my horse and handed Garrat the reins. "I feel nothing," was his answer.

"The call is not for you, brother."

"Don't let this delay be for long," Romelda warned. "As it is, we shall reach the cavern by nightfall."

At that, Garrat's stomach grumbled.

I nodded to Romelda, then left them and headed out into the fog. I wove a slow path as the mist clung to the trees and every obstacle that would trip me. But I didn't have to go far before the mist danced in violent swirls, then parted like a curtain to reveal a massive bear-like beast looming over me. Its brown pelt flowed with striations of rich gold. Around its face, sprouts of gray grew thicker with each passing decade. Once its green eyes glowed with menace, they were now dulled and partially covered with the encroaching milky white of blindness.

"Igthredia, old friend. You've traveled far."

The beast lowered from its hunches and prowled closer. I held out my hand as a greeting, taking the butt of its wet nose as the warm welcome it was.

Its body shimmered as it loosened its hold on its animalic form, flowing and merging into the frightful contortion of a man-beast. Huungardred were not true shape-shifters; they couldn't take on the full physique of a human. One half was distinctly human, while the other was a contorted amalgamation of human and beast.

He heaved himself down on the ground with some creaks and a groan and nudged his head to welcome me to sit beside him. I nestled myself on a log so that my head reached his middle.

"I lumbered long to Ironhelm, only to hear you ventured west."

A heavy, craggy brow overhung his eyes, setting them deep into his face. The left side remained in its human-beast form, covered with thick, coarse hair. His snout had flattened, and his thick, dark lips were drawn back in what seemed like a permanent snarl, exposing long, pointed teeth. It made conversation awkward, but I understood all the same.

"I'm sorry you had to make the extra journey."

"I needed the exercise. Lazy I've become, and the years keep passing me by."

On the left side of his body, at the tips of his massive, hairy hand, black claws curled downward like deer antlers. I waited to hear his reason for hunting me down, while Romelda's impatience drummed at the back of my mind.

"I'm here for Thaindrus."

The thread of alarm itched the back of my neck. "Is Thaindrus alright? I sent a rider four days ago but had to leave before his return."

"Thaindrus is old, my friend. He fares little better than me, and I feel the aches each morning when I wake. He longs to see you."

I nodded, feeling a heavy weight lodge itself on my heart. It was the heavy sadness the living endured when loved ones crossed into the death realm.

"When my duty here is done, I shall head north to Thaindrus's court."

"You're traveling with the Nazeen."

I nodded.

"Prepare, dear friend, for the augur's ramblings may lead you on a twisted path."

"That's one of my concerns. But I trust Romelda. She believes him."

"Yes. The Nazeen carries a great deal of fear. And a great deal of promise. Your path is not that of the Huungardred. But you are still of our blood, and I would caution you, young Tamas. You are but an infant in our eyes."

"But not so in the eyes of man. And unfortunately, it is within that world I must make my mark."

"That I understand. But the Nazeen guides you toward a

dark path. Many falter on such a path. Many lose grip on who they are."

"I fear it's the only one I can take, and I'm the only one who can take it. I can't hide here in the north any longer. It's in here..." I patted my chest over my heart. "I feel it. Romelda's right. The Etherweave is calling me."

"There is no doubt within my heart that you are a king. But are you ready to take your place? It is more than sitting on a throne that makes you a king. As it is more than wielding power that makes you strong."

I huffed a laugh I didn't feel. "Am I ready? I cannot say. Do I have to be ready? Yes. The House of Tannard must not claim the Etherweave."

"Always remember, Tamas, their blood is also yours, as are their fragilities, and so too could be their sins."

How could I ever forget?

"It's well that my blood is also yours, that of the Huungardred. Your bloodline shall be my strength and keep me honest."

"Then the fates of the seven realms are safe." Igthredia snorted as he barked a hard, quick snap of a laugh before dropping his smile. "Our bloodline stretches far deeper than the coming of man to this realm. Our ancestral lore speaks of the great wrong committed by the first weavers in bringing the Etherweave forth. It is not a power that was ever meant to be in this realm. The unnatural gives rise to darkness, and darkness so easily corrupts."

I placed my hand on his arm, feeling the leathery skin under my palm. "While it was a great wrong to bring it forth, it is here now. We cannot deny or dismiss it. The best we can do is ensure it's not held in the hands of those who know nothing but evil. I have to try. You know that don't you?" But what if I could be just as evil?

"It is so, as much as my heart wishes it not."

"Then, my friend, I must head back to my party. Tell Thaindrus I shall be there as soon as I can."

I patted him on the back, then rose, his warning like manacles around my ankles, hauling me back. I could make no promises that if I succeeded, the Etherweave would not corrupt me.

OUR HORSES WHINNIED and snorted with unease as we neared the cavern tucked deep in the forest. It was the cusp of night, and my senses tingled, sending a wave of unease through my body. I instinctively rested my hand on my sword, though I knew there was nothing to fight. Perhaps Igthredia's warning had left its mark. Hours after our parting, his words lingered. His fears were my fears; I questioned my strength to withstand the darker lure of the Etherweave.

According to Nazeen legend, King Ricaud, the last great king to sit upon the Bone Throne, had a thirst for knowledge, not war. He invited scholars from all the kingdoms of the seven realms, eager to discuss science, philosophy, and religion, seeking to discover the perfection of living. He then built a library to house the scrolls and tomes he gathered or commissioned. He refused to see the Nazeen as a rival power to his own, but as a source of ancient wisdom. Perfecting farming practices, trade, and wisely managing the wealth of the land was how he built Tarragona into the wealthiest and most powerful kingdom within the near realms.

Was I worthy to take the Etherweave? There seemed to be only one desire within the heart of men, a thirst for power, and I judged myself no better. I questioned my strength to withstand the darker lure of the Etherweave.

We secured our mounts and followed Romelda into a narrow rock corridor. The early evening stars caught the fine white flecks in the rock surface, making them appear covered in a dusting of snow. The natural corridor opened out into a basin covered in moss and creeper and the blackened ground where a fire had been lit. A dark cavern, like a gaping mouth, sat at the far end of the basin.

Romelda led us to that mouth.

"Sirillious," she called before entering the darkness. Not waiting for a reply she waved us forward.

We'd not gone far in when the flicker of candlelight danced across the cavern walls ahead. The choke of smoke singed the hairs at the back of my nose, but the smell of cooked meat drew saliva into my mouth.

"Be gone. I have no need for your maledictions today," the augur muttered as we rounded a corner, forced to stoop forward or bang our heads on the cave's ceiling.

Old, but not stooped, the augur was the smallest man I'd ever seen, reaching to my chest or just below. He was thinner than a child, with sunken cheeks, bulging eyes, and arms like old twigs ready to snap. He smelled like he was already dead, and his clothes hung off his body in tatters. Romelda had abandoned bringing him new clothes long ago, as he only used them as firewood.

He lifted his head from the pile of stones he'd placed in a circle long enough to glimpse Romelda. "It's you." Then he went back to staring at the stones.

I knew little about augury, so I wasn't sure if the stones were his implement for divining or if this was yet another sign of his madness. Did he think they were alive?

Romelda waved Osmud, Garrat, and I farther into the cave, toward what looked like a stone plinth lying on its side. The perfect seat to relieve us of a crook neck.

"Sirillious, old friend," Romelda started, sitting cross-legged on the floor.

He held up a hand to silence her. "Speak and you infect this place with your scorn."

I squeezed the bridge of my nose, fighting the sinking feeling I had wasted valuable time taking the journey.

"You bring me the bloodborn and two other sons of beasts. To steal my meal?"

It had been a long time since I'd heard that title, so it came as a shock. I looked over at the fire, crackling in its circle of stones. A blackened lump of meat inside an earthen bowl sat abandoned beside the fire. Something too small for my eyes to determine crawled across the top of the meat. I smirked on seeing Osmud release a small shudder as he turned from the sight of the meat.

"We're here for your wisdom," Romelda continued.

"Because they have no wisdom of their own," he snapped.

"Because you see what others can't."

Sirillious darted sideways and snatched up his bowl of charred meat and huddled it into his chest. "Because they are too lazy to feed themselves." He took a bite, tearing flesh and gristle and chomping it noisily. I turned away on seeing the small, crawling creature disappear into his mouth.

"The bloodborn will fail," he said, finishing his mouthful. Then he turned it into a song. "Will fail, will fail, will fail." And he jiggled about in some weird hobbling dance and bumping his head on the cave's ceiling.

"Sirillious, please," Romelda pleaded.

"Yes, yes. I've proclaimed. And you won't listen. But do you like my little song?"

Romelda closed her eyes. I watched her chest rise with a steadying breath. Perhaps she regretted this waste of time, too.

I was still looking at Romelda when something hit me between the eyes.

"Hey," I groused as a small bone, wet from Sirillious's mouth, landed in my lap. Beside me, Garrat and Osmud sniggered.

"Are you worthy?" the augur intoned, his voice seeming to bounce around in my head as he glared at me. Jerking his bowl to his chest once more, but losing the meat into the dirt at his feet, he hunched forward. "Evil little boy," he cackled wagging a finger at me.

Garrat rolled his eyes and sank his head into his hands. I glanced at Osmud. He simply shrugged. If only I could care so little, but it seemed the augur had the power to see right into my heart, surfacing my fears from deep within. Was his silly little song my future? And how would I fail? To win the Bone Throne? Or to keep the Etherweave from infecting me?

Romelda launched herself to her knees. "Enough, Sirillious, please." She seized his wrist and jerked him around to face her. "Speak to me, old friend." She pulled him toward her, holding his gaze while dragging her fingers down his face. "It's just you and me. Tell me what you see," she crooned.

Sirillious pulled from her hold as if she'd stung him and hobbled toward the back of the cave to where there was a mound of reed and furs. There he slumped down and ducked his head like a child sulking before throwing himself on his bed and staring up at the rock ceiling.

I shared a look with my two friends, then turned to Romelda, opening my mouth to tell her we wouldn't remain to waste more time when the augur started.

"When the tapestry of night is stripped of its obsidian cloak, and the celestial vaults alight in a radiant blaze akin to the sun's embrace, the rightful heir, a descendant of the fallen, shall rise."

He stayed silent. The three of us shared another look. There was nothing new in what he said, which made this journey a definite waste of our time.

"From the sepulchers of the departed, the one holding ethereal authority and the spectral bond to ancestral spirits shall descend the hallowed steps to claim that which was forged from the essence of destiny's marrow and holds the bloodlife of mortality itself. Those under the veil shall bow to such a claim, and the might of the Bone Throne shall once again be glorious."

We waited, but he'd fallen silent.

Osmud leaned in and whispered, "We traveled all this way for that."

I nodded.

"Did you understand any of it?"

"Not a word."

"Right. I'm not the only fool."

"We agreed to come. So, yes, we're all fools," Garrat added.

"South is our enemy. I didn't need to travel all these miles to understand that," Osmud finished.

"The time draws near when the barriers between realms fade. Darkness shall yield to brilliance. Boundaries will blur and realms intertwine."

Osmud sighed. "Do you think he'll do a translation?"

"Within the yawning depths of a cavernous abode, in the annals of antiquity, where the ethereal whispers of forgotten knowledge intertwine with the very essence of existence, lies an ancient text, ensconced in the heart of darkness. To behold its sacred verses is to embark upon a perilous journey through shadowed corridors where ancient runes breathe life into dormant incantations. Seek not the comforts of light, for within these chambers, the boundary between worlds wavers, and the realm of the arcane reveals itself to those worthy. The tethered secrets of Etherweave, once unleashed, shall breathe vitality into those who dare to wield its power, transcending the mundane shackles of existence. But heed this warning, for the pursuit of such forbidden knowledge demands resolve, and the guardians of these hallowed texts are not easily placated. Only the steadfast and the valiant may lay claim to the coveted whispers that shall reveal the elusive path to the realms where Etherweave magic breathes eternal."

"And I understood that even less," Osmud grumbled.

"Did any of that tell us where to find the Senjel Oracles or the Etherweave?" Garrat said.

"Not that I could tell." I looked at Romelda, but I wasn't comforted by her frown.

Sirillious convulsed, then arched his back off his reed bed, head tipped upward, and howled. Romelda crawled toward him. Before she reached him, he convulsed again, and I waited for another howl. Instead, Sirillious jerked to the side and vomited the burned meat onto the dirt floor, releasing the stench of reed rotted in a bog.

"Curse the dark night," Garrat spat, pulling his cloak up to shield his nose.

"I think the deer in my stomach will go the same way," Osmud complained, patting his belly.

Sirillious looked like a limp fish in one breath, the next he jerked upright in bed. "Twain is the bloodborn."

"Someone needs to shut him up," Osmud grumbled.

"The end, Sirillious," Romelda intoned.

"Twain is the veiled ones' curse."

"Siri—" Romelda began.

"Wait," I said.

But Sirillious said no more. He flopped back down onto his bed of furs, rested his hands across his chest, and closed his eyes. Within breaths, his head rolled to the side as if he'd fallen asleep.

"That's it?" Osmud said.

We waited for moments longer with only the crackle of fire as our answer. Romelda was the first to move, motioning us to follow her from the cave. Eager to escape, I followed her out into the basin and fresh air, then along the natural corridor to our horses, the others close on my heels.

"That went well," Osmud said, once we left the rock corridor to stand in the small clearing.

"I remember little of what he said. We should've brought a scribe," Garrat replied.

I stayed silent, as did Romelda. The moment we exited, she separated from us and turned to stare up at the stars, something she had a habit of doing when deep in thought.

"And someone to translate. I'm sure he twisted everything up so we wouldn't understand," Osmud continued.

By now, the conversation was between him and Garrat, for I moved to stand beside Romelda. Her profile was stark in the moonlight as she continued to gaze up at the stars, ignoring me. It was not Sirillious's claim that I would fail that now set my mind on a new path, but his last words. And I would say by Romelda's expression she was worried about the same thing.

"You were right. I have no time to gather the clans. I shall send Osmud and Garrat in my place. Garrat is a far better negotiator besides. We still need the north united, I'm not turning my back on that, but I'll do as you say and ensure Prince Juel's bride doesn't reach Tarragona's shores."

Romelda turned her attention back to the stars. "I had not expected this."

"Do you now question your choice of heir?"

"Never. Sirillious's last words changes nothing, Tamas. You are the rightful heir."

So she had been as surprised as I to hear his last pronouncements.

"And once you see to Juel's bride, what will you do?"

"I shall enter the House of Tannard and take it down from within."

Romelda turned to me. "Then why do you need your army? Why not take Osmud and Garrat with you to the south?"

"War is inevitable. There's no guarantee the nobility will accept us on the king's death. And the Salmun will fight. We need to crush the south so they may not rise again. We need the Nazeen's help to do this."

"You'll have it. But I warn you, there are less of the blooded these days."

"We'll take everything we can get. I shall visit Thaindrus on our return journey, then I shall take a small party and depart for the coast."

CHAPTER

FIVE

TRESSYA

THE TREACHEROUS SEA curled back upon itself, then mounted another attack, pounding mercilessly against the dock. The timber dock shuddered under my feet as a fine mist of sea spray dampened my hair. Having never sailed before, I wouldn't dwell on the time I would spend in cramped confines with Radnisa and Anderline, who would replace Lucia as my lady's maid, since Lucia was not a disciple of the Sistern. My family was conspicuously absent from the farewell party, which consisted of no one.

The docks bustled with noisy chaos. Men scurried up and down the gangplank, carrying cargo and herding reluctant livestock to be kept deep in the hold, while hungry gulls screeched overhead. Apparently, fresh breeding stock was also part of the deal. I could imagine what the ship would smell like halfway through the voyage. They cautioned us to expect peasant food and warned that water would be scarce.

Ten seamstresses had fattened my trunks with dresses of exquisite craftsmanship, embellished with jewels to grace the halls of Emberfell Castle. I might be a bastard with few features to recommend me, but Father was determined I would not disgrace the House of Whelin.

I turned away from the disordered mayhem and looked back at Aldorr Castle, nestled high on the mount. With the weak sun's rays reflecting off its stone walls, the castle appeared like a ghost hovering above the sprawling city below. And just like a ghost, I had always thought of it as a lonely place.

In the weeks since my father's announcement, I had tried to gather as much knowledge as I could about my future home and husband. But everyone dismissed me. Unlike Edilene, no one bothered to educate me about the Tarragona court, its laws, religion, or history. No one expected me to play any political part, just that of the docile, pregnant queen, hidden from public life for the shame of her ancestry.

Pregnant queen was the only role the Mother expected of me. The Sistern of Silence focused on bloodlines, secretly intervening and manipulating for their desired outcome. While kings concerned themselves with their male heirs, the Sistern focused on far more important fates: those of the female line. Daughters of important marriages were fostered into the Sistern's care and trained as loyal disciples. This ultimately strengthened the Sistern's political power within the near realms. But I was puzzled why the Mother chose me, ignoring Edilene, the more accomplished daughter, banishing her to the House of Stafford, though I doubted she cared much for a bloodlink with Prince Guillenet. No wonder Edilene was furious. I felt a smug satisfaction at that.

I turned back to the large ship, standing taller than any ships docked alongside or anchored out to sea. This was one insignificant fact I would be grateful for; perhaps I would find some space away from my two Sistern shadows.

A small boy with wild, shabby hair, dressed in stained clothes and smelling of fish, tugged at my skirt. I smiled down at him. "Hello, young sir."

"There's a man over by the crates," he motioned behind him. "He wants to speak with you."

Carlin. I'd managed one message to him since Father's announcement and had yet to see him. I thought perhaps it would be best for us both if I left without a teary farewell, even if the idea broke my heart. Now I knew he was here, the pounding of my blood through my ears obscured Radnisa's approach.

"No."

I jerked at her harsh voice, spoken over my shoulder. The boy scampered away.

"I have time. There's still more to be loaded onboard."

She seized my elbow and jerked me around, then stepped close to keep her voice low. "Your future is across the sea with an heir at your foot to appease the king and a daughter in your belly to please the Mother. That is your only purpose. Your life here is over."

I pulled my elbow from her hold. "I will say goodbye to him. I suggest you stop delaying me."

Her green eyes darted between mine as her lips pinched

tight. I read her struggle to hold her anger within. Hidden away from onlookers, I was sure she would slap the insolence out of my mouth. "Now is not the time to grow thorns."

"And you'd best tend to your own preparations."

I spun from her and the fury roiling in her eyes like an angry sea. With my skirts lifted above the damp grime, I strode across to the empty crates stacked beside an old warehouse. Seeing Carlin's face poke around the side of the stack, I forgot about the stench of rotten fish, which turned the food in my stomach. His eyes widened, then a broad smile spread across his face. My heart tore in too many places; I was bound to leave many pieces behind.

He snagged my hand as I neared and pulled me around behind the crates. I breathed into his mouth as our lips smashed together and our chests collided. His mouth smothered my gasp at the lingering pain of my wound. With our bodies pressed as one, I felt his heart beat in tune with mine as tears burned my eyes.

We savored each other with a long, languid kiss to stamp upon our memories until we both needed to breathe.

"You didn't think I would let you go without saying goodbye?" he said with a cheeky smile.

"I thought it would be kindest to both of us if I slipped away." My arms wrapped around his neck, and I entwined my fingers through his hair, staring into his muscovite eyes. "I'm so glad you're here." Then I kissed him again, desperately, showing him all that was in my heart, inhaling his seed oil smell and knowing that smell would never leave me.

My salty tears broke free and streamed down my cheeks

and into our mouths. I had few words strong enough to bridge this moment, so I poured my pain through our kiss, wanting it to find a home deep within him. I was a disciple. I knew this day would come, but I'd not expected it to hurt so much. I didn't want to let him go. He struggled to pull back, but I clutched him tighter to me.

"My beautiful princess."

I placed my hand over his mouth. "Don't call me that."

"You're right. I should call you queen."

I closed my eyes. "That I want to hear even less."

"Tressya." He won, setting me back a short distance. "You'll be a magnificent queen. There's no woman as wise as you. That is what you take with you. And this." He pressed a hand over my heart. "Loyalty to your people. They'll fall madly in love with you. I know I did." He feathered a finger down my cheek. "They won't be able to help themselves."

The pain was like nothing I'd felt before. I'd let Carlin into my heart. *Mother forgive me my weakness.*

"You would hate the life of a farmer's wife even more. It's beneath you."

"I never would've hated you."

"Someday maybe you would've done. You're too intelligent and too courageous to be anything other than queen. Don't compare yourself with your sister. Or that snake of a lady-in-waiting. You outshine both. It's no wonder the king chose you."

I circled my arms around his neck and pulled us close, unable to meet his eyes any longer.

You don't know me. The painful stab in my heart at thinking those words brought more tears to my eyes. I fulfilled my promise never to lie to Carlin in all ways but one, the most important way, the way that opened the true depths of my soul. Love was not one of the six pillars, so the Sistern gouged it from our hearts. It was a manacle, diminishing our purpose and placing an obstacle in our path. The perfect disciple's heart would not bleed. That mine did showed my lack of discipline.

"The prince will be kind and unselfish. Oh, and did I mention adoring of you?"

"How can you be so generous?"

"I don't know. It comes naturally." Then he chuckled, but I sensed the underlying melancholy in his voice.

"You'll give your children a title that does not begin with bastard. Something you and your mother never had."

I nestled into him even more, my hot tears against his neck and drenching his shirt. Only now, in the wrenching pain of separation, did I realize that Carlin had found a dormant place in my still-beating heart. For a brief moment, I had loved. But I had been weak to fall. This beautiful man was not meant to be my life. He was too honest, generous, and wonderful to exist in my world, and I was too torn, beaten, and dangerous to live in his.

I wanted to stay in his arms forever. *Discipline.* I loosened my grip on his neck and let my hands fall to my sides. While it would have torn my heart to depart without a proper goodbye, I needed to remember who I was.

"Forget me," I urged him. "In your children's eyes, see only the woman you loved and married."

"That is an impossible request."

"And one you will fulfill." I darted in and kissed him to

silence him, to remember him, to sear his presence into my pain for a little longer.

"I have something for you." He captured my wrist before I could retreat, with his other hand he pulled a silver chain from his pocket, a piece that would cost six months' worth of wages if not more.

"No, Carlin. You shouldn't have."

"But I did. You can't refuse it."

I shook my head, fresh tears blurring my vision of the small, intricate carved series of circles dangling before me.

Carlin took my hand, turned it palm-side up, and placed the carving in the center, allowing the chain to slip through my fingers.

"I carved it from bone."

"Bone?"

"I wanted to do something different, something special. You likely have plenty of expensive jewels in your trunks, but I bet you have nothing carved from bone."

He took it from my hand. "Turn around."

As I obeyed, he told me. "Circles have no end. Remember that my love for you will have no end."

I held the bone carving in my fingers as Carlin fastened the chain. Then he spun me around to face him.

"Your courage will have no end. Even in the darkest moments."

I closed my eyes as I placed my fingers over his lips, unable to bear his words any longer. Already they'd torn out my heart. My strength deserted me. I would give me life at this moment to stay by his side.

"I have to go," I whispered, drowning in my warm tears as slashes brutally tore my heart to pieces.

He nodded, wiping his eyes. "I couldn't let you go without a piece of me."

I tortured myself a breath longer, falling into his silvery-gray eyes, memorizing for the hundredth time the perfection of his ordinary face.

Then I let him go and fled, knowing that was the last time I would feel my heart; the last time it would be ruined.

THOUGH SPACIOUS FOR A SHIP, I already felt caged. King Henricus spared little expense in collecting his son's bride while taking the opportunity to display Tarragona's wealth. Father's ships were little more than barges alongside the Sapphire Rose, with its black and white ensign rippling in the gentle breeze.

The crew was numerous and busy, leaving the three of us forgotten. I slumped on one of my many trunks, already feeling my stomach roll in time with the ship, already sick of the smell of the salty air. Radnisa stood beside me, arms folded and wearing her usual deep frown. She shuffled from one foot to the other and huffed a sigh before finally uttering, "This won't do. You"—she snapped at a passing sailor—"do something about these." She waved at our trunks. "Do you expect us to wait here until the ship leaves the dock?"

He eyed her, seemingly unperturbed by her snappish

manner. Then he flicked his eyes to me. Equally unimpressed, he turned and slouched away.

"Mercy to the Mother, these Tarragonans are half savage." Radnisa caught me smirk so turned her body to face me. "I wouldn't start with your exaltations. You're not on the throne yet."

Slowly, I turned away, pressing my lips together to suppress my smile. I was free from my family and Father's court. That was enough to lighten some of my burdened heart.

"A flirtation with the stable boy, and now you think you know a man's heart," she continued.

I closed my eyes, preparing for the lash of Radnisa's words. She never allowed me the upper hand in any argument, knowing how to wield her tongue to cut me deep.

Facing the dock, I heard the fabric of her skirts crinkle as she leaned closer to me. "The crown prince of Tarragona won't differ from any man. Ruthless, greedy, and vengeful, with a wandering eye and disdain for the one whose bed he's forced to share. Wives are easily shoved aside." She straightened. "It's a good thing you are so compliant. It will be easier for him to dismiss you."

Perhaps her words were tinged with personal experience. "What about Baron Ledredon?"

"He was happy to let me go."

I'm sure he was.

"Besides, he would've found a knife in his chest had he made a fuss," she added, her sarcasm cutting through.

Placed there by his wife, who would've paused long enough to take some celebratory wine before raising the alarm. Radnisa was high-born but forced into a marriage with a lowly baron. I'm sure the indignity was responsible for her permanent ill temper.

"Someone else has likely already filled his bed. And that is the way of men. Now get up, we're finding our cabins."

A man dressed in a regulation uniform of breeches, a gray frocked coat with white trim, and large white buttons approached us, trailed by a band of sailors. He had tied his dark brown hair into a small bun at the nape of his neck. The only facial hair he wore was a small mustache that barely covered half his top lip.

"Forgive me, Your Highness." He made a show of his bow. "I am First Officer Hindemill. I see the men have been tardy in securing your trunks. You must forgive us. The captain says there is a storm coming and wants to be away as soon as possible. There's much preparation I need to oversee before then."

I stood. "You're—"

"Ensure Her Highness's trunks are stowed first. The princess is not herself since boarding the ship," Radnisa interrupted.

Hindemill shared a knowing smile. "It's not uncommon for those who've never been onboard before. It will pass." He dipped his head before spinning on his heels to bark orders at his men.

The first officer escorted us to the stern of the ship, boasting that my cabin was the best onboard and placed Radnisa and Anderline elsewhere. If not for the wound in my heart, I would be elated they weren't cramped in my cabin with me.

I pressed my hand over my heart as if that would hold the dozen pieces together, then feeling Carlin's necklace, I seized it in my fist. He was my past, so he shouldn't be filling my head or remaining lodged in my heart like he did. Prince Juel should be there instead. Since no one had told me anything about him, all I had were my hopes. And if I let my fantasies free he was a brave, generous, attentive, handsome prince, though the latter wasn't necessary for my happiness.

Instead of dwelling on those thoughts, I leapt to my feet, intent on exploring my cabin, only to land back on my bed when my stomach rolled with the ship. I pressed my hand over my bodice, swallowing the queasiness down before standing again. Hopefully, as Hindemill said, this sickness would pass.

The sun flooded through latticed windows, creating blocks of light across the furniture, and stretching as long columns across the floor. At least they hadn't housed me in the depths of the ship, which had been a momentary fear. I had a large wooden desk with stationery and a comfortable couch for relaxing, and if I opened the window, I could release the stuffy smell all enclosed spaces held and let in the briny sea air.

The crew had set my trunks against the opposite wall to my bed. Perhaps if I unpacked a few things, I would forget about my stomach moving in rhythm with the ship. But before I made it halfway across the cabin, a shimmering light appeared above my trunk. I watched as muted colors emerged through the floating mirage, swirling in on themselves before coalescing into the form of a man wearing the clothes of a sailor. The top half of him was visible while the bottom half disappeared inside my trunk. For the first time in my life, I was seeing a spirit. Any gift in the death arts manifested in infancy, which meant if I was a spiritseer, it would've manifested already, not at the late age of twenty-three.

"By the looks of yer expression, I'd say yer'd be seeing me."

He moved forward, his bottom half emerging from my trunk. Rather than walk, he floated, his legs less formed. I could also see through him to the wall of my cabin behind. There was no death echo for me to read because, I guess, the man was already dead.

"A shock, aye? Same 'ere. This ain't never happened to me before. What might the lass's name be?

"Tressya. And you?"

"Scregs." His eyes roamed down my body.

"I see the dead lose their manners."

"The dead think like the living. Even if we've no more desire. Habit, I guess." He chuckled as he floated around me.

"Yer the princess?"

"And they eavesdrop."

"What else I gonna do? No one to talk to."

"You're alone?"

"Nah. Yer try talking to the same dumbasses for a century more and see how interesting that would be."

"Why don't I see them?"

"Yer will. No doubt. At some point." He came to a stop in front of me. "Curious, ain't it?" He slowly reached out his hand, but his finger passed through me like a spear of ice.

I shuddered. "That we're talking to each other?"

"Yeah. And more."

"Which is...?"

"Yer."

He floated closer. I refused to step back as a wall of cold pressed against my skin.

"What about me?"

"Why aren't yer on the floor? Fainting is what fancy ladies do. Or screaming?"

"I'm familiar with spirits. I've never seen one before, but..." There was little point in explaining.

"Hmm..." And he rubbed a finger along his chin, but it passed through his face. Perhaps gestures were a habit the dead retained, even if they couldn't feel what they were doing. "It might explain yer ways."

"My ways? Do you mean my ability to read death echoes?"

"Don't know what yer talking about. Death echoes?" He uttered it a few more times, playing with the word. "Never heard that one before."

"Colors are intricately linked to a person's fated moment of death. The taint of their death echo, the aura surrounding them, will change depending on where they exist in their life-death cycle. A healthy baby's death echo glows like the sun. A person close to death is surrounded by a choking, dark mist. Those are the extremes. Every key moment on their way to death is signaled by a change in their death echo."

He nodded, then scratched his ear, but his hand slipped through his head as a heat rushed up through my body. I swayed greater than the gentle roll of the ship, and I spun from him, a hand over my mouth, one pressed firm to my stomach. That didn't help. As the burning wave rode up my throat, I had little time to rush for the windows. The latch wouldn't budge. In my desperation, I banged on the wood paneling. "Curses, why won't you open?"

"I'd show yer. But I ain't got the fingers." Scregs wriggled his fingers in my periphery.

I palmed my mouth once more, pressing my lips firm to keep the constant roll of sickness inside. Fighting with the latch would not win me through. I closed my eyes. *Discipline.* I focused on my sudden, unexpected well of panic, swelled with the rise of sickness from my stomach and finding the window wouldn't open, then used my deep exhale to dislodge the panic and drag it from its clutch on my chest.

Once I'd tamed my wild racing heart, I found the latch wasn't hard to undo. I swung open the window and leaned out as far as I could, breathing in the cold sea air. The back of the Sapphire Rose stood almost as high as the dock, but I stared ahead out to sea with the noisy squawk of gulls overhead.

Scregs appeared at my side, the windowsill splitting his body in two.

"It happens to many. Best to empty yer guts into the water. Yer'll feel better."

I ignored him as I pressed my palm to the wound. *Mother, what have you done?* It was the only explanation for my deepening ability within the death arts.

CHAPTER

SIX

TAMAS

Snow blanketed my fur cloak, along the horse's withers, and in its tracks, obscuring the trail I left behind. I pulled the fur around my neck and slumped further into my saddle.

It was a long, slow journey I made alone. The Huungardred bloodline flowed through Garrat and Osmud as much as it did through me, but I sent them on a mission to gain loyalty from the northern realm instead of joining me. I'd decided to go see Thaindrus myself, to check on him. Mostly I sought his wisdom.

While I hoped to bring down the House of Tannard from within, many within Emberfell would rise against me, even without their king. A swift war against the senate and nobility would put an end to any potential insurgency, though it would not address my greatest concern: the Creed of Salmun.

The horse threw up its head, then gave an anxious snort.

"Scare my horse, and I'll scare you," I said without bothering to raise my voice, for the Huungardred had the ears of a wolf.

Snow fell from the branches of spindly pines as something moved toward me, snapping branches in its path. A great shadowy beast lumped out of the thicket and into the thin veil of falling snow. I soothed my prancing horse with a warm hand at its withers. "That's close enough. Or you'll have me on the ground."

The beast gave a soft growl, rumbling deep in its throat —which I took as an apology—and lowered to its haunches.

For years, I'd traveled this far north and had learned to distinguish most of my distant kin while they were in their preferred form. The blood-red streaks through her pelt, the mixed color of her eyes—the left honey, the right rich brown —and the scar running a hairless line down her left foreleg told me she was Thaindrus's daughter.

"Bryra." I nodded in acknowledgment. "This is a pleasant surprise."

On all fours, she turned in my direction and settled into an easy lope beside my now-settled horse. Calm as he was, my horse would refuse to carry her, so there was no point in her shifting now. Besides, in form, she could outdo my horse's speed in a full gallop.

We continued in silence as the snowfall gained momentum. Bryra's thick pelt kept her warm, but the cold found ways under my clothes, making me dream of a blazing fire and spiced mead to burn the throat. The dampness flattened my hair to my head, and melting snow dripped from my chin down the front of my cloak.

By the time we neared Droshrar, the great hall of Thaindrus, I could barely see yards in front of me. I relied on Bryra to guide me through the dense undergrowth, until she moved ahead, swallowed by the snow-coated branches as she disappeared amongst the thick-trunked trees.

I was familiar with these parts this close to Droshrar and spurred my horse into a brisk pace, heading for the centuries-old pine rising high above its neighbors. The pine stood as a sentinel to the trail leading to the great hall doors.

The Huungardred had little need for added warmth while in beast form, their thick coats providing plenty, so I was glad to see smoke spiraling up from the large stone chimney—a sign that Thaindrus awaited my arrival.

Through the curtain of heavy snow, I barely made out the half-form that appeared from the side of the hall. Instincts told me it was Bryra again. Few Huungardred cared about changing into their half-form in front of outsiders, except Bryra, and I suspected her shyness had something to do with me.

She was half a century older than me, but in Huungardred years, she was still a youngling, though old enough to marry. A fact that grew more awkward with every year I returned to Droshrar. I was a man with many loves but inept at loving. A cherished friendship was not enough to pull me into marriage, so my visits to Droshrar grew less frequent in recent years.

I slid from my horse as another half-form appeared through the snow to take charge of my mount. His head reached my chest, and he walked with a cumbersome gait, which was common among Huungardred who spent most of their lives in their natural form. Because of the uneven growth between their beast form and their human bodies, the boy stooped, his back hunching to the left, the human side. With time, it would even out, his beast side stretching his human side to gigantic proportions. The young boy took my horse's reins without comment and led him toward the stable.

Bryra smiled as I strode toward her. The beast side of her face peeled back into what looked like a snarl. Both sides of her half-form were beautiful. Her beast side kept its rich pelt of lush reds, her eyes their mixed colors, her body strong and muscular. The skin on her human side was deep brown and as smooth as that of any highborn. The scar ran down her left arm, the human side, as a dark brown mark, from shoulder to elbow. Her hair flowed down her back as a thick mane of mahogany splashed with streaks of red.

Bryra was a fierce fighter, a kind and loyal friend, a woman any man would desire to marry. Many times, I wished that man was me, for there were few women around with such strength of character, capability, and will. But I could not convince my heart to feel differently toward her.

"You are welcome, my good friend. It has been too long."

"Far too long." About to speak lies as excuses, I pressed my lips firmly. It was not how friends treated each other.

"News has reached us all the way up here that you traveled with the Nazeen to see the augur."

"Igthredia is fond of a tale."

"He wasn't filling our table with fanciful stories to keep us all guessing?"

Even standing at the top of the steps, I remained half a foot shorter than Bryra, and I was not a short man. "Romelda has always had faith in the augur."

She quirked an eyebrow on the human side of her face. Strangely, the two sides of a Huungardred's half-formed face could move independently. A smile on one side could end up in opposition on the other.

"What do you believe?" The question was half innocent, half daring, tinged with a wisp of flirtation.

"Many things. But it's never too late to stop listening to your elders."

Her cheeky smile faded as she dipped her eyes to the ground. Something in what I'd said changed the easy flow of our conversation.

"Do you believe this is your fate?"

Bryra didn't need to ask what the augur had said. I had shared my concerns and doubts with her over these many years when it never crossed my mind she would feel any differently toward me than I for her.

I hesitated before answering because I felt this answer needed careful consideration. Whatever I uttered aloud, I could not take back. "Yes. Yes, I believe."

"What happened to the Tamas I once knew?" A sad stain lightened her voice. "There was a time when you scoffed at the Nazeen's words. What has changed your mind?"

"There was once a time I had the leisure to doubt. But I'm not a boy anymore. I can't deny my responsibilities. There is... It's hard to explain. It feels like there's something inside of me urging me forward." How could I explain? "I believe it's the Etherweave. Though I could be wrong." Because it sounded ludicrous. I sighed, slapping a hand to my thigh, finding I had lost the impetus in my answer. "I can no longer turn away from my Fate."

"Did the augur say anything of worth?"

"The augur said a great deal. I've yet to decide if it was of any worth."

Four of us heard Sirillious's pronouncements, but two of us, Romelda and I, seemed to understand their implications. I had yet to speak of our visit to the augur with my two friends, finding the last words the augur spoke a dark prediction. *Twain is the bloodborn.* I wanted to think on these words and their implications before I shared them.

"But if what he said was true, I can't ignore it."

Bryra nodded. "In your heart, you already know."

"You know me."

"Maybe too well." She stood aside and welcomed me into the great hall. "Father will be happy to see you."

Thaindrus sat at the far end of the great hall, his enormous chair placed so he stared into the dancing flames. The hall was twice the size of Ironhelm, with a ceiling high enough to touch the stars.

The Huungardred had lived in the wilds of the north before the great war with the Levenian a millennium ago. They'd crafted their own legends of their ancestry, and these tales are deeply intertwined with nature. They believed they emerged from the wilds, embodying the link between nature and humans. They gradually gained wisdom in understanding the complex and delicate balance of nature. And, as nature intended, they were able to communicate their knowledge with humans, enabling them to comprehend and respect the wilds just as profoundly.

Perhaps that was so, but it seemed many had forgotten or no longer cared for their legends and their purported purpose, for they chose to spend a good deal of their time roaming the wilds in their natural form, returning to Droshrar hall at certain times of the year to take part in their yearly celebrations or when called by Thaindrus, but rarely in-between. For some, it made them less willing to accept their half-form and less tolerant of humans, which was a growing concern for Thaindrus.

The echo of my boots reverberated across the hall as I closed the distance to my good friend. He kept his eyes on the fire, looking comfortable but tired. And old. The sight of him wedged a spike through my heart. My guilt seeped out. I should never have left it this long before returning to his hall.

After I had won my place as the head of Ironhelm, I often fled to Droshrar hall, seeking Thaindrus's counsel. It turned out living a long life slowed a man's lust for power, dented the vice of revenge, and gave him much wisdom.

Thaindrus looked from the fire to greet me as I slipped into the large chair placed opposite him. It was so large, when I sat, my feet dangled off the ground, and I had to shuffle backward into it if I wanted to relax against the high-back.

His mouth peeled back into a warm smile, revealing mostly gums on the human side, and dark yellowed fangs on the beast side of his face. Once glistening and lush, his coat of silvery-gray was now dulled to the color of a murky morning mist and lank, as if he'd just come in out of the rain. His eyes were the color of the flames, with the beginning patches of milky-white in the center.

"You look younger by the day," I jested.

He nodded. "You were never a good liar."

He stroked his long nails across the armrest, a habit of his that left deep grooves in the wood.

"Young Razohan, you have been busy."

"As is expected of me."

"Forgive my absence at your feast. I fear my body refuses to move as it once did."

"It's I who should ask forgiveness. It's been too long since I returned to Droshrar."

He waved his hand to dismiss my remark. Only then did I notice the cracks and chips in his long nails.

Wild, fierce, and loyal. These were the three biggest traits of the Huungardred. They valued courage, bravery, and grit in their principal, so overlooked the hereditary line when deciding their next ruler. In his youth, Thaindrus was all these things. I never knew him then, but in old age, he reminded me a lot of my father.

"There is much the young Razohan thinks upon. I see the restlessness in your eyes, the weight bearing on your shoulders."

I nodded as I smiled, knowing a solemn face would disguise nothing from my dear friend.

"Your venturing has sparked rumors across the north."

"I can hold no secrets."

"Everyone in the North has a great deal of interest in

what the young Razohan leader does and says. You are very important to all of us. But especially to me."

I leaned forward and took his hand. "As a good friend, your health is especially important to me."

"Do I look that bad?"

"Not for a man of your age."

He chuckled. "Ah," he said, looking across to Bryra, who'd entered the hall, carrying a tray with two large tankards. At the site of them, my mouth watered.

"These days Father speaks long and slow." She smiled. "Perhaps you'll need more than one of these." She handed me a tankard full of warm mead.

Thaindrus accepted his tankard, then waited as Bryra straightened, waited more as she looked down at the two of us. She frowned at her father, then rolled the one eye on the human side of her face.

"Secrets, Father?"

"Men's talk."

"Since when do you shield your gossip?"

"When it's not gossip I speak." He kissed the back of her hand. Releasing it was his signal for her to leave. She huffed but strode across the grand hall, casting me a look over her shoulder as she left. There was once a time when a look like that meant fun and mischief. Not so now, and all I could do was flash a weak smile. She disappeared out into the frigid evening air, sending drifts of new snow inside.

"The Huungardred never waste time on small talk."

I nodded and took a swig of the mead in preparation.

"My time draws near. That I can no longer disguise."

"The Huungardred will deeply mourn your passing. As will I." Already I felt the loss in my heart.

"I must secure my predecessor before then."

"And who do your people choose? Why have this conversation with me?"

Thaindrus glanced over his mead at me.

"You won't name Bryra?"

"I love my daughter very much. And while she is deeply respected amongst my people for her courage and bravery, she does not understand the human realm."

I slowly nodded, staring into my mead, knowing Bryra would be disappointed with this conversation. She'd spent her life preparing to take his place, proving her worth through bravery and ferocity alongside her brethren, hoping they would accept her as their next principal.

"You must know the respect I hold for you?" Thaindrus continued.

"And I you." I shuffled in my seat.

"That is why I wish to name you as principal before the council of elders."

I almost choked on my next swig of mead. "That's too much of an honor you place on me."

His shrewd, flaming eyes leveled on me. "You're struggling to find your excuses."

"I don't believe the Huungardred would accept me over one of their own."

"Are you in such a hurry to distance yourself from your own blood?"

"What? No. Thaindrus. You know how much I honor my connection to the Huungardred. But what of your second? I struggle to understand why you would choose me over your second."

"Malinth is a loyal second. But he is brash, easily offended, and as quick to temper. He does not understand the ways of humans. He would not welcome sitting with the council of the clans. I fear he would provoke unease with the men of the north.

"Long gone are the days when the Huungardred roamed all the north. The coming of man has blunted our rule and shrunk our territory. They are many as we grow less with each decade passing. We need a strong leader, someone cunning, who understands the world of humans and the importance of negotiation if we hope to survive."

The sacrifice of living long lives was their difficulty in birthing children. Only a mere two offspring were ever successfully born to a woman in her extended life, which meant the clans of the north outbred the Huungardred. Slowly human settlements pushed them further north into the deep wilds inhospitable to humans.

I clasped my tankard, feeling his eyes on me as I stared into my mead. My love and respect for him meant I wanted to think hard before I answered. "I am deeply honored. But my fate lies to the south."

"I feared the Nazeen had gotten through to you."

"It has always been my fate. It's only now I accept it."

"Remember, young Razohan, your fate is also our fate. Our destiny is your destiny. Your allegiance is with us. It is our blood in your veins. It is through us you have the power and strength to defeat your enemy in the south."

"I couldn't be prouder than I am carrying the blood of your forefathers. But my blood is also from the Tannard line. Something I can't ignore. The time is coming as the augur foresaw. The Etherweave will rise. With it, King Henricus will seek to destroy me and everyone who calls the north their home."

He banged his fist on his armrest. "Then take your place with the Huungardred as their rightful leader. Lay claim to your heritage, and you shall have a loyal and savage army to face the king when he comes."

"I fear it won't be enough." I sunk into my seat. "You know I've never desired Henricus's throne. My place is here. But I can't deny what I need to do. For the sake of the north. For the sake of the seven realms. You know the Levenians seek the power of the Etherweave. We must ensure it's in our hands if and when they return."

"You're sure these sea people will be a terrible force with the Etherweave in their grasp?"

I stared at him, shocked by what he said. "A millennium is a long time, but you can't have forgotten what they did to the people of Tarragona."

"I do not, young Razohan. But power has a seductive force no matter who wields it."

"You think I'll be no better."

"The line of King Ricaud runs in your veins. He was a good king. You'll be the same. But stay true to those loyal to you. Without friends and allies you are nothing."

I sighed, seeing no way clear of this argument that wouldn't offend my old friend or compromise the certainty I felt for the path I had to take.

"Have you thought about what Malinth would say to this? The council of elders respect his opinion. Do they not?"

"There will be no issue once you take Bryra as your wife."

This time, I choked on my mead.

Thaindrus ignored my spluttering and continued. "An alliance of marriage between a Huungardred and a Razohan will give you the authority you need to take my place. The elders could not refute it. Even Malinth would accept your pledge."

"Thaindrus—"

"Do not be an idiot and tell me you're ignorant of my daughter's feelings toward you."

I nodded. "Aye. I have suspected for a while."

"While we accepted the descendants of King Ricaud's granddaughter as our blood, we have long sought to keep our bloodline pure. But I believe such wisdom will be the death of my people. Your marriage to Bryra will be the survival of my kind, and my people will accept such a marriage. We must strengthen our bloodline through the line of humans."

"I can't speak."

"I have spoken of my plans with Bryra. And she agrees."

I sat forward, my head hung low for all the thoughts it held. "My friend, there will be a way." Still, I didn't look at him. "I know there will be a way to save your people. Please give me time to think."

With the tasks in front of me, now was not the time to take a wife. Had Bryra agreed for the good of her people or because she really loved me? As the Razohan's leader it was expected of me to marry and have children, but I was not prepared to do so without love. A lifetime of respect and companionship, I could bare, but why take only that when there was the possibility of so much more with the right woman.

"I fear I have little time to wait for your answer."

My loyalty to Thaindrus and his people ran as deep as my loyalty to the Razohan. I didn't want to see his people fade from the north, neither did I want to hurt Bryra, but I couldn't say yes.

"You age slowly, old friend. I think you have time for me to find an answer."

"I ask you to save my people, Tamas."

Finally, I lifted my head to meet his eyes. Just as I was about to give him an answer, not one he would like, but one I had to say, Bryra appeared in the doorway.

"Tamas, you have a messenger."

I launched to my feet.

"He's ridden hard."

I placed my tankard on my seat. "Forgive me, Thaindrus." But before I moved for the door, Septus rushed inside.

"My lord," he spluttered, shaking the snow from his head. "The Nazeen has sent news."

I glanced down at Thaindrus, but he kept his eyes on the fire.

"What is it?"

"King Henricus's ship set sail from Merania two days prior."

Prince Juel's bride was on her way. "That's all?"

"Yes, my lord. The Nazeen told me the news was urgent."

"Thank you. You've ridden hard, I see."

"Accept Thaindrus's hospitality for the night," Bryra said.

Already the day had darkened outside, which meant I would go nowhere either. "Go," I said to Septus. "Enjoy Thaindrus's generous hospitality." Then I turned back to Thaindrus.

He flicked his eyes up to meet mine before returning them to the fire. "Nazeen schemes? They never bode well."

"I can't ignore what she says. Neither can I ignore the threat King Henricus poses to all in the north." I moved my tankard and sat on the edge of my seat. "I've made my promise to the Nazeen. I must deal with this new issue. And now I make my promise to you. The Huungardred will never disappear from the north."

Thaindrus rested his tankard in his lap. "A grand promise. How will you keep it?"

That I couldn't say without accepting his request. "I will keep it. But if I fail to keep the House of Tannard from taking the Bone Throne, then any failed promise to you won't matter."

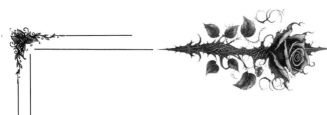

CHAPTER

SEVEN

TRESSYA

It was the first time since our departure that the sea didn't toss us about in our beds. I slumped forward, clinging tightly to the railing, my head feeling too heavy to lift. My hair stuck to my cheeks and hung limp from the spray. At some point soon, I was bound to lose more of my supper. Though the sea was calm, the rolling of the ship pressed the railing into my old wounds.

Hindemill said the sickness would pass, yet we had been traveling for five days and there seemed to be no end to the time I spent emptying my stomach into the ocean. By now, I felt weak with hunger and too sick to keep anything down.

"Your Highness, you shouldn't be up here." It was Hindemill, who had become my shadow whenever I came on deck.

"I shall take care of the princess." As if summoned, Radnisa appeared behind him.

It seemed she had taken a disliking to Hindemill or the attention he gave me. I couldn't decide if she feared me finding an ally or loathed the idea of anyone showing me kindness. Why had the sickness not affected her? My only consolation was that Anderline, too, suffered and never rose from her bed.

Hindemill's eyes rolled skyward upon hearing her sharp voice. I would smile at him as a show of unity if I didn't think my stomach was about to betray me again.

The first officer turned to the side. "Of course, my lady. I wouldn't dream of standing in the way of your duty to the princess. You are her servant, after all, not I."

To that, I did smile, especially upon seeing Radnisa's mouth pinch tight and her eyes flare with fury. Maybe I should warn Hindemill to sleep with a dagger under his pillow for the rest of the voyage.

He swept into an exaggerated bow. "Your Highness, seek comfort below."

"I will. Thank you."

He left without acknowledging Radnisa, who followed his departure with a lethal stare.

"He's vital to the sailing of this ship, so I wouldn't do what you're planning."

She turned to face me, chin held high. "What's one man lost when there are plenty more sailors on board to fill his shoes?"

"Discretion, dear sister. Don't let your claws show, or I'll think you're jealous."

"The sooner we reach Tarragona, the better. I'm eager to

see you bound to a man's fate. We'll see how smart your mouth is then."

I snapped my head away to stare out over the ocean, not wanting to give her the satisfaction of knowing her words cut me. I had long suspected that her assignment was not simply as my lady-in-waiting all these years, but as my tormentor. Her life had become less about studying the pillars and practices, and more about devising ways to make me feel inadequate.

Her gaze flitted down my body. "You're a disgrace. Go below and clean yourself up before gossip makes its way to King Henricus. Since he's lost the daughter he favored for this marriage, you need to take extra care of your behavior and appearance, lest he refuse you. We cannot disappoint the Mother."

"I'm sure we'll have greater concerns once he meets you," I breathed, losing my sharp tongue as another wave of nausea threatened me.

"Marriage will not remove me from your side," Radnisa hissed. "I'm your shadow. Always. Remember that."

"Do you plan on sharing our bed, too? Because I'm only too happy to move aside and give you room."

She folded her arms across her chest. "And there are the reports I must make to the Mother."

Curses. Once again, I swallowed any further remarks with her final blow.

"I'll head below once I've..." And I spun my head away, leaning over the railing.

"Praise to the Mother," Radnisa cursed with an exasperated tone and fled.

I lifted my head, wiping my limp hair from my face, finding a smile after all. My bed called to me, but the rocking ship felt worse below, and I was fed up with telling Scregs to leave me alone so I could wallow in my sickness. Instead, he brought friends, and they insisted on filling my small cabin and badgering me with questions about Merania, my life, my family, and every conceivable question they could think of. After a day of confinement with the sailor spirits, I pretended I didn't know enough to answer any further questions. Perhaps if I concentrated on developing my skill in the death arts, it would allow me to shut out the spirits until I found them useful.

Around this time of evening, when the sun grew close to the horizon, a mist bobbed its way across the deck. A sudden chill racked my body as the temperature dropped. I was wearing damp clothes from the constant spray and about to get sicker if I didn't change into something dry.

Before I made it two steps to the stern and my room, Scregs and Longhorn blocked my path. Longhorn was short, scraggly, with one eye and full of scars. He talked with a stutter, which meant he rarely spoke, a blessing, but Scregs always made up for his silence.

"If we could, we'd send that one over the edge," Scregs said, while Longhorn nodded.

"Women like her are no good except for bedding, and even then only while gagged," Scregs continued.

About to laugh, I palmed my mouth when my stomach churned. After inhaling deeply, I felt ready to speak. "Radnisa has spikes in hidden places. And I'm sure they can even reach the dead."

"No doubt. Like I said, bedding is all they're good for."

"While I welcome your conversation more than—"

A sailor walked my way, staring at me with a heavy scowl. I turned back to the railing and watched the mist thicken until he passed. In the few brief moments of talking to the spirits, the sun had slipped below the horizon, leaving a grim gray in its place.

When I turned back, Scregs and Longhorn were floating along after the sailor. Decades of living on the boat as spirits, they still showed a lot of interest in the sailors' lives. It was the spirit of an old, stout sailor with drooping cheeks who told me of the longing in all their hearts. Not only did they continue to perform habitual gestures, but they also remembered what it was like to feel sensations. Losing that ability plagued them from the other side of the dividing veil.

Since my stomach no longer threatened me, I left the railing and headed back to my cabin. Inside, I crawled across to my bed in the dark, feeling my stomach already complaining from the stench of the livestock in the hold below and knowing my cabin's walls surrounded me. Halfway there, I diverted to the window. Perhaps if I let in some fresh air, I wouldn't feel so bad.

The moon had risen, but the mist obscured its light. I stumbled with the roll of the ship, using the desk to help me reach the window without tripping over my feet.

I stalled when a flicker of shadow flashed across the window. Perhaps I was mistaken. I waited, but seeing nothing else, I continued to stumble forward. A thud sounded from over my head. Noises were common. But that was quite a thud. Next came the cries.

The beat of my heart pulsed down into my fingertips. Taking one slow breath, I listened to the eruption of chaos above, the heavy thuds that sounded like barrels falling to the deck, shouts of fear, cries of pain.

Abandoning the window, I headed for my trunk, the one with the small green jewels of no value embedded within a circle of wood carved to look like lace on the lid. I retrieved my two sheathed daggers wrapped in cloth and buried beneath my embellished dresses. Shutting out the sounds of fighting, I focused on shortening my dress, using one dagger to slash the hem to knee length. Once done, I stepped out of the discarded fabric and sheathed the dagger.

Scregs pushed his way through the wall of my cabin, followed by Longhorn and Stede, son of a captain and, sadly, too young to die.

"What yer doing, woman?" Scregs cried.

"How bad is it?" I replied, while focusing on strapping my daggers to my hips for easy reach.

"Ya can't go out there," Stede said.

"How many are we up against?" I continued, ensuring my buckle was tight. I couldn't see in the dull moonlight and wanted to ensure I wouldn't lose my daggers halfway through a skirmish.

"Yer crazy woman. Yer listen to us. Stay here. Ain't nothing but death up there."

Finally, I glanced at the plaguing spirits, but I had nothing to say, so I headed for the door to my cabin. Scregs maneuvered his spectral body in front of me as if to bar my way. "Yer daft, bloody woman. Maybe we should step aside. We could do with some fresh meat on board."

"Fine. Move aside. I don't want to pass through you." An involuntary shudder racked my body at the thought.

He made a grab for me instead, and his arm passed through my chest. My breath hitched as the icy chill tunneled deep through to my heart. Gritting my teeth, I passed through his body, then stumbled for the door as I punched out a held breath. My hand shook as I fumbled for the latch to my cabin door. "I won't be doing that again."

"Go on then. We ain't following yer body overboard. We'll wait for yer to come back to us."

I would've slammed the door in their faces, but they could simply come through the wall. Besides, I had to be quiet lest the enemy hear me.

Faint starlight streamed down the stairs leading onto the deck, guiding my way. I used the wall on one side of the corridor to keep my balance from the roll of the ship as I headed toward the dull light. A harsh guttural sound, like a roar, turned my body to ice. What could make that sound?

Scregs reappeared in front of me. "If yer going to be so foolish. This is what yer face."

I would've stepped around him, but this could be useful. I pressed my back to the wall for balance and waited, hands resting on the hilts of my daggers.

"It's them ruddy beasts from the north. Fierce as they come. They're powerful, those lot. Stronger than any man. Yer be needing more than those knives to cut through their hide."

Another thud rumbled through the deck directly above, sounding strong enough to split the wood. I dived sideways and into the opposite wall, one dagger in my hand.

"What beasts are those?" Curses that my father and the Mother failed to educate me properly. There was no mention of marauding beasts in the limited education I had received. How did they get on board?

A death scream followed every roar, which pierced through my ears and tightened the choke on my lungs.

"They call 'em the Huungardred. Monstrous, evil things. Unstoppable by normal means."

Oh yes, I had heard of those, but only as legends to scare children at night-time. "Are they possessed? Why are they attacking us?"

"They have two forms. Beast and man."

"They're intelligent?" The legends said as much, but I was no longer a child, and the legends told to me as a child held no sway over me now. If they were intelligent, then they would know how to fight like a man, reading body language, using counterattacks, and counterstrikes.

"Lethal fighters. So they say."

"Enough. I have to join the fight." We needed as many as we could get if we hoped to survive the night.

"They have keen eyes."

That stilled me. Night was their advantage.

I took one breath, gripping my dagger tight in my hand. Mother be with me. I used one more breath to steady myself and with the slow exhale, I focused on the noise above me. Radnisa would likely already be above deck; Anderline in her cabin. There she could stay to go down with the ship or be killed. Whichever came first if we failed.

Once my hands felt like steel around my daggers, I pushed off the wall.

"Where yer going?"

Ignoring Scregs, I hurried deeper into the bowels of the ship, but he annoyingly kept pace. "That's it. Go hide yerself. It's the only way to survive."

Hoping he would understand what I meant when I didn't reply, I quickened my pace. But Scregs kept me company as I climbed down to the livestock hold. The stench of excrement burned my nose, but I continued forward, pushing my way through the herd. Animals could sense danger, and the stock shuffled restlessly in their confined space, crying out in distress, as if I was the beast.

"Good plan. Hide amongst the cattle."

I pushed the rump of one animal aside, held my breath, then bent to pick up some of the dung and smeared it over my body.

"Gods, woman. That's gross, but smart."

"If they can see in the dark, they can smell in the dark. And the meat they're after tonight is not cattle."

"Yer smart. But I doubt it will do."

"It will have to do," I said, caking more dung across my body. My delicate stomach would revolt if I'd not already smothered all else except my focus on winning this fight. But when I smeared the dung across my cheeks, my stomach roiled violently. I convulsed forward, unable to stop the retch. Having spent the day with my head over the railing, there was nothing left in my stomach to empty.

"Yer making me sick."

I shook the remaining clumps from my hands, then wiped my hands on my skirts. That would have to do.

"'Ere now what yer doing?" Scregs yelled at my back as I

retraced my steps toward the ladder. "I told yer all that to stop yer."

The noise of the fight grew louder as I climbed, but the roll of the ship made my progress slow. I staggered through the bowels of the ship, bouncing off of the walls, and twice lost my footing on the ladders. Scregs persisted in pestering me until I stopped at the bottom of the last ladder leading above deck.

"If you want to help me, get up there and tell me when it's clear for me to come up. I don't want to exit in front of one of our *friends*," I said as I gripped firm the ladder's railing. Already my hands itched to feel the hilts of my daggers in my palm again. Looking up to the night sky, a blur rushed past overhead, so fast I couldn't make it out.

"Yer sure 'bout this?" Scregs's head popped up between me and the ladder.

"Go," I growled.

"You'll end up with a claw through your heart."

"If I could, I would put a claw through you."

Scregs disappeared. I scrambled up the stairs, losing my footing once more in my haste when the ship dropped into the trough of a wave, but my grip was like a manacle on the wood railing. Nearing the top, I slowed, waiting for Scregs to reappear. But he didn't. Of all the times to abandon me, now was the worst.

It wasn't Scregs's head that appeared in the hatch, but Stede's. "Ya stupid or brave. I'm going with stupid."

"Is it clear for me to come up?" I whispered.

"What ya mean to say is, are there any fighters up 'ere? A ship full of 'em, but ya don't seem to care."

"Curses," I whispered. I would have to climb up and see.

"'Ang on." Stede held out a hand to stop my climb.

A dark figure rushed past him.

"Blimey, that was close," he said. "Nearly barreled into 'em, ya did."

"And what about now?"

Stede stared over the hatch, perhaps at some fight happening nearby. I was about to reiterate my question when a blur of darkness rose behind him. On reflex, I let go of the railing and jumped from the ladder as a hulking man, too big to be a sailor, fell through Stede and down into the hatch. I landed on my feet, but my momentum sent me tumbling backward onto my ass as the roll of the ship dropped the ground from beneath me. The man crashed down on top of me, pinning my legs to the ground.

The two of us moved as one: me reaching for a dagger as he rolled toward me, fumbling with his hands to reach me. Before he caught me in a situation I couldn't escape, I jerked up and stabbed without aim. My speed caught him unawares, my blade piercing him through the shoulder. Not a fatal wound. That's what my other dagger was for.

His body went rigid as he growled his pain-driven fury. That moment was his mistake. With my other dagger in hand, I struck again, this time straight through his heart. For a breath, he turned to stone, then he fell sideways, leaving me coated in spurts of his blood.

Stede released a long whistle, hovering above me. "Where did ya come from, little lady? That was bloody awesome."

Too busy rolling the large man off of me, I didn't bother

to glance in his direction. "This time, look. You didn't even see him coming."

"Sure thing, Captain. Whatever ya say."

I glanced the enemy over. In the dark, he was nothing more than a large, dark mass sprawled in an awkward pose. On my knees, I shuffled closer, feeling for his chest, then shoulder, hunting for my daggers. My blood slicked hands slipped on the hilts, but my blades were sharp, making it easy to pull them free. I wiped them once across his clothes, then re-sheathed both and climbed to my feet.

Hearing a soft noise behind me, I spun, a dagger in my hand.

"What's happening?" Anderline said, slinking closer.

"North men are attacking us," I whispered, nudging the dead man at my feet. "Look at the size of him. They're shifter people."

Anderline came up beside me. "Mother on high, you stink."

"And you smell like prey. But that can't be helped. Come on."

"Wait." Anderline grabbed my arm. "You stay here."

"What? You're joking?"

"I'll go above and fight, but you must return to your cabin." She moved past me, pushing me backward.

"Anderline." Too shocked, I couldn't reply for a wasteful breath. Then, tumbling into action, I yanked her around to face me. "No way. We fight together."

"You're loyal to the Sistern, are you not?"

"You don't need to ask that."

"Then follow orders."

"The Mother would require us all to—"

"You must reach Tarragona. It's your duty to birth the next heir to the Tannard line. Do you hear me?"

"The Mother did not foresee this—"

"Are you questioning your orders?"

"No."

"Then do as I say." She pushed me back and fled to the steps.

Anderline was halfway up when something far from human dropped through the hatch, swiping her from the ladder. In the dull shaft of starlight, I couldn't make out what was happening, but I knew Anderline was compromised.

My delay risked her life. I leapt forward, stabbing hard and fast into the monstrous creature's back. The size of my enemy meant my strike hit lower than I would have liked, but if I was lucky, I would hit an important organ. Before I could use my second dagger, it swept its arm back and knocked me off my feet. Such was the strength of its blow, I left the ground to hit the wall behind me, blowing the wind from my lungs and smacking my head on the wood paneling.

My head spun, tunneling the half-muffled cries of fury and tumultuous sounds of fighting to a distant place. I struggled to claw my concentration back, keeping enough wits to know I was in trouble as I was. Above the cacophony, a woman's wails pierced the air. Anderline. She needed me.

I rolled to my side, pulling my second dagger, when I heard breaking bone and Anderline's horrifying silence echoing with finality. A coldness swept through my chest, then spread throughout my body, freezing me in place.

Discipline. I took a deep breath, then scrambled away as the giant beast charged toward me. It caught my shoe, wrapped a hand like a manacle around my ankle and yanked me back with force, sweeping my arms out from under me. I bit back my cry, still holding my dagger firm in my hand. Splinters dug into my wrists and any exposed skin, so I used the pain to sharpen my focus.

Close now, I could feel the heat from its body blanketing me in a suppressive hold. While I struggled to suck in air, the beast drew in deep, lumbering breaths with a low, rippling snarl. Its claws split the skin on my ankle as it yanked me to where it wanted me.

Feeling the creature shift above me, I tensed, straining to listen over the chaos of the continuing fight on deck. I had one chance.

I rolled, at the same time curling myself up, plunging up with my dagger. The beast loomed low. It wasn't far for my strike to go, but a hand seized my wrist, halting my strike mid-air. Tightening its grip, my fingers numbed. I lost hold of my dagger, and it clattered to the wood floor.

Crying the fury of my failed strike, I kicked upward and hit the creature between the legs. I could only hope it would suffer the same pain in beast form as it would a man. With an ear-piercing roar, it tumbled forward, blowing hot breath across my face as it landed on top of me, crushing my breath from my lungs.

The beast roared again, dousing me in the stench of stale blood. I turned my head aside, feeling as though my bones would break, growing hot under its fiery body heat. Spiked hairs tickled my face and neck. Its claws traced tracks along my wrists. Perhaps these marks would be permanent.

Caged, my mind raged, but the beast's body held me firmly in place. I had no hope of escape. No daggers, no room to move. Mother Divine, this couldn't be the end.

I felt it transform, saw its outline in the faint light shift and ripple as it lost its beast form and became human. The hairs that had tickled my skin disappeared. The fiery burn of its body heat lessened, and I felt the surprisingly soft skin of its hands against mine. Its size shrunk, though the man now on top of me remained heavy and too strong.

"You're next." His deep voice was part growl, part thunder, but I couldn't see his face in the dark hold.

"Why have you attacked us? What are we to you?" I spat.

"These people are nothing to me."

"Then you're after wealth?"

"No."

"You're lying. Either you've come for us or for our wealth. You wouldn't be here otherwise. Call off your attack, and I will make a bargain with you."

"That's impossible."

"I have means at my disposal."

"It's impossible because there is nothing you can give me I want."

He sounded sane, which meant I could reason with him. "Please. Just call off your attack. Then we can talk. No one is above bribery. Whatever bargain you've been offered, I can offer better."

I was half-conscious of the words pouring from my mouth, desperate words to keep his attention elsewhere while I grappled to gather my focus and funnel it into him. I hoped impending death was the impetus I needed to overcome whatever blocks I had with finding soul voice.

I concentrated on loosening the confines within my mind and opened my awareness to the surrounding spaces. Apparently commanding the skill went beyond listening for sounds; I had to become a part of those sounds; beyond feeling the deck below me, I had to become the solidity of the wood holding me in place. Only then could I pierce the boundary of another and merge so that my heart beat in time with theirs and their pulse filled my veins. I would have no access to their thoughts, emotions, or sensations. Rather, to find their soul word, I had to delve into the ethereal places where sense was an illusion, where life became indescribable, and you were left with a knowing that couldn't be voiced. Through this mystery came a unique word that held no meaning on its own or power when voiced to any other. I had never found such a word before.

This was all according to the Sistern's training; a level of skill I'd failed to achieve.

"What do you offer, princess?"

His question caught me on the cusp of feeling my heart miss a beat to form a rhythm with his. It lurched to snap back to its own tempo.

Dammit. I'd been so close.

It was the shift in his tone that dragged my focus to the surface. Gone was the deep, threatening rumble of an angry storm. Instead, it sounded smooth, like velvet, with a subtle edge. In human form, was his eyesight comparable to his keen vision as a beast? It was an uncomfortable thought, given his face was merely a hand-span from mine. I could feel his warm breaths, no longer smelling bloody now he was a man, nor did his body smell animalic.

"What do you want?" I tried to dismiss his presence, the heat of his body pressed against mine, the welling panic threatening to consume my control, and corralled my focus once again.

"A dangerous question, princess."

I wasn't the virgin princess fluttering her eyes in court, so I wasn't ignorant of the reasons behind the deepening tone of his voice, laced with a silken caress. If I had a leg free, I would aim once more between his and show him all the ways I would like to play with him. Better if I had my daggers. His prized cock would become fish food.

"Why are you calling me princess?"

"Only royalty can be so conceited as to make demands when they should be begging for their lives. But I must say, royalty usually smell better. It's an interesting perfume you favor."

I was momentarily dumbfounded by his pathetic attempt at humor. If I had a hand free, I would slap myself to my senses. "Why have you attacked us? If I knew—"

"Can I trust your promises?"

He caught me unawares. "Those within my power to make," I said.

"Go home. Never step foot on Tarragona's shores."

"That's one I can't keep. You must know a woman has no mastery over her fate."

"Is that a lament in your voice? If mastery over your fate is what you desire, I could give you that."

What was happening here?

"All you have to do is promise to abandon Tarragona."

"And I would say you have no sense of duty."

"You'd be wrong there, Princess. It's my unwavering sense of duty that brings me here."

Curses. This conversation would get me nowhere. I renewed my concentration on working my way inside his soul.

"I feel you would fight any who tried to control you."

I didn't understand what he meant by saying these things. He arrived with one purpose, and now he danced with his goal. Was this a game he liked to play before he killed? "And how would I do that? What command do I have in a man's world?"

He snorted a laugh, which shocked me. More so because it sounded light and filled with genuine humor, rather than dark and filled with malicious intent. "You don't believe any of what you're saying."

And now I was confused, but I refused to dance with him. "I'll grant anything within my power. Tell me what you want. King Henricus will be generous, my father more so." He wouldn't. King Regnier would curse his missed alliance. That was all.

His fingers tightened their grip on my wrists, guaranteeing black bruises for weeks to come. "What King Henricus owns is already mine."

What did he mean by that? "Who's your master?" I'd lost my ability to concentrate, so I stood no chance of finding his soul word, and it was too dark to see his death echo. It was unlikely he would die by my hand tonight. But would I die by his?

He leaned down, his face blotting out the starlight. "I'm the master."

"Then who is your informant?" His woodsy smell lingered faintly under the grim of blood and death. How did he know where to find us and who he would find on board?

"You haven't made your bargain."

"Call off your attack."

He released a soft snarl, which rippled across my skin. "You dare give me an order?"

"I'll make no bargain with you while your men slaughter my crew."

He laughed, a deep throaty laugh, resonating against the grizzly noise of death that continued to be dealt above our heads. "Then there is no bargain."

For one fruitless moment, I struggled against the tight binds of his hands on my wrists. His weight and my arms still pinned to the deck: it was all in vain. "Am I meant to live or die? Tell me and be done with it. I won't be your entertainment any longer." I would be no one's amusement.

If everything King Henricus owned was his, then I was his goal; the bride his son shall never meet.

He left the chaos of the fight as his answer. Hearing the cries of fear, the howls of pain, I lost my tight hold on my panic. It wasn't for me I struggled again, but for the men who played no part in this beast-man's cruel game. "Please, I beg you. Spare them. They're only doing their duty. I'll give you what you want."

He stayed silent.

I would have to aim to lure his heart. "I believe you love a fight. I offer you this bargain. Let us decide our fates in a duel."

"Are you not afraid?"

Yes, I was, only that was now mixed with a budding fury that heated me more than the flames of his body. "I harness my fear." I spat at him.

I was crazy, but better to end in rage than silence.

Three heartbeats lapsed, then he lifted his head and let out a deep resonate sound, close to a wild animal's howl. It took more heartbeats before the noise of the attack diminished, leaving wails of lingering pain and unrecognizable softer noises, which swiftly diminished breaths later.

"Give me time to gather my weapons."

"No."

"Then you're not an honorable opponent."

"I never claimed to be." And he pulled my left wrist off the ground as he leaned over. I felt the sting of his bite, fangs piercing through my bruised flesh.

It lasted seconds before he pulled away and dropped my arm. He sprung to his feet, leaving me to suck in lungfuls of air now I was free of his weight. For one moment, I fumbled across the floor for my dagger. Not feeling it, I sat up, nursing my wrist close to my chest.

"What did you do?" My fingers smeared the slimy wetness of my blood.

"The Huungardred bite is poisonous."

"You wish me to suffer a slow death? I ask you to give me my bargain. A duel."

"The wise are never in a hurry to die."

"What makes you think you'll win?"

Head tilted back, he released a deep rumbling laugh. "I like your spirit." Then he stepped toward his fallen friend.

"Excuse me for not finding anything nice to say about you in response."

He looked back over his shoulder at me. "What if I told you there is a cure?"

Traps and tricks. Curses, he'd bound me. "Would you tell me what it is?"

"Who is responsible for the death of this man?"

I swallowed. Would the truth condemn me? "I am."

He turned to face me. "You're quite the surprise... I'll tell you if it gives you hope."

"Tell me?" I snapped.

"I'm the cure."

I whimpered, my arm propping me up, giving way. I was going to die. "How can that be?"

"I'm your only cure, princess. Which means you need to seek me out with whatever means you can, so you can beg me to grant you life. Please my wishes, and I may be lenient."

"Is that so?" I rolled to my side, and the tip of my finger felt the sharp edge of my dagger.

I froze for a breath, then awkwardly shifted to my knees, giving my fingers time to crawl up the hilt, to clasp it firm in my hand. I rose to my feet, balancing my weight, measuring in my mind his height to mine when in a crouch, the position of his heart, the angle of my aim. *Precision.* I really couldn't afford to miss.

I released the dagger as fast as I spun. The starlight gave insufficient light for my aim, but I didn't always need to see my target; one glance and the mental image was all I needed to go by.

The dull light caught a faint glint of the dagger. It flew swiftly, but I wasn't expecting the reflexes of the beast-man. He snapped his arm up without a grunt or cry of pain.

"Never underestimate your opponent."

Curses. He must've caught it. "Likewise," I replied.

He paced toward me. I wouldn't step back.

"I heard the faint scrape as you pulled the dagger from the floor. Your slow movements were too suspicious. I was ready."

"I'll remember that for next time."

"It was a perfect shot. In the dark, too. I congratulate you."

"Next time I won't miss. I'll take your heart as my souvenir."

"Ah, now a promise I believe you'll keep. Goodbye, Princess." He gathered his fallen friend, then fled up the ladder with speed unnatural for a man burdened by another. He left without my promise, which meant he expected the poison from the bite to end me before I reached Tarragona's shores.

CHAPTER

EIGHT

TAMAS

OUR PASSAGE WAS hard and relentless. The ocean turned against us as waves battered against the bow of our rowboat. For days we'd rowed, drenched, without food and water, hands frozen to the oars, and our stomachs growling and churning. The days felt grim, the nights savage. My men continued, taking turns at the oars to spare their strength to ensure we made shore by the night of the split moon. Tonight.

We waited offshore, working against the current to keep out of sight until night broke, then we slipped in using the dark as our cloak. Lustuif leapt out along with Tremmin and guided the boat into the rocky shallows.

The half-moon gave us some light as we made our way across the rocks and up to the edge of the marshes and the hedge trees behind. After our time at sea, I welcomed the powerful stench of rotting marsh weed released as we trudged through the mud, drenched by the salty spray.

I stopped, raising my hand, then sunk into the marsh and kept watch. Within breaths, two figures appeared. I hooted a soft bird song, the signal to my men it was safe to move on and rose to join the two approaching figures, tasked with waiting our return.

"Well timed. The stew should be about ready," Waylen said.

I took his hand, and he swept me close for a chest press and back slap.

"Now that I want to hear," Garrat said, coming up behind me.

"What about the ale?" Osmud asked, crossing his arms to slap his shoulders, a sign he was ready to leave the cold behind and drown himself in a tankard or ten.

"The deed is done?" Kintore asked.

Garrat made a snort and pushed past Waylen and Kintore, tramping back the way they'd come through the marsh and into the hedge trees.

"We're one less," I said. "We'll remember Micale tonight and give thanks for his bravery. Then we set our sights forward to our next plan."

Kintore nodded but said nothing in response. An honorable goodbye should follow an honorable death, but we'd had little choice but to send Micale's body over the side of the boat while silently giving our thanks for his bravery. Those by the fire would appreciate their chance to say goodbye.

I had yet to reply to Kintore's questions and still felt

Osmud's glare and the heavy frown I'd spied the morning after our attack. Neither Garrat nor Osmud had questioned me during our row to safety. Their silence hung on my shoulders and rippled around the boat. I'd sought solitude to think, and now I'd made my plan.

Our landing was obscured by swampland few could farm. Settlements were rare around these parts, but reaching shore within Tarragona territory, we had to be careful.

A dance of flames flickered through the hedge trees, growing steadily before us. The bearer left the trees and squelched through the marsh, heading for the boat. I clapped his back as I passed, not sure which one of my men it was in the dark, but confident he would fulfill his duty. Before I passed into the hedge trees, I glanced behind to see the first flicker of fire lick the boat. By morning, there would be nothing but ash.

We trudged the rest of the way to our campfire in silence. Thanks to my Huungardred blood, the cold bothered me less than a normal man, but days wet at sea, and the cold penetrated into my bones. The fire was a welcome sight, as to the dozen men who rose on seeing our approach. I'd taken twelve strong Razohan to attack the ship, another twelve to await our return. Twenty-four was a safe number, good numbers in a skirmish, but few enough to move through the kingdom undetected.

And then one more. Bryra moved in beside me when we reached the fireside. She, too, had said nothing about our attack on the ship and the aftermath. I had avoided her eyes the most on that cold, wet journey, feeling guilt for what I'd not achieved for reasons other than duty.

Ayllip circled the fire, two tankards in his hand. "The task is done?" He handed one to me and gave the other to Bryra.

I averted my gaze, but there were no more chances for silence. Instead, I made myself comfortable on one of the many logs pulled around the fire. "She still lives. But we've crippled the ship. There are not enough sailors for them to reach Tarragona's shore."

A long mournful howl resounding in the distance broke the ensuing quiet.

"Her death was the sole purpose we came here," Ayllip continued. "Why did you let her survive?"

Bryra eased onto the log beside me, her human side closest to me. I gave in to the distraction, eyeing her muscular thigh a finger's width from mine. She'd been responsible for most of the deaths, but the blood had washed free from her body early on our return voyage.

As a pureblood, in their true form, Huungardred measured twice the size as any Razohan. Bryra insisted on coming, claiming with so few men, I faced failure. It was a slight, and one I swallowed given I'd withheld my reply to Thaindrus's request and Bryra knew. With her at our side, there was no question of us failing, and she would be of great value on the return journey to the north should my men run into any trouble.

"It was for the best. I have a new plan."

"It would've been kinder to kill her," Kintore said.

I took a long drink from my tankard, having no answer they wanted to hear. Neither could I explain my leniency to myself, not yet. When I found solitude in the days ahead, I would be able to parse apart the sudden and conflicting emotions and thoughts and devise a solution.

I'd seen her features in the darkness while in my shifted form. There were three traits in a woman that won a Razohan's eye: beauty, curves, or strength. She had none of those. But there were other traits about her that stilled my hand. Courage, bravery, ferocity, and will. Those were the traits a Razohan fell in love with, and what I admired in anyone above all else. Such rare gifts, yet the princess of Whelin held all four. My now healed wound was a testament to her prowess with a dagger. And she wielded two with the ease of a skilled fighter; that I couldn't help but admire even in my toughest enemy. The last trait to eclipse all else, honor, won her her life; to bargain her life for her people in a duel was her savior.

But it was more than mere admiration that restrained me. I'm certain the Salmun had no idea whom they were admitting into the House of Tannard.

"The bride's survival doesn't change your task." It was time to push forward from what I'd failed to do onto more important matters.

I took my bowl of stew, eager to find something else to do other than talk. Conversation disappeared while the twelve of us were given time to fill our bellies. I stared into the fire, trying to stop from mulling over the problems I'd likely created in allowing the princess to live. The first tight situation was sitting beside me.

Thaindrus said nothing to dissuade Bryra from accompanying us, even though the Huungardrerd strove to stay neutral in men's affairs. I knew why he allowed her and why she came, and it made this campsite moment tough to bear. Added to that, I felt the interrogating weight of Osmud and Garrat's glares. Both waited for my reasons, and I had none that would satisfy them, doubling my guilt for asking them to risk this venture.

Finally, the unease in my head drove me to my feet.

"I give thanks to the cook. It was well needed."

"There's plenty more in the pot," Waylen said.

"Then save some for me." I left my bowl where I sat and moved away from the fire, taking my tankard with me.

I moved far enough to keep others from hearing and waited for Osmud and Garrat, knowing I had run their patience dry. After days of heavy cloud, strong winds and rain, the stars were a welcome sight. I searched the sky, wandering what signs I was supposed to look for according to the augur's prophecy. Night lit as day. I couldn't comprehend how that should be. And how long were we to wait until the phenomenon appeared? Thinking about that, my mind slipped to the rest of the words he'd spoken until the soft tread of footfalls drew me back.

"Okay. Out with it," Osmud said with a sigh, leaning against a spindly tree.

"I was close. So close. I had my hand raised to strike."

"Then what stopped you?" Garrat said.

"It was your cock. Wasn't it?" Osmud said before me.

I snorted. "Like I'd let that interfere with an important task."

"You've been withholding too long, my friend. It's not natural and plays havoc with your head."

"She's not to my taste." The lie was acid on my tongue.

"Then explain to us why the Razohan leader spared one woman at risk to the rest of his clan. That is not like you, Tamas," Garrat said.

"Because I'm sure she has a part to play. More than we believe." It was out before I could censor it. Having lost the taste of my mead, I threw the tankard's content away.

"You're not wrong there." Osmud said. "Only she's on the wrong side of this war. We don't want her playing her part. And I would've finished that for you."

"What if it's an important part?"

I didn't expect Osmud's fist to my jaw. It sent me stumbling backward, losing my tankard in the scrub.

"Did that knock some sense into your head?" he said.

I straightened, rubbing the pain away. It was nothing less than I needed. My two trusted were right to question my sanity, something I'd done these last days during our journey.

"A conversation with hands isn't going to get us anywhere," Garrat said, stepping between us.

"She's a disciple?"

"How can you be sure?" Osmud said, flexing his fingers.

"I felt her awareness probing me. She was looking for a way in to command me."

"Even more reason to have killed her," Garrat said. "I'm surprised it has taken the Sistern this long to force one of their own into the Tannard bloodline. That we can't allow."

"She's much more than a disciple."

"Would you listen to yourself?" Osmud said. "You've totally lost your head."

Garrat moved alongside Osmud. "What do you mean, Tamas?"

I rubbed my forehead, then shook my head. "I need to think on this."

"You better think fast," Osmud said.

Ignoring him, I continued. "You'll return with the rest of the men to the north and continue your efforts to win allegiance from the northern clans. Tell them they must prepare for war."

"So that part of the plan has not changed."

"Whether the princess lived or died, war was inevitable."

"And the augur's ramblings?" Garrat said.

"Not even Romelda can give us a precise time."

"The augur made it none too clear." Osmud downed the last of his mead.

"We'll act with speed. It's all we can do and hope the events foretold do not arrive in the meantime."

I looked at the two of them, my trusted. Both accepted my failure without argument or judgement. It was well I had them by my side, for I was the harsh judge of my actions. Had I condemned my people by allowing the princess to live?

The sound of approaching footfalls disturbed us.

Bryra's silhouette obscured the campfire. On seeing us turned toward her, she stopped. "Am I interfering?"

"What needs to be said has been said," Garrat replied. "Come on, Osmud."

I would've given them both spearing glares if I knew Bryra wouldn't see. They knew of Thaindrus's request, and both had the audacity to question why I'd refused.

It was our bloodlink to the Huungardred that ensured

the Razohan's strength in the north. Few dared speak against us, but many of the larger clans were growing restless with our authority. Marriage between Razohan and the Huun-gardred would strengthen our position in the north and secure their survival. As leader of the Razohan, it was my duty to make strategic alliances, especially through marriage.

Garrat slowed on passing Bryra. "It's thanks to you we returned in almost full number. When you're finished listening to his morose ramblings, come sit by me, and I'll give you far better entertainment."

Maybe respect and friendship were enough in marriage to live a happy life. That's all I could give Bryra. That half of her was always in beast form meant nothing to me. She was breathtaking in any Razohan's eyes, a true leader for her people. If only I could love her.

"Have you come to berate me, too?" The awkwardness I'd felt toward her these last few years would never diminish our long-held friendship.

"I would never question your judgment."

"Then perhaps you should take those asses aside and have a strong word using your claws."

"They don't know you as I do."

Those few words drew the night down around us, sheltering us from the rest of my men at the campfire. The coward I was, it twitched my legs to turn and flee. When it came to the heart, honesty was tougher than political negotiations or war.

"I know you don't act without a secure plan. You see a benefit to the princess being alive. I understand."

I dipped my head, staring at my feet. If only Bryra's faith in me was not absolute. She was blind to my flaws. I already drowned under my own expectations; I couldn't shoulder hers. Truth be told, when I spared the princess, I'd acted on instinct, destroying most of my original plan. I'd never expected to discover a woman as intriguing as her. As I spiked my claw ready to strike, the augurs words played in my head, forcing me to question if she deserved to die. Perhaps her part in all of this was more important than any of us thought. All I could hope was I'd not condemned myself and my people.

"I don't have enough thanks in me for what you've done for us. This is none of the Huungardred's concern, and yet—"

"It's your concern, and so it's my concern. You know I would fight beside you without question."

"You are one of the few I would choose by my side." I loathed to hurt my good friend. Perhaps it wasn't wise to have allowed her to come. Things between us were now awkward and that pained me.

I inhaled, then turned to face her. "Bryra—"

"I know you have not answered Father. And I know why. And I understand."

I sighed. "I'm glad. I want nothing to destroy what we have."

She nodded. "It won't. Don't listen to my father. He was wrong to rush you. In his old age, Father has grown fearful. But I am young, with countless years to come. I can be patient. I know what you must do, and I understand the importance of that, for the good of us all."

"Thank you." But I wasn't sure exactly what I was

thanking her for because I couldn't decide if she was referring to our friendship or something more. "Bryra—"

"And I'm glad you didn't kill her. The House of Tannard
are the ones deserving of that fate, not an innocent woman
whose only flaw is having a womb."

"That means a lot to me. Thanks. Maybe you can
convince the others."

If I was right about Tressya, she was more than a woman
with a womb. So much more. Having met her only once, I
couldn't be certain, but my instincts told me I was right.

"They're men. Of course, they never stop to think of her
powerlessness in deciding her fate."

Was Bryra thinking of her own predicament here? Was
she sore her father placed her in the middle of his own
strategic alliance? "Are you—?"

"She's not from the House of Tannard. So she's not our
enemy. You still have time to stop the marriage and send her
home."

"I do." Did Bryra want something else? Someone else? Or
no marriage at all. Perhaps she wanted to rule alone.

"I have every faith in your judgment."

This was too much. I couldn't let her continue. Everyone's faith in my ability to do the right thing, succeed where
none had tried before weighted every decision I made.

"You're a good man, Tamas. Strong in your heart, strong
in your convictions. You will succeed for all of us."

"I will." There could be no question.

CHAPTER

NINE

TRESSYA

THE OCEAN WAS CALM, the only mercy we had received these last two days. With too few men, we bobbed about on the water, too wounded to unfurl all the sails. The captain and Hindemill were gone, but thankfully, we weren't directionless. There was one among the handful of sailors remaining who could read the captain's papers and navigational instruments, but our progress was slow.

The day after the attack, we spent disposing of the bodies, followed by cleaning the deck. Since there were so few of us remaining, Radnisa and I joined in. Once finished, I struggled to find it in myself to do anything more. The spirits tried to keep me occupied, but ignored enough times, they left me alone. Two sailors had brought me a bucket of seawater because they couldn't handle the smell or perhaps out of pity. Then Radnisa insisted I change, and she hurled the shredded dress covered in cow dung over the side. I'd covered myself in stinking cow dung for no reason, which would be mildly funny if I wasn't now poisoned.

Today, I sat on the deck, leaning against the mainmast, and stared out to sea, interspersed with staring at the bite mark on my wrist encircled by bruising from his cruel fingers. I had yet to feel the poison's grip on me, but that meant little. For all I knew, it would take weeks for its effects to take hold. The puncture wounds were large circles, showing the size of his fangs, and had mostly healed—most likely the result of magic, just like his ability to change form.

There had to be a way to cure this poison without involving the man who put it inside of me. I knew as much about the tales and legends of the other kingdoms as I did about Tarragona's political hierarchy, which was to say little. Edilene would know more, thanks to our diverging education. Once I reached Tarragona, I would learn everything I could, both about my new home and about these Huungardred. The next time I saw him, I would force him to cure me, then cut out his heart.

Unable to control this poison, my thoughts went to the sailor spirits, who came and went with no command from me. Spiritseers saw spirits; spiritweavers commanded them. The latter was a deeper level of the arcane talent. If someone was born a spiritseer it didn't mean they would develop the advanced skill of spiritweaving. Given I had recently developed this talent—thanks to the Mother and the black mist she put inside of me, I was sure—I didn't know if my skill would advance to spiritweaving.

After a while of trying to conjure them with thought, I

grew frustrated, more so because of our crippled state than my failure at spiritweaving. I hated being stuck on this ship, hated seeing nothing but blue, hated how easily our enemy had decimated us and how powerless I felt. Most of all, I hated my inability to master soul voice. The outcome of the attack would have been different had I succeeded in my discipline and training. The Mother was right to be disappointed in me, but she could never be more disappointed than I was in myself. And now it appeared as though I would die a slow death from this beast-man's bite if I didn't find him in time.

I clenched my fists, digging my nails into my palms. Perhaps if I narrowed my focus to Scregs rather than all of them, it would be easier. I closed my eyes and pictured his translucent appearance in my head. *Scregs.*

I cracked one eye open. No spirit.

"Scregs."

"You're talking to yourself now?"

Deep in concentration, I'd missed Radnisa's approach, which was not something a good disciple would be proud to admit. I was yet to decide if I was happy to learn that she'd survived, escaping with only a large gash that ran down her left arm and across her neck, plus bruising to the left side of her face and an eye swollen shut.

We had said little to each other since the attack, neither of us mentioning Anderline. Radnisa had shown compassion by closing her eyes, and I had reached out to touch her arm with no sadness in my heart. Loyalty to the Mother meant loyalty to my fellow sisters within the Sistern, but it didn't mean I had to like them.

Radnisa leaned against the mast, an unusual display of idleness. Perhaps the attack had unsettled her more than she wanted to admit. Or was losing Anderline the cause? Though I would never accuse Radnisa of having a heart capable of feeling.

"What do you know of the Huungardred?"

"Some. The Sistern stay away from them."

"From what I've overheard, they're fierce fighters. I'm surprised the Sistern hasn't sought to form a bloodline with them."

"Isn't losing a sister to them enough? Now you're fascinated by them?"

Perhaps I was mistaken about Radnisa's lack of emotions. Maybe losing Anderline weighed heavily on her heart.

"I want to learn about our enemy. I won't let this go unpunished."

He'd told me to seek him out to cure the poison. I took that to mean this northerner didn't plan on going too far from Tarragona.

Radnisa made a derisive sound.

"Once the prince and I marry—"

"Don't assume more power than you'll ever possess. King Henricus and his son know better than to risk moving into the north. Tarragona has yet to claim that territory, and not for lack of trying. They won't go to war at the request of a bastard princess who's had her ass kicked."

I arched my head back, the sun's rays warming my neck as I practiced my calming breaths. I never dreamed I would hold any sway over my husband, especially not one as powerful as the Crown Prince of Tarragona. That didn't mean I wouldn't devise a plan to ensure someday the Huungardred would pay for what they'd done.

"They came here for me."

"You really think you're that special?"

"Perhaps dangerous. King Henricus must've plenty of enemies. All powerful men do."

"And what danger could one woman possibly pose?"

"They hope to destroy the House of Tannard," was all I said.

"What better way to do that than kill the bastard princess of an insignificant kingdom?"

"Maybe they want to prevent any heirs to the Tannard line."

Radnisa rolled her eyes. "And you're the only woman who can give the House of Tannard an heir? You're not even queen and you've elevated your importance."

Even with all my years perfecting a shield against her sarcastic remarks, many still found their way under my armor, making it harder for me to find my calming breaths.

My hand involuntarily found the old wound above my left breast. Upon realizing, I jerked it away, casting a sideways glance at Radnisa, but she was staring out to sea and hadn't noticed.

"Many would love to see the House of Tannard, the House of Whelin, and every other ruling family brought down. That's the way of men," she said, pushing off the mast. "You know, they weren't the Huungardred."

She strolled around to stand in front of me. "None of us would be alive if the Huungardred had attacked. They were men of the north. Men who've bred with those beasts and birthed beasts themselves." Disgust dripped from her mouth. "They say the Huungardred can't take on true human form, but the descendants of such creatures can."

My mind whirled with that information, but before I could ask anything else, a shout from the sailor high in the crow's nest rent the air. "Sail ho!"

The bellow sent the remaining crew scurrying to the starboard side of the ship. I found my feet, but Radnisa had already joined the crew, looking out to the horizon.

"The King's ship," shouted the man from the crow's nest again.

Excitement rippled through the crew, which brought on a sudden queasiness in my stomach, unrelated to sickness. While I welcomed an end to our endless drifting, rescue meant moving closer to my fate. I clenched my teeth, then eased my hands to my sides. I would give myself this moment to succumb to my trepidation, then I would banish the feeling.

I came alongside Radnisa, squinting at the small speck on the horizon, not entirely convinced the sailor in the crow's nest was right. I had taken to wearing my daggers belted to my hip, dismissing the queer looks I received from the crew. Radnisa hissed at me to remove them, saying it was not how a princess should be seen, but after my confrontation with the beast-man, my daggers would stay where they were.

In the past few days, the implications of his poison had plagued me. He could have easily achieved what he came to do. Instead, he bound my life to him, ensuring I would survive only by his whim. While I doubted he would return so soon, even if eager to watch me beg, I couldn't calm my unease. I loathed the idea of feeling bound to anyone. The Mother was the only person who had the right to my allegiance. By his actions, this beast-man bound me tighter than a sanctified marriage ever could.

"We should ready ourselves in defense," I said.

Radnisa snorted. "With what? A handful of dispirited men against a fully manned ship?"

"I never thought I'd hear you speak in defeat."

"You've lost your head. This voyage—"

"Soul voice, sister. You only need to control the captain."

She folded her arms. "Why don't you do it then?"

"You know I haven't mastered it." I gritted my teeth, anticipating her reaction.

"I never question the Mother's actions," she said, leveling a long look at me. "Since the announcement of your betrothal, I've done nothing but ponder her choice. Perhaps she made a mistake this time in sending you instead of Edilene."

"The Mother knew what she was doing." I turned away, focusing on the approaching ship, all the while conscious of the poison crawling its way through my body and the strange tentacle mist now residing in my veins. "She knew exactly what she was doing," I whispered, my voice so low I doubted Radnisa had heard. Edilene was superior to me in all ways but one—I now had a connection to the dead.

Under full sail, the ship was upon us before the sun reached its peak. I never thought I would be relieved to see another ship, nor eager to climb aboard, but when I saw the ensign flying at the stern, the black and white symbol of Tarragona, that's exactly what I felt.

As it maneuvered alongside us, the remaining crew sprang to life, preparing the Sapphire Rose for boarding. Men crowded along the port side of the arriving ship, peering across at us, and that too was a welcome sight. One figure stood out amongst the rest, distinguishable by his elaborate, decorative, and expensive attire. He clearly wasn't a captain or first officer.

The crew stood aside after fastening the plank in place to join the two ships, and the elegantly dressed gentleman crossed first. He leaped down onto the deck with the agility of a fighter and bounded towards Radnisa and me with an enthusiastic stride. His free-flowing locks, reminiscent of fine silk the color of the sun, bounced in the gentle breeze. But my eyes were drawn to his wide smile—a genuine smile that illuminated his face and reached deep within, touching my heart. In that moment, I thought of Carlin.

This man could be none other than a prince. The embroidered gold trim on his long cloak, the double gold buttons adorning his chest, the long cuffs concealing his hands, and the intricate patterns of fur, silk, and jewels stitched into his attire left no room for doubt.

I straightened, aware of my wild hair, the lingering scent I failed to wash away despite my sea water scrub, and the creases in my clothes. Was this my soon-to-be husband? With that thought, every fear lodged in my heart fell away. He was beautiful in the way kind eyes, a gracious smile, and a welcoming and generous face made a person beautiful. At the first glimpse of my fate, a thrilling tingle tickled my insides.

"Princess Tressya," he announced with a high lilt in his voice, then swept into a deep bow. "Prince Andriet to your rescue."

Crown Prince Juel's younger brother. I curtsied. "Your Highness." Then he turned to Radnisa. "My lady."

Radnisa's eyes widened a fraction as she inhaled. Not even Edilene bothered to acknowledge Radnisa once inside the castle walls of Aldorr.

"It seems you have suffered a great deal of hardship." He scanned the deck, his eyes traveling over the darkened bloodstains patterning the wood. "This is most grievous news." He looked solemn for a moment before his face brightened once more, leaving me to wonder if Prince Andriet was ever one to wallow in darkness. "Come, we shall settle you aboard the Silver Wing and make haste to Tarragona. Once you're settled, you can tell me about your adventure." He held up a hand. "Forgive me. Perhaps you're not willing to relive the moment."

"If you're looking for a princess easily distressed, you'll have to search elsewhere. I'll fill you in on every detail if that's what you want."

His beautiful smile returned. "Well, Your Highness, you're quite the adventurer. I adore bold ladies." He crooked his elbow, inviting me to link arms.

Radnisa sucked in a breath at the inappropriateness of the gesture. Like Andriet, my smile was genuine, mixed with relief and sincere happiness. I slipped my arm through his and let him guide me toward the makeshift bridge, giving

Radnisa a smug smile as I passed her by. How alike were Andriet and Juel?

"I shall stay by your side and guide you across if the idea of crossing the plank is terrifying."

"That's unnecessary." I slid my arm from his. To prove myself, I attempted to climb the makeshift steps before me but stumbled when Scregs appeared in front of me.

"Not without leave from us," he growled.

"Are you all right?" Andriet rushed to my side.

"Yes, I'm fine. It's nothing." I gave Andriet a reassuring smile, then faced the plank with a heavy scowl and a small jerk of my head, a subtle sign that Scregs needed to move aside.

Scregs either didn't understand or ignored me, blocking my path while attempting to fold his arms across his chest, but failing to perform the gesture correctly.

"Yer can't leave. They'll abandon the ship for sure. Leave us to a watery grave depths below the sea."

I half-turned. "Prince Andriet—"

"Just Andriet. We're almost like siblings."

I pressed my lips together to stifle my smile. I wouldn't be forced to endure my marriage if Juel was anything like his brother.

"What do you plan to do with the Sapphire Rose once all our things are across?"

"I shall leave enough men on board to sail her back to port. She's a mighty fine ship. One of my father's best. He'd never send scrap to return the treasure of Tarragona."

My smile mixed with a frown as I wondered what he spoke of.

I didn't have to wonder long. "You, dear princess," he said. "You're now the treasure of Tarragona."

Radnisa made a derisive sound behind him.

His brown eyes radiated warmth, and suddenly the dark shadows encasing my heart cleared, allowing in a small amount of light. I inhaled as if to take in fresh air after years of suffocation. For one embarrassing moment, I couldn't turn away from him. How could I distinguish flattery from praise when we'd only just met? I should trust my instincts, and right now, I wanted to believe in him. Would Juel be as thoughtful and kind? Please, let that be the case. I would survive my sentence if that were so.

I caught Radnisa shifting slightly to the side, a reminder of who I was and my purpose. There was no time for fanciful thoughts in my life. Stupid me for forgetting that. There was also no returning to my life before and the one person whom I would do better to forget.

I flashed Andriet an inadequate smile to match the friendship his words offered and turned to face Scregs, raising an eyebrow and giving him another small jerk of my head.

"So he says." Stede had appeared beside him. "And full of sweet talk. He's too pretty. I don't trust 'im."

"Me either," Scregs agreed.

"Your Highness." Andriet's touch on my elbow was feather-light. "Let me cross first. You will see it's sturdy and safe."

"Just yer wait. Once yer aboard, he'll do with yer as he likes. I know those eyes," Scregs continued.

"Yeah, greedy, they are," Stede added.

I would slash through these two if it didn't make me look utterly mad, and if I knew my daggers would find their mark.

"It's not that," I snapped and waved my hand at the two spirits to shoo them away, trying to make it appear as though I was dismissing the idea of an unstable crossing. "Call me Tressya," I added, trying to soften my harsh reply, and gave Andriet another fractured smile.

"Tressya, may I say you'll have to cross or stand aside and allow me to guide you? The men are waiting to carry your possessions aboard."

I looked over my shoulder to see my trunks lined up on the deck. From my height on the makeshift step to the plank, all eyes were on me. I spun back.

"Yer can't cross."

"I can do this," I announced. "I will do this."

"Great," Andriet said with false enthusiasm. He probably thought me a fool now.

More spirits gathered to bar my way. "I can easily pass through you," I whispered. But it wasn't easy at all. I loathed the freezing sensation it gave me. It penetrated deep into my bones, carrying with it a profound loneliness that threatened to swallow me whole.

"It's a mistake!" another spirit yelled from further along the plank. "We beg you not to leave us."

I'm sorry. But they weren't my responsibility. And I would have to walk through a line of them to reach the other side.

I pressed my lips together firmly, gathered my skirts, and climbed the last few steps to the plank, tensing myself as I passed through Scregs. His spectral form caught me in a chilling grip, the biting cold seeping through my skin and feeling like icy fingers squeezing my heart. Though I knew what was coming, the shock still caused me to stumble forward, and I flailed my arms to regain my balance. The plank was wide-ish, but not wide enough for someone stumbling around.

I heard Andriet shout my name, but I was already passing through Stede's body, the freeze taking hold of my legs. My mind played tricks on me, convincing me that more frozen, claw-like fingers gripped my shoulder. I jerked sideways as if to release the grip and felt my foot skim the edge. I needed to calm my mind, use my breaths to find the control I always sought through practice. But more icy hands clutched at my shoulders, around my legs, across my waist, tugging me backward. I glanced down, but there was nothing there.

It's in your mind. I had to focus. But it was too late. My mind had become sluggish. Fear had become my enemy.

Somewhere in the back of my awareness, Andriet's voice rang out, but it seemed too far away and receding. The moment I heard my name, I felt plunged deep into a darkness as black as a moonless night. Pale figures moved around me, through me, filling me with an ache of longing so great that tears prickled my eyes.

"Don't leave." A wail filled my head. I think I wailed too.

A vibration shimmered up through my feet. Then came the sounds of thumping to match the reverberation. Andriet's voice drew nearer, calling my name, pulling me back. My arms flailed against the spectral fingers; my steps unsteady as if on uneven ground. Before I knew it, the side of my foot gave way to nothingness, and my body fell to the left. For a moment, I was convinced it was my mind creating more illusions, but then I felt a cold wind pass close to my hand and heard Andriet let out a desperate cry.

I fell, my shouted name spiraling down behind me. It was only one breath, if I had breathed at all, before I hit the water. The sudden cold felt like a blow to my head. My mind, freed from its frozen spectral grip, danced wildly. I was suddenly alive and fighting. But it was too late.

I couldn't swim. The weight of my clothes pulled me down. With my skirts entangling my legs, my arms were all I had. My body had become an anchor.

I had never come so close to death while feeling so helpless. No amount of training could prepare me to accept it or guard my mind and heart against the fear of losing the fight.

Discipline: controlling the mind to harness fear. This was not my grave.

Something solid wrapped around my waist and yanked me upward. The seawater burned my eyes as I looked through the blur to see sun-kissed hair waving through the churn of the current. Looming beyond were the spectral faces of my new tormentors.

"Yer ours," Scregs's voice raged through my head.

My thoughts raged back. *No.*

I worked my arms, not knowing what to do, but instincts took over in the absence of knowledge. Andriet's firm grip held me tight as he swam for the surface. I looked up, seeing us drawing near. The fierce will to live gave my legs the strength to kick free from the tangle of my skirts, and my arms found coordination to assist Andriet in hauling me to the surface, even though my lungs burned for a breath.

When we breached the water, I sucked in lungfuls of air,

my arms wrapped around Andriet's neck. Lowered ropes dangled down the sides of both ships. Andriet pulled me toward the Silver Wing, the closest of the two. Our progress was slow, allowing some spirits to move alongside us, but none of them reached out to touch me. And gradually, they fell behind, anchored to the Sapphire Rose.

The swell tossed us about, and I wasn't much help in swimming, but I tried my best, refusing to look back at my tormentors.

Mother, you have truly cursed me.

CHAPTER

TEN

TRESSYA

TOLUM'S SPRAWL reached down to the waterfront, its dock a lively place full of bustle and noise. The smells of dead fish, oil, and brine reminded me too much of home and the person I'd left behind. I clutched Carlin's necklace and tried hard to shut the vision of him out; mourning his loss wouldn't help me survive.

"I can't wait to show you the sights," Andriet said, snapping me out of my reverie. He was standing close beside me, closer than a married couple would stand in public; only in private and deeply in love.

He turned to face me, leaning his hip against the railing of the ship. "Tell me, what're your secret hobbies? Not stuffy pursuits such as needlework and weaving." He leaned down, bringing his dark eyes level with mine. "I mean the pursuits your father would frown upon." And he quirked a brow.

147

I couldn't help but look at Andriet on the voyage to Tolum. He was handsome in a classical way that would send the court ladies into a huddle of chatter at balls. However, my reason for staring had more to do with the shadows cast upon my soul. His bright manner, smile, and vivacious conversations filled me with joy, and I couldn't help feeling as though we were in a cheerful dance. The clouds vanished from my future when Andriet shone his dark-colored eyes on me.

"Tell me all, dear sister, and I'll see if I can match them with the delights Tolum offers." He swept his arm wide toward his city. "Every treasure is at your feet."

"I'm not interested in treasure."

He reared back, eyes flaring wide. "What?" he exclaimed in mock surprise. "A princess not interested in treasure? That cannot be. You jest."

I made to slip one of my daggers from my hip, only to remember they were now stowed below in a trunk, thanks to Radnisa. "My blades need sharpening."

"Oh, those. Yes, I saw those. That's not a very lady-like pursuit. Perhaps you should take up needlework."

"I doubt a needle through the enemy's heart would have much impact."

He lowered down, leaning an elbow on the railing. "You're quite the treat. A blade-throwing princess. Are all Merania's ladies taught to fight? If so, I would very much like to visit."

"Only a special few."

Andriet took my hand, winked at me before bending to kiss the back of my palm. "Then Tarragona is lucky one of those special few shall sit beside her husband on the throne."

A warm feeling bled through my chest as Andriet squeezed my hand. I pressed my lips tight to stem the smile, then strained against the fight. The lightness in my body made me want to dance.

I wanted to ask about Prince Juel, but the words seemed to ball up in my mouth. For days now, questions mounted, and my mouth felt fuller with every passing hour, but I couldn't bring myself to ask. Instead, I envisioned a man like his brother; I thought of sunshine and laughter and moments where no words needed to be spoken because we understood each other. That wasn't like me. I blamed Andriet and his infectious mood for weakening me to the point where I dared to dream.

There was, however, one thing that kept me firmly grounded. Radnisa stood within my periphery, eavesdropping on everything we said while sharpening her spite. Later tonight, when we were alone, she would get her chance to share her thoughts with me, whether I was interested or not. Andriet had stayed by my side these last few days, giving Radnisa no time to swoop in with her cruel taunts and douse the budding happiness I felt. For all the times she had sniped and snapped about my future marriage, now she had a slap on her face. Tarragona was my home, and I was welcome.

"This is us, dear sister," Andriet said, taking my hand and guiding me toward the plank, which was lowered across to the dock. "I shall walk beside you and hold your hand the entire time. Can't have that gorgeous dress or fancy swirl in your hair drowned."

Radnisa, whose glare could forge iron, had to stand aside or be run down by Andriet's stride. My arm woven through his, I allowed my silly smile to show, feeling for the first time like all those ladies at my father's court when noblemen fawned upon them.

When I was younger, I had never wanted to be like them, but I had desired to be with them. Lucky for me, I soon discovered they were little more than the fancy dolls that had lined my nursery shelves: hollow. I welcomed being ignored rather than forced to engage in their frivolous conversations and petty concerns.

And what about the court at Emberfell? I hadn't asked Andriet a thing about his home, instead staying under the spell of his fantastical stories. Only now, as I made my way onto the dock, did I understand why I had held my tongue. The queasiness in my stomach returned, and I pressed my fingers into Andriet's arm.

I glanced up at him, taking in the high cut of his cheek-bone, the slight up-tilt of his nose, and the soft curve of his full lips in profile. He looked nothing like Carlin, but in many other ways, they were identical.

"Is...? Is your brother like you?"

"I'm much more handsome."

Finally, I pushed myself to ask the one question that concerned me. "Why did you come to meet me and not the crown prince?"

"Juel must bother himself with boring stately affairs. Whereas I, as the second-born, get to do what I damn well please. And if I grow sick of my idleness and decide I want to sail out and meet the treasure of Tarragona, then that is what I'll do."

Apparently, a passing fishing vessel alerted Emberfell to our plight, but once again, I loved his embellishments in that tale.

An exquisite, closed carriage, iron-wrought with intricate detail, waited for us on the dock. Behind that, a plainer open carriage.

Six black horses snorted by the carriage. Eight black-clad guards waited; their horses restless. There was no sign of Prince Juel or any other member of the royal family. Seeming to sense my thoughts, Andriet squeezed my hand. "Anticipation is best. Don't you think?"

"Of course." Not in my experience.

To my surprise, Andriet did not release my hand once we'd crossed the bridge. When I glanced up at him, I found his eyes fixed on the row of guards.

Like Aldorr, Emberfell rose above the city sprawl, perched atop a hill. Unlike Aldorr, heavy cloud cover and its dark stone walls tainted the castle a deep, morose gray. It stretched across the mount like an imposing lump of rock, carved by a giant's hand into spear-like spikes fashioned skyward into the clouds.

To the west rose another mighty edifice, black as night and just as imposing as Emberfell. A temple, perhaps.

"After you." Andriet distracted me, helping me into the covered carriage. "Father has planned a great many delights in celebration of your arrival and your impending marriage." He climbed in and sat opposite me. "Balls, street parades, and of course, the grand trials."

The footman closed the door behind us, shutting Radnisa out. She glared in at me, her expression a promise of repercussions, and all I could do was shrug as I smiled.

"Trials?" I asked, losing my concentration on what Andriet said because everything about what was unfolding was too delicious to miss.

"A Tarragonan tradition. Dates to the triumph of the Levenians over the unjust king. The Creed of Salmun have assured the tradition remains. No royal marriage is considered sanctified without one."

That drew my focus back. "Who competes?"

Andriet slid across the carriage to sit beside me, then slouched, stretching his legs out to rest his boots on the seat opposite. I inhaled the spicy florals of his scent, still fresh after days at sea. "The nobility. It's a chance for a man to show off his prowess and bravery. The courtiers get to swoon, we get to look good."

I peered out the window, disappointed to see Radnisa led to the plain carriage as our own moved away. Better if they forced her to walk the distance to Emberfell, but I couldn't have it all my way.

I turned back to Andriet, taking a moment to remember our conversation. "Is it dangerous?"

"Savagely so. There are deaths, to be sure. But the strongest and bravest always triumph, and receive great honors to their name, titles, lands, jewels, wealth, favors from the king, these are not trivial goals to strive for. Half the peerage in Tarragona won their privileges in the trials. Besides, it's hardly a trial if it doesn't involve great risk.

"The gentry ensure only one of their sons enters, so they

152

don't lose all of their line. But if they only have the one, then, perhaps, most think it's worth the risk."

"If the trial takes place proceeding a royal marriage, then that would mean you've never witnessed one."

"Petty details, my sweet. I've read all the accounts on them. I could recite some of the gory details to you if you would like."

"It seems a senseless thing to do for honor and wealth."

"Spoken like a woman; the gentler sex, full of charms and graces and a far wiser brain on top their shoulders. Of course, it's a ridiculous way to gain a title, but my dear, if you're not born or married into peerage, then there is little chance of gaining it. Some will do anything."

"Will you enter?"

"Alas, no. It's Juel's wedding. All eyes must be on him."

"So he'll enter?"

"His will be the first name called. You needn't worry, he'll be well protected. The Creed of Salmun won't let a perfect hair on top of his head be damaged." I couldn't be sure, but I thought I detected a hint of spite in Andriet's tone. I'd not known him for long, but it seemed out of place. Before I could think on it, he continued. "He'll arrive to you on your wedding night very much alive and ready for..." He glanced at me and snorted a laugh.

"Don't be prudish, brother," I said with a grin.

He sat up, dropping his legs to the carriage floor. "Wonderful. A bride who wields blades and isn't afraid to fuck."

I chuckled. When I stopped, I found Andriet's dark eyes fixed on me, his expression caught between excitement and seriousness. "You're not what I expected. And I mean that from the depths of my heart."

"What did you expect?"

"Someone who would never be my friend."

"Is that what we are already?"

"Totally. I knew the moment I saw you. You're not..." His gaze flicked to my hair, my dress, then back to my face, and I knew what descriptive word he struggled to use. I was plain.

I had fought a successful war with Radnisa on my choice of dress for my first meeting with my future husband. I selected a simple one, or rather the simplest I could find in my trunk. Radnisa insisted on something elaborate until I reminded her Juel would bed me no matter how I appeared. An heir was his responsibility as the crown prince, after all. He'd seen Edilene's portrait, she'd argued. I countered by saying any account of me was bound to be accurate; there were few impressive features about me someone could embellish.

"As a princess should be," I finished for him.

But a royal guardsman, who had ridden up beside the window, caught his eye. I waited until I had his attention again, and when it wasn't forthcoming, I looked over my shoulder to the dusky-skinned guard keeping pace beside us. High cheekbones, powerful jaw, straight nose with a neatly cropped beard, a combination of features to capture any woman's attention. Or man. I turned back to Andriet. He shifted his eyes to me, then blinked.

"He's supposed to keep pace at the back of the carriage so as not to block your view during our procession to the palace. That he should know. I'll have a private word with him when we arrive. I don't want him to get into trouble."

"I don't suppose you do."

He sat back in his seat, obscuring his view of the guard outside the carriage. "What were we saying?"

"You were promising to teach me everything there is to know about Tarragona's politics, court intrigue, and history with the northern realm."

"I'd never promise that. How about I promise to show you the inside of all the reputable taverns in Tolum? Though the disreputable ones are more fun."

"Are they places for a lady to be seen?"

"Absolutely not. And that's why you'll love them more."

Everything about Andriet was pleasantly contagious.

"I guess as the crown prince, your brother doesn't get to sneak away to taverns."

"That's why you have me."

Andriet had drawn my focus away from the docks and into the narrow streets of the city, where the buildings seemed to lean against one another. The further from the sullen gray and grime of the docklands, its people moving with a listless edge that stooped their backs and aged their faces, past the heaving choke of the factories, Tolum transformed into a vibrant city full of many colors. I leaned my head out of the window and looked ahead to Emberfell, rising like a monstrous claw over the city, its dark walls an affront to the sprawling city below.

The wheels crunched the stones until we arrived at cobbles, then the horses' hooves clattered us into the grand sweeping gates of Emberfell castle.

Andriet rushed off to have a quick word with the striking guard while I took the time to smooth my clammy palms down the sides of my skirt. The castle loomed over me, its vast columns of dark stone standing like spears pointing to the sky, creating an aura of ominous power and ancient majesty. The colossal structure, seemingly carved from the darkest depths of the earth, absorbed all light around it, casting long, eerie shadows across the barren landscape. Menacing statues of weird creatures adorned the battlements, their eyes seemingly following every movement with a silent threat.

Radnisa's carriage hadn't shown by the time I disappeared inside Emberfell, much to my delight. It seemed my good fortune would continue for now. I fought with myself not to see this as a sign of hope that my life had finally shifted to one I could enjoy, rather than one I simply endured.

I arched a quizzical brow at the bounce in Andriet's step as he returned, pressing my lips hard to hide my smile. It seemed his talk went well.

"Shall we?" He crooked his arm in yet another shocking gesture of intimacy, and I slid my arm through, surrendering to my smile. Never had I smiled so much in one day. A funny fluttering feeling churned in my stomach when I thought of the man I was about to meet inside Emberfell. *Please let him be like Andriet.*

The dark stone of the interior walls, lack of sizable windows, and scant torch brackets along the walls dragged the night in early to Emberfell's corridors, as though it had left some of itself behind on passing. I hoped somewhere in my trunks of gowns I would find something fitting for Emberfell's chilly halls.

I pulled my travel cloak closer around me as I glanced at the long tapestry, intricately woven with miserable colors of dark reds, dirty oranges, tortured pinks, and differing shades of browns and grays.

Andriet slowed beside me to keep pace. "A history of Tarragona told by the hands of its skillful weavers."

"It looks like a violent history." More than half the tapestry depicted a bloody battle.

"Not as violent as you would think. The tapestry was commissioned centuries later in commemoration of the great war."

"I know very little of Tarragona's history. Even my knowledge of the near realms' history is poor. What was the great war?"

"To us, it's legend. A pivotal moment in our history, bringing monumental change. Our power and wealth are all thanks to the Levenians' success in defeating the unjust king, King Ricaud, who ruled in tyranny."

"Levenian was a name I'd heard whispered when I was young, though none of my studies have ever mentioned them. Unfortunately, none of my studies mentioned anything of interest."

"Oh really? Where did you learn to fight? I find that of great interest."

I gave him a coy smile—something I was sure I'd never done before, but it was difficult to stay detached in Andriet's presence. "It's a secret."

"Secrets are my favorite form of gossip. I do hope you'll tell me before long."

"Perhaps. For now, it's leverage."

Andriet laughed. "I love you already. You're wicked."

Forgetting the tapestry, I stared up into his dark eyes, following the tiny black lines moving out from the center of his eyes to the edges of the whites.

"What color eyes does your brother have?"

"Curiosity from the bride is a good thing. They are green, depending on the color of the day. Sometimes they may look closer to a sludge-like gray, and nowhere near as noticeable as mine."

"What about the color of his hair?"

"You'll find out soon enough." He gently pulled me along, but an unusual image on the tapestry caught my eye.

Slipping my arm from his, I moved closer. "Who are they?" I pointed to gray-hooded figures with their faces and bodies obscured under long flowing cloaks.

"Our strength. Thanks to them, Tarragona has rebuffed many attacks over the centuries. Our continual dominance within the near realms is all down to the Creed of Salmun, a wizard cast who arrived with the Levenian one thousand years ago, or so the legends say.

"When the great war was won, the people of Tarragona rejoiced at the end of King Ricaud's harsh rule and begged the Levenian to call Tarragona their home. They didn't. They returned to their realm across the sea, but placed a strong and fair ruler upon the Tarragonan throne and left their wizards to protect our lands."

"Did the war stretch as far as the north?"

"The north is inhospitable. Only fools and Huungardred would care to fill the place. They say the unjust king's daughter was taken into the north rather than face the same fate as her father. There she bred with those beast-men. Her offspring were an abomination and have remained as such ever since. You have suffered greatly by their hands. They are cowards with no remorse or honor to stay hidden in the north. But you don't want to hear any more of that tale. Come, Father will be waiting."

Andriet guided me deeper into Emberfell until we approached two large wood doors, guarded by two sentinels on either side, baldrics slung over their left shoulders and spears in their hands.

We were almost at the doors when three figures drifted out of a shadowy alcove. They kept their faces and bodies hidden under large hooded gray cloaks that reached as low as the stone floor. Their hands were the only part of their skin showing, which they kept clasped in front of their bodies.

"Your Highness." The one who spoke inclined his head. His voice was like a serpent's venom, poisonous after time had elapsed. "This is the woman?" The pungent smell of resin and burned herbal oils followed him as he stepped closer.

"Tressya," Andriet corrected him.

Dressed as they were, these three had to be the Levenian wizards Andriet praised for strengthening Tarragona's borders and keeping the kingdom safe.

"She seems adequate," came the serpentine voice of the tallest, standing before his brethren.

"Tressya's more than adequate. She's an indomitable fighter. And we're already good friends. I think she will add much-needed light into the darkened halls of Emberfell."

"I meant no disrespect, Sire." This time he bent forward into a stiff bow.

Andriet turned to me, dismissing him. "We shouldn't keep Father waiting."

He spun and faced the door, straightening himself and shifting his shoulders backward. In my periphery, the tall wizard moved in behind me, heating my neck with his crackling breath. My fingers itched for my daggers, hidden in my trunks, as a ripple of unease coursed across my shoulders. Since I couldn't fight, I released the shutter on my mind, smoothing away the sensory barrier between myself and the wizard.

A fast beat rushed inside, echoing through my body like a hammer at my back. I sneaked a look in my periphery at Andriet, head held high, staring at the closed doors. Feeling his wild, erratic heartbeat, I realized his outward display of gaiety was a facade. He was nervous.

He'd come into my body so easily, but his presence was not the essence I was looking for. I squinted my eyes in an effort to push Andriet's essence aside and instead focused on the cloaked man behind me, but my mind slammed against a shield. At that moment, the doors swung wide, snapping my awareness to the large room in front of me and the long stretch of polished stone leading to the foot of a wood dais and the king sitting upon his throne.

Andriet led me into the room. The wizard came on my heels, his robes whispering across the floor as he moved on silent feet. I couldn't help but stay focused on the unknown person at my back, but I needed to concentrate on the people before me: the king, sitting proud upon his iron throne, but more importantly, the man sitting upon an impressive seat of his own to the right of his father. Crown Prince Juel.

The similarities to Andriet I saw first, those parts of Andriet I had quickly learned to appreciate. Both had the fine features their father lacked: sloping foreheads, slim faces, aquiline noses, and skin the color of uncooked pastry. It was predominantly their eyes that linked them as brothers, but also drew them apart. Andriet's eyes shone with the light in his heart. Juel's eyes remained like stone, his expression the harsh edges of a cliff face. Here was my husband, staring down at me from his seat perched atop the dais like an eagle on a ledge.

I had been a fool to dream.

I shifted my attention to King Henricus. Unlike his son, the king sat heavy on his throne. An imposing man with strong features, broad shoulders, and a rounded middle. Except for the gray sprinkled through his hair and heavy beard, he looked too young for children so grown. He had the eyes of a hunter, shrewd and all-seeing. By the way he watched my approach, I could tell his mind was already writing an unsavory letter to my father, outlining his deceit in offloading his bastard daughter.

Andriet bent into a sweeping bow. "Father." His voice remained cheerful. If I'd not felt his racing heartbeat brush alongside my own, I would have believed his facade. "I wish to present Princess Tressya, who's arrived safely into our care."

The king rested his elbow on his chair, taking the time to walk his gaze over me. "So it would seem." His tone was flat, as if bored by his duties and wanting to be elsewhere.

"The reports were true. Northerners att—"

"What do you think." King Henricus turned his head to Juel. Juel unfolded his legs and rose from his seat.

"Noble of you to rescue her, brother. You've done your bit." And he flicked his hand, dismissing Andriet. The boredom in his voice oozed over me like a slurry.

"Perhaps we should send scouts to the—"

"Or you should leave the important decisions to us," Juel drawled, cocking his head to the side and eyeing Andriet as one would stare at a fool.

I flexed my fingers, then admonished my instinct to reach for my daggers as Juel swaggered down the steps toward me. He was taller and broader than Andriet, with a lush mouth that wore no hint of a welcoming smile. Instead, it was drawn into a line and drooped downward at the corners. Those hard staring eyes were the color of glass.

Juel paced around me, holding his head on a tilt as his eyes traveled across my body. Once behind me, he leaned close to breathe across the back of my neck, and a shiver ran along my spine, reminding me of spirit hands with its creeping chill. The sound of his inhale, the tacky warmth of his breath at the base of my neck, and I closed my eyes, imagining the exact position of his face behind me, seeing in my mind's eye the arc I would need to make so my elbow speared into his nose. He would stagger away, shocked by my bold, unladylike assault, during which time I would force him to his knees with a solid kick to his...

Eyes closed, I struggled to find my discipline and those calming breaths.

"That is all, Andriet," Juel intoned. "Return to your playthings and leave me to inspect my bride."

I kept my eyes closed, needing more time with my calming breaths. Andriet's retreating steps echoed through the cavernous room in time with my breaths. The heavy clunk of the door closing left me alone in the darkness behind my eyelids, alone and falling into a deep void of...

"I was promised a beauty." Standing beside me, Juel yanked a strand of my hair free from its tie. I opened my eyes, lips twitching with the pain, but I kept my features smooth. "With hair spun like gold. Not ink." He lifted my arm, inspecting it as if studying something he found inside his horse's shoe. "And skin the color of milk. Not mud."

It doesn't matter. The Mother emboldened me, gave me strength to endure. That's what was inside of me, ice running through my veins. It's all I needed to survive.

The king remained slouched in his seat. "Harsh words, my son. True, there is no resemblance to her sister. But beauty leads to trouble. The plain are always best."

"Your Highness, an alliance with Merania is not without benefit." The wizard's voice was like a snake, slithering across the floor to entangle amongst our feet.

Juel dropped my arm. "Question is, do I want her in my bed?"

"Orphus is right, remember that. The alliance was signed. You have your bride. As Crown Prince, you will uphold your responsibility. In time you'll grow to appreciate her skills."

"What skills? Name me a skill." But Juel wasn't looking at me when he asked the question because he wasn't interested in hearing me speak for myself.

The king glanced around, appearing lost for words. "As with highborn ladies, the princess will be appropriately educated in the feminine arts." For the first time, one of them addressed me. "You have the rudiments of reading, science, and philosophy, I suspect?"

"Yes, Your Majesty."

It was my fate that Juel was the first born.

"There, see. She's not without skill."

"What am I going to do with the offspring? Keep them veiled?"

And what should I do with you once the heirs are born? Perhaps a blade to your prized jewels would change your attitude and give me some sport.

The king snorted. "You're unkind, son." He rose from his throne and descended the steps with powerful lumbering strides. "The princess is not a sow."

"Lucky for her, or the stalls is where she'd stay."

I exhaled slowly. *Discipline.*

Like his eldest son, King Henricus towered over me. He was broader, and slouched, pronouncing his rounded middle. "She has intelligent eyes."

"Dull, if you ask me."

"As for the rest of her, there's no requirement for beauty in the king's wife. What is your duty as wife to the king?" Henricus asked me.

I had the strength to endure, thanks to the Sistern's training.

"To remain in his shadow and to support him in all ways," My voice was clear, even if my fingers itched to throw a dagger.

He flashed me the barest smile, or was it a grimace of pain? "Excellent. There see. The perfect wife. I find myself quite pleased with the match."

Juel was sullen. "We're keeping her then?"

A gruesome death for him was not without merit. The Mother would care little if Juel survived for as long as I bore heirs. My blade in his heart could be my birth present to myself once the breeding was done.

"It took me far too long to arrange the alliance."

"Fine." Juel breathed heavy through his nose, then tugged on the strands of hair he'd worked free. "We're finished with you. You can go. Orphus, find someone to show her to her rooms."

I stepped back, then curtsied to them both, dipping my head to avoid looking at either. Acting as though cruel words never reached my heart was the thing I excelled at best. In my periphery, I caught the flutter of the wizard's robes. There were too many enemies within these walls. My best defense was silence; to listen, learn, and plan.

Still avoiding the eyes of both men, I spun on my heels and strode away with my back straight, head high. I was such a stupid, stupid woman to ever think my life would change.

CHAPTER
ELEVEN

TAMAS

To find a nobleman out at night, one had to visit the seediest taverns hidden down forgotten, narrow streets in the darkest reaches of the city. Asking the right questions led me here, to a rowdy place frequented by those who traded in secrets and sex. I was here for neither. Instead, I stayed at the far end of the bar, where I had the best view of the raucous drunks and serving ladies doing their best to avoid wandering hands.

My deer stew was now cold, but I had eaten all the meat and didn't fancy whatever was left floating in the thin gravy. The loaf left the taste of mold in my mouth, so I filled my belly with ale as I eyed the table in the far corner, close to the hearth.

Four men sat in varying stages of undress, three with ladies on their laps, also in varying stages of undress. The aristocracy was easy to pick. They were the foolish ones who flashed their leather coin pouches, alerting the three young boys employed by the tavern owner to the exact location of their wealth.

I took a swig of my ale and watched one lad skulk his way around the tables, seemingly keeping his gaze on the other side of the room when, in reality, his eyes wandered to the pockets of the men he passed. A quick slice of the small knife in his sleeve, and pockets and pouches were emptied of gold, or gold buttons on jackets disappeared.

I had traveled for three days to arrive in Tolum, reaching the sod-soaked streets of the barrios by early morning. Then, huddled in a dark alleyway next to a stack of crates with my back against the cold brick wall, I took some sleep.

The alley smelled of shit, piss, and the pungent stench of rotten vegetables. Traveling nonstop, the stench failed to disturb my few hours of sleep. When the sun broke, slanting its early morning glow across my toes, and the first of the street hawkers wheeled his carts through the sludge, I was ready with a plan.

The thieving lad who'd foolishly thought he could trick me out of my coin assured me the White Shale was the perfect hunting ground. The tavern was small, stank of tobacco, sour bodies, and ale, and was filled with half of Tolum's male nobility, allowing me to be fussy about my choice. Already, my eyes stayed on the four noblemen, growing drunker and rowdier with each sip I took of my ale.

When one of the party lurched to his feet, I lowered my tankard and straightened. As he stumbled around the tavern, bouncing off tables and tumbling into passersby, I assessed his height, build, and clothing for a suitable fit. Once in a neat tie at the nape of his neck, some of his hair had come loose and hung limp against his sweat-drenched cheeks. His fair complexion contrasted against my own, as too the feel of his skin, I was sure.

A young woman, her breasts spilling over her bodice, swept into his path, grabbing his waist and pressing her curvaceous body against his. That was my cue to move. I slunk through the crowd, dodging the swaying drunks and a couple grinding against a large oak barrel, and slipped up beside the nobleman, whose face was now buried in the lady's generous cleavage.

Her eyes darted to me, then widened. In a heartbeat, her face transformed as she worked her lips into a salacious smile. Fisting the nobleman's hair, she yanked his head from between her breasts.

"Fuck off," she growled at him and shoved him away before turning to me. "What may I do for you now?" Her eyes raked my body in one breath.

"I'll be taking my friend," I quipped and spun to haul the nobleman off the table from where he fell.

Jostled and yanked about, he staggered to his feet. Eyes hazy and unfocused, he slurred a jumble of words I had no ear for, then tumbled over his feet as I dragged him across the crowded tavern to the rear door.

Outside, the frosty night air tightened my skin. I let go of his arm, and the nobleman collapsed against the back wall of the tavern. We were in a narrow alleyway cloaked by the night. At the mouth of the alley, rowdy passersby failed to notice us hidden in the depths.

"I need a piss," he mumbled before swaying across to the brick wall of the neighboring building.

With a sigh, I waited for him to finish and button himself up. On turning, he got lost in his feet and fell sideways into the wall, bracing himself against the brick as a means of keeping himself upright.

"What's your name?"

He ran a hand through his hair and straightened his velvet jacket. "Lord Magnus Bloodwyn. And you—" He tripped over his feet crossing the alley toward me, and I dashed forward to catch him, not wanting his clothes to be drenched in mud and who knows what else rotting in this alley.

I straightened him and dusted off his jacket, then swatted his stale breath away from my face. "Lord Blood-wyn. I've heard you mentioned favorably in court gossip, but I can't recall your demesne."

"Mush obligsh." Once again, he attempted to tidy his hair. "My lands...are north."

"Iredale, Celnaer, Burneside?"

"Raebershire."

"Ah, close to the Ashenlands. You're a braver man than I to hold title in those parts."

"Ish a trouble, to be shure. The king gives ush no aid and demands more tax."

A discontented nobleman was nothing new, and not why I chose him.

"There must be a good reason to travel this far into Tolum."

He squinted his eyes as he looked at me, then raised an eyebrow. "The wedden."

"Oh, yes. Crown Prince Juel has his bride. And you have an invitation. That's fitting."

I had thought she held a slim possibility of making it to shore and now felt a grim satisfaction in knowing she had survived. These feelings I would never dare share with Garrat and Osmud. I wanted to disown them myself, but she had grown more compelling in my head during my travel to Tolum.

Garrat and Osmud were right to question my weak heart in keeping her alive; I questioned myself. The princess was caught in a dangerous game, played over a millennium. Though I would struggle to call her innocent. Her precision with a blade was unquestionable; her links to the Sistern were concerning. The woman herself was persistently annoying in the amount of time she stayed in my head.

Why had I bitten her? My actions shocked me. It would have been better for all if I had slit her throat and finished what I had intended to do. Yet, in a moment of weakness, I spared her. Please don't let it be the worst mistake of my life.

I shook my head, forcing her out of my mind yet again. She had reached Tolum. That was all I needed to know. If I acted swiftly, I could spare her the burden of carrying the Tannard heir, thereby saving her life from me, yet again.

I gritted my teeth, shedding the thought, and focused on my reason for standing in a stinking alley talking with a drunk who couldn't hold himself upright. I eyed Bloodwyn as he swayed in front of me. It wasn't his fault he was the perfect fit for what I needed, and I couldn't help the smidgen of guilt I felt for what I was about to do. Some necessities were evil, but not always wrong.

"Where are you staying while in Tolum?"

"Letmesee." He patted his pockets. "Daswood Manor."

"And the burro."

Bloodwyn rubbed his lips. For a moment, I thought he wouldn't reply. Which was no matter. I would have no trouble tracking down such a salubrious place.

"Ah, no, I 'aveit. Upper Heedlemain."

I slipped the small deep red berries from my pocket as I clapped him on the shoulder. "You've been most helpful. Here, why don't you chew on one of these?"

"Whashtish?"

"It'll clear your head. You can get back inside and drink some more."

He leaned in close, squinting to look at the berry I held between thumb and forefinger.

"They're an expensive treat." I popped the one I held in my mouth, then rolled my eyes back and moaned. "Delicious."

"'Ere." And he held out his hand.

I dropped the malec berry into his palm and watched as he slipped it into his mouth and swallowed without chewing. Slowly introducing the berry into a northerner's diet afforded us protection from its lethal effects, but unfortunately for Lord Bloodwyn, he had only moments left. I eased myself back against the wall and waited. Soon I would know more about Bloodwyn than I particularly wanted, so I felt little inclination to talk.

I caught him as he staggered to the left and pushed him up against the tavern wall. "Easy there. Can't have you dirtying your clothes."

Bloodwyn clutched at his throat, his eyes bulging, his cheeks flushing the same color as the malec berry.

"My sympathies, Bloodwyn. Just know you're playing your part in the deposition of the cruel king. I'll ensure they compose a ballad on your behalf."

Bloodwyn opened his mouth to speak, but the malec berry's poison was rapid. Gasping for air, he grappled with me, fisting my shirt front as his knees buckled. I took his arms and guided him to the alley floor, laying him on a narrow patch of dry ground.

It took only moments more before Bloodwyn took his last breath. I knelt beside him and held my hand over his mouth, checking for his warm breath. Satisfied he was dead, I placed my hands on his chest while I stilled my mind, searching for Bloodwyn's soul.

As descendants of Sophila's line, the Razohan inherited the Huungardred's ability to shift form, but unlike the Huungardred, the Razohan were not limited to the form of a beast. We were true shape-shifters, and no Nazeen alive could explain how this phenomenon emerged.

My talent was both a boon and a curse, for the only way I could take the form of another was through their death. And so, with my hands upon his chest, I sought Bloodwyn's essence deep within his soul. The surface of his body beneath my palms heated as I corralled my focus, searching for his life force. It wasn't an easy task and required great concentration, but once I had found the thread of his essence, the flow poured into me, searing through my chest like an iron rod in a smithy's forge, branding me with Bloodwyn's soul. All that he was in life entered me and found a home, and that was the curse of my ability. The hardest to accept were a person's memories, followed by their desires, and lastly the burden on their souls. For this reason, we rarely killed to assume another's body. The drag of their life's sorrows was enough to drive any Razohan insane. When it was done, it was for a good reason and done with care.

Once his body turned cold under my hands, I began the task of stripping him to his undergarments. I had chosen him for his build and—to be honest—his handsome face, but now that I was wearing his clothes, I discovered the shirt buttons pulled tight across my chest and the legs of his breeches were short on my ankles. The jacket I wouldn't bother to close. I jiggled his coin pouch hidden in an inside pocket and judged it ample. Finally, I redressed Bloodwyn in my clothes with the idea of burning his body: the most honorable burial I could give him.

Dressed in Bloodwyn's clothes, I stilled, funneling my mind inward, searching for Bloodwyn's soul. His life was new to me, so it took time to find it amongst the ethereal mass I held within. Following a trail of memories from our last moments together, I wrapped my mind around the amorphous essence and pulled it forth, releasing the binds of my mind and body so both merged with his, enabling me to take his form.

Once done, I glanced down at myself, then stretched my

neck from side to side. While young, Bloodwyn felt half as fit, half as capable, and far less intelligent. Good thing his body was only the shell, and the man that I was remained inside.

I straightened my sleeves, then bent and shouldered Bloodwyn's body as I planned how to leave the alley without calling attention to myself, or the body I carried.

CHAPTER

TWELVE

TRESSYA

RADNISA KEPT HER SMIRK, regardless of what menial task she was required to perform. Two days since our arrival, and she'd witnessed Juel's dismissal of me enough times to please her until death.

"I suggest you keep your mouth shut," she added to the long list of suggestions she'd already unhelpfully made. "No need to embarrass yourself so soon. And avoid those wizards. They mustn't know our business. Give the king an heir, the Sistern a daughter, and the Creed of Salmun won't be able to interfere."

She yanked my hair extra hard as she wove my strands into a messy style on top of my head. "They mustn't know we're daughters of the Sistern."

Henricus had appointed me a string of lady's maids, but for the first time since Radnisa walked into my room as my lady-in-waiting six years prior, she insisted on doing every-thing herself, so she could gloat at every moment.

"You're lucky Queen Gusselan is ill and keeps to her bed. I've heard she has quite the tongue." She sighed. "The gossip in this place. It spreads faster than the pox." Then she smirked, forcing me to wait for whatever malicious treat she hoped to share. "Juel can't keep to one woman in his bed. It seems the prince has quite the appetite."

Her cruel glare flicked to my reflection in the mirror, wanting to catch my response.

"He's no different from any man?"

She arched a manicured brow. "It would seem."

My lips twitched at her sour tone. She'd not made the wounds she hoped to make. I didn't need court gossip to learn about my future husband. Remaining invisible at my father's court won me the seclusion I'd wanted to observe and learn. I had seen and heard enough court intrigue and inflammatory gossip to know court life was more dangerous than living in the wilds, perhaps more dangerous than the feared Huungardred.

"I've heard he gifted a very expensive necklace to his current mistress for your betrothal ball. You'll just have to wear those."

She nodded to the jewelry laid on the bureau before me. The jewelry I'd always worn to the balls back home.

"You mean the set I love." I didn't care what I wore around my neck or in my ears. In fact, I was happier with nothing at all. Jewelry was a hindrance in a fight.

Radnisa pinched her lips tight and tugged more strands up into the ugly knot atop my head, taking delight in dressing me to look a fool. It was the reason she'd shooed the other maids away. I was within Emberfell now. King Henricus had accepted me. There was no need to preen and fuss over my appearance, so Radnisa would do her best to turn me into the court jester, which I welcomed. I'd been foolish to wallow in fantasies. Now I was cured. My duty was to birth an heir and a daughter for the Sistern, not to love my husband or have him love me in return. And since I despised my future husband, the less time I spent in his bed, the happier the two of us would be.

"Juel will do his duty as I'll perform mine, and then we won't bother with each other again."

But maybe I would find a way out of this mess through the poison in my veins, thanks to the beast-man. I still felt strong, so the poison had not progressed, which made me wonder if the beast-man told the truth. However, it made no sense for him to lie.

"You'll likely be called upon to perform certain duties outside the bedchamber. Then there will be the balls and festivities and the many other appearances you and your husband will be required to make. I'm afraid it will be difficult to stay out of his way."

She placed the remaining pins on the bureau in front of me and stepped away. "You'll never be free of him."

I rose from my stool. "True. But at least I'll be a queen."

As queen, I would have certain privileges, such as choosing who would attend me. If it was my choice, Radnisa would be the first to go. Except, it would never be my choice, even as queen, for the Mother had chosen Radnisa as my shadow.

I spun to leave, only to be hit by Radnisa's glare. Her hatred spread like a living presence, clawing its way with vicious talons toward me. I turned my back on her, the only recourse I had, and faced the mirror once more.

One calming breath, and I was ready to leave my room, but Radnisa's footsteps held me in place. I listened to their soft approach, then looked at her reflection as she stepped up beside me.

"Remember, sister." Her voice, like syrup, poured over my skin. "I command soul voice. Not you."

I turned my head to face her, my eyes on the smug curve of her lips. Even as a loyal disciple, I knew Radnisa would do the forbidden and command my soul word just for the pleasure of watching me suffer. And who would know? Not the Mother or any of the Sistern, only Radnisa and I.

I shifted my gaze from her lips to the hard edge of her glare, the watery-green of her eyes like the ocean depths that had almost swallowed me.

I couldn't breathe with all the thoughts cramming my head. The Mother wanted me linked to the Tarragona throne because of my connection to the dead—else why enhance my gift in the death arts—and she chose Radnisa to come with me because she was uncertain I would do what needed to be done. If that was the case, Radnisa would have permission to use my soul word against me. Under the command of my soul word, what would Radnisa have me do? No, that had to be wrong. The Mother knew I would do anything she asked. I'm no less loyal than Radnisa. Perhaps this was nothing more than yet another of Radnisa's taunts.

As if she read my mind, she smirked and arched a brow,

daring me to voice my thoughts.

My composure lost, I spun from her and hurried to the door. Not even my calming breaths would work for me now. Every hasty step I made was a revelation of my inner turmoil for Radnisa to pick over and savor. I loathed giving her so much, but I couldn't remain in her presence any longer. Already a fist squeezed at my lungs, leaving me with shallow, pitiful breaths.

In the corridor, I pressed against the wall, clutching Carlin's bone carving while I tried to find my years of discipline.

"At last, I have found the treasure of Tarragona."

I jerked at Andriet's sudden appearance. This was the second time someone had slipped under my guard and caught me unawares. "Andriet." Even so, he was the one person I would happily let surprise me. The noose of what I'd learned still hung around my neck, but Andriet's smile was like rescuing hands loosening it and allowing me to breathe.

He frowned down at me. "Are you nervous?" The concern in his voice eased the noose some more.

I pushed off the wall. "A little. But not now."

"Of course you would be nervous. This is your first time appearing before my father's court. You needn't worry, though. I'll stay by your side until you're confident to stand on your own."

I fell into his dark-colored eyes, dark for mysteries and secrets, but I doubted Andriet held too many of those. At least nothing malicious. I shouldn't trust so easily, but there was something open and honest about him, something that reminded me of... I pressed my hand over the bone necklace, the only reminder I could allow myself to hold of what I'd left behind.

"You can dance, can't you?"

"Yes, but poorly."

He wrinkled his nose. "You just have to follow me. I'm an adept partner. I won't let you trip."

His gaze shifted to the shocking mess Radnisa had made of my hair. "What a fabulous style."

"Radnisa has a way with hair," I responded deadpan.

He feigned surprise. "The snake likes to do hair? I never would've guessed." He crooked his arm at me.

"Tell me," he continued once we were walking. "How did you get stuck with that one? She's all bristles and spikes. I would say if I stripped her bare, I would find jutting hips and spiked tits." He shuddered to make his point.

"I doubt you'd ever get that far. Radnisa is... capable." I shouldn't reveal any more than that.

"Like you?"

I stuck out my bottom lip, pretending to think, but Andriet beat me to my reply. "Impossible. No one's like you."

He patted my hand, then guided me down the sweeping staircase. I was no humble woman with a provincial upbringing, but Emberfell was worth a gasp. The ceiling towered above us, cut skyward as coarse and violent as the spears of the steeples outside, and dark, like a half-moon night.

"Tressya..." Andriet stopped us on the stairs, touching my hand, then frowned and continued on down the stairs.

I didn't press him, seeing the conflict in his expression. If it was important, he would find the right words to say.

Instead, I looked down on the vast hall in front of us, empty of any furnishing that might make it feel like a more welcoming place.

We reached the bottom step when Andriet turned to me, taking my hand. "I want to apologize for my brother."

"You really—"

"I'm sorry, but he can be a swine at times. Not always easy to get along with. Father indulges him because he's the crown prince." He patted my hand again, like a parent soothing a child. "The two of you shall get along—"

"Andriet. You don't have to pretend. I'm no stranger to the royal court and its tight circle of personalities. There's nothing you need to apologize for."

"It's just... Juel needs to be handled in a certain way."

It was my turn to pat his hand reassuringly. "I know exactly what you mean."

His eyes narrowed before he shared a devious smile. "I believe you do." Then he winked at me, taking my arm in the crook of his once more. "You have no idea how delighted I am that it's you who shall be queen."

Radnisa and her cruel taunts and my sudden revelatory thoughts faded when I was with Andriet. Curse my fate he should be the youngest brother.

Andriet moved close beside me, as he tucked my arm into his. It seemed he was determined to keep his promise to stay by my side. That I was grateful for, and the fact Juel felt it beneath him to escort his bride to the ball.

"Are you ready to shock the foundations of Emberfell's court?"

"I am." I glanced up at Andriet's broad smile and wide

eyes, unable to believe my luck in finding such an ally. Hopefully for once my fate would allow me to keep someone kind.

Swallowing my sudden emotions, I stared ahead to the grand doors. I could already hear the music from the other end of the cavernous hall. Sentinels flanked the doors, dressed in bone-white doublets and breeches, rather than the outfits I had seen through Emberfell these last few days.

We walked to the entrance, Andriet pausing on hearing my inhale as I took in the ballroom's expanse. In a balcony high above the crowd, the musicians perched with their instruments. At the opposite end, on the ground floor, stretched a large table the width of the room and brimming with food. King Henricus commanded the head of the table, flanked by nobility and other important figures. Those seated at the king's table were people I would make it my business to learn everything about, as most who sat there were usually enemies. That was my first lesson upon entering my father's court.

The queen's seat was vacant, as was Juel's to his right.

Andriet guided me through the throng of dancers, and with each step we made, the music faded, and the dancers parted to create a path leading to the king.

Whispers flared all around too low for me to hear, which was a mercy, for I was sure they said nothing nice. The seamstresses commissioned to improve my wardrobe were half as skilled as those who created the clothes of the Tarragona courtiers. The women's gowns were voluminous, covered in lace, silk, jewels, and every vibrant color. My pale green gown looked heavy and drab in comparison. Ladies wearing adornments in their hair seemed the style in Emberfell, something Radnisa would have paid attention to and ignored while preparing me for tonight.

The herald pushed off the wall and scuttled to take his place before the king with a sweeping bow. "Your Highnesses, Prince Andriet and the Princess Tressya."

"I know my son, you fool," the king grouched, then his shifted his gaze to me. "You look quite fine." His eyes trawled over my body with no hint of his thoughts. "I shall instruct the royal seamstresses to dress you in the latest Tarragona fashion. It's a shame the queen is not present tonight to lend you advice. These matters are beyond me." He waved a hand as if to be rid of us. "Andriet take her around the floor. Everyone needs to see her dance."

My eyes scraped the table, memorizing faces, as Andriet drew me away toward the middle of the room and the dancers, who'd already resumed in time with the music.

Far behind the king's table, lurking in the shadows, were two hooded figures: the Salmun. I had rarely seen the wizards during the last two days. Andriet had said they preferred to stay in the shadows, interfering little in court life. Although they were present at every meeting of the king's council, they never spoke a word but regularly attended the king in private. The shadows were the best place for the cunning and schemers.

Andriet squeezed my hand, offering me a thin smile as he spun me around and into his arms. He was an accomplished dancer and a strong partner, ensuring I didn't embarrass myself by missing my steps. I kept my eyes on him to avoid the stares I could feel hammering into me as we swung around the room.

"There," Andriet began. "The short, stout man with the generous belly, wearing a mustache wider than his face, is Marquess Mendel. Owns titles across the eastern lands and has a seat within the king's council. His voice on the council is the loudest."

Andriet guided me further along the room. "His wife, the marchioness, is the one with the red hair."

He nodded to the three women huddled together and deep in conversation. The chalk color of their skin, thanks to a thick layer of white paste, made them all appear like ghosts if not for the rich red they'd painted on their lips.

"She's in love with the Duke of Eerlie. He's the one standing by the last pillar. We're about to pass him now. Also on the king's council. He loathes Mendel, by the way, but not as much as he loathes Lord Arobet, who's gambled all his money and is in deep debt. And we shan't tell the duke's wife about his indiscretions."

Andriet continued to move me around the ballroom, weaving me through the crowds like he'd been born to dance. He held my hand in a firm grip, and his arm against my back was strong. There was no way I would fall.

"Uh-oh. Off to your right. Danger approaches. The old dragon in the wig is Baroness Magenta Deflume. Avoid her, whatever you do. She killed her husband."

"Oh." My eyes flickered to the baroness, intrigued.

"That's not how the story goes. They found him with his face in his dish of smoked duck and peas. Sir Willbrie Stokrest, the baroness's long-term lover, conducted a closed investigation and concluded that there was no sign of poison. I should say Baron Deflume was also on the council, and his widow has been pushing ever since to place Stokrest in his vacant seat, but Father won't have it. His titles are a poor claim, I'm afraid. And his family are power grabbers."

"Is there anyone here you know little about?"

"Good gracious, no. It's in my best interests to gain an intimate knowledge of all who sit on the king's council."

"What about Juel?"

"Are you asking me to divulge the secrets of my brother?" There was a light tease in his voice.

"I meant, does he pay as much attention to everyone on the king's council?"

"He would think such trivial details beneath his notice."

"In my experience, problems arise from those closest to the king. It pays to know them very well."

His eyes lit with his smile. "So you're cunning and bold. Juel won't know how to handle you."

Neither would his brother care to know what I could offer our alliance.

In my periphery, I caught a couple walking our way. I turned to see Juel approach with a dazzling woman on his arm. Dressed like a bride, her white gown, cinched at the waist and spilling like a fountain of stars to the floor, contrasted against her midnight skin. She looked every bit the princess with a garland of tiny white flowers and golden jewels woven through her elaborate plaits, which pinned into loops and swirls. My eyes couldn't miss the large diamond necklace sparkling against her skin; the jewels Juel gifted her for tonight's ball. Once he turned her aside for another, she would likely sell them in a fit of rage and jealousy, as Arnaud's lovers always did.

"Brother," Andriet announced. "My lady." He gave a curt nod of his head to the stunning woman beside Juel.

I resisted glancing at their clasped hands. He didn't bother to hide from the royal court his infidelities, and it seemed no one expected him to.

"Lady Astaria, this is my bride." Juel drawled the introduction, already sounding bored.

"Your Highness." She dipped into a graceful curtsy, then shifted her gaze to Juel with an innocent, sidelong blink.

For the first time tonight, I glanced at my almost husband. He looked elegant and regal, every part the desirable husband, except for those ice eyes that grew into glass shards as he glared down on me.

"Once again, brother, you seem to have rescued her. You'd better be careful, or the court will tell tales. Can't have them questioning the legitimacy of the infant she'll soon carry."

I blanched at the jab at my heritage but tried my best to keep any further emotion from my face. Juel arched one brow as he continued to stare at me, hoping to catch my reaction, no doubt. Then, slowly, his eyes roamed over my gown.

"Brother, you know—" Andriet began.

"I believe the Earl of Vaelorin wants a word." He wriggled his fingers. "Off you go."

"I've promised—"

"You've already fulfilled that promise," I said, releasing his arm. I didn't want him to suffer humiliation by his brother's tongue over me. Andriet frowned at me.

"Yes, brother, do as you're told."

Lady Astaria smiled behind her gloved hands.

Andriet looked stricken, but I nodded and somehow found an encouraging smile. "Thank you, Prince Andriet. Now that I've found your brother, I'm in good hands." While Carlin had saved my heart from turning to stone, the Mother had ensured I was far stronger than anyone believed. I didn't flutter my eyelashes or seek praise, and I kept my words to myself, but I wasn't meek.

He looked as though he was ready to refute everything I said, his eyes flicking between his brother and me. For my part, I kept my smile and my head held high, but I wouldn't bother to look at Juel to read his expression.

"Well... if you're happy, Princess." Andriet bowed to kiss the back of my hand.

"Thank you for the dance." I dismissed him by facing Juel.

The further his brother retreated, the broader Juel's smile became.

"She's quite plain, as you can see, Lady Astaria."

Lady Astaria stared at me as she sucked in her cheeks. She made an obvious show of looking at my hair, then wandered her eyes down my pale green gown, allowing her thoughts to play across her face. When her eyes finally climbed to mine, she smirked.

Having completed the formalities etiquette required, she shifted her gaze to Juel. Lady Astaria was a beautiful woman, but the demure smile she gave Juel made her stunning. No wonder Juel was transfixed. I could only imagine his dry mouth on receiving such an adoring gaze from such a magnificent-looking woman. His eyes dipped to the subtle slope of her cleavage, modestly exposed. I thought of clearing my throat, but Juel retrieved his senses before I needed to.

"I was thinking, Lady Astaria, perhaps you could advise my new bride on what to wear. It seems Merania has fallen behind the times in fashion. The trials approach, and you know how the ladies like to parade around in their finest fashion. I would hate for the princess to draw attention to herself for the wrong reasons."

"Of course, Your Highness. Anything you desire, Your Highness." She dropped into a deep curtsy, low enough to place her face level with his groin. Juel's nostrils flared, his eyes shifting like that of a hungry animal.

Thank the Mother he had her and all the many women that likely spent a night in his bed. It meant Juel would stay clear of my bed beyond his required duty. My future already looked promising.

"Your gown is quite stunning, Lady Astaria. You have impeccable taste. I would appreciate your advice on my wardrobe. The prince is right. Merania is far behind in fashion."

Her smile faltered. She glanced at Juel as if requiring his advice on how to react and what to say next. Juel's smile had also slipped.

"If you'll excuse me." I gathered my skirts and curtsied, lacking all the grace Astaria held. Which was the point. Neither did I bother to explain my departure because Juel was not my master.

No one paid me any attention as I hurried from the ball-room out to the balcony. Holding my composure in front of

Juel and his mistress pressed against my chest; I felt I couldn't breathe or swallow. Outside, I could finally take a gulp of air.

I clasped the railing and ducked my head, inhaling a deep calming breath. I had trained for years to maintain my outward calm but internalizing it deep within me was never easy. Unlike the Mother, Radnisa, and the other disciples, I'd not mastered the soul voice, and neither had I mastered a stony heart. But I would one day become the perfect disciple.

Confident, powerful strides interrupted my solitude. I leaned against the pillar and stared up at the stars as if dreaming, all the while focusing on the slow steps that sounded reminiscent of a hunting predator. A man, for sure. My hands itched for a dagger, but Radnisa had opposed the idea. Considering my daggers were too large to be hidden discreetly under this gown and retrieving them quickly from beneath all my layers would be impossible, I relented.

Something I was currently regretting. I flexed my fingers. Why should I feel at risk?

"Princess Tressya," came a low voice, dripping in darkness.

I spun to find a tall, striking man approaching, dressed in deep green velvety breeches and matching jacket, a cloak of fur thrown over his shoulders. A thin mustache matched the color of his light brown hair, neatly tied to his nape. Half of his face was lit by the many chandeliers that adored the ballroom; the moonlight shadowed the rest. But it was his amber-colored eyes I found startling.

A weird feeling, like a tiny fluttering of insect wings,

danced across my wrist, in the exact spot as the bite mark. I rubbed at it with a frown. "I'm at a disadvantage."

"Lord Bloodwyn." He bowed but kept his eyes on the hand rubbing at my wrist. The way his eyes seemed to sharpen at the movement sent a sudden chill across my chest.

"The princess doesn't like to dance?"

"The princess has danced too much and wants to be by herself."

Something about him made my heart thump hard underneath my ribs. He spoke with the cultured voice of an aristocrat and dressed like one too, but something lurked beyond what I could see. I couldn't explain the feeling. My chest tightened as I assessed his size against mine. If I moved swiftly, I could go for a jab to his throat, a kick to his groin. It was strange I should suddenly plan an attack when he appeared pleasant and harmless, but I never questioned my instincts. If this was my first thought on meeting this lord, I would go with it.

"I apologize for the intrusion, but is this not your ball?"

"It's the Prince's ball."

"Ah, quite. It seems the princess is already weary of her husband."

The funny, fluttery feeling around the bite mark intensified. My brow twitched as I fought the urge to rub it. I didn't want to draw his attention to it again. The feeling became too much to bear, though, and I grabbed my wrist, pressing my fingers to the mark as if that would ease the irritation.

Bloodwyn stepped toward me. "Is the princess all right?"

"The princess is fine." And before I could stop myself, I took a step back. I never stepped away from anyone.

"Hmm... that's an interesting necklace you're wearing."

I covered it with my hand, not wanting him to see it, which, again, was a strange reaction for me to have. At some point, he'd stepped even closer, and I hadn't realized. How had I not realized? My pulse deafened me, so I inhaled, blowing the breath out slowly through my nose to calm my body and my thoughts. *Discipline.* Why was I acting like this?

"It's a present from home."

Who are you to make me feel like this? I relaxed the barriers in my mind as I focused on Bloodwyn's amber eyes, now staring at mine with a curious smile quivering on his lips. The more I practiced harnessing soul voice, the more I would succeed.

"It's bone, isn't it?"

The way the word bone came out of his mouth, half accusation, half denouncement, I tensed as if ready for a strike.

"Perhaps."

"A gift from someone important, no doubt."

I dropped my hand from it then, not wanting him—or anyone—to know of my attachment. "You're wrong. It just reminds me of home."

Downward, I funneled my mind into the depths of his existence, into the place where a disciple of the Sistern held true power. And there, I fell into a confusing swirl of misty darkness, a deafening chorus of cries, a stranglehold of chaos that seized me in a grip so fierce it felt like my ribs would break.

This couldn't be real. It made no sense. It was as though there were many souls within this man. Or at least more than one... The northerner?

"That's rather rude," Lord Bloodwyn drawled before he swiped an arm toward me.

But I was ready and dodged low, then cracked my forehead up into his mouth. Hearing the clash of his teeth, I spared no time and kneed him hard in the groin. He doubled back with a suck of air, and I followed, ready to cut him hard through the throat with the side of my hand, but he seized it and spun me around with a yank that shot pain to my shoulder. My stomach slammed against the pillar, and his scent—earthy, woody, leather, and smoke—enveloped me as he pressed against me.

"Now, that's not the way to greet the man who holds your life in his hands," he growled in my ear.

It had been dark in the hold of the ship when we fought, so I never saw the beast-man's face. I remembered the size of him pinning me to the floor as he threatened to take my life. This man was of similar size. Was it him?

"You're lucky they made me wear this ridiculous dress, or I would've fulfilled the promise I made on the ship."

He huffed a laugh. "Like a feral cat, hissing and scratching even when caught. But I'm curious. What alerted you?"

"As if I'd tell."

"I believe it was the bite."

"The poison," I corrected him.

"Perhaps," he mused, sounding disinterested. Of course, he would be. What did it matter to him if I died? As long as he got to play his cruel game for as long as it pleased him.

"Tell me why you did it?"

"Sorry, princess, but I'm not about to tell unless you wish to be more obliging and answer my questions."

I bucked against him. "If you'll get off of me."

"Are you bargaining already? You have a habit of that when you're most disadvantaged."

I inhaled, needing my calming breaths more than ever, but all I got was the leathery spice and woodlands of his smell. A northerner was in the south, dressed as a nobleman and mingling among the king's court. How did he get this close to the king?

"We both have questions," I said, filling my voice with anger.

I felt the pressure of his body lighten on mine, but he didn't step away or drop his hands from the pillar. Instead, he allowed me room to wriggle while keeping me caged. It was a threat, an intimidation. I kept my back to him rather than try to turn in the tight circle of his arms.

"What did you see when you looked inside of me?"

I couldn't stop my sudden gasp. Neither did I realize I'd spun around until I felt his breath on my face. He was suffocatingly close, too close. The amber in his eyes faded out to a striated black around the edges. They were...mesmerizing. I blinked once I realized I'd been staring too long and saying nothing. Then he smirked. Its power was better than a slap to my face to steel my focus. This asshole thought me a blushing princess.

"Come now. There's no need to be coy, my princess."

I snapped up my knee for another groin kick, but he caught my leg under my thigh and held it in place.

"Uh-uh. That's not good for political relations with the north."

"Let go," I snapped and attempted to pull my leg from his hold.

He released me and stepped back, giving me the room to suck in fresh air and not... him.

He was fast and cunning. I needed to be smart.

"You really are quite the surprise. Not what the prince expected, I'm sure."

I crossed my arms in front of me. Then I dropped them again on realizing I did it out of defense. I felt like I needed a barrier between us. He stood too close, his presence suddenly everywhere, overwhelming me, overpowering me.

I snapped. "Are you here for me or him?"

"There are rules to our conversation. You answer my questions, and I'll... We'll see how we go. What did you see when you delved inside of me?"

I stared at him, the shock once again stealing my ability to speak.

"Come, princess. You didn't honestly believe the Sistern's talents were a secret to all?"

The Sistern spread their reach wide, but into the inhospitable realm of the north?

"I'm sure it was quite a surprise. But I'm genuinely interested. I've often wondered what my soul would feel like." I followed his hand as it slipped into his pocket. "Not necessarily my soul, of course, rather..."

Rather, what? What other surprises did he hide? "First,

the attack on the ship, and now you turn up here. What's your purpose?"

"You don't want to know my purpose, princess. Or can I call you Tressya?"

"Princess will do." I glared at him as he leaned on the railing, seeming immune to the tension thinning the air surrounding us. I hated that I noticed the way he did the simplest movements with powerful grace.

"Is it disruption you want to cause? You want to incite a rebellion, befriend the nobles of the south to rise against their king?"

He huffed as he nodded his head. "That would be interesting, but far too easy and rather boring."

"You didn't kill me on the ship, so you won't kill me now. But what about Juel?"

He tilted his head, his amber eyes considering me. They were so unsettling. "Would that upset you if I did?"

"I would thank you. Then I would put a dagger through your heart."

"And what of the younger brother? Would you thank me if I did away with him?"

I stiffened. He'd been watching me. "You really think you're that good?"

He shrugged. "Perhaps." Spoken with a nonchalant voice, and I wanted to punch that smile off his face—if he wasn't so intriguing. He exuded a confidence I found compelling, coupled with an arrogance I found grating.

A creeping sickness filled my gut at how careless he'd been in revealing himself to me, because it may not be a careless move at all. "You've made one mistake."

"I have? Please tell."

"I know your face now."

A vile smile crossed his lips. "Do you now?"

The sickness drove a lump into my throat. Knowing nothing about him or his people, I was disadvantaged, but I sensed there was something more to him than a link to a half-beast people.

"Why are you here?" I demanded. "If it's for me—"

"Sweetheart, you're the least of my concerns."

I was getting nowhere in this conversation. "How long do I have before the poison kills me?"

He shook his head with a wry smile. "I wouldn't let that worry you. Not just yet anyhow."

I still had time then. Time enough to learn everything about him and his people. I didn't need him to reveal his plans because I could already guess. The end of the House of Tannard. There was no other reason why a northerner would sneak south. Assassinating Henricus would make Tarragona vulnerable to an attack. If it were true, it made him my enemy.

"Answering questions with questions gets very tedious. I hope that's not how all our interactions will play out."

The arrogant ass wanted to taunt me. Unfortunately for him my years with Radnisa made that a hard task for anyone to achieve. "I'm not the only disciple to have arrived in Tarragona, you know. So I'll tell you this, beast-man. You can't stay hidden. Not now that you've revealed yourself."

He rubbed his chin, appearing thoughtful. "You mean the rather severe-looking woman who shadows your every move. She certainly has the scary look down. Besides her, I

196

believe you are alone. Your—what do you call her, Mother Divine?—must really have faith in your talent to send just the two of you across."

He'd closed the distance between us, and my refusal to step back meant we were too close for my comfort. His height forced me to arch my head back to meet his eyes.

To my horror, he leaned down, bringing his face far too close, ensuring I had the misfortune to see deep into his striking amber eyes. For some inexplicable reason a spark fired deep inside my stomach. A worthy adversary. That's what caused this sudden stabbing beat of my heart. It was the only explanation.

"Threats, little princess, won't work. It makes no difference to me how skilled either of you is in your talent. Your skills are useless against the Razohan." He dragged his finger along my chin. "We have no soul to command."

Before I could respond, he disappeared over the balcony and into the night. My anger boiled in my throat as I peered over. He'd disarmed my defenses and muddled my thoughts, and now he was long gone. "Curses," I spun away, fists clenched.

He could only be here to disrupt or destroy the House of Tannard. How many more of his kind came with him? The wizards were lax to let this happen.

I turned back and stared over the railing into the darkness. My duty was to bear an heir, but I couldn't fulfill my duty if there was no House of Tannard. The Mother would want me to protect the Tannard sons.

At least now I knew my enemy's face.

CHAPTER

THIRTEEN

TRESSYA

FEELING unable to handle the choking confines of the ballroom, I walked further along the balcony. A thin sliver of glowing candlelight slanting across the ground drew me closer. I found a narrow gap in the heavy drapes and peered through. In the dim candlelight, I saw a large bookshelf reaching to the ceiling, crammed to bursting. A library was just the place I longed to be right now, so I tried the latch on the window and found it unlocked.

I was halfway through opening the window when a man inside the room spoke.

"We have the Earl's backing," the voice was dry and crackling.

"We need more than his backing. We need it written down. Leverage. That way, we're assured he'll fulfill his promise," the other voice was forceful and rough. The man sounded younger than the first.

"Getting it will delay our plans. He's unlikely to oblige."

"Then it's delayed. I refuse to take the risk. If there's the slightest problem, he'll betray us to save his skin."

"We can't delay." There was a third man in the room. "King Henricus is pushing the wedding forward. Juel and his bride will leave Tolum for their honeymoon. We must have our men in place before then."

Someone chuckled. "I doubt the prince will be willing to travel with his new bride. Unless he keeps that whore, Lady Astaria, hidden in his trunk somewhere to ease his aches." It was the forceful younger man.

The rest of them laughed.

I closed my eyes as I ground my jaw.

"Something must be wrong with the prince if they've stooped low enough to accept a bastard as a queen." It was an old, dry voice, coming from a man I envisioned to look little better than aged parchment.

I wrinkled my nose, then pressed my lips firmly. Curses, it hurt to hear that word, even if I'd heard it uttered repeatedly my entire life. Please, let its jabs fade from my heart.

"And one that isn't even fine to look at," said the younger man.

"That's easily fixed. You simply blow out the candle," came the third voice, and they all laughed.

The creak of the library door opening cut their laughter short.

"Forgive me, gentlemen, I had no idea you were all hiding away from the ball."

Andriet. My heart raced.

"Your Highness," came the voice of the third man. It sounded as though he was trying to rise from his seat.

"There's no need to leave on my behalf. I'm completely danced out. We can all share a brandy and have a good chat."

"Your Highness. I'm sorry, but I must head back to the ball."

"No need to apologize, Lord Dowel. Besides, I think your wife needs rescuing. Lord Trevel had her caught in his arms for most of the night, and he seems intent on refusing her a breath. She's still smiling and laughing, so I guess she's enjoying herself."

"'Er, what? Excuse me," Lord Dowel barked. His footsteps hurried from the room.

"What do you say, gentlemen, shall we—"

"I have something I wish to say to the Earl. Good evening, Your Highness," said the younger man. And he too departed, along with the third older man with the dry, crackling voice, or so it sounded as more than one set of footfalls vacated the room. The door closed with a heavy clunk. Next, I heard Andriet's voice dimming as he disappeared with the two remaining noblemen.

I deliberated with myself about climbing through the window for two breaths, then I hiked up my layers of skirt and did just that. It wasn't easy, but I made it through with a good deal of fumbling and puffing.

Once inside, I headed for the hearth, only to hear fabric rip. I turned to see the trail of lace I left behind. Shrugging, I bent and finished dismantling my hem, then balled up the material and headed for the fire. The flames burned through the lace, fanning the flares into a welcoming glow.

Slumping into a large leather chair, I thought about all I'd overheard. It was a treasonous plot. No surprise. Every royal court had them. Such a shame I knew only one of their names, but I would remember their voices, and I was sure Andriet suspected something was going on between them.

And what was I to do about the Razohan?

"What is she doing in here? This library is a place for gentlemen," came the aggrieved male voice behind me.

"She is in my chair," announced another.

"Did you see how she got in here?" came a third. "Through the window. What sort of—"

I lurched up from the chair and spun to find three spirits hovering behind my chair. Would I ever find time on my own tonight?

"She is looking at us," declared a reedy gentleman, dressed in richly adorned yet antiquated fashion.

"Do not be absurd," said the man next to him, half a head shorter than his companion, and half a body rounder. "The woman cannot be looking at us. She is simply looking in our direction, more likely something behind us has caught her attention."

"No. The lady is definitely looking at us," said the third, who was dressed less fine than the other two.

I folded my arms across my chest. "I am looking at you."

"Stars and fire," cried the third man. "She is talking to us."

I groaned as I slumped down into the chair once more. Spiritseeing was turning into an annoying talent. With time,

I'm sure I would learn how to control my new ability by shutting them out of my mind to call upon them at will. That way, I would keep these pesky spirits from interfering with my peace.

It took the three noblemen little time to recover from their surprise. They drifted through the furniture to stand in front of me, staring down at me like I was the half-beast.

"Are you sure she—" said the third spirit.

"I can see you, hear you, and talk to you."

"Mercy. That is unheard of," cried the tall, reedy spirit.

"So too in Merania, for some time now. That I'm now a spiritseer is thanks to the Mother. I'm sure of it."

"What do you suppose she is talking about?" said the tall spirit.

"A spiritseer? I can see and talk to spirits. So, gentlemen, make yourselves comfortable. I have questions I want to ask."

"I beg your pardon," the shorter spirit huffed. "That is my chair. And this room is strictly—"

"Shut up, Albert. The lady can speak to us. How that is, I cannot say. But after all this time..." The man with the less distinguished clothes sunk to the rug. If his lower half were better formed, he would be cross-legged on the floor. "This is a miracle."

"What's your name?" I said.

The man sitting in front of me wafted up to his full height again and bowed. "Forgive me, your ladyship, I am Sir Truett Monbasora. This is Earl Albert Elvistan. And finally, Lord Borrat Wickenbro. This is quite the honor."

"Do not fall all over yourself, man. Have some self-respect," Albert said as he lowered himself down into the seat next to me, his lower half sinking through the leather cushion.

I entwined my fingers and rested them on my lap. "Gentlemen, let's get down to business. What can you tell me about the discussion of the three men who recently vacated this room?"

"Wait. Wait. Wait. Your ladyship, with all respect, you must give us time to recover from our shock. This is a tremendous moment. We have been stuck here for centuries, or longer, without a chance to touch the world beyond. And here you are," Truett said.

Albert tutted and rolled his eyes. "Get a hold of yourself before the lady laughs at you." He drew a hand to his mouth, then sighed as he dropped his arm to his lap. "Oh, how I want my pipe. After all this time, it is the one thing I miss."

"Albert, old chap, you are a lucky dead man if that is all you crave," Borrat said.

"I'm sorry, but I can't fulfill that wish," I said to Albert as Truett floated across the floor toward me. He would be crawling if he had legs. Instead, it appeared as though he was dragging his lower half behind him.

"Stop right there," I held up a finger. "You'll keep your hands to yourself."

"Please, lady, I just want to see if I can feel you."

"You can't. But I can feel you when you touch me. And it's not pleasant." I shivered at the memory of passing through Scregs and the other spirits before I plunged into the ocean. "Talking to you is as close as we'll ever get."

The fire cracked and sent up a fine spray of red sparks up the chimney.

Borrat lowered himself onto the small wood table beside my chair. "What is your name, my lady?"

"Tressya."

Truett gasped. "The princess."

"Who is that? Why do I not know about this?" Albert demanded.

"You have buried your business for too long below the stairs with the servants. Namely one servant, to be exact," replied Truett. "You pervert."

"She is dishonest and disloyal and needs a firm hand. If I were—"

"You are not. You are dead and have been so for a very long time," Truett rolled his eyes.

Borrat turned on Truett. "And you are little better. You did not even know who she was at first sight."

"Neither did you," Truett snapped back. "But you are her, am I right? The bride of Crown Prince Juel?"

"Yes. But, gentlemen, please. Have your arguments another time. I'm more interested in what Lord Dowel and his companions were talking about."

"We choose not to divulge such things," Albert settled himself back in his chair, only to partially sink through. It wasn't hard to guess that he was one of those noblemen who saw a clear line, forged by privilege alone, between the deserving and undeserving.

"Why not?"

"We do not interfere with the intrigues of the living."

"Because you haven't been able to until now."

"Huh. She has you there," Truett said.

"We simply allow them to play their games and watch each triumph or fall. It is the way of life. There are always winners and losers. As spirits, it is not our responsibility to govern their destinies."

As a spiritweaver, it would be within my power to command these spirits to answer me. Instead, I would have to win him to my side.

"I believe I'm in your seat, Lord Albert." I rose and strode to the fire, taking my time to stare into the flames. When I turned around, Albert had taken his seat and crossed his legs, staring up at me with a satisfied expression.

"As a woman, my head is full of balls and gowns and all manner of pretty things. What would I know about treasonous talk?"

"To be sure, princess, that is what it is," Borrat interjected.

"Lord Borrat, you are a fool," Albert drawled. "A lady, especially a princess, should never concern herself with the affairs of men." He shifted his gaze to me. "As the wife of the crown prince, your place is beside your husband, your duty to him likewise. It is unseemly to act otherwise."

"I see your wisdom, Lord Albert. But isn't it my duty to ensure the stability of my husband's reign and, therefore, do what I must, feeble as I may be, to protect the House of Tannard? A quiet word in my husband's ear, perhaps?"

"What she says has merit," Borrat said.

"Yes, but we cannot have women believing they can influence the ways of their husbands, especially when he is the crown prince. Imagine, next they will think to insert themselves within the council and dictate the laws. Mercy knows what would happen to the legacy my forefathers and I left behind were it to end up in the hands of women."

If I were a spiritweaver, I would force Lord Albert to choke on his words.

"I understand your fears. I can assure you I am ill-qualified and lack any interest in such responsibility. However, imagine the praise the Crown Prince would receive in uncovering a treasonous plot. I would, of course, ensure he stumbled on the information seemingly by chance, happy as I would be to remain in my husband's shadow."

Albert folded his arms as he eyed me.

"They are planning to force the king to abdicate," Truett said.

"Hold your tongue, man," barked Albert.

"Interesting, Sir Truett. Thank you for—"

"The Earl of Vaelorin is of my line," Albert said.

"And a traitor," snapped Truett.

"Who is not a traitor?" Albert sighed. "It is how I lost my head."

Borrat huffed as he looked at me. "It is in the blood."

"Gentlemen, please. Such gossip is spinning my head." I moved over to the chair Albert had vacated in favor of his and eased myself into it. "For a treasonous plot, many would be involved. I may not be able to keep up with all you're saying, seeing as I'm unaccustomed to understanding such complex matters. Maybe you should start from the beginning."

Borrat leaned forward. "The king has gathered his fair share of dissenters. Many lords are fed up with his taxes, the unfair land laws, and the queen's gambling debts and expensive tastes. Need I go on? It is the curse of all who rule."

"Can you be specific about this treasonous plot? I fear too much talk will confuse me," I asked.

Albert sighed. "Their plan is quite simple. They wish to force the king's abdication by kidnapping his eldest and his bride and holding them ransom in the demesne of Burneside. That is Lord Dowel's lands. The king must give up his throne in favor of the Duke of Eerlie." He spoke matter-of-factly as if he had not recounted how I would be kidnapped.

Seeming to realize what he had said, he continued, "Oh dear. The bride-to-be is you, is it not? I am afraid you are going to lose your head."

"No, she is not," Truett snapped. "The princess will reveal the plot, and all will be dealt with." He glanced at me. "You get to keep your head."

"Come now, gentlemen," Borrat interrupted. "It would never have worked. Prince Juel and his bride," he dipped his head at me, "will never be far from the sight of the Salmun. I believe the lords have yet to come up with a solution to that problem."

"Have you not noticed? They are withdrawing more of late. I see little of them within the castle. Something has drawn their attention elsewhere," Truett said.

"It is a honeymoon, you fool," Albert continued, as if Truett had not mentioned the Salmun's unusual behavior. "Were you not listening? The Salmun cannot always be at their side. There the matter of the..." He arched an eyebrow. "It is a delicate matter. Not to be mentioned in the lady's presence."

"Are you referring to our wedding night?"

Albert coughed. The other two glanced at each other.

I waved my hand to dismiss their awkwardness. "We can forget about that." Then I steepled my fingers and held them to my lips. I would have to think about what I did with this information. Obviously, I didn't fancy losing my head, but valuable secrets such as this were worth keeping close until I needed to use them. And there was my duty to the Mother I had to uphold. Bearing an heir to both the Tarragona throne and the Sistern came above all else.

"Tell me, what do any of you know about the Razohan?"

"That is not—" Albert began.

"Filthy beasts," Truett proclaimed.

"So you know of them?"

"Our lands were rarely plagued by them thanks to the Salmun. They were ruthless in their destruction when they dared to venture south. Then the Salmun created the Ashenlands, and now they do not cross."

"We have given the princess a lot to—" Albert said.

"They believe they have a rightful claim to the throne of Tarragona. Which is all hogwash," Borrat added.

Removing the House of Tannard was the northerner's aim, as I had suspected.

Truett snorted a laugh. "No more right than I."

"Then that is why Lord Bloodwyn took the risk of venturing this far south. But on his own? It makes little sense. Unless he's not on his own. And Bloodwyn is probably not his real name." I forgot about the spirits as I spoke aloud my thoughts.

"Lord Bloodwyn is an oaf," Borrat interrupted my thoughts.

"You know him?" I said.

"His great-great-grandfather swindled me out of half my lands, which Lord Bloodwyn has promptly lost because of his love for gambling and whoring. The crown prince will do the same as soon as he inherits his title. He and Bloodwyn are firm foes across the card table. But they often share the same women."

"But... how is it he lives in the south?"

"I beg your pardon, princess, I am missing the point of your question," Borrat said.

"I met... He said he was..." I stared into the fire, my mind whirling. Recalling the chaotic swirl of Bloodwyn's soul, the cries, I gasped. "Is the beast form the only form the Razohan can take?"

"Mercy no, princess," Truett said. "That's the Huungardred. The Razohan can take whichever form they choose. They are said to be true shapeshifters."

Curses. I was a fool for the things I'd said to him. Taking Bloodwyn's form was how he infiltrated the palace. I didn't know his face. How he must have laughed to himself at my naivety. Why had the Mother not prepared me well enough for this role? Because the only role I was supposed to take was that of the pregnant wife.

"It is the Salmun who protect the south from the Razohan. The rest of us are defenseless against them," Truett said.

I shifted my gaze back to the fire. "The Salmun are no longer the only ones."

"What did she say?" Truett said to his spirit companions.

"The princess says strange things indeed," Borrat said.

I rose to my feet. "Thank you, gentlemen. You have no idea how helpful you've been."

"No. Wait. We have much more to talk about." I was too slow to prevent Truett from reaching for me. His hand grazed down my arm to my fingers. I snatched my hand away on feeling the ice of his touch. I stumbled away, my pulse a sudden noise in my ears. For a heartbeat, I swear I felt beyond the chill, to the touch of his hand.

Truett gasped, his eyes growing wider than any dinner plate. "I felt you," he uttered in awe.

"No." I shook my head. "That's impossible. Your mind is playing tricks on you because you wish it to be true."

I stepped away from him and the other two who'd now risen to standing, so to speak.

"I did. I did. I swear it is true."

"Don't let your mind fool you," I snapped.

"You are dead, you imbecile," Albert said. "It is as the princess says. It is impossible."

I tried to steady my voice. "I need to leave." I spun to go.

"Please, princess, wait."

I glanced over my shoulder to find Truett gliding toward me. "No." I held up my hand, not wanting him near, desperate not to feel the chill of his touch and the solidness underneath. "Stop." A wave of something rushed through me, out of me.

Truett halted in place, dangling like a curtain, his ill-formed legs swirling as if in agitation. He looked as though he was in pain or struggling.

I turned and fled the library. Choosing the opposite

direction from the music, I hurried down the long corridor. Finding a darkened alcove, I darted within, seeking solace in the shadows.

Could it really be possible I had just commanded the dead?

Mother, what have you done to me?

CHAPTER

FOURTEEN

TAMAS

OSMUD AND GARRAT would question my sanity. In quieter moments, I'd question myself too, but hiding before the eyes of my enemy was an excellent sport. Still, I couldn't shake Romelda's persistent warnings. The people of the north relied on my success, and I was whittling away precious time fooling the Tannard heirs.

Unfortunately, it was only after I'd taken possession of Bloodwyn's soul did I learn he wasn't favored among the elite of Tarragona and was often shunned from important events. This meant it would take some work on my behalf to ingratiate myself with the royal family. Juel, in particular, loathed Bloodwyn because of his expertise across the card table and his stamina with the ladies.

I worked the blunted sword, assessing its weight and balance in my hand. Shoddy craftsmanship had gone into fashioning its blade, and the guard was severely dented, but it was evenly balanced and lighter than what I was used to. It would do.

I waited opposite the royal box, in the shade of the pavilion, my attention fixed on the woman sitting beside Juel. Tressya had yet to see me; her gaze was on the two noblemen fighting in the arena. I was sure she soaked in every move the nobles made. Given I suspected her sword skills to be excellent, I would assume she found them lacking, as did I. Already, I had a dozen offensive and defensive moves playing out in my head to counter every blow either made.

Having placed two gold gowl on the tall redhead winning, I left the pavilion and headed for the royal box.

A united groan rippled through the onlookers to signal the end of the fight. I didn't bother to glance at the winner. Tressya settled back in her seat. Beside her, Juel turned to his mistress, Lady Astaria, giving Tressya his back. I smirked, enjoying the thought of the humiliation I would deal Juel on her behalf and for my pleasure.

Tressya did a double-take when she caught my approach. The closer I came, the more her brows knitted together. When she glanced around to Juel, I was sure she contemplated ways to avoid our meeting.

"Your Highnesses," I exaggerated my bow, keeping my eyes on Tressya as I rose.

"Lord Bloodwyn," Juel drawled, looking down on me from his seat. Seeing the sword in my hand, he quirked a brow. "Are you here to ask me to put money on your win?" He snorted a laugh as he turned to Lady Astaria, who fluttered her fan as she sniggered.

"I've come to ask if you would join me in the arena?"

"No," snapped Tressya.

Juel stared at her in stunned silence.

"I see Your Highness is practicing her charm for her duty as wife." I gave a short bow, adding salt to the injury. Her furious glare made the win all the more rewarding.

"His Highness does as he pleases," she announced, raising her voice so everyone in the royal box could hear.

"Spoken like a dutiful wife," Juel replied.

I regretted forcing everyone's attention to Tressya in this way.

"I feel such a fight is beneath you, Sire. Surely you could find yourself a more worthy opponent," Tressya responded with a strong voice.

Good. Juel had failed to humiliate her. My smile broadened. Juel was about to suffer some hard knocks thanks to Tressya. I was going to savor every moment of this.

"What you say has merit," Juel sounded mollified.

"To refuse a request in front of his royal court..." I faded away, leaving everyone's minds to wander on my suggestion.

"To beg in front of the royal court is little better," Tressya countered.

"To stand behind the skirts of one's betrothed—"

"Return to your card games, my lord, and leave sports to the men."

"You've asked about me. I'm flattered." I locked my eyes on hers and gave a small wink.

Having remained in stunned silence through our banter, Juel, along with everyone else within the royal box, now stared at Tressya. My cue to rescue her.

"Your Highness, I apologize for the intrusion."

"Wait," he demanded. "I can make up my own mind." He rose from his seat, looking down on Lady Astaria. "I leave your side momentarily. I'll finish this soon enough, and then we shall retire to the pavilion for tea."

Tressya's glare turn sharp as an arrow when I gave her another wink.

"Ten minutes, Bloodwyn." Juel waved at his squire to attend him as he strode away.

"Take your time, Sire." I strolled toward the preparation tents close to the entrance of the arena, keeping my attention on my back. She had ten minutes to accost me with her whip-like tongue before I ground Juel into the sand.

"Last night was a mistake," she panted, hurrying toward me from between the tents.

She wore a deep green gown that set off her blue eyes, practically glowing in her fury. I wasn't a romantic, but the blood-red streaks of color glistening through her black hair made me ponder a poetic line or two. "Because you failed to kiss me?"

"I left you alive. That's not a mistake I'll make again."

I waved my sword. "It's blunt. Now's the perfect time." And I opened my arms, offering my chest.

Compared to me, she was so small, yet her demeanor was anything but meek. She inhaled deeply. "I'm smarter than that, but you're an imbecile, so I should warn you of your failure should you do anything out there."

I could crush her in one hand if I chose, but I'd rather anchor her to me while I kissed the fury out of her. "A good thrashing is all I plan."

215

"Coming from a man who loves wine, women, and gambling."

"Wine, not so much. But I'm touched you've taken the time to get to know me."

She folded her arms. Stars, I loved teasing her. "I'm interested in the man underneath."

It was an attack, not a seduction, but my blood boiled all the same. "Well, well, you have got to know me."

She took a step back when I advanced forward, dropping her arms as her haughty expression faltered. A flicker of some emotion crossed her face—self-admonishment, I would say—before she drew herself straight.

"It was hard. Few find you interesting enough to talk about."

"But that's not who you're interested in, remember?"

She briefly closed her eyes while exhaling. Calming breaths. I knew all about those. And I was getting under her skin. Excellent. It's where I wanted to be; under her skin; in fact, inside of her any way I could.

"Tell me if I'm going to live long enough to be queen?"

"I'm not an augur, but if you eat well, drink less, and stay away from dangerous men, you should live a normal lifespan."

She pulled up her sleeve, baring the scar I'd made. "This," she demanded.

"Do you really want to be queen?"

"I want an answer."

"Beside Juel, I'm sure it'll be a loathsome duty."

She growled, bunching her fists. "Not as loathsome as time spent with you. Now tell me."

"It won't kill you."

"Then why did you do it?"

"So I could hunt you." Really, where was my head? The words just came out. I probably made a terrible mistake in revealing that. Her eyes flared as her lips parted in horror.

"Then it's poison," she hissed.

"It depends on your point of view. If you were Huungardred, you'd be flattered."

"I'm appalled."

That wounded. "Though it's never done without permission. I apologize for that, but it was necessary," I wasn't going to tell her everything about the bite.

"The Salmun will have means of nullifying it."

"You haven't revealed me yet, so I doubt you'll do it now." I could only hope. Osmud and Garrat would gut me for this. Romelda would burn me on the spot.

"I bit you, so I didn't have to kill you. I needed a way of keeping track of you, and that was my only option at the time."

"What does that mean? Tell me what it does specifically."

"You don't want to know the specifics, trust me. Let's just say you're never far from my mind now."

She took a step toward me. "Listen to me, beast-man. Either you tell me the truth, or I'll—"

"The bite is part of a love ritual between two mating partners when they surrender themselves to each other. It's a Huungardred tradition."

Her mouth sagged open as she stared at me.

"It's usually very well received by both partners in the relationship."

"We're not in a relationship," she shrieked. "Unless you want to count enemies until death."

"Death is usually the only way to separate a mated pair."

Tressya's eyes could go no wider. I closed her mouth with a finger under her chin, but she jerked her head away. "Then I shall have to make yours swift."

I chuckled.

Then she surprised me by saying, "So you've just blown your chance at..." She swallowed. "Mating..." A faint flush filled her cheeks. I couldn't be sure if it was embarrassment or fury. "With someone else."

At the time, I was desperate and had shunned thinking about the implications of what I'd done.

"Essentially, yes."

This meant I could never accept Bryra as my mate, not in the full sense, not as a Huungardred would like. I pushed the guilt aside for not speaking with Thaindrus first before committing myself as I had. But if Thaindrus knew the reason for my actions, he'd understand; at least I hoped he would.

"This makes no sense. You make no sense. Why would you do that? Why are you being so honest with me?"

"I plan to lull you into trusting me."

"Huh," she snorted. "That will never happen." She jabbed her hands on her hips. "Tell me how it makes me easier to... hunt?"

"I'm all out of confessions for now."

"Then I'll have to find my answers elsewhere."

"Is that a threat, little princess?"

"Take it how you like, beast-man."

Hurrying footsteps disturbed us. I looked beyond Tressya to see Juel's squire rushing over. Saved. Thank the stars.

"Your lord—"

"On my way." I bowed to Tressya, giving her no time for a rebuttal, and headed toward the arena.

You fool, Tamas. I should never have told her the truth.

I watched her stomp away, feeling more convinced than during our first meeting that Tressya was my foremost rival in the race for the throne. Yet it didn't have to be that way. She could be a valuable ally. I really hoped she would be. In fact, I'd gambled the safety of the north, and my chance of choosing a mate, on the belief she would be more than just an ally.

I entered the arena, facing Juel, who was slashing his sword through the air in preparation.

"I thank Your Highness for the honor." I bowed, then brought my sword up to the ready. Juel was perfectly placed to help me expel some tension.

Bloodwyn was an ass at blade-dueling, and Juel knew it, having set him on his backside on more than one occasion. Which meant I had a full inventory of Juel's favored maneuvers. The prince was a skilled swordsman, but his talent was born from arrogance, his attention drawn to how he appeared to those watching and not on the fight itself. Diverted attention meant death.

Once we'd started, I wasted no time using offensive strategies and deception to maneuver myself into a favorable position, ensuring the sun was at my back and in his eyes.

Juel expected a bumbling idiot with two left hands, which played to my advantage.

Keeping just out of reach of his sword, but not far enough that it gave him time to read my moves, I taunted him with a few half-hearted slashes and thrusts.

Timing, distance, and footwork were key beside mental discipline. Juel's rhythm was predictable. He used repetitive moves coupled with flamboyant flourishes, but he was fast, agile, and determined to win.

We parried back and forth as he tried to force me around him, giving himself the better position. I relented, allowing him to think he'd fooled me.

I shifted my balance, raising my foot, deliberately signaling a move, which he fell for and took the advantage, lunging forward. But I was ready, dodging while half turning to sweep my blade along the length of his. My strength was greater, and I could've disarmed him at that point. But I allowed him to keep his sword.

I danced with him for longer, gaining fresh insight into his skills until I saw his growing frustration. Time to harry him some more. Juel fought for his reputation, which made him an angry and desperate opponent.

"You've been practicing," he quipped.

"Just a little."

This was too fun to end, but I caught sight of Tressya as she moved closer to the side of the arena. Her eyes would be on me while she tried to learn as much as she could of my sword skills, and I had to resist turning my attacks into flourishes.

Beads of sweat ran into Juel's eyes. With a savage swipe,

he cleared them away, then lunged while I blocked. He grunted, lunged again, opening himself for my counter, but I stopped shy of poking him in the stomach.

Tressya fisted her hands, her body tense. *Stop paying her attention.*

I blocked his thrust, dodged his lunge, then closed the distance with my sword raised. He fell for it, raising his own to block, and I kicked him hard in the midsection, knocking him backward four steps. A gasp rippled from the royal box.

Tressya had folded her arms, a hand pressed against her lips. What was playing through her mind?

My distraction gave Juel time to recover his distance. He came at me with a series of aggressive attacks, which forced me off balance.

Dammit. Now who's the fool?

I maneuvered so she was at my back, robbing me of temptation.

"I'll end you, Bloodwyn," Juel panted, his face flushed.

I smirked. "Try."

His eyes flared. This time he bellowed as he attacked. I went with him, flowing around each stab, thrust, and lunge. Losing one's mind to anger led to failure in this game.

So far I'd been kind. With my next reversal, I jabbed him hard in the stomach, technically a win. Another united gasp from the onlookers shook the restraint from his fury, and he redoubled his attacks, ignoring the rules.

I cut from up high, which he blocked, but I swiftly followed by feinting a harder cut high, which Juel fell for. Meeting his eyes, keeping my true target in my periphery, I sidestepped his potential counterattack and dropped my attack into his foremost leg, swiping it from under him.

Juel went down hard on his back, and I followed through, digging the hilt of my blunted sword into his throat. It took one breath for him to move, stunned as he was. Then, with bared teeth, he attempted to rise, but I refused to relent the pressure.

Our eyes locked. An instant of surprise, then horror passed over his face as I stared dispassionately upon him. It would take a sudden force of pressure to puncture his windpipe and sever his spine.

I looked over my shoulder to see Tressya running toward us.

Out of time. I flicked my sword away and held out my hand. In my periphery, I caught Lady Astaria making her way from the royal box, perhaps hoping to beat Tressya to his side.

"Your Highness," I said.

Juel glared at my hand, then took it, smacking his hand into my palm as if he dreamed of punching my face.

"I want to thank Your Highness for giving me the win," I announced loud enough for the courtiers in the royal box to hear once I'd pulled him to his feet.

Tressya had slowed to a walk, but Lady Astaria pushed past her and flung herself upon Juel. "Are you hurt, Sire?"

His ego, perhaps.

"Not at all," he said in the most pompous voice he could muster after such an embarrassing defeat.

"His Highness took the fall for me. In fact, His Highness held back his most lethal attacks to give me the advantage, and to save me from yet another humiliating loss. I'm most humbly grateful." I bowed deeply.

When I rose, it was Tressya's eyes I sought, but she turned away, unable to hold my gaze, and I swear I caught a twitch on her lips.

"Yes. Well." Juel was lost for words.

I ducked and retrieved his sword, but Tressya suddenly appeared at my side, snatching the sword from my hand.

"My lord has proved himself adequate with a sword, I'm sure you're ready to retire." She handed the sword to Juel, who looked at her askew. Forthright and outspoken was not how a princess of the Tarragona court ought to act.

Juel took his sword without thanking Tressya. "Come, my lady, I've earned some refreshments. Bloodwyn, you're welcome to join us."

"Bloodwyn looks in ill health after his blade-dueling, Your Highness. I fear he's—"

"More than happy to accept His Highness's invitation."

"Excellent." Juel ignored Tressya as he guided Lady Astaria away with a slight limp, but Tressya was too busy staring at me to notice the limp. And I doubted she would've cared.

I bowed in front of her. "My lady, was the spectacle worth your time?"

She glanced to the royal box, perhaps checking who was watching. "I've seen better." And she turned and walked away.

Hurrying to catch up, I said, "You really thought I would be stupid enough to kill him in front of the royal court?"

She didn't stop. "I believe you're stupid, yes."

"But you're impressed."

She spun on me. "Leave now, and I'll ensure your excuses are plausible."

"I can't wait to sample what His Worship dishes up."

"I'll gut you if you try anything."

"Is this intense antagonism toward me because of our almost mating?"

Her eyes narrowed like the end of an arrow. "Courage. Never waver from what must be done. I know exactly what must be done. Your end, beast-man. It's only a matter of time."

"It seems I bring out the best in you."

"You make me want to stab something, preferably you."

"Love and hatred. Both are passionate emotions."

She stalked away. I followed, counting in my head how long it would take her to spin around and verbally assault me again. I knew I was in her head, as much as she was in my veins.

Since Tressya had yet to reciprocate in the bond by taking my blood—if she ever did—we'd never reach the level of intimacy mated partners could achieve; a knowing of each other that needed no words. I was the one to benefit from this one-sided union, and I had to admit my shame. Especially since a Huungardred would never impose a mate bond on another; it is considered sacred.

It was either kill her or claim her, and I'm sure in time she would appreciate my choice. Tressya was inside of me in more ways than she could ever imagine now I'd tasted her blood. She could never escape from me.

"You held back from using full force with most of your strikes."

I knew she couldn't make the distance to the prince's private pavilion without saying a word, but what she said surprised me.

"I doubt he noticed."

"Why did you do it?"

"I'm overcome by generosity at times."

She cast me a sideways glance. "He was a poor opponent. He was too arrogant. He underestimated you and misread every move you made. Worse, he failed to compensate for his earlier mistakes by taking you more seriously, and he was driven by pride. That makes for terrible concentration."

"So you *are* impressed with me."

She groaned. "You were sloppy at times."

"Deliberately so. I couldn't set him on his ass at the start."

She harumphed.

"Did you see any maneuvers you'd like me to teach you?"

She sighed as she halted. "I'd rather stick a knife in my eye. Better still, I'll stick it in yours."

"Tressya, Tressya, Tressya, you do deserve to be queen." I bowed on seeing her surprise and shuffled backward, spun and walked away, leaving her gaping.

CHAPTER

FIFTEEN

TRESSYA

IT WAS A MISERABLE DAY, but the king insisted on a procession through the streets of Tolum as part of his grand festivities for the impending marriage of the crown prince. We were to travel in an open-top carriage, regardless of the weather, so the people of Tolum could see their prince and his future bride.

For this occasion, they had dragged Queen Gusselan from her bed. She was a refined woman, tall with a long slender neck, graceful in everything she did. Her beauty was the silent kind— becoming apparent the longer you looked.

I sat across from her in the carriage, noting her sallow complexion and pale lips. Her chambermaid had attempted to put life into her face by adding a little color, failing to hide the ashen hue of her skin. She avoided my eyes and said little. I wondered if she needed to harness what little energy remained in her frail body just to stay upright.

I had nothing to do but look pleasant and occasionally wave, so I dared to shift my vision and gazed at the queen. Darkness hugged her body, discoloring to a dull hue of silver. Death was already clawing for her, but she wouldn't die yet.

Judging by the distance between the king and queen, I felt sure Henricus wouldn't mourn her for long. The steps it took to place her on the throne were likely similar to mine; men of power making alliances through the women in their lives.

Andriet shared our side of the carriage, forcing Juel and me closer together. We kept our hands in our laps to avoid accidentally touching each other. Andriet sprawled in his seat, playing the enthusiastic prince, waving at the crowds, laughing, pointing, and clapping through the cheers.

Juel sighed and paid no attention to the crowd. Radnisa informed me they'd forced Juel from Lady Astaria's bed, grouching he would rather ride beside his mistress in the carriage than beside the ugly sow he was supposed to call wife. Radnisa filled me in on the things Juel said behind my back, even though I showed no emotion. I couldn't care less for Juel's opinion; savage words can't affect a heart that never opened, and for Juel, my heart was bolted closed.

"Juel. Smile," the queen said, the only words she'd managed to say. Once uttered, she collapsed back into her seat and closed her eyes. No one seemed to notice her struggles. Andriet was busy adoring the crowds. Juel stayed in his world, slouched in his seat with eyes hooded as if he was about to fall asleep, and the king stared blankly at the road we'd traveled, lost in his thoughts. No one except Andriet paid any attention to the people.

Behind and in front of us rode the royal guard. Flanking us either side on large gray stallions rode two wizards, their faces obscured by their hoods. The procession was a test of endurance, so I focused on seeing more of Tolum. Half the crowd seemed happy to see us. The other half were the reason we traveled with guards.

In pockets where the bustling crowds dissipated, I caught glances of the streets and noticed tiny stone shrines nestled amidst market stalls or at street corners. Despite their lovingly adorned exteriors graced with fresh flowers and meticulous care, these shrines exuded an ancient aura, seemingly on the brink of crumbling from their stone pedestals into dust.

I nudged Andriet to get his attention. "Whose small shrines are those?"

"That's the old religion. It's surprising they've survived so long. The Levenians freed us from enslavement to a complicated pantheon of gods and goddesses and showed us the truth."

"Which is?"

"That we control our own destinies and that no supreme ethereal powers are responsible for our failed crops or lack of rain. There are those who still hold to the old beliefs, though only a few. These small shrines are what's left in Tolum of their religion. They cause no harm, so Father is tolerant of them and allows them to continue their worship."

"Who worships at that temple?" I nodded toward the towering monstrosity I'd seen on first arriving in Tolum.

"Emberforge, the stronghold of the tyrants from millennium past. After the war, the victors abandoned Emberforge to build Emberfell and shifted their seat of power to the north of Tolum. The Salmun are the only ones now to regularly walk its silenced corridors. Within sits the Bone Throne, an artifact of their time, and the seat of their power. Only now it's nothing more than a relic built on death."

"It sounds like an impressive tale."

"Prophecies proclaim the resurgence of the Bone Throne's power. But that's a long and tedious tale to tell. It goes hand in hand with vengeance and war, but with a happy ending."

"What happy ending comes from a tale of vengeance and war?"

"It's said an heir from the House of Tannard is destined to win and claim the throne."

"It sounds like a narrative woven by someone with ancestral ties to the House of Tannard," I joked.

"Indeed. Are you bored yet?"

"Not with Tarragona's history."

Andriet arched an eyebrow. "What a peculiar woman you are. No one cares about those old stuffy tales, except maybe the Salmun and the king's council, and father, I suppose. As a child, I was brought up on these loathsome tales, but as the second-born, it's not my concern. I keep my mind free of them. They bore me senseless, but I was never a diligent pupil, and now prefer to squander my life in idle repose, which makes me the most agreeable and exciting of the two of us." He leaned in. "Personally, I would say you've lucked out on your betrothal. I would've ensured you spent your days in recline and your nights drinking, dancing and, well...whoring's not quite the word I'm looking for, but we all like to keep a few scandalous secrets, don't we?"

"Some people more than others."

Andriet leaned over, so I could hear his lowered voice. "She'll likely stay in his bed once the ceremony's over, but I sense that wouldn't displease you. Then, you can revel in satisfaction when he eventually dismisses her because of waning beauty or his fleeting interest. There'll be more after that, but it's only you that counts. After all, the sole enduring female legacy lies in the queen."

"As the second-born, what's your destiny beyond drinking, whoring, and idleness?"

"Nothing. I'll bow to my brother upon his throne and hope never to find myself in his place. An heir is all that father and the Salmun desire. Once that's settled, the spare can fade contentedly into the shadows."

Our heads close together, we muttered as though no one else was in the carriage. "That's not true. You have an astute mind and are keen to protect your heritage. I learned that listening to you the other night at the ball. I suspect Juel will rely on your counsel more than on those who sit at the king's table."

"You're dangerous, my queen," he winked at me. "I believe Juel will need you more than me." He settled back into the carriage. I joined him, our heads leaning against the seat, turned toward each other. "I'm joking, of course. You've caught me out. I could recite the prophecies and legends in my sleep. They filled me with many vivid dreams in my youth. I was always the victor.

"I'm not a boy anymore. And while I struggle to maintain any form of serious façade, I'm dedicated to Juel's destiny. I'll gladly step into the role of knight, advisor, confidant, brother —whatever he needs from me. But never king. I have my limits."

"I hope that role also includes being a close friend and confidant to his queen."

He took my hand and placed it in his lap. "I promise you this, my queen: you'll be the only lady in my heart." He squeezed my hand before returning to look out at the crowds.

I stared at his profile, grateful I had found another man like Carlin. Though, it was my cruel fate he would never be my husband. But I was accustomed to knowing I would never have the life I chose. At least Andriet would always be by my side, even if never as a lover.

There was no better time than now to reveal the Razohan to the Tannards, but for some strange reason, I kept him a secret. He was here to destroy the House of Tannard, which made him my enemy.

Tell Andriet. I could still remember his smell. Fresh, wild, and free, it reminded me a little of Carlin.

And why should his smell make me abandon my duty to the Mother by allowing a threat this close to the House of Tannard?

"Andriet."

"Hmm." He drew his gaze from the crowd, bathing me in his generous smile, the smile he gave me on our first greeting.

I couldn't let the Razohan take him from me. "There's a threat to your family."

He chuckled. "There's always a threat to the royal family. One treasonous plot or another. I'm alert to most of what goes on amongst the courtiers. The Salmun take care of the rest." He patted my hand. "Don't be afraid. You're in the Tannard household now. Nothing will happen to you."

I remembered how silently the Razohan came upon me on the balcony, the power in his body when he pressed me into the pillar that night, the agility and grace with which he moved. His sword skills were hypnotizing. He was the perfect predator.

"I'm not afraid for myself." Perhaps I should be, but if he wanted to kill me, I would already be dead.

To hunt you. I was furious to learn that. Better it be poison than to force a bind around my neck; a love bind. I couldn't fathom his motivation. It wasn't much of a love bind as it gave me nothing; I felt nothing when he claimed he could now hunt me. Typical of a man to gain all the advantages in such a joining.

"Neither should you be." And he turned back to the crowd.

The words had haunted me through the night, but not as much as the traitorous spark of desire that had risen unbidden on first hearing the words. As a disciple, I should be infuriated, not... tantalized by the promise they offered, and that I wanted him to keep; I couldn't lie to myself. But only so I could keep my promise to cut out his heart.

Striking amber eyes stared down at me.

I blinked to clear the plaguing vision. The Razohan had cursed me.

Tell him.

My confession wouldn't come. I was keeping the Razohan *my* secret when he needed to be revealed, set before the Salmun. What foolish mistake was I making? I would give myself time to find out more about him, then deal with him myself. If it proved beyond me, I would confess what I knew.

I gazed across the carriage to find the queen's gray eyes narrowed into a steely glare. Andriet still held my hand, resting it on his thigh. Her eyes, however, stayed on me.

Etiquette dictated that I look away, but rather, I held her eyes with curiosity more than malice. Growing up in a royal court, I knew women rarely found allies amongst each other, and I knew little about Queen Gusselan. As an accomplished liar and manipulator, I wouldn't take Radnisa's word for the queen's character, but there was no question about the thoughts behind her glare. I was familiar with the expression of distrust.

Just as I was wondering who would look away first, the clattering of hooves on the cobbles, echoing louder than the carriage wheels and drowning out the cheering crowds, drew the queen's gaze over my shoulder.

Andriet and I sat straight in our seats. The king craned his neck to see the source of the commotion. "Halt," commanded the king. Beside me, Juel stirred and sat up.

I glanced around to see what had attracted everyone's attention to find some of the king's guards rushing up behind us. Between them rode a man dressed in the smart clothes of a nobleman.

Their sudden appearance stirred the crowd, but they soon settled when the king stood in the carriage. "What is the meaning of this?" he bellowed.

The two Salmun blocked their path to the king. After a brief discussion, they allowed the party to ride toward our carriage. It was only when they moved closer did I notice another man, whose hands were tied behind his back, running along behind the nobleman's horse, a thick rope ensuring he kept pace.

"Forgive this intrusion," shouted the nobleman.

I didn't recognize him from the ball.

"I've apprehended this treasonous wretch to present, so you might determine his punishment," the nobleman stated, bowing his head.

A heavy silence enveloped us. The king's glare settled on the nobleman, and I half-expected a command to bind the nobleman's hands and join him with the man sprawled behind the horse. The queen seemed engrossed in her hands. Juel appeared disinterested, and Andriet shifted beside me.

As the king prepared to speak, I found myself more attuned to Andriet's murmured words. "Lord Rudolph—the very example of how far one can fall from the king's grace. Penniless, dishonored, and despised. His survival depends on his sister's generosity. With her wealth dwindling, he's desperate to mend his reputation and regain the king's favor."

"Bring this traitor forth," commanded the king.

The guards jerked the man to his feet. He struggled to

find his balance and collapsed to his knees, where they dragged him to the side of the carriage.

I turned slightly toward Andriet. "Do you know of his supposed treason?"

Perhaps he was in alliance with the nobleman I over-heard in the library. Did the king already know about the plot? There went my potential leverage if ever I needed it.

"No treason," he murmured.

I dragged my eyes from the man, lying on his stomach beside the carriage, to face Andriet, ignoring the nobleman as he spoke.

Andriet's expression stayed solemn. With a finger on my cheek, he gently turned my face away so he could speak in my ear. "Not all men need to be desperate to do wicked things. This is one exception. Lord Rudolph is desperate. His enemies, and they are many, now circle him like wolves, hungry for his demise."

"He's made everything up?"

"It takes little to incite the poison of paranoia in every king's veins."

I caught the last of Lord Rudolph's conversation. "I beg the king's pardon, but I had to act with haste before any further damage was done. Shall I deliver the rest of the trai-tors' heads to you before sundown, so you may see for your-self the terrible canker growing beneath your feet."

I turned to the king. He looked pensive as he slowly nodded. "Very well. You have paid your blood debt to the crown."

"Sire, you are most generous."

The king shifted his attention to the guard. "Take the

traitor to the dungeons. The Salmun will learn all he has to say before his head is staked on the gates outside Emberforge, alongside the other traitors."

Henricus motioned for the nobleman to move his horse closer to the carriage. "And if you ever think to disturb my official duties again, it will be your head staked outside Emberforge."

The nobleman's eyes flared, but he ducked his head. "Understood, Your Majesty."

"Blood debt?" I raised my eyebrows as I whispered.

"After one too many ales, Lord Rudolph gets loose with his dagger. He's left a few bloody corpses in his wake. Murder done outside the king's command is not warmly welcomed. His title has saved his head thus far, but Father's patience with him has run dry. He knows that. Hence the supposed traitorous plot."

"Does your father truly believe him?"

"Probably not. But he'd rather deal with a dead traitor, even if falsely accused, than face a live coup."

Henricus dismissed Lord Rudolph by turning his back on him and arching his head to gaze up the face of Emberforge. The nobleman quickly faded away with the guards, dragging the poor wretch behind him, and seeming keen to disappear from the king's presence. There was nothing I could do for this poor man's plight. I could only hope when Juel was king, I would have some sway over whose heads he took.

I drew my gaze from the sorry sight and turned my attention to Emberforge. This close to the temple, I could understand why they included forge in its name. The temple of black stone looked as though it had been forged from a giant's furnace and fashioned on an anvil into a mighty weapon.

"It's not part of my plan for today, but since we have stopped, I would like to step inside," announced the king.

On hearing that, a footman dismounted and rushed for the carriage door. Juel rose next. I was about to follow him, but Andriet squeezed my hand, sharing an apologetic smile with a small shake of his head. "Only the royal male bloodline." He looked embarrassed to say the words.

Juel smirked down at me as he straightened his dress cloak and swaggered as he dismounted the steps of the carriage. For the first time, Andriet didn't bother with a quip.

"The guards will keep you safe," was all he said, avoiding my eyes, before he dashed from the carriage to join his father and brother, now led by the two Salmun as they made their way toward the massive iron doors of Emberforge.

Alone together, the distance between the queen and me shrank. I watched the king and his sons disappear inside the temple doors, then turned to look ahead, casting a fleeting glance in the queen's direction. Her eyes were closed, her head leaning back against the seat rest. It surprised me little that the king would leave his sick wife exposed to the crowds under the weak sun while he visited the temple. The guards maneuvered their horses, which acted as a curtain between us and the crowd.

Waiting on the king was a primary lesson for any member of the royal court, so I settled back in my seat and stared up at the face of Emberforge.

"You've fooled many," came the strained voice of the

queen. Soft and fragile, I almost mistook it for a comment from the few milling people beyond the wall of horses.

I glanced across at her to find her looking at me. Her breaths seemed heavy. Dark smudges, like shadows, hung under her eyes. After a few moments, her eyelids fluttered closed, as if breathing caused her strain. The first words she had spoken to me were accusatory, but I couldn't help feeling sorry for her predicament and hating the king's loathsome disregard for her condition.

"I'm sorry," I said.

She opened one eyelid. "Why would you care?"

"You're dying."

She nodded, as if I'd told her tomorrow would rain. Then she sighed and arched her head back on the seat. "It doesn't take a genius to see that."

With her eyes now closed, I took the time to stare at her, noting her smooth complexion despite having grown children. How old had she been when she married Henricus?

"Your Mother's plans are doomed. I've seen to that."

I was caught off guard this time, my eyebrows shooting up and my mouth hanging open in disbelief.

She flashed a smirk, but even that seemed too much for her to hold. It vanished within seconds, leaving her complexion blank and sallow.

"No link to the Sistern will sit on the Tannard throne." It was the longest sentence she'd made so far and left her inhaling heavy breaths.

I exhaled, gathering my composure. "I think there is little you can do if the Salmun want it." I didn't want to antagonize a dying woman, but the shock of her confrontation left me with no smart defense.

The queen snorted, a faint sound of disagreement. "You think that?"

Who was this woman? Why had the Mother not warned me of her? Had the Mother even known? The Sistern liked to move in the shadows. I'm sure there were other orders who did the same.

"How do you—"

"Know," she interjected with surprising force. She closed her eyes, gathering her strength with deep breaths before speaking again. "Your naivety is appalling." She took another slow inhale. I waited, rigid with tension. "Your Mother knows less than she believes." I could tell she would say more, and the wait had me climbing out of my skin. "The Nazeen to the north. The Salmun in the south." She paused for another breath. "Tarragona is a void in their knowledge. Until you."

Instead of replying, I focused my attention, gathering the threads of my mind. Since leaving Merania, I'd not dedicated enough time to my practice in developing soul voice. Now was the perfect time.

"Don't think to control me."

It was like a punch to my face. My eyes snapped open to catch another smirk sliding from her lips. She rolled her head, looking beyond the carriage as if dismissing me. "I'm simply saving you the bother." Her lips twitched with a faint smile. "It wouldn't work anyway. I'm well trained in countering your pathetic mind games."

"Tell me who you are?"

"Is that a command?"

"No. But you're dying. Does your anonymity really matter now?"

She rolled her head away.

"I know about the treasonous plot."

She slowly rolled her head to face me again. "What plot is this?"

Her surprise sounded genuine. Maybe the conniving plot to kidnap Juel and me was not part of her plan to keep the Sistern from the throne. "It wasn't hard to find out."

"What plot?" she demanded. In her weak state, the demand was little more than a quiet plea.

"Perhaps it's connected with the dastardly treason Lord Rudolph uncovered. The king needn't worry now, I suppose." I mirrored her by turning away to glance up at Emberforge. What had she done to ensure no blood link to the Sistern would sit on the Tannard throne?

"I see through all your lies," she whispered just loud enough for me to hear. The queen was tiring.

"I truly am sorry for your condition, but you're the fool to think me blind. You were better off staying quiet, but now you have my attention." It wasn't a threat. In fact, I was grateful for the warning.

I sat forward and snatched her wrist before she could react, then turned it over and pushed up the flimsy lace sleeve of her gown. She was too weak to fight me, even though she tried.

"If I were you, I would have those I trusted prepare my food and drink." I ran my thumb over the mark I found on her inner right wrist, the one I'd thought was a bruise made by Henricus from grabbing her with uncaring, rough hands. It wasn't a bruise.

When I let her hand go, she dropped it into her lap, seeming to sag further into her seat as if she was about to fade into the leather and disappear.

"That gives me questions. But you're not willing to provide me with answers. But I'll get them."

The queen simply closed her eyes and rolled her head away as if in defeat.

CHAPTER

SIXTEEN

TAMAS

THE STREETS WERE abuzz with activity. At any minute, someone was bound to stumble upon us. Finding his soul was taking too long.

My focus was distracted—that's why I was having trouble. When I closed my eyes, the distant noises filled my head. I tried extra hard to force them out of my mind as I reached out for the apostle's soul. Dare I say, it seemed to be hiding from me. A devotee of Emberforge and the Salmun, the soul seemed to recognize an enemy in death. Just when I was about to growl in frustration at its elusiveness, I felt its presence like a frost at the edges of my mind. Once found, I latched on, drawing the soul from the shadowy depths into me. A long stream of unsavory memories filled my head, which I shoved to the back of my mind before they could falter my concentration.

Once the task was complete, I took his form and stripped his clothes but left him in his undergarments. The poor man didn't need the indignity of being found naked. Besides, I wasn't keen on wearing anything worn that close to his skin.

Hiding the body proved easier than hunting for his soul. And once I'd finished the grisly deed, I slipped two of my daggers into the belt, hidden under the cloak, and headed for the alley's mouth. There, I found a street full of people and guards on horseback shielding the king's carriage.

Curse my luck. The king had arrived at Emberforge. The crowd surrounded his carriage.

Rotten idea, Tamas. But I couldn't stop myself. I had to know if Tressya was here.

Focus on your task.

It was foolish, but my curiosity won out, and I pushed through the crowds, edging my way closer. The apostle was a slim man, smaller than average height, which meant I was able to duck and weave my way through the crowd like a child, positioning myself close.

A horse's rump blocked my view of the inside of the carriage, so I dodged around a rounded lady and her husband. Being slight had its advantages. Keeping low in the crowd, I squeezed myself between two horses to give myself the perfect view.

And there she was, gazing up at the face of Emberforge. The sight of her sent a sudden thrill through my blood. It had been a long time since I'd felt such exhilaration; was it the challenge or the woman?

Go. I'd satisfied my curiosity; now it was time to complete my task, but my legs stayed anchored in place. The king was in Emberforge—a possible blessing. His presence would draw the attention of the Salmun and the apostles, leaving me time to explore unhindered. I really should be gone.

Before I could depart, Tressya dropped her gaze from the face of Emberforge. Her eyes landed on me. They felt like a barb piercing through to my heart; *my* heart, not the skin I was in. An impossibility. She wouldn't suspect. But her eyes stayed locked on me.

Curses to her perceptiveness. The penetrating probe of her inquisitive mind brushed the edges of my awareness. Instead of fleeing to protect my identity, I remained still, feeling the exploration of her mind dust the surface of mine. When it should have felt like intrusive hooks, I found it a pleasant tickle.

The moment those captivating blue eyes widened, then narrowed, I winked at her, then ducked backward into the crowd and scurried away as fast as I could. This was not a hunt, yet starting the chase sent a vein of exhilaration through my core.

Pulling the hood of my cloak over my head, I hurried across the front of Emberforge and headed for the apostles' entrance on the western flank of the temple, bowing my head low and quickening my steps on passing the guards stationed by the massive iron doors. Once out of sight from the crowds and guards on the main street, I slowed, moving in the shadows cast by the hoardings as I made my way toward the entrance.

There I waited, leaning against the cold stone wall.

You're a bloody fool. And in danger of destroying all my plans.

Revealing myself at the ball was the first and biggest mistake, followed by ever worsening decisions. And here I was, waiting, ears tuned to any approaching footsteps, because no way would the disciple stay content in her seat when she knew I was lurking close to her precious Tannard heirs.

I smirked at the sound of hurrying footsteps, which faltered when a guard called out. *Don't go to her aid.* I shouldn't make it easier for her to follow me. Except, I was waiting here for her to find me.

The argument continued. She sounded frustrated, demanding he return to protect the queen, but the guard stubbornly insisted she couldn't walk alone.

Don't, Tamas. I shook my head against the irresistible urge spiking into my legs. *Don't.* It seemed I was destined to continue making terrible mistakes where Tressya was concerned, for I left my place, hugging the wall as I retraced my steps, whisper quiet.

As enemies, we danced around each other, playing a game where neither of us could foretell the outcome. This excitement was driven by more than danger, and I wanted to know what drove her to join me in this game.

Tressya had closed half the distance, ensuring my attack would go unnoticed by everyone on the main thoroughfare. The guard's back was to me, obscuring Tressya's view of my approach. He was a head taller and twice as broad, necessitating a blade or a claw for the job. I preferred the latter, needing the added boost of Huungardred strength to take him down silently.

A subtle shift to my beast form granted me the strength I needed. I flexed my fingers, careful not to stab my wrist with my lethal claw. Using the extra Huungardred strength, I leaped at the guard from behind and slashed across his throat in less than a breath. I threw him sideways, careful to keep his spraying blood away from Tressya's gown. Once done, I released the Huungardred strength and lost the claw.

She sucked in her breath. "I should gut you for this," she growled.

"With your teeth? Unless you have a surprise hidden under all those layers of lace."

Taking advantage of her stunned silence, I lunged toward her, grabbed her hand, and dragged her down the alley toward the small entrance into Emberforge. She remained silent as we ran, but once inside the narrow, airy passageway formed by the girdle wall, she yanked her hand away from my grasp. The outer passage had no ceiling, and the weak sun reflected off the left side of the wall, revealing glittering silver specks in the black stone.

"Someone will find the guard," she stated.

"Then we better move quickly."

"I'm not going anywhere with you."

"That's your choice. There's the exit. Goodbye." And with that, I headed toward the central inner courtyard, smiling to myself as I went. No way would a woman like Tressya accept that dismissal.

"Wait."

I stopped, forcing the smirk from my lips. Being an apostle, I was her height, allowing us to look eye to eye.

"An attendee of the temple. Very convenient." Her eyes skimmed down my body.

"A necessity. No one will question an apostle moving about within the temple."

"And what did you do with the apostle your masquerading as?"

"Is that really what you want to know?"

She frowned. "Fine," she huffed. "Did you find me with this pathetic love knot?" She held up her wrist.

I quirked a brow. "Love knot? Now that's an interesting way of thinking about it. I wouldn't have thought you'd use the word love in relation to the mark."

"Don't twist my words, Razohan. It was, wasn't it?" The look in her eyes would shoot daggers.

I returned her stare with the hint of a smile, which muted her nicely. In our interactions, there would probably be more instances where she gained the advantage, so I would savor my victories whenever they occurred.

She speared her hands on her hips. "Are you here for the king and his sons?"

"In the Salmun's stronghold? I'm much smarter than that."

"According to whom?"

I chuckled.

"Why are you here?" she demanded.

"Follow me, and you may find out."

"Follow the man who's turned me into prey?" She shoved the bite mark in my face.

"Princess, you're far from being prey. I'd say you're more the hunter than the prey."

"I'm not flattered."

"If not, why am I your secret?"

She gasped. Reading the shock on her face, I knew I'd chosen the right word. She thought of me as her secret—a lofty position I very much enjoyed.

She stepped closer. "I plan on bringing you down *my* way. That's why I've said nothing." She straightened, lifting her chin. "Do you honestly think I find you enigmatic?"

I shook my head slightly. "Not until now. I'm flattered."

She growled. "I put myself to sleep dreaming of my blade in your stomach."

I held out my hand. "Shall we call a truce?"

"Not on your life."

"We pretend we don't hate each other—"

"Impossible. I can't pretend that much." She crossed her arms.

"And we work together to solve a puzzle."

Her arms fell to her sides. "What puzzle?"

I walked backward, beckoning her to follow.

"You're unnerving when you look like that," she snapped. When she saw I wasn't stopping, she tentatively followed.

"The name's Petrulus. Pleased to meet you, Your Highness." I gave an elaborate bow.

"Give me a good reason not to scream right now."

"You'll never find out what I'm after."

She looked skyward as she groaned, then followed me begrudgingly. I turned around and moved along the narrow passage, very much conscious of the woman who followed after me.

The passage opened out into the central corridor. To our left was the great court, leading to the Arunian Hall with its massive pillars and rising floor that gave the impression of ascending to the sky. To our right, we had to pass through massive pylons to reach the temple sanctuary. The sanctuary housed numerous minor temples built to revere various gods of the old religion, creating a labyrinth of passages to the grand hall and the Bone Throne upon which the rulers of the ancient kingdom sat.

Voices reached us from the temple sanctuary, too faint to discern if it was the king or his sons. There were also the Salmun and other apostles to consider. Tressya was a liability in this endeavor. I should've entered the temple alone, leaving her in the carriage, oblivious to my activities. Why I hadn't was a question I would ponder for days to come, even though I was fairly certain of the answer. Facing it required too much inner reflection for the moment.

I jerked my head to the right and whispered, "We're heading into the temple." Glancing at her dress, I added, "And you're going to need appropriate clothing if you don't want to get caught."

"I won't let you kill anyone else."

"That's not what I had in mind."

She glared at me, unmoving, so I took her hand and pulled her alongside me as we passed between the great pylons and into the first sanctum, which was also filled with pillars. The central pillars, taller than those on the outside, lifted the roof away from the walls, allowing light to shine through.

We slipped into a smaller temple, and I hid Tressya behind the first pillar. "Stay here. I'll return soon."

"I don't trust you."

"You should've told me that before following me."

"You practically dragged me along. I could scream at any time and alert everyone to our presence."

"Your presence, little princess. I'm an apostle. Please, just trust me."

She jabbed her hands to her hips but said nothing, so I took that as her agreement.

I wove further into the temple sanctuary, following low-spoken voices and the faint sounds of humming. The Salmun never encouraged religious fervor, but they turned a blind eye to the burgeoning rituals created by the apostles.

Over a millennium, living within Emberforge, the apostle caste had begun writing their own stories, building upon the myths of the ancients, written in tomes within a chamber beneath the grand hall, and creating their own rites.

The humming was part of one such ritual, which Petrulus was missing. I slipped into the temple where I knew the attending apostles would be deep in prayer, missing my approach. Selisimus, the target, stood at the back, obscured by the pillars holding the thurible. Petrulus knew him well.

Silently, I approached, partially shifting to draw on Huungardred strength, and struck him on the side of his head. He was in my arms before he hit the floor. Selisimus was larger than Petrulus, so I maintained my partial shift as I dashed back to where I had left Tressya, carrying him in my arms.

Before entering the small sanctuary, I released my hold on the Huungardred and dropped the apostle. Then I took his hands and dragged him the rest of the way across the stone floor and back to where Tressya waited.

"He better not be dead."

"The cloak should cover the ill-fitting clothes," I said as I crouched beside Selisimus and stripped him of his clothes. "As we move further into the labyrinth of the temple sanctuary, the light grows dimmer, which will hide you from suspicious gazes."

"How do you know so much about this place?" She didn't realize I took the souls of my victims to take their form, giving me access to all their memories. She might find that reprehensible, so I chose not to fill the gaps in her knowledge.

Instead, I handed her items of clothing as I stripped them from Selisimus. "Put these on."

"When you turn your back." Thankfully, she seemed not to notice my silence.

I took the chain from his neck before standing, placing it in my pocket. At the entrance, I kept an eye out for anyone approaching while listening to the rustling of fabric behind me. The humming continued, as did the distant voices. If we didn't hurry, the king and his sons would depart the temple and discover Tressya missing. That would start a search, during which the dead guard would be found. The temple would be stormed, and... It was best not to think about the conclusion.

Tamas, you bloody fool. At this rate, I would soon be revealed, bringing the might of Tarragona down on my head.

"Curses," she hissed.

"Having trouble?"

She growled. "I need your help." She didn't sound pleased about it.

"I'm only too willing to oblige, Highness."

She was half out of her voluminous clothing, revealing a heavily ribbed bodice, which concealed her breasts behind what could only be called a suit of armor. Her face was flushed from the effort of trying to climb out of her layers by herself; her accusatory glare was filled with anger, no doubt for the predicament I had placed her in.

"You do know how to do this?" she asked, then rolled her eyes as she gave me her back. "Of course you do."

I smirked. "I do have a little experience in undressing a lady."

"Be quick, then go back to where you were standing."

Truth be told, I'd never dealt with a dress like this. The ladies in the north never had use or cared for anything so elaborate. I hesitated, trying to decide where to find the end of the thread tying the suffocating ribbed armor close to her body.

"What are these?" I rested my hands on her hips over the pouches on either side, tied in place with string.

She jumped. "You're supposed to be untying me, not criticizing."

"You're full of surprises, little princess." I delved a hand into one of the pockets and felt the blade sheathed inside.

She jerked away, but with my hand still inside the deep

252

pocket, she succeeded in pulling me into her. This close our breaths mingled, which sparked disastrously good feelings in my groin. My gaze drifted to her lips, because I was a weak-hearted man when it came to anything I wanted, but the look on Tressya's face was like being forced to stand in a blizzard.

"I thought we were in a hurry," she hissed, leaning away from me. Maybe she found Petrulus repulsive. Not a good thought.

I pulled her dagger from inside the pouch and unsheathed it.

"Turn around."

Her arched brow was her argument, then she did as I asked. And that did more disastrously good things for my sanity.

Carefully, I sliced through the threads. "Done."

The ribbed bodice fell to the floor before Tressya could grab it. "What am I going to do when I get dressed again, now that you've ruined my stays?"

"Torture device, you mean. And I think we can improvise with something around here."

"Get back over there," she barked, folding her arms over her chest, even though it wasn't necessary as unfortunately there were still plenty of petticoat layers to conceal her breasts.

I returned her dagger hilt first, then strolled back, half-listening for intruders and half-listening to Tressya dress.

"They're pocket bags if you must know. Though I'm surprised you know so little about women's clothing."

"I prefer my women naked."

She snorted, but said nothing in return.

A lesser man would've peeked. I was sorely tested, but restraint won.

"What am I going to do with my clothes?" she announced, coming toward me, still tucking the shirt into the belt, alongside the dagger.

"I'll take care of that." I doubled back and gathered all her things, then stashed them behind a far pillar where most would normally never go.

Then I took care of Selisimus, taking his arms and dragging him to the far pillar as well. Back at the exit, she'd finished tucking her clothes in and had pulled the hood down over her face.

"This way." I led her deeper into the temple sanctuary.

The Bone Throne lured me, but I had to resist my curiosity, unless I wanted to run afoul of the Tannards and the Salmun. As much as I wanted to see it, it wasn't the reason I'd risked so much by sneaking into Emberforge. Somewhere hidden within this temple were the Senjel Oracles. I felt sure of it. And thanks to Petrulus, I knew of the chamber beneath the stone floor, and the stairwell that would lead us there.

"Keep your head bowed and your hood low," I cautioned Tressya as we shuffled along the passageways between the many temple sanctuaries.

We passed apostles, but all moved like us, shuffling along with their eyes on the ground. Now was the hour for silent contemplation and prayer, which meant none of the apostles would meet our eyes or question us.

The voices continued to echo through from the grand hall because the Salmun ignored the apostles' traditions and practices, and Petrulus could give me no explanation for why they allowed the apostles to continue their existence within Emberforge since they held disdain for their growing religion.

"Here," I motioned toward an archaic-looking door. I pulled the chain from my pocket, slipping the single key into the lock. There were three keys to this lock: one kept by the scroll guardian, Selisimus, one for Tortilus, the lore keeper, and the last for Plesy, the scribe master.

"I don't understand how this is so easy for you."

"That's a conversation that requires endurance."

The door creaked its age as I slowly pulled it open. The noise echoed through the passageway like a shriek, sending tingles of dread up my spine. Tressya shook her head as she looked at me. I simply pushed her through the slim gap I'd made, slipping through behind her. It was lucky Petrulus was so slight.

With the door ajar, the slither of light revealed a steep descent of stone steps and a dim flicker of yellow torchlight at the bottom.

"Don't break your neck," I warned as I took the steps first.

The air was dank, cold, and held the scent of dust and age. We descended in silence, and once at the bottom, I stopped with a small groan. Beside me, Tressya inhaled sharply.

Since taking his soul, I had delved into Petrulus's memories for information to aid my search for the Senjel Oracles. However, I discovered that Petrulus was merely a liturgy steward. He knew the location of the chamber, known as the sanctum of solmira, but not its contents. I would have taken the time to kill Selisimus and plunder his soul, but with Tressya watching and our time constraints, his clothes and the chain were the best I could manage.

Though Petrulus did prove useful. I learned he suspected Selisimus, along with Tortilus, Plesy, and a few others, of forming a secret enclave within the temple. It seemed they were sowing seeds of dissent, cultivating an atmosphere of mistrust, and even animosity against the Salmun. Something I wanted to explore further when I had more time.

The sanctum of solmira wasn't large by any standard, yet it was choked with the written word. Scrolls filled most of the shelves, which were chiseled into all four stone walls. Some shelves contained bound volumes, and on the bottom ones, there were stone tablets.

"A library," Tressya observed.

"Filled with ancient lore," I headed toward the nearest shelves.

"From before the great war?"

I brushed cobwebs from the spines of the tomes. "These are more recent. I doubt they were compiling books that far back."

The light from the flaming torch flickered as Tressya picked it up and moved to the wall opposite me, where the scrolls were crammed into every available space, most now pressed flat.

"You're searching for something from the past," she noted. It wasn't a question.

I let her statement hang in the air as I ran my hand along

the spines. "The newer volumes are the apostles' own works. They're busy creating their own religion."

"Since I haven't screamed and given us away, you can answer this: How do you know all this? That this room even existed?"

"Are you bargaining with me, little princess?"

She rolled her eyes. "I'm sick of your questions instead of answers."

"Sounds like we need a bargain. You answer mine and I'll answer yours."

She straightened. "No. And I refuse to help you find what you're looking for unless you answer me this: You wanted me to join you in here. Why?"

"A one-sided bargain. I guess I can go with that for now." I arched my head back, my eyes traveling up the face of the shelves. "That's a good question. One I have no answer for."

"I don't believe you. Is this a trap?" She sounded alarmed.

"Petrulus has no authority to be down here, so no, this is not a trap. I'd be in as much trouble as you. And no, I honestly can't tell you what led me to bring you here." I glanced over my shoulder at her. "I've risked a lot letting you follow me."

"Dragging me here, you mean."

"I enticed, not dragged. And if you really want to know, I'm chasing knowledge."

"To help you bring down the House of Tannard."

"I can do that blindfolded, little princess. I'm surprised you need to question that." Again, I looked over my shoulder at her. A woman of her skill had to be impressed with my swordsmanship yesterday.

She stared at me, looking unimpressed.

"Besides, I'm chasing something far more important. And given the king and the Salmun will be leaving the temple sometime soon, I suggest you keep quiet, so I may search for what I'm after."

"Amongst all of this. You've lost your mind."

"After everything I've done these last days, I'm inclined to agree with you."

I headed toward the next wall, away from the books, and stood with my hands on my hips, scanning the expansive shelving, scroll upon scroll packed deep. I stood no chance of finding it now. My idiocy was in choosing to spare Selisimus, for Tressya's sake. And that was another mistake I'd made because of her. She was going to cost me my throne at this rate.

I pulled back the hood and went to run my hand through my hair out of frustration, forgetting Petrulus shaved his head regularly.

"You've no idea what you're after, do you?"

"The contents, yes, but not how they'll be presented."

"How far in the past are you searching?" She stared at the shelves in front of her. "I've not seen any of Merania's ancient text, so I'm unfamiliar with the medium they used to capture their words."

I watched her finger her way through some of the scrolls, smiling through my surprise at her sudden enthusiasm.

"I doubt anything as far back as the great war would be

found in bound books. More likely written on scrolls. Am I right about the time frame?"

"There abouts." My focus should be on the search, yet her presence was irresistibly distracting, especially now her mind was actively engaged in solving a puzzle.

"Before or after the great war? After the war, there would've been a gap in knowledge keeping, starting again when life resumed some normalcy. The Levenian influence may have led to change in the materials they used to hold their knowledge. That might give us a way of separating pre- and post-war writings. So which is it?"

"During. Or after. Soon...after."

If our little venture softened her prickly demeanor toward me, I wouldn't mind, but I adored a challenge, and this little ferocious creature was proving a challenge too tantalizing to resist.

She was becoming much more than I'd anticipated when I first made the pivotal decision to leave my mark on her. With every moment spent together, my conviction that keeping her alive was the right choice only deepened. Her intelligence matched her boldness, and her decision to keep me a secret revealed she was as far from being a loyal disciple to her Sistern as I was from being a woman. And that gave me hope.

With her back to me, she remained still, and I could imagine the look on her face as she tried to work out the puzzle. Then she turned to face me. "You're trying to find proof of your bloodlink to the Tarragona throne."

"No proof needed."

"You want to know how the Levenian defeated the king."

"Dark and dangerous magic." I paced along the wall toward her.

"The losers will always say that." She paced away from me, starting us in a slow dance.

"Surely you must sense the Salmun's malevolent presence."

"They're creepy, sure. But that doesn't make them bad."

"How would you explain the Ashenlands if not for dark magic?"

"I've heard mention of this place. I know nothing about it."

"The Salmun cursed the land, forming a belt running across the kingdom right down to the sea. Inside, they released their pets—vile creatures brought with them, along with many more they created since then."

We continued our dance. "I heard it was created to protect the south from the marauding Huungardred beasts," she said.

"Lies."

"Who am I to believe? My enemy or my people?"

"These are not your people," I snarled. "Don't ever make the mistake of thinking that."

"I'm to marry Juel. Which means they are my people."

Hearing her say that, I fisted my hands.

But her eyes widened. "What about on stone?" And she doubled back to crouch beside the stone tablets stacked on the bottom shelves. There weren't many, which meant less to search through if she was right. She drew the flame close so she could see.

"The king may be heading for the carriage."

I'd been selfish in luring her from the carriage because I desired her company. The last thing Tressya needed was attention from the Salmun. I should get her back. Given I now knew what apostle's soul to take, I could return at any time and retrieve what I wanted.

"Wait." She stopped, staring ahead as she thought.

"You're best staying beneath the Salmun's attention, which you won't be if they catch you snoopy around in here."

"I'm a dimwitted princess. I simply got bored and wanted to look inside." She continued to peruse the tablets.

I gazed at her, enjoying watching her astute mind pick at the possibilities.

Then suddenly she straightened and spun to face me. The torchlight softened her features, making them appear more attractive. Or maybe it had nothing to do with the soft yellow light and everything to do with spending more time with her.

"It was common in Merania for the scribes to translate our most important ancient texts into bound volumes to preserve the knowledge."

I couldn't keep up with her fast mind.

She headed for the books lining the shelves I'd just vacated when voices came down the stairwell. I dived for Tressya, swiping the torch from her hand and dousing it on the stone under my boot. The darkness enveloped us when the voices became clearer.

CHAPTER
SEVENTEEN

TRESSYA

With a firm arm around my waist, Bloodwyn—Petrulus—
pulled me away from the steps, burying us deep into the
library.

"The torch has gone out. Fetch another," came a male
voice.

There were no places for us to hide.

"We'd look less guilty if we let them know we're here. I'll
tell them I insisted on you showing me around," I whispered.

"And the explanation for the key?"

"Wasn't that your key? I mean, Petrulus's key?"

"I took it from the guy whose clothes you're wearing.
Only three apostles within Emberforge have a key to this
place."

"And you know that how?"

"Explaining Selisimus will be difficult."

"Who's Selisimus?"

"And the fact you're wearing his clothes."

He'd wanted me to join him here—for reasons I couldn't fathom—but I shouldn't be surprised he wasn't going to play fair and reveal all his secrets. And I could only believe this excursion was meant to turn me in circles.

"They're a perfect fit, by the way."

I struggled in his arms, and he relented, but only to snag my wrist and yank me close. It was dark, and I couldn't see his face, but I could feel his stale breath across my lips. If he was Bloodwyn, my heart might have betrayed me and kicked up a beat, but while he wore the apostle's skin, I found it easy to control my reactions.

I pushed away from him. "You don't smell like Bloodwyn." *Oh Mother, did I just say that?*

"Does that bother you?"

"We're about to get discovered, and that's your focus?"

Old clothes, a body in need of a good bath, and the fragrance of smoke—that's how Petrulus smelled. It turned my nose.

"I have a plan," he whispered.

"Not if it involves more dead people."

"Do you want the Salmun to find you like this?"

"Bloodwyn," I growled, then jumped when I felt his finger pressed to my lips.

"Shh."

A small tingle sparked low in my stomach, but then I remembered whose finger it belonged to and swiped it away.

"Petrulus gives me the creeps."

263

"You should've told me earlier. I'll ditch him at the first opportunity."

I smirked at his sound of disgust.

"Where's Tortilus? Perhaps it's his key," came a male voice, followed by a long creak as they swung the library door wide, bringing down a stream of light.

"Who'd be down here during the vigil of devotion?"

"I can't explain. Go see who it is. I'm wanted in the grand hall."

Bloodwyn pushed me back against the shelving, then leaned in close and whispered, "I'll deal with him. In a non-lethal way."

There was no point arguing. Petrulus was my only hope of getting out of here without being seen. Strangely, I wasn't worried about the king discovering I was missing. No one could blame a foreigner for getting bored and curious, but the dead guard was a problem, and the apostle Bloodwyn hid behind the pillar along with my clothes. If he woke and found a noblewoman's dress, it would make my actions harder to explain.

Bloodwyn rushed to the bottom of the stairs to intercept the new arrival before he could reach the bottom.

"Petrulus," the apostle said in surprise.

"Rewas. No one's allowed in the Sanctum of Solmira during the vigil of devotion."

It was possible Bloodwyn knew the apostle's name, and every other damn thing about this place because he'd already entered. Many times prior, it would seem, which led me to wonder how long he'd been in Tolum. Whatever he was chasing in Emberforge was important to him, which meant it was important to me. Knowledge was power.

"And you, Petrulus. How do you have a key?"

"Selisimus needed something, then he suddenly took ill and asked me to fetch it for him."

"But that's... It's..."

"Yeah, sorry, but I don't have time for this stilted conversation."

I rushed forward when I heard the scuffle followed by a muffled cry. Already Rewas lay unconscious in Bloodwyn's arms. The apostle looked an impossible weight for Bloodwyn —Petrulus—to hold, but Bloodwyn moved him down the last steps with ease, then dragged him across the floor and dumped him at the back of the chamber.

"We're accumulating too many bodies," he said as he grabbed my elbow and hurried me up the steps. "The other one was called to the grand hall. It means the king and the Salmun are still there."

I needed my breath to run up the steps, sparing Bloodwyn my questions.

At the exit, he steered me back the way we'd came, but at the sound of a group marching toward us, Bloodwyn yanked me left down a narrow passage. On our right, a wall of iron lattice gave me a glimpse inside the small temple, lit with bracketed torches along two thirds of the wall. As we dashed past, I caught sight of a large stone altar at the far end.

Suddenly Bloodwyn pushed me against the wall, shielding my face as the group moved past our narrow passage.

"The king," Bloodwyn hissed.

"They're leaving?" I'd thought my luck would last. Curses, that I was wrong. How long before they found the dead guard?

"Not Emberforge. But we still could have a problem. They're heading in the direction of the library. If they find Rewas..." He never bothered to elaborate on that outcome, instead hurried us along the narrow passage.

We continued to weave our way through a confusing maze of ever narrowing corridors, passing pillared court-yards and small temples while my eyes became accustomed to the ever dimming light.

"Do you know where you're going?"

"Yes."

"I thought we had to get out of Emberforge. This feels like we're heading deeper inside."

"We won't be long. No one's heading for the carriage just yet."

"Getting into my clothes takes time."

"I'm here to help."

I slanted him a sideways glance, struggling to see Bloodwyn under his disguise. Bloodwyn's hands on me. The idea was pleasing. But Petrulus...

"I'll ditch the skin," Bloodwyn said, seeming to read my thoughts, perhaps it was my expression.

"Don't bother. Neither is an improvement."

He smirked. Normally I was good at hiding my emotions, but he seemed to penetrate through to my heart. As a disciple that was not an easy task for anyone, especially a man. It was concerning how he'd managed such a feat in a short space of time. I was rarely swayed by a man's handsome features, yet something about Bloodwyn had slipped under my shield. I would blame the bite. There was some poison at work, making me more than easy prey, now I was his accomplice.

"It's just up ahead. We won't stay long."

"Why the crazy maze." It was a sarcastic spill of frustration, but Bloodwyn answered as though it was a question.

"The ancients believed a person had to earn the right to stand before the power of the Bone Throne. They had to pass through a series of temples devoted to various gods. If they were worthy that god would grant them passage to the next temple and so on, until the truly worthy were granted an audience with the bone king."

"And that's the king who sits upon the Bone Throne?"

"Yes."

"That's where we're heading."

"Yes."

I stopped asking questions, suddenly as eager to see this fabled Bone Throne as Bloodwyn. Hurrying along beside him, the small temples on either side held no interest for me. Our path led us along more passages until we stumbled out into a cavernous room.

In the flaming torch light, flecks of white stone seemed to dance along the floor's surface, making it appear like ripples on an oily sea. Above, the same flecks of stone gave the ceiling the appearance of the night sky. The only other color in the vast chamber was the throne of bone erected on a lump of black stone.

The Bone Throne rose imposingly within the chamber, a colossal testament to its grandeur and grotesque elegance.

Forged from skeletons, its sheer size dwarfed the standard of ordinary thrones, making it not just a seat but a monument to the dominion it represented.

Each vertebra and bone had been meticulously interlocked, sculpted by the hands of a master. The throne's back was a macabre pantheon of elaborate carvings, each bearing the face of a—I presumed—forgotten deity, their expressions contorted for eternity in a meld of creation and destruction.

The armrests swooped downwards, morphing seamlessly into the colossal heads of serpents bearing crowns of thorns on their heads.

Entranced, Bloodwyn let my hand go and moved forward, seeming to forget about me. I followed, feeling exposed in this vast hall with no space to hide if someone should enter.

"I take it this is the Bone Throne."

"I'm not surprised in the short time since your arrival you've already heard of it." he said as he strolled toward it as if in a daydream.

"Once, briefly. I know it was the throne of the last king before the great war."

"It was so much more." Bloodwyn climbed the rock, but rather than sit on the throne he ran a hand along the arm rest as if stroking the serpent's head. "King Ricaud was the last king to sit on this throne. That was a millennium ago."

I blinked, thinking I saw some movement rising up behind Bloodwyn. The flaming torches provided little light and plenty of cover for anyone to hide.

"A just king," he continued.

"Some would say otherwise."

"He who currently sits on the Tarragona throne is not worthy of his ancestral bloodline. Neither are his sons."

"Don't tell me. You're worthy."

Bloodwyn glanced over at me, but my eyes flittered to the shadowy movement coming up from behind. With the tingle along my arms, the shiver across my shoulder blades, I knew it was a spirit.

"What do you think?" Bloodwyn said, moving around to sit on the throne, splaying his arms on the armrests and crossing his legs. "Am I worthy?"

The spirit rose up behind the throne, his transparent body dull in the flaming torch light. A man, seeming as proud and regal as any king, even with no crown upon his head. He wore the chain mail of a fighter and carried a sword in his hand.

"Where was King Ricaud killed?"

Bloodwyn frowned. "I'm not sure. Why?"

I shook my head. "Why would you think you're worthy? Are you claiming to be a Tannard heir?"

Andriet had said only an heir from the House of Tannard would sit upon the throne. But that could simply be an elaborate story woven by the victors of the great war.

The spirit stared down at me from behind the throne, and I struggled to keep my eyes on Bloodwyn; my developing skill in the death arts was a secret he wouldn't have.

Then suddenly, the spirit rushed forward, passing through the throne and then through Bloodwyn. His arms seized as he thrust his chest forward, head arched back, sucking in a noisy gasp. In that moment, he lost the form of Petrulus and turned into someone else. His skin was darker than Bloodwyn's, his body broader, more muscular, but with his head thrown back, I couldn't see his features.

Once the spirit left him, he collapsed forward as if kicked in the gut, then kept going until he rolled off the throne and onto the lump of black rock. Curled in a ball, I saw only his night black hair.

I rushed forward, intent on seeing the real Razohan, but by the time I reached the throne, Bloodwyn was back, pushing himself up to sitting.

I glanced over my shoulder at the spirit, and groaned, when behind him, I spied more spirits filling the chamber. A rank of soldiers behind their king, each dressed in battle armor.

"He made his last stand before the Bone Throne." And I didn't mean to say that allowed.

Since Bloodwyn was still dazed and not paying me any attention, I glanced back to King Ricaud, hoping he would speak to me. I had so many questions I would ask him if I was alone. He stayed silent, only now he was staring at Bloodwyn.

"He has many faces." Finally King Ricaud spoke, and I wasn't sure if his words were meant for me or his men.

Bloodwyn scraped his boot across the rock, righting himself, and I turned back to face him. "Are you all right?"

Head bowed, he hung his legs over the edge of the rock, supporting himself on his arms.

I sat beside him, giving him time to gather himself together, knowing too well what it felt like to be invaded by a spirit. Still with his head bowed, I took the chance to look at King Ricaud and his men again.

He appeared little older than Bloodwyn, with a crown of wavy hair falling below his shoulders and a heavy beard. Even as a spirit, his presence was imposing.

He wafted toward us, shifting his eyes from Bloodwyn back to me.

"You are looking at me, are you not, young woman in an apostles clothes?"

I slowly nodded.

King Ricaud came closer still. "How is it the living see the dead?"

I shrugged.

"That was rough," Bloodwyn groaned.

"You looked as though someone speared you through the stomach."

"Hmm." He didn't seem to be listening to me.

"He dared to sit upon my throne. He dared to claim himself worthy. The Levenians' filthy dogs seek to sit upon my throne. But this man is not of that line. I felt something inside of him, something which reaches to me across the veil and touches my soul."

I gaped, desperate to hear more of this. "You're a Razohan." I patted Bloodwyn on the shoulder.

I caught King Ricaud's frown.

"Are you implying as a Razohan I'm weak?" Bloodwyn lifted his head and gave me a thin smile.

"What is a Razohan?" King Ricaud said.

"You turned into someone else before you collapsed. Your true self. Beast-man from the north."

Finally he lifted his head, forcing me to snap my gaze from King Ricaud to him.

"You're saying strange things, Tressya, or is my hearing affected.

"The north you say. The Huungardred inhabited the north a millennium ago, but none could take the true form of man."

"You're a descendant of the Huungardred, so..." I didn't know what else to say. It already sounded ridiculous.

"Did you hit your head while I was passed out?"

"No. But that's a fact isn't it. Your ancestors bred with the Huungardred and—"

"My last command was for the Nazeen to flee east with my Ammelle to Strathembrook."

"Who were your ancestors that bred with the Huungardred?" I implored.

"It's the wrong time to have this conversation," Bloodwyn said.

King Ricaud moved closer. "Did my Ammelle survive?" His question sounded desperate. A millennium of not knowing if his daughter survived or not. "Is that how this... Razohan claims a link to my throne?"

"You're a descendant of King Ricaud's daughter, aren't you?" I shouted.

"Easy now. You're determined to unravel me, secret by secret, aren't you?"

"Just tell me, yes or no."

"Yes."

Ricaud rushed toward me. "My Ammelle."

Without thought, I reared back, avoiding his grasp.

The king would've collapsed to his knees but since his lower half was ill formed he slipped through the floor.

Bloodwyn grabbed my arms. "Tressya, what's going on?"

"My bloodline survived through my daughter?"

I opened my mouth to answer the king, then slammed it shut, remembering Bloodwyn. "I'm fine."

The king surged to his feet. "There is hope." He turned to face his men. "There is hope."

Even if I was alone, could I refute him? Listening to the spirits cheer, I knew I wouldn't be honest. I wouldn't have the heart to tell him I was here to make sure the House of Tannard remained on the throne, and a Tannard heir, my child, secured that line.

Beside me, Bloodwyn said. "That was unexpected."

I flicked another glance at King Ricaud, but his attention was now solely on Bloodwyn. "Good unexpected, or bad?"

"Unexpected," he repeated, then pushed up. "We need to go."

"What? No way." I joined him, but he was already marching off toward the exit.

"Wait!" I shouted. He was heading straight for the line of spirits.

Bloodwyn spun around. "Come on, princess, I've got to get you dressed." His sudden energy confused me.

"You're Bloodwyn not Petrulus." His clothes were askew, buttons burst, seams ripped at his thighs.

"I thought you'd prefer it that way." And he turned and marched away.

I opened my mouth to shout again, but the spirit king

and his soldiers disappeared, clearing Bloodwyn's path, so I scurried after him.

At the exit, Bloodwyn stopped me, placing his finger to his lips. I sucked in my bottom lip and held my breath, but heard no one coming. He then grabbed my hand and dragged me along beside him, weaving us down the passageways like dogs were on our heels.

"Now you're in a hurry," I puffed.

"I need to get you back in that carriage."

"You weren't in a hurry before. What's changed? What happened in there?"

His hand wrapped my waist, and Bloodwyn yanked me off my feet and into one of the small temples, crushing me against the wall.

"Not a peep," he whispered, then locked eyes with me while we waited.

My sole focus was on his amber eyes hypnotizing me and my heaving chest caught between the solid warmth of his body and the cold stones. I wasn't even assessing the risk we faced. Moments passed and the flutter through my body had turned my brain to mush.

"All clear. Let's go." Bloodwyn dragged me out of the temple and hurried us on our way. I stumbled after him, unable to switch my mind from the heat in my body to escaping as easily as he seemed to achieve. Unless he was unaffected by what happened back there.

"Are you going to answer any of my questions?" I forced the annoyance into my voice.

"I had a moment. It's passed. Now we need to get out here."

"What about Ammelle—" I didn't mean to say her name.

Bloodwyn yanked me off my feet once again, spinning me around and into another small passage, pushing me against the wall with a hand over my mouth.

He leaned down to whisper. "Too many questions, princess."

My mind fuzzed up with the smell of him, and his large hand smothering anything I would say. The amber in his eyes seemed to sparkle alive. With his eyes fixed on mine, expression solemn, I forgot everything including my ability to breathe. Especially when his hand slipped from my mouth and rested on my throat, large enough his fingers almost wrapped around my neck.

An untamed soul was behind those eyes, staring down at me. His body both taut and relaxed, large and powerful, strong and beautiful, yet his hand resting on my throat was anything but threatening. I was unaccustomed to feeling vulnerable around any man, something I should feel acutely being so close to such an excellent predator, but I knew if I told him to release me, he would; if I told him to back away, he would; if I told him to leave me alone, he would, just as soon as he returned me safely to the carriage.

Cobwebs could form for how still we stayed. Then Bloodwyn blinked. Placing his hands either side of my shoulders, he released a low rumble in his throat, which sent small vibratory ripples along my skin to my heart. I still had yet to breathe. Every hair on my body reached toward him, every inch of my skin prickled waiting for a hint of his touch.

"How do you know that name?"

"What name?" My mind was a mess.

Ammelle, that's right. That conversation seemed a life time ago. "Wait? You don't remember what happened back there?"

He leaned his elbow against the wall, bringing him suffo-catingly—mesmerizingly—closer. With a finger, he twisted a stray strand of my hair. "Things are rather fuzzy. And that's a tale very few know."

"I asked around a lot, and I'm very persuasive." I couldn't think straight. Mostly because every time he twisted the strand of my hair, his knuckles dusted my cheek, like a care-less caress.

"I bet you are, princess. Tell me, what would you—"

"Forget it."

"I have a lot to offer."

"Is it clear now? I'm in a hurry." I wanted to stay pinned by his body, struggling to breathe while I waited for the tease of his knuckles on my skin. But I wouldn't allow the Razohan to realize how much he was effecting me right now.

He heaved out a deep breath. "It's clear." Once again, he dragged me off down the passage.

"Is there actually anyone coming, or are you enjoying throwing me about? Because I don't hear anything."

"You don't have my hearing."

That had to be a Razohan thing.

Finally I recognized our path. The passages widened, natural light seeped through and the sconces along the wall became few.

"If we're lucky Selisimus is still unconscious and yet to be found," Bloodwyn said, as he diverted us into the temple where I'd changed.

Behind the last pillar, we found the apostle and my clothes.

"What are you doing?" I said, as Bloodwyn scooped them up in his arms.

"Wait until we reach the outer passage and the exit. It's safer that way." And he marched out of the temple, retracing his steps back into the open air passage we'd first stumbled along.

There he handed me my clothes. "This is as good a place as any." And turned his back.

I stared at him, my mind still back with the Bone Throne, King Ricaud and what had happened in the mad dash that followed; especially what had happened during the mad dash. Bloodwyn's actions made no sense. Maybe he was possessed.

"You do realize Selisimus will be found without his clothes."

"We'll have to let him explain that problem."

"What about Rewas unconscious in the library? That's too many weird occurrences. The Salmun won't like it."

"Then we'll leave them to try and figure it out. So far only Petrulus has been spotted."

"And where is the real Petrulus?"

"That's a whole heap of questions for someone who should be worried about being caught out of the carriage."

I spun him around to face me. "Which throne would you choose to sit upon if, say, you actually won."

"The only throne that matters. The Emberfell throne is for imposters. The Levenian bloodline pollutes it." Disgust laced every word he spoke.

He turned his back on me again so I discarded the smock.

"I will win, little princess."

"You know I won't let you."

I was trying to attach my pocket bags when he turned around, catching me off guard. On reflex, I covered my breasts with my hands.

He gave me a wry smile. "All you're wearing is petticoats and already you're hidden under so many layers."

"That's not the po—"

Bloodwyn's hands were on my waist, turning my back to him. "You need help."

"I was doing adequately."

I stared up at the sky and tried not to focus on his hands as they tied the pocket bags' strings, fastening them to my hips.

"My blade." I bent to retrieve it, but Bloodwyn beat me to it, slipping the dagger inside one of my pocket bags. As he did so, I repeated what I'd said before. "You know I won't let you."

When he stood this close, staring down at me, it reminded me that we were alone; it brought back what I had seemed so easily able to forget—that he was my enemy. It also reminded me that, despite my skills, I had little defense against him.

"Do you think you can stop me?"

Said as if he'd just read my thoughts.

"I'll try regardless."

"Then we're going to have some fun."

I was sure I would hate his idea of fun.

CHAPTER

EIGHTEEN

TAMAS

I CIRCLED, catching a turbulent ride from the winds racing down the Draghunn Mountains. With my keen eagle eyesight, I spied Ledbric Hall nestled on a small plateau above the forest line.

It was perhaps the most imposing structure in the northern realm, which suited Kaldor's personality. The last I heard, Garrat remained at Ledbric Hall, using all his diplomatic guile to convince Kaldor of the benefits of an alliance for the people of Wilhelm. Kaldor would need the promise of glory or money to commit his men to a war with the south, but if anyone could succeed in convincing him, it would be Garrat.

After my experience in Emberforge, I wasn't ready to face probing questions from Kaldor regarding my legitimacy in claiming the Bone Throne. He gave scant attention to augury, believing all of them crazy, and thought little of the Nazeen because they had refused to recognize him as over-lord, which he believed would give him legitimacy to claim their magic as his to command at will.

Instead of landing at Ledbric Hall, I penetrated the thick forest on the eastern side and found Garrat already waiting.

We embraced. "How're things in the north?" I asked.

"Progress is slow for now. Kaldor senses the need for haste, so he's dragging his feet. He's hoping to extract a few more promises before he commits."

"As was expected. For the Huungardred's sake, don't give him rein to make too many bargains."

Men like Kaldor were the reason Thaindrus had asked me to marry Bryra. Kaldor wanted Huungardred land, expanding his lands to abut the borders of his rival, Malun-drad. Huungardred land, while buried deep in snow for half the year, was extremely fertile, rich in mineral wealth, and excellent for hunting, and that would add to Kaldor's wealth.

"He requires special handling."

I patted Garrat on the back. "You're up to the task. I have faith in you." Then, I turned from his questioning gaze before he asked if his faith in me was misplaced.

We both turned in the direction of Osmud as he crashed through the forest. My breath hitched upon seeing Bryra coming alongside him. *Damn you, Osmud.* Of course, he'd do something like this to annoy me. I had secrets she couldn't hear, and I felt uncomfortable around her now, which saddened me.

"Have we missed the important bits?" Osmud said, stomping through the thicket toward us.

I rubbed my forehead and glanced at Garrat, who held up his hands as if to say 'keep me out of it' and leaned against a tree.

"Bryra, you look well." A lame comment to make to a dear friend.

"We're keen to hear the progress you've made in the south," Bryra said.

I glared at Osmud. He simply shrugged. "Please, give us all the details."

"The Salmun's eyes are everywhere."

Osmud turned to Bryra. "See, I told you he'd start with an excuse."

"When dealing with wizards, things can't be easy," she countered. Never before had I felt suffocated by her persistent belief in me and enduring faith in whatever action I took. Now, I wondered if it was a need to please me. I loathed the idea. She was a bold woman, a fierce fighter, a loyal friend. I never wanted to see her diminished, not even for love.

After I murdered my father—I could give no other name to my action despite what others said—to claim my place as Razohan leader, Bryra, along with Osmud and Garrat, was the first to stand by my side.

My actions pained Thaindrus deeply. It took him a full turn of the seasons before he was willing to listen to my reasons. Not even Romelda could get through to him, but, without a doubt on her behalf, Bryra believed my actions were justified. The guilt at not answering Thaindrus's request gnawed a hole inside my heart. Even more so now my attention was utterly divided by Tressya.

"Let's start with the basics. Are all four of our enemies still alive?" Osmud said.

I rubbed my temples. "Tell me the fourth, and I'll reply." I should've spoken to Garrat alone.

Osmud gave me a long look, as if he thought me a child. I returned it.

"How about we stay with our three greatest concerns," Bryra said.

I flashed her a grateful smile, but she held my gaze, and I could feel the choking hands of guilt tightening around my throat. As my dearest friend, she deserved honesty.

"The king and his sons still breathe. The Salmun stay close."

"Are you trying to tell us as a Razohan you can't get close without raising suspicion."

"You've never stepped foot in Tolum. You wouldn't know how it is."

"Is that an invitation?"

I forked a hand through my hair. "I entered Emberforge."

That got everyone's attention.

"This is good," Osmud said. "It's progress. Just hold the conversation. It was a long flight." And he headed off through the trees some ways to find himself some privacy.

I took the opportunity to berate him, so I nodded to the other two and headed after him. Caught taking a piss, I had his undivided attention.

"Why did you bring Bryra?" I growled, attempting to keep my voice to a whisper.

"To make you feel awkward."

"Did you not think it would also make Bryra feel uncomfortable?"

He glanced over his shoulder at her through the trees. "She looks perfectly at ease. If she were uncomfortable, it would be because she felt guilty. And since she has nothing to feel guilty for, she's not uncomfortable." He quirked a brow. "You, on the other hand, look ready to climb out of your skin."

"I'm dealing with things the way I know how."

"Not the Razohan way to be sure," he said as he tied himself up.

"She's not meant to die?" I snapped, then regretted it. Osmud was there when the augur spoke, but he understood nothing. "And I won't let it go this time if you think to punch me again."

"It didn't help you the first time," Osmud grumbled. "I know what this is about, Tamas. Stop dragging that burden around. Your father..." He looked back at the other two, deep in conversation. "He wasn't the same after he lost your mother. Everyone saw it."

Having shunned augurs all his life and driven to near insanity by grief, Father sought one out. In the augur's teachings, he either learned the truth or heard a lie; no one would ever know. He became obsessed with becoming the next Bone King, driven by the belief that the Etherweave was powerful enough to bring his dead wife back.

I looked past Osmud to Garrat and Bryra. Both would echo Osmud's words.

"Don't question your right to the Bone Throne. And don't question your fidelity to your people. None of us do. It's what makes the difference between a good king and a wicked king."

I clamped a hand on Osmud's shoulder and gave it a squeeze. "Thanks for that, but you'll want to take it all back when I tell you I bit her."

"What the fuck?" Osmud exclaimed, pulling away from my hold.

The other two looked our way.

"You better have a damn good explanation for doing that," Osmud lowered his voice and glanced over his shoulder. "If I'd known you'd lost your mind, I never would've brought Bryra. There's no way you can accept Thaindrus's request now." He stepped away, shaking his head. "What were you thinking?"

"Not enough and yet too much all at once. I never wanted to accept Thaindrus's request, you know that." I strode a few paces, running my fingers through my hair as if I could pick out every jumbled thought to lay before me, giving me a chance to understand more clearly.

Due to my profound connection with Thaindrus, I was not as naïve as many Razohan, including Osmud and Garrat, about the true depth of the mate bond. Since all mated partners in the north paired with their own kind, none had the opportunity to fully appreciate what I gained by bonding with Tressya.

"This was a cock thing, wasn't it?"

"No, that's far from..." Did I want to keep lying? "I'm..." Feeble-brained when around her. "Did you understand anything the augur said?"

"Not a word."

I placed my hands on my hips and bowed my head. I wasn't ready to divulge my thoughts about Tressya just yet. For now, I clung to a deep-seated hope, kindled in Emberforge, that sudden flush of confidence that my instincts about her had been correct. I believed something extraordinary could emerge from this, provided I could gain her trust.

"The other two need to hear this." And I left Osmud glaring at me and returned to Bryra and Garrat.

"Tell us," Garrat said. "What does it look like?"

"It's a mighty thing, the likes you've never seen. I sat upon it."

Osmud laughed, losing all the anger of moments ago. "Getting a feel for it, were you?"

The memory was filled with a certain someone, a detail I would never reveal. I paused a moment, losing my narrative as I remembered hiding in the narrow passage while she changed back into her dress. She promised to stop me from ever claiming the Bone Throne, with no idea how true those words might be.

"That's not the end of it. This is going to sound crazy," I glanced at Garrat. "I swear King Ricaud's spirit came to me."

"You're right, it does, but I'll go with it," Osmud said.

"What do you mean, Tamas? How did he come to you?" Bryra asked.

"When I sat upon the throne, suddenly I was filled with... I can't explain, but for a moment, he moved through my soul. I felt... like I was a king. It's the only way I can explain it."

"That has to be an omen," Garrat said, surprising me. He

was never one to give credence to anything mysterious. My father's misguided actions had entrenched his steadfast disdain for augury.

"It's good news, indeed," Bryra said. "I believe his spirit has chosen to reveal itself to you in a favorable way because he sees you as worthy."

For a breath, I feared she'd overheard Osmud's rousing speech, but if she had, she wouldn't be smiling at me encouragingly. My admission about the bite wouldn't be pleasant for her to hear. But no, this was Bryra being Bryra, a loyal friend. And damn that the thought stung.

"Perhaps so. I felt undefeatable." I held back from mentioning the Etherweave. I believed that was what the King's spirit had bled inside of me. For one moment, I felt its raw power.

"That's what we want to hear," Osmud said.

"I also found a chamber under Emberforge, some sort of library. It was stuffed full of ancient texts. All the teachings King Ricaud gathered during his reign, I would say. I'm sure the Senjel Oracles are hidden in there somewhere."

"What makes you so sure?" Garrat asked.

"I don't know. It seems logical. Emberforge is the Salmun's stronghold now. What better place to hide it? Somewhere they would believe no one can penetrate? I need another apostle and more time in there."

"Not yet," Garrat said. "We need to stick with Romelda's plan. First, we fight. When we win, the Salmun will have no choice but to surrender all to you."

Garrat was right. Killing the heirs and winning the war would get me the Senjel Oracles without too much bother on my behalf. What I didn't reveal was my urge to sit upon the Bone Throne and feel the majesty of King Ricaud's spirit residing within me again.

Or was it the power I chased?

****

Upon returning, the first person I sought was Tressya, reaching out through our mate connection. Although the bond was weaker than most—since she had not taken my blood—as long as she didn't escape to the north, or across the sea, she was within my grasp to find.

At the moment, her heart raced unusually fast. The bond allowed me to delve into the nuances of her emotions, but I had to contend with the faint connection we shared, lest I risk breaking a sacred soul vow: never to intrude without consent. And consent, which was symbolized by mutual bite marks among mated partners, was something Tressya had yet to grant me.

Curiosity pricked, I probed for her whereabouts. "Strange indeed."

She was not in Emberfell. The princess had missed the second ball, an event celebrating her nuptials. Turning on the steps of Emberfell, I closed my eyes and tilted my head back, searching for that elusive sign that would lead me to her.

A chuckle escaped me upon the discovery. It was certainly intriguing. I made my way down the steps, crossing the gravel grounds toward pockets of wilderness now shrouded in darkness. Before reaching the trees, I let go of my human guise, spread my wings, and soared into the night sky.

Settling in a quiet alleyway across from Daswood Manor —a grand manor situated in the borough of Upper Heedle-main—I whispered, "What brings you here, little princess?"

I straightened my jacket and removed a few stray feathers from my collar.

With the streets nearly empty at this late hour in Tolum, her choice of time made sense. Smiling, I crossed the road, scaled the iron fence with ease, and landed among the flowers, their sweet scent released underfoot. After selecting the most vibrant among them, I placed them in my breast pocket.

There was no need for such a covert approach to Bloodwyn's residence, but I had chosen not to alert the staff of my return. I slipped along the right side of the manor, heading for the kitchen entrance—a modest adjunct to the main house.

I had left no instructions for dinner, allowing the kitchen staff a night off—a decision that now seemed providential. In the corridor, I paused to pinpoint her exact location. Sensing her, I continued, slipping into the dining hall to avoid a servant, then hugged the wall into the reception hall. The library lay across the room, its large wooden doors firmly closed. Entering through them would betray my presence.

Instead, I crossed the reception hall to the right chamber room. Through a private door, I could access the library. The chamber was dark, lit only by moonlight streaking across the floor, as no candles burned within.

I clenched my teeth, hearing the small door creak, then waited for two heartbeats before sliding through.

In the library's far right corner was a circular room with a view over the front garden. The drapes were drawn, and a single candle's soft yellow glow cast shadows around the space.

Tressya was at a large oak desk, rifling through a stack of papers likely retrieved from the shelves or the cabinet. Bloodwyn had been a hoarder, and that extended to documents detailing his financial dealings since inheriting his title. I puzzled over what she hoped to uncover in what must have been a tedious search.

Approaching her with the silent stealth of a Razohan, I positioned myself behind her and drew the flowers from my pocket. I leaned over while encircling her with an arm extended to the desk for support, my other hand presented the bouquet.

She let out a shriek and swung her elbow back swiftly, aiming for my face. I dodged to the left, giving her space to slip from her seat, which she pushed into my shin. The candlelight glinted off the silver of her blade as she stabbed at me. Anticipating the attack, I seized her wrist, pulling it wide and driving the blade into the chair's wood.

"Asshole," she spat.

"That's hardly the way to welcome someone into his own home, especially if you're a thief."

"I'm not stealing anything."

"You're pilfering information, princess. And you certainly weren't invited to my home." I tugged her arm toward me, forcing her to release the blade.

Her right hand, balled into a fist, swung at my nose. I ducked, captured her around the waist, and hoisted her onto the desk, sliding her backward until she was pinned beneath me—my body compellingly nestled between her legs.

"Let go of me, beast-man," she growled.

I tussled with her until I had both her arms pinned over her head."Now why would I do that?"

"That's right. You're no gentleman."

"And tonight, I'm more beast than man, so mind your tongue."

I stared down at her, watching emotions flicker across her face. Then, for one moment, I lost myself in the thrill of my lust, pumping down into my groin, and tuned in to the flow of her feelings before I realized what I was doing. Dammit, I'd crossed the forbidden threshold. Snapping to my senses, I pulled back, but not before I momentarily linked with the wild rush of an insatiable hunger, and I just about grew fangs, intent on trailing them down her throat.

Before I could quell my growl of frustration, it was out. I clenched my teeth, forcing my ragged breaths to calm. Once I felt sure my breathing was even, I said. "I'm curious what you hoped to find amongst all this boring paperwork."

"You'll be in debt soon. All that gambling and whoring."

Bloodwyn no longer had to worry about his mounting debts. "I'm unlikely to be around long enough to suffer the consequences."

"What will happen to Bloodwyn when you leave?"

"Do we need to talk about that man?" The truth would ruin her mood.

"Fine. We'll talk about the Razohan?"

"I find any conversation about you more stimulating." I

tried to keep my concentration on our conversation and not on the fact I was nestled between her legs.

"The Razohan are descendants of King Ricaud's daughter, Ammelle."

"Is that a question?"

"I'm gathering my thoughts. Which is impossible in this position," she snapped.

"I'm glad you feel it too."

"Frustrated, yes. Angry, you betcha. Like I want to scream at the top of my lungs."

"Passionate emotions are always a good place to start." I stifled an inhale to avoid smelling her fragrance. There were already too many things about this moment wrecking my concentration.

She struggled. "Get off of me."

I relented, fighting my desire to steer a tendril of my link into her heart. I squeezed my eyes shut. Since I'd forced this connection on her, that would be the ultimate betrayal.

Begrudgingly, I released her, then retrieved the chair and slid down into it, feeling wrecked from all my restraint.

"The Razohan as a topic of conversation are off-limits."

"That leaves us with nothing left to talk about." She slid off the table, but I snagged her around the waist and hauled her onto my lap. She gasped, but to my surprise and delight, she didn't fight me.

"You're too fond of manhandling me."

"You feel too good to stop manhandling."

I caught her inhale but won the fight with my smirk, else she would jab me in the ribs or climb off my lap.

What flared my nostrils and set my blood on fire was her

leaning forward, using one hand on my chest, as she reached over the back of the chair and dislodged her dagger. I should know better than to let her have a dagger in her hands, but her hand on my chest pinned me in place like a boulder.

The cold bite of steel caressed down the side of my neck and around to rest on my throat. "Am I going to turn into a beast?"

"No."

"Thank the stars."

"On the contrary, you'll miss much as a human."

"And be constantly picking stuff out of my fur? I don't think so."

I took note that she didn't lean back when I leaned forward. "What I really meant was our bond."

"We have no bond." She held up her wrist. "Except for this unfortunate thing."

"Mated partners benefit a great deal from their bond. Especially during sex." I let the word hang, staring into her expressive blue eyes as I did so, absorbing the full impact the word had on her.

It lasted breaths longer than I thought it would, her gaze staying with mine for tantalizing heartbeats.

She blinked. "It doesn't bear thinking about." And slipped off my lap.

Liar. I saw the pulse in her neck jump, saw the small flare of her eyes. I let her go, thinking about sitting myself in the cold water trough outside.

A knock sounded at the main door, and given my current problems, I growled at the disturbance this created. Maybe it was for the best. Nothing good was going to come from constantly being in her presence, except having my mind twisted about, making me forget who I was and why I was here.

"Curses," I growled, launching to my feet and stomping across to the window.

Parting one side of the drape, I peered out onto the portico, then groaned upon seeing Lord Dowel standing at my door. Tressya came up beside me and looked out.

"Lord Dowel," she hissed.

"The oaf has got his days wrong."

"You invited Lord Dowel?" Her voice rose at the end.

"Not tonight." I released the drape. "The idiot."

I glanced at her outraged face.

"By your expression, I'd say you know of his plot against the king."

Her mouth gaping, she shook her head. "And you hope to join him."

"You know why I'm here, Tressya." I speared my hands through my hair, feeling on the spot with her accusatory glare. "It's in my best interests to know all the goings-on in Emberfell. I plan to pick apart his scheme and see if there's anything useful."

I caught her hand before it connected with my jaw. "You're under my protection, so you needn't be so mad about it. Nothing will happen to you."

"Arrogant asshole. As if I need your protection. Whose protection are you under?"

He frowned. "That's not necessary."

"So you think." She pulled her hand free. "I should thank you."

"I agree, but will you?"

"Yes, I will. Sometimes during our interactions, I forget who we are. I forget we're, in fact, on opposing sides, and that it's in my best interests to learn to hate you. At some point in our conversations, you always end up reminding me of the truth. So thank you."

I wanted to save her the bother and stab myself.

"*Learn* to hate me. That means you currently don't."

"I slip between loathing and disgust."

It was too late; she was already marching out of the circular room. I slumped onto my desk, frustrated with the way I continually mucked things up.

"Tressya," I said.

She kept her back to me.

"The hunt is tomorrow."

Slowly she turned to face me. "I hope not to see you there."

"There's no one better than me in a hunt. You can be sure I'll be there."

Her quizzical gaze lingered for moments. I could see her mind working hard trying to work out why I'd even brought it up.

"Then I'll take two daggers."

"That might be wise."

CHAPTER

NINETEEN

TRESSYA

So far there was no news of any disturbances at Emberforge. The queen had fallen asleep and missed my arrival. I'd made it back to the carriage with enough time to practice looking bored.

The deep skirt and coat with doublets was a ridiculous riding habit, but it was the only outfit I had that was appropriate. Back home, I shunned convention, riding in breeches, and got away with it because I mostly rode alone. Radnisa had risen early and laid the outfit out. She glared at me while I dressed, not wanting to miss another moment to gloat over the misfortune of my life.

Father kept a stable of purebreds for hunting, and King Henricus housed them in a castle. Not even the stable hands were up, so I could take my time strolling along the stalls, eyeing each of the horses. There was a pinch in my chest, and

I clutched at the bone carving while I swallowed the lump. It would get easier with each passing day to forget Carlin and the small things that reminded me of our time together.

The animals were in perfect health, large and muscular, and I longed to ride freely by myself rather than being confined to the crown prince's side. Expecting food, the horses came toward me as I passed, some snorting and pawing at their hay, disguising the noises coming from the last stall.

I stilled in shock, my mind slow to recover, so I remained staring at Andriet and his guard lover locked in a feverish kiss, torsos stripped bare, limbs entwined, so thoroughly lost in each other. I should've ducked back to the previous stall or averted my eyes, and I was about to, but something in their shared hunger for each other stilled me. The guard's midnight skin contrasted against Andriet's pale body like the night sky meeting the soft glow of a silver moon. My body tingled alive at the wet sounds of their intense kisses and the fever they both shared. It hadn't been long ago I felt that desperate passion, and yet it felt like an eternity. I almost sobbed at the ache that cleaved through my heart. The loneliness tore a wound through my soul.

I'd made no sound, so it had to be the heat of my stare that alerted Andriet to my presence. Our eyes locked as he broke their kiss. An instant wash of heat flared up my throat into my cheeks as he jumped away from the guard.

"Tressya," he cried.

On seeing me, the guard covered his face as if in shame, then turned away, slinking down to the hay to retrieve his clothes. Too many people in my life had made me feel that way. Curses, that I would be someone to make another feel so wrongfully judged.

"I'm sorry," I snapped. "I didn't mean to..." *Stare.*

"Tressya. It's not—"

"No, don't." *Apologize.* This was humiliating. Not because of what I'd witness, but that I'd lingered, gawking at them.

The guard hurried to dress, doing a poor job. And I was perhaps making things worse by remaining to watch.

"I'll just—"

"Please, Tressya, let me explain." The pale skin on Andriet's chest turned red, the flush making its way up his neck and into his cheeks.

"There's nothing to explain." Then I winced. Did that sound dismissive? I turned my back, allowing them to dress while trying to shut out the sounds of their whispered exchange.

Once dressed, the guard rushed out of the stall and past me without glancing my way. Then, remembering himself, he doubled back and bowed, but he couldn't raise his head to meet my eyes. This was a disaster, but he fled before I could say anything to ease his shame.

I swiveled to face Andriet, wanting to soothe his humiliation, and found him buried in his tunic as he slipped it over his head. Now was the time to avert my gaze. I didn't. My eyes followed the striation of muscle along his flank as he bent to retrieve more clothing. He was lean but muscular, with a fine sheen of fair hair across his chest.

He took his time dressing, averting his eyes all the while until I could no longer hold my tongue. I moved across to the stall door as Andriet straightened, boots in hand.

"He... Ah... buttoned himself up crooked." Really? That's what I had to say as comfort?

Andriet looked as though he would curl in on himself, and I almost wept from the mortification in his eyes. I couldn't bear the devastation shadowing his features to make him look drawn and aged.

On seeing he was about to speak, I raised on my toes and placed my fingers over his lips. "I don't want to hear any apology. It's I that should apologize."

He pulled my fingers from his lips. But I used my other hand, smothering his mouth again. "I'm not that kind of princess, remember?"

I took both his hands and guided him along. "We can't steer our hearts." Then I slipped my arm through his, tucked myself in beside him, and walked us back along the horses' pens. "It's very clear you love him."

"I..." he shook his head.

I turned to face him, taking both his hands. "This is the most important thing you must learn about me. I would never judge a true and honest love. So few will ever feel it. So if you're one of the lucky few to have found it, then I say keep it safe and treasure it."

He seized my face between his palms. "I can't believe you. How did my brother become so fortunate and be such an idiot not to realize?"

I pressed my hands against his. "All we can do is take pity on the fools."

He chuckled, then sighed, dropping his hands as his expression turned, reflecting the sodden days that seemed to plague Tarragona. "You're right. I love Daelon. I've always loved him. We grew up together, you see. Sword fighting with wood until we were old enough to use blades. We were both confused by our feelings toward each other and too shy to voice them. Until they became too big, too intense to ignore."

He collapsed against the wood pillar, staring out the stable door. "But we're doomed. I have my duty as prince. Father's already scheming his next alliance. My head's on the block. I'll be married and forced to spend my life with someone I could never love. How will she ever understand?"

I went to him and rested a hand on his cheek, feeling the warm clamminess of his partially dry sweat. "Believe me, there is no one more understanding of how you feel than the woman standing in front of you."

He stretched his neck back and groaned. "It happened to you, didn't it?"

"Forbidden love. It's a joy. And a curse."

He leaned down and gently pressed his forehead to mine. "We can only rejoice in feeling the pain of our loss, for if we felt nothing, our hearts would be nothing but stone." He then placed a finger under my chin to lift my eyes to his. "We shall endure our broken hearts together."

"No. We'll do more than that. We'll survive. That I fervently promise because I am sick of enduring."

I'd endured my life in my father's court to Carlin. Far away from my seat of peace, I would find a new way to survive. The Mother had forced her will upon me by burying the mysterious dark mist within and nurturing a dormant talent. I would harness what grew inside of me to whatever end so that I would have the strength to shape my fate beyond my constraints, by whatever means necessary.

Andriet leaned close, so I felt the moist warmth of his breath on my cheeks. "I love your vehemence." He bared his teeth as he said the last word. "I wish it was mine own."

"Don't worry, I'll hold enough for the two of us."

The vehemence Andriet spoke of was liquid iron in my veins, fast hardening to form the mold of my body. Perhaps it would surround my heart until that too became encased in iron. Maybe that would be a blessing.

The stable hands disturbed us as they arrived to prepare the hunting horses. We ambled out to sit on the grass, where we exchanged love stories as if we were carefree, forgetting for the while both of us were chained to lives decided for us. Nothing about this moment felt real. Not even with Carlin had I found the chance to be honest about my heart. If only the moment would last for eternity; if only this was who I could be.

It wasn't. And soon the king's party arrived.

Andriet helped me to my feet while Lady Astaria's gaze roamed over my now creased skirt before skimming to Andriet with a secretive smirk. "Your Highnesses," she said in a wispy voice.

"Brother," drawled Juel. "This is really becoming a problem." He waved a finger between Andriet and I. "I fear what people will say."

It meant little to anyone that Lady Astaria arrived everywhere on Juel's arm.

"Nothing you won't encourage yourself, I'm sure." I curtsied in my usual graceless manner, then turned my back on

Juel, so I wouldn't have to look at his face. "Which horse is mine?"

"I believe it's this magnificent dapple gray."

My eyelids fluttered closed with my inhale on hearing his voice, but nothing could stop my wild raging heart. Already the strange tingling feeling bothered my wrist at the site of his bite.

Blowing out my held breath, I turned, hating how my deep inhale did nothing to ease the chaos raging inside of me.

I avoided his gaze and instead looked the horse over. "She's magnificent." I meant it, along with my genuine smile. I loved a powerful, headstrong animal, one that required skill to manage. I ran a hand down her neck, feeling a muscle quiver under my palm.

Bloodwyn moved close to the horse's face, his voice dropping low, narrowing the conversation to the two of us. "She'll require a strong hand. She's barely tame."

"Spoken like a true male. According to your kind, all powerful females are untamed and in need of strong handling."

My body reacted standing this close to him, burning a hole up through my core, incinerating my common sense. Two days on from our time at Emberforge, mercifully away from his suffocating presence, and I remembered I was a disciple, but my body continued to fight against me.

Discipline. As a disciple, he was my enemy.

Do not forget that. If the Mother knew about the Razohan claim, maybe she wouldn't have tied me to the House of Tannard. But she didn't. Which meant my duty hadn't changed. The Tannard line currently upon the Tarragonan throne remained mine to protect. I would marry Juel and birth the next heir. It didn't matter that the Razohan filled my senses, so I could think of no one else when he was around.

Since my duty was clear, I should let everyone know who drank and danced and reveled beside them, and who had joined the hunt, while plotting the House of Tannard's end. But I didn't even know his real name or his real face.

Bloodwyn had convinced everyone of who he was, moving amongst them like he was one of them and no one noticed anything unusual in his mannerisms or countenance. Had the Razohan changed his features to look like Bloodwyn, or had he assumed Bloodwyn completely? If the latter, it would explain how he knew so much about the goings on in Emberforge. He'd skillfully milked Petrulus's mind of all his knowledge.

By the way they all accepted Bloodwyn, I knew I would have a hard time convincing anyone of my sanity if I announced him as a traitor. That was the sort of dangerous skill I was up against.

I couldn't help my eyes from following the gentle strokes he ran along the horse's cheek, like a loving caress. I licked my lips and turned away. The prickly heat coursing through my body turned the stupid riding outfit into a prison.

"Your Highness is an accomplished rider?" The purring sound of his voice speared a shard of longing like a red hot lance into my groin.

"Her Highness is a more accomplished hunter."

He arched a brow. "Excellent. I look forward to the chase."

"It will be hard to look forward when you have two stakes stuck in both eyes."

His chuckle left me speechless. I gritted my teeth and turned away. Damn that I liked the sound of it.

It was a good thing I'd finished dressing myself once Radnisa left the room after delivering her usual diatribe. Beneath my voluminous riding habit, I'd strapped one dagger to my thigh. I'd yet to devise a plan for how I would retrieve it in a hurry, but it was now warm from my body heat and pressed solid against my thigh as a reminder I was not without help. If he continued to distract me, I would stake him and be done with it.

"A friendly warning. Stay out of my way on this hunt. I'm guaranteed to mistake you for prey." I kept my voice low.

"Come now, princess. We had such fun the last time we met."

I looked around, fearing Juel and Lady Astaria were still close. Silly me. As if they would find my conversation of any interest. Juel was helping her onto her horse across the courtyard.

"I woke up with my sanity intact today."

Bloodwyn dipped under the horse's head, and I jerked away in surprise, but he caught my waist and pulled me closer. I slapped his hand away, tempted to step back, but I never stepped back from anyone.

He took advantage of my reluctance to step away and leaned down, our faces too close for decency. "You know who I am."

"And you're one breath away from everyone else knowing who you are, so move away and let me breathe."

A muscle in his jaw twitched. "I'm the legitimate heir to the throne."

"Two other males here can also claim that title." I was serious. I couldn't breathe because if I did I would smell...him.

"I said legitimate." He spoke with clenched teeth.

Discipline. No way would I allow him to think his proximity was affecting me. "Is this how you win hearts?"

"It's how I tease my enemies." He winked. He bloody well winked at me.

Curses to my body. What was it doing to me? I was showered in hot ash every time the Razohan got near me. My skin pebbled and prickled wanting to feel his touch.

When he leaned down to whisper in my ear, my heart felt like it tried to punch out of my ribcage. "I'm going to win, Tressya. The throne is mine."

"That's a problem because I intend to win." I held my breath rather than allow the smell of him to become a memory. *Good luck, Tressya.* I feared it already was lodged deep inside my mind.

"You don't understand what's at stake. If you did, you would abandon Henricus and his sons and come to my side."

"Because you told me to?" I scoffed, my voice rising too loud.

Bloodwyn glanced over my shoulder.

"Your arrogance is typical—"

"Listen." The amber in his eyes became more like the glow of flames. "I mistook you for an intelligent woman, one who knew how to survive. I hate to learn I was wrong."

I ignored his belittling remarks. "I'll ensure you fail."

Bloodwyn sucked in a breath, baring his teeth. "You have no power to stop me. You can't control my soul. I've already warned you."

"Do you really think that's all I'm capable of?"

"Make haste, princess," Andriet came up beside me, breaking the stalemate of our hardened stares. "The others are about to leave."

I looked around to see the court had already mounted and was preparing to head through the gates.

"Yes," I said, sounding like I'd woken from a dream. Nightmare more like it. "I'll be right there." I gave Bloodwyn one more narrow-eyed glare. "You can never hide from me, no matter your disguise," I whispered, flittering my gaze across his body.

"I don't intend to hide from you."

"You can't take all of her attention," Andriet grumbled to Bloodwyn, grabbing my arm and pulling me toward my stirrups.

The cacophony of barks and whines from the hunting dogs filled the air as the horses snorted and pranced, growing jittery to the excitement building through the gathered party.

I swung up into the saddle before the stable hand could place the footstool on the ground, or Andriet could put a hand to my waist.

"Well done," he said. "You're a masterful horse rider as well, I see. Is there no end to your talents?"

"As if I would share my weaknesses," I teased, then, remembering who was present, I swallowed my smile and looked over Andriet to Bloodwyn, who waited on his large black gelding, his eyes on our exchange. I glared at him, wanting his attention far from Andriet, even if it meant placing it all on me.

The Mother would be furious if she knew how much I risked the House of Tannard by allowing their enemy to walk amongst them unchallenged. But I would allow him his secret for now. Besides, I was not without skill. His soul may be protected from the Sistern's power, but I was not defenseless, and growing even less defenseless over time thanks to my developing skill in the death arts. I welcomed him to be my shadow. As I would shadow him.

The horn marked the beginning of the hunt. The budding excitement unleashed once the king led the hunting party clear of the gates, and many spurred their horses into a mad gallop, inciting the dogs into a frenzy of barks as they raced the horses across the field. If the barking dogs weren't enough to alert the forest creatures of the hunt, the thundering hooves would send them scurrying to escape. It seemed the hunt was more for showmanship and not a successful kill.

****

After hours of riding, there was still no sign of our quarry, and the hunting party was now spread out. Some had lost interest, while others grew more interested in enjoying the beautiful day.

The king was intent on catching his stag and drove a group of noblemen to the south of the forest. I could hear the baying dogs, still wild with excitement, and their horses' pounding hooves. Andriet rode alongside his father. I wondered if the reason he was intent on keeping pace was to prove his riding skills in front of the king.

I slowed my mare, savoring my solitude. After hours on the move, she didn't fight me. Instead, she slipped contently into a gentle pace. At home, few could keep my pace once I was on a horse. Whereas now, I preferred to waste as much time as I could meandering over fallen logs and pretending there was no one else in the forest but me, so my frustration was real when I heard the heavy thuds of a horse's hooves.

Please, let that be Andriet. It wouldn't be because I last saw him leaning far over his horse's withers, determined to lead the hunt. It could be none other than my shadow. Fine. I felt ready to unleash some of my venom. Who knew, maybe during the process, I would trick him into revealing more of his schemes.

I glanced over my shoulder as the horse neared. To my dismay, I saw it was Juel approaching. Never mind. I had no intention of gaining my future husband's adoration, so he might as well feel some of my mood at being disturbed.

"The hunt has left you behind," he said.

"And Lady Astaria, it would seem."

"On the contrary, she's neck to neck with Andriet. The hunt stimulates her passion. She's quite the fire when she gets going. Not you. It would seem."

"I don't kill for pleasure. Only when the need arises."

He humphed, then his wane smile dropped, and he frowned, perhaps trying to work out my meaning.

"For the happiness of both of us, we should make an

agreement. You're obviously thrilled with Lady Astaria and—"

"Are you trying to dictate our marriage terms?" He sounded affronted.

"I'm trying to find a way forward between us that will stall my dreams of killing you."

"I beg your pardon," he spat.

"Let's not play games, Juel. Neither of us wanted this marriage. I'm offering you—"

"Wait." He snapped. "You're marrying into the House of Tarragona, the wealthiest, most powerful lineage in the near realms. I command legions your father, ruling over his miserable little kingdom, could only dream about. Power lies at my command. I need only click my fingers, and women fall to their knees and beg for my attention. And you're what Merania gives me. The Crown Prince of Tarragona." He snorted a derisive sound before turning away.

With the hunt moving ever more distant, a lark sung out a call.

"A woman like you," Juel continued, just when I thought he'd exhausted himself, and hoped he would ride on. It was obvious I would get no cooperation out of him. "There would've been few offers coming your way."

He shook his head as he huffed a breath. "Your father deceived us, and yet we upheld the alliance when it was within our right to refuse."

I strove for my calming breaths. "Look, Juel—"

"Who would want to marry a bastard? It's only because our heritage is so strong we bothered to contemplate such a union."

That word. After all these years; after all the times I'd suffered hearing that word and all the ways people twisted it like a knife through my gut, why did it still hold the power to diminish me? It was as though Juel knew it, stabbing it around whenever he could. His circumstances were far superior to mine, even without the title of bastard. He knew that, which meant he used it with pleasure.

Perhaps now he'd exhausted his anger he would stay quiet. Our marriage was coming too fast, and I wanted us to agree before I was forced into his bed. I had to make this as pleasant for myself as possible. That hope diminished now I had wounded his pride.

"What of the claim from the northern men?"

He reined in his horse. "What of it?" he snapped, then laughed, but it was dry of humor. "Are you suggesting they're more worthy? Maybe we should send you north. Those beast-men might well mistake you for one of their own. I'm sure you would take great pleasure in being—"

"Oh look. There's a stag." Not a stag at all, but a young doe. Still, it would shut him up.

He glanced in the direction I pointed, then looked ready to share another scathing remark. Bother, he wasn't interested.

"Fine. I'll make this one mine." And I dug my heels into the sides of my horse.

She exploded from under me, but I was ready. Gripping my legs firm to her flanks, I leaned forward to give her her head. In my periphery, I saw Juel react likewise, and I couldn't help but smirk. No way would he allow a woman, and a bastard at that, get the better of him in a hunt.

Juel's horse was larger than mine. Its strong powerful legs vanished the distance with each stride, but the mare was swift and agile, weaving through the trees faster than the larger horse could manage. Even so, it would be hard to lose such an accomplished rider.

With our sudden turn of speed, the doe fled. Being so small, it disappeared into the thicket without a trace. For me, this was not about the doe or the chase, so it didn't bother me we'd lost her. I spurred my horse on, giving her as much rein as I could, determined to be the one to win because this had turned into a race.

Our horses soared across the ground as if they had wings. One misplaced step, and a fall could be deadly, but I was as caught in this challenge of wills and skill as much as Juel. Weaving through the trees, clearing fallen logs, we paced each other as though our lives depended on our success. It was more than our lives. It was our pride. The doe was long forgotten.

In places, the forest grew dense, forcing our horses apart. In other places, it cleared, giving us a glimpse of each other hunched low in our pursuit. Whenever our eyes met, I could read the furious determination set as ugly creases across his brow and around his mouth, his body hunched, tense, out of rhythm with his horse's stride. When his horse veered around a tree, he looked ready to topple from his seat, and my heart rose in triumph. It was his strength and skill that kept him in place.

We rode so fast the wind snagged my hair and sent it billowing behind me. The cold bit hard against my cheeks and found many ways to get beneath my clothes to chill my skin.

As we raced toward a large fallen log, I gathered the reins and prepared to go with my mount as she cleared the thinnest end. When her hooves hit the ground, Juel's sharp cry ripped through the air. I reined my mare in hard and spun to see he'd gone down. His horse lay across the lower half of his body.

I would be lying if I said I didn't feel a thrill, but the pleasure vanished when I realized his horse wasn't moving despite his howls of agony and punishing fists as he punched the animal's body.

There were two choices I could make; one I would love to take without a second thought, but that was not the choice I made because I was yet to be so hateful and cold as to turn my back. He was of the Tannard line, the man I was supposed to marry.

I dismounted and led my mare back toward him. His howls of agony silenced the birds and muffled my horse's clomping hooves, but not the beat of my thumping heart. My body felt numb, and a strange emptiness filled my heart the closer I came.

The blood quickly coated the dead leaves and moss on the forest floor, before mixing with the loamy soil to create a sludge under his right thigh. So much blood, it had to have come from his horse.

"I'm injured. Get help, woman."

I slung the reins over a broken branch and approached.

"Stupid woman. Can't you see I need help?" he squealed.

"Of all my luck, I'm stranded with an imbecile." Then he let out a series of curses and long, drawn-out howls.

"It looks as though the horse's neck's broken."

"What do I care about the horse?" His voice rose into a high-pitched hysteria. "I don't care about the horse. For mercy's sake, you stupid woman, get me help."

The horse, he no doubt took much pride in, now pinned him to his possible death.

I crouched. "I can't move the horse myself. And I doubt anyone will reach you in time."

I was sure now the blood was his.

"What are you saying? You murdering whore. What are you saying?" He screamed at me, eyes flaring wide in horror. "Father will take your head for this." He looked at the sky. "Mercy on my soul." His eyes rolled back to me, his face a mask of vicious fury. "You murdering whore," he spat with as much venom as he could muster, but I could see his energy waning, see the exertion it took to mount such hatred.

The luster of his complexion, the soft pink drawn from the hard ride, drained from his cheeks, and a fine sheen of sweat broke out across his brow.

I bent lower, positioning myself so I could see his leg better as I tried to determine where the blood came from. His sword, which he'd not removed from his waist, had pierced through the leather sheath protecting the sharp blade. The glint of its polished metal caught in the weak sun's rays. When he fell, it must have severed through his thigh.

"Mercy, you wretched whore, have mercy," he cried. His voice broke, and his eyes filled with tears. Neither triggered any of my mercy. Was this the true feeling of a heart made of stone?

"I'm your betrothed, the crown prince," he croaked. Fear filled his eyes and dribbled out with every word he spoke.

I looked into his pale eyes, thinking how glass-like they were now, easily shattered. "And I'm sorry mine is the last face you'll see."

"Arrrrh," he growled, but his voice lacked vigor despite how much his fury clung to him. "You fucking bitch. I'll kill you." Then, mustering the last of his strength, he screamed for help.

It could've been instincts. Maybe it was my one chance at revenge, or perhaps my heart really had turned to stone because I smothered his mouth with my hand. "Die with honor, not as a baby crying for its mother," I hissed.

His eyes grew so wide I saw the rimming white, filled with fine red veins that were now pale. He grabbed at my wrist, but there was no strength in his hold.

I couldn't look at him as I held my hand to his mouth with my heart thumping so hard it felt like my body vibrated. A small part of me screamed, but a bigger part of me held my hand firm to his mouth and tried to ignore the way he feebly pawed at my wrist. I was going against the Mother's command, suppressing the screams from the man she sent me here to marry.

Would it curse me to act so vile and cruel? *Mother, I hope you don't hate me for this.* She was a disciple herself. Of course she would understand.

When he released my wrist, I still couldn't look at him. I stared out into the forest, my pulse violating my body with its harsh rhythm. I would never know what effect my choice had until it was too late, but right now, this felt like freedom.

Finally, when the warmth of his breath ceased, I removed my hand and turned away, rising to my feet. It was too late to make another choice, too late to act as a good disciple should.

"This is your home now," I said. "This is where you will reign, over dead trees, fallen logs, moss, and insects." I turned around to find his spirit hovering above his glazed eyes, staring vacantly at the sky. He looked at himself, at first in shock, then horror, once he realized what it all meant.

"You," he snarled and rushed forward until he was right in my face, his expression twisted in vengeful fury, and I tried my hardest to stay where I was and not stagger away from him to avoid his touch.

"Say what you want to say."

The fury vanished. "You... you see me?"

"Yes. That's my talent. But right now, I wish it wasn't."

"You murdering whore. We should've sunk your ship before you reached the shore," he growled.

"But you didn't, and here you are now, through no fault but your own."

"This is how you wanted it. Wasn't it, you conniving wench? You'll never be queen. You ruined your chance when you let me die. Father has no use for you. In fact, he loathes the sight of you. Bastard whore."

For once, hearing the word affected me little. "The dead can't reach me." I patted my chest. His words held no power to pierce my heart.

"No one will love you. Who could ever love a bastard? And an ugly one at that."

He jutted his face forward, and I feared he would get too close and force me to endure his icy touch. As of yet, he didn't realize how the dead made me feel. If he knew, there would be no end to his touching me. His handsome face was contorted with the poison in his heart, but I stayed where I was, meeting his glare as the thundering of horses' hooves grew steadily louder.

"They'll know you did it," Juel laughed. "You'll lose your head for murdering me," he shouted into my face.

We were eye to eye, with only a hand's width separating us. The pounding hooves of the approaching horses trembled through the ground and into me.

I screamed.

Juel's hands grasped for my neck. The ice of his fingers, like sharp shards, stabbed through my throat, filling me with the suffocating well of his rage. Losing my balance, I stumbled sideways, my vision blurring to an oily darkness. My legs gave out, and I went to my knees, sinking into a mud pit of Juel's loathing. His icy grip choked, while fear clung to me like a fierce giant's fingers.

I tried to rise to my feet. "You're mine when you die," he snarled into my ear.

My hands were at my throat, pulling at the collar, trying to release a grip that wasn't there, desperate for a breath. "Let go," I groaned, but his sudden and relentless assault left me without my wits. I couldn't think straight to summon enough determined energy into my voice.

"You're bound to this forest," I gasped. "Your power is over the insects now."

I screamed. It warbled out of me, dying and hoarse at the last. Juel loomed up in front of me. Leaning close, all I saw was the ugly sneer on his face. I doubled forward, violently retching my breakfast, my body falling through his as his wicked laughter echoed through my head.

Once I finished vomiting, I tried again to lurch from the ice of his grasp and his unending venomous emotions, but he clung to me like mud. This was my punishment for the choice I made, so I surrendered, allowing his spirit form to pass through me as I screamed. Again, and again, and again. No matter how much I drowned in Juel's chill and his unending hatred, I kept screaming until it hurt my throat.

"You can no longer affect the living," I gasped, panting my breaths.

"I seem to affect you," he sneered, holding his mouth to my ear.

"You're now a part of history."

The hunting party burst into the small clearing. I fell to my hands and knees, taking Juel with me.

"Help him," I begged through forced tears as Juel clung to my back like a cloak. "Juel, please, help him." Then I dissolved into wails as Andriet, the king, and many others jumped down from their horses.

"You fucking bitch. Stop it," Juel hissed, his face still close to my ear.

"He's..." I swallowed, striving to find my way clear of the ferocity of Juel's emotions. "He's... there's so much blood." I stumbled to my feet, tripping over my skirts, the hem now heavy with grime. "His horse went down." I palmed my mouth, then let out a wail. "Juel." The agony in my voice surprised even me.

Men were running. The small clearing turned to chaos. On seeing his father approach his body, Juel finally released me and shadowed his father.

"It was her. Father, it was her. Take her head. Take that fucking bitch's head."

My mind swam free from the weight of his emotions, but after such a struggle, I was exhausted. And I would play on that exhaustion. After all, trauma would make any woman faint. I covered my face but saw partial movement through my fingers and the concern in Andriet's eyes as he rushed toward me.

I gave into the heaviness in my limbs having struggled in a mental battle with Juel for so long, having worn every foul emotion his vengeful heart contained, and buckled into the hands at my waist, allowing them to take my weight and sweep me into strong arms. I turned to look up at Andriet, but it was Bloodwyn who held me secure to his chest.

He smiled down at me and murmured, "That was an excellent show, princess."

CHAPTER

TWENTY

TRESSYA

"Stupid, stupid girl. You've ruined everything."

I sat at my bureau, watching Radnisa's reflection through the mirror as she strode toward me. Her expression matched the fiery hatred of Juel's spirit as Bloodwyn had carried me to my horse.

She stood over me, staring down at my reflection. "You know I had a word with the Mother the day of our departure. I told her I would do my utmost to ensure you fulfilled your duty, but that I felt sure you would fail."

She leaned close to my ear. "All you had to do was spread your legs." She straightened. "But you couldn't even do that. Instead, you went and killed him."

Our eyes remained fixed upon each other. "You've lost your chance now. You've destroyed the Mother's plans. She'll cut you off. The Mother has no use for disciples who can't

318

uphold their duty. Especially disciples who can't even command soul voice."

She arched a brow. "You've always been a disappointment to her. I believe it was because of your mother she kept you, trained you, though you showed no promise, even when you were little. And now, it's amounted to nothing."

"The king wants his alliance. There's still Andriet."

She laughed. "With you?" Then rapidly dropped her false amusement. "The king didn't even want you. Gossip below the stairs says he was bitterly disappointed on seeing you and was half tempted to send you back. Well, he'll send you back for sure now." She sighed. "Back to your father's court. And without the Mother's protection, where will your fate land? Nowhere good, I can assure you."

Once she was no longer glaring down at me, instead pacing away while she continued to whip me with her malevolent words, I dipped my head, closed my eyes, and exhaled long and slow. As much as I raged to refute every word, she was right, unless I could persuade the king to marry Andriet and I.

I lifted my head to stare at my reflection. My skin looked as pale as Juel's shortly before he died. I placed my elbows on my bureau and covered my mouth with my hands, staring at my reflection and seeing only defeat. I couldn't go back, not to the hostility of father's court. But I would rather endure an eternity of barbs from his court than face the Mother and the disappointment in her eyes.

Mother, you can't abandon me.

A knock at the door silenced Radnisa.

"What is it?" snapped Radnisa as she strode for the door.

The young maid flinched as the door swept wide. "What do you want?" Radnisa barked.

The young maid dipped her gaze and curtsied. She slunk past Radnisa and into the room. "Your Highness. The king has summoned you."

It seemed the king needed only one day to decide. That did not bode well for me.

Radnisa folded her arms and paced into the middle of the room, running her tongue inside her cheek. "That didn't take long," she mused.

"Thank you," I said to the young girl and rose from my stool.

She fled from the room, avoiding Radnisa's arrow sharp eyes. Once she'd closed the door, Radnisa strolled across to my bed and perched herself on the edge. "I hadn't thought he would move so quick." She ran her hand over the covers, as if smoothing away any wrinkles. "Don't worry. I'll pack your things while you're with the king."

"Do as you please," I said as I strode for the door.

In the corridor, I took a moment to steady myself. I knew there would be repercussions upon Juel's death, but I'd been disconnected from my feelings and couldn't think straight. How could I not feel triumphant in his death? The feeling, however, was sour, interlocked with doubt, and I'd sat at my bureau for hours trying to work out what it meant for my future.

Radnisa had spoken the words I feared. I released a sob, then muffled the noise with my hand and gritted my teeth, exhaling a shaky breath. I could make this work; I could save myself. I just had to be smart. The king had no reason to hold his end of the alliance when there was no prince to marry, but there was Andriet: my only hope.

I ran a hand down my skirts to straighten them when a young woman appeared in my path. "You gotta be 'er."

I glanced over my shoulder, checking for living servants in the hall, then back to the spirit servant girl with hair so thin in places I saw her pale scalp underneath. That wasn't the only thing about her that was thin. Her cheeks were hollow, wrists and collar bones were jutting angles, and her eyes were bulging as if about to pop from their sockets.

"I'm sorry. I have no time to talk. The king's waiting." I felt I couldn't dismiss the little waif without at least acknowledging her.

"Yeah, I know 'bout that."

"I suppose you do. What's your name?"

"Deliah."

"I'm sure you know mine."

She nodded, then did nothing else but stare at me.

"Can you tell me what the king wishes to say to me?"

"His son's dead, and he ain't shed a tear. Yeah, and he's gonna send you back."

"I thought as much." I sighed, as I stared ahead, already thinking of ways to make him change his mind.

"You got to change his mind 'cause you're the only one we can talk to. It ain't no good 'round here when all you got is the same pricks you been talkin' to for a century."

I ignored her plea, instead concentrated on making my plans. "What can you tell me about the Creed wizards?" Did they know of the treasonous plot between Lord Dowel and others. If so, perhaps they'd already told the king, and I would lose my leverage.

She made to spit on the ground. "Don't trust 'em. Wicked lot. They only care 'bout another Tannard sittin' on the throne."

"How many are there?"

"Too many. I ain't know for sure since their home is Emberforge. Rumor has it they hope to claim the Bone Throne."

"What's so important about the Bone Throne?"

"Powerful it was. As was he. It's the reason the Levenians invaded. Greedy lot. They wanted to steal the power for 'em elves."

"Wait. Who held the power, the king or the throne?"

"Both."

"I don't understand you."

"The king had a mighty power. But he needed the Bone Throne to...I don't know. I'm only repeating what I 'eard. It's confusin'. You'll 'ave to ask one of 'em pricks if you want to understand."

She had to mean Truett, Borrat and Albert. "So this Bone Throne is no longer powerful?"

"You gotta ask 'em lot. I'm dead. What do I care about anythin' anymore?"

"That explains why they've claimed Emberforge as their temple," I mused to myself.

Hurrying footsteps distracted me. Through Deliah's translucent body, I saw a maid reaching the top of the stairs.

"Oh, curses, the king," I said. Only at the last did I stop myself from accidentally passing through Deliah in my haste to get to the throne room. I skittered on my feet, then ducked around her, which must have looked queer to the maid, for she gave me a quizzical look.

"I know. The king's waiting," I said as I dashed past her and raced down the stairs.

I was almost at the throne room doors when a hooded figure emerged from the same shadowy alcove as he did on my arrival in Tolum. I yelped to a stop as he glided across the stone floor toward me. Half a head taller than me, he kept his neck angled in such a way as to keep his face in the shadow of his hood, giving me the slimmest glimpse of the ruddy color on the tip of his nose. "Princess," came that similar slimy voice.

Orphus.

Covered entirely in those thick woven gray robes, height was their only distinguishing feature; and now I had the tip of Orphus's nose I could use to discern him from his hooded Creed. As he neared, I called on all my resolve to stay where I was and not shrink away in revulsion.

In the few days I'd been at Emberfell, I'd spent little time in the presence of the Salmun. Andriet said they were the real strength behind Tarragona's wealth and power and yet they seemed content to float in the shadows, playing little part in the day to day running of the kingdom.

"Orphus, isn't it," I said.

At our first meeting, he smelt of rituals. Now I thought perhaps he'd been interrupted from cooking his dinner as the smokey smell of burned hopweed and fat overwhelmed me.

"Indeed, young princess." Like a snake, he trailed the

word with a long hiss. "Shall we?" He gestured toward the doors with a bow.

Curses. I didn't want him present but was in no position to demand he stay outside the throne room. For a foolish moment, I lost my composure and slipped my mental barrier, probing outward, looking for a crack in that hard wall I'd encountered on our first meeting.

The hard wall was gone. My mind pierced inside without restraint, down, down, deep inside, down, down as a syrupy ooze bound to my mind and pulled me under, like my heavy wet skirts around my feet when I fell into the ocean. I floundered, unable to penetrate to the heart of his essence, unable to force my focus on my purpose. Instead, I drowned. This time, there was no one to save me.

Interesting. The ferocity of my beating heart was the only thing to mute the sinister voice as it echoed through my head. I flailed inside an ocean of shadows without a grip or a saving hand to help me heave myself free. I had to save myself. I tried to withdraw my awareness, but the syrupy feeling coating my mind hardened like dried sap.

I haven't finished with you yet.

No surprise, his mental strength was much greater than mine. I had no hope of wrenching free. Blessed Mother, my fate was not to be brought down by a ruddy-nosed, hooded creep.

I dragged in a sharp breath. *Discipline.* No one caged my mind. Then exhaled. At some point, fear had leaked into my veins. I yanked it close, wrapped it around my mind to use as spikes. Fear harnessed became a weapon, summoning my focus, sparking my awareness, amplifying my determination.

My jaw ached under the strain of my concentration, and my nails dug into my palm. The fine pain was my anchor, the place I pulled against to heave my mind free.

Discipline. This was a fight of wills, and I had to win. I focused on building my barrier, the void I buried my mind behind, but already, I felt a lethargy seeping into my mind, the exertion from the war between our wills as the binds of his mind towed me under. I thought of the ocean, what it had felt like to flail yet to find nothing, grasping for a hold that wasn't there. I clawed in a breath. The Mother had taught me to be better than this. I won't lose this fight. I couldn't lose this fight. Orphus would not master my mind.

You will not win. That was my solemn promise. I tunneled all my focus on the amorphous mass of my darkness, the emptiness that was my pit for all who dared to cross. I could feel the hollow expanse building around me, my body growing weightless. Unlike floundering in the ocean, I was floating, despite the weight of Orphus's hold. And it was freedom. It was empowerment. Then, out of that void, something grew, a feeling that tugged at a place deep inside of me, something so familiar yet ancient and comforting.

Aetherius. The illusionary, the indescribable, the true essence of myself. My soul word, the very thing that came to me from the depths of the void I'd created. *Aetherius.* The word resonated through my mind, like a volcano to blow the binds of Orphus's mental chains free.

I gasped, swaying for balance as I sprang forth from deep within my mind and into the corridor. I panted breaths as my heart raced. *Aetherius* was my savior. Our soul words as protective barriers against the mind control of soul voice was not something the Sistern taught in training. It was up to us as disciples to learn the truth. Neither was it logical to think the word that bound me when uttered by another was the same word to set me free when uttered by me. My soul word was my power.

The first prickle at the back of my neck rose in time with the soft *shush* of his cloak across the floor. He moved closer. The heat of his presence scorched along my side like a raging fire.

"The princess is not as we expected." His voice slithered across my shoulder like an unwelcome hand.

"I'm nothing more than a woman with a little mind trick, which would win her some coin at a town fair."

"Those who stay out of the light have the most to hide."

"I'm hardly hiding."

He was standing at my side now. "I fear the House of Whelin has played King Henricus for a fool."

This close, I could see underneath his hood to a face steeped in shadows. There was nothing distinguishable about his features except his hooded eyes, white as snow, and the dark smudges underneath. He had tattooed over his left eye two black ink-like lines forming a cross. The thicker line ran from brow to cheek, and the second, smaller line, started close to the base of his nose and ran across his cheek to slash through the other line close to its end.

"Father fulfilled the treaty under difficult circumstances. What happened to my sister was out of his control."

"Juel was an excellent rider."

The prickles were no longer confined to the places on my body closest to where he stood. They invaded my entire being, itching and crawling like beetles. "If you're searching for a killer, then you need look no further than his pride. I, too, am an excellent rider. He simply wouldn't let me win."

It was hard to say where his gaze landed on me, until he lifted one hand, pointing a long, yellowed nail at my chest. "What is that?" It was as though his voice glided through the air and across my chest.

I looked down, unsure what he meant, and saw the carved bone necklace. I covered it with my palm. "A trinket from a friend." It was strange Carlin's necklace should gain so much attention. I liked Orphus's attention on the necklace even less than the Razohan's.

"Bone." It wasn't a question.

"He worked with whatever he could."

Orphus tapped his two fingers together, so the long nails clicked against each other.

"Most interesting."

"The king is waiting." I had to flee from him and his serpentine voice.

"Indeed." Orphus inclined his head one more time. "The king does not like to be kept waiting."

I continued to the doors, conscious of Orphus following behind. He moved silently if not for the *shushing* of his cloak across the floor, but I couldn't shake the feeling of his essence, the binding of my body until I felt I couldn't breathe. My heart beat wild again, forcing me to take calming breaths as the sentinels swung open the large doors.

The king sat on his throne, half turned in his seat and

staring out the vast stretch of window. Everything about today reflected the solemn mood that seemed to crush the atmosphere in the room, from the king's clothes to the deep gray clouds outside, to the weight laying heavy in my stomach.

Standing at the bottom of the dais and to the left of the king stood three men, one I had seen at the ball, Lord Arobet, but the others I didn't know. Each wore velvet and silk doublets adorned with embroidery and fine jewels and cuffs to cover their hands. They belonged to the king's council for sure, which meant any or all could be involved in the treasonous plot.

I shifted my gaze from them to the king, who'd yet to turn his attention from the window.

"Your Majesty." I bowed, for once trying to find the grace I lacked. There was only one man who I'd ever bothered to please, yet today was the day I would attempt to please the one man who could save me.

King Henricus stayed like stone, staring out the window as if *I* was a spirit.

Orphus glided past me, leaving me awash in tingling chills, and glided up the dais. He leaned over and murmured in the king's ear.

The king grunted, then turned to face me. I stayed in his hard gaze for a long time, averting my eyes to the floor so as not to antagonize him.

He huffed, then rearranged himself on his throne. "I'll be direct." He slouched into his seat. "Your presence in Emberfell is no longer needed. Your purpose was to give me an heir. And now my son is dead. You no longer have a purpose."

The king couldn't send me back to Aldorr, not to my father's court. While I adored the idea of seeing Carlin again, I couldn't face the Mother having failed her. I just couldn't. Was Radnisa right in saying the Mother would reject me if I returned?

"Your Majesty, if—"

"The weather is against us, but come the first change in the winds, you'll be on that ship. You may stay at Emberfell until then, but I shall restrict your movements to the castle and its grounds."

"Your Majesty," Orphus said. "Perhaps it would be wise to rethink—"

"My eldest is dead," the king shouted. "There is nothing to rethink. We no longer need her."

"Andriet...Your...Majesty," I stammered, which was met with huffs of derision from the three councilmen. Desperation had made me raise my voice, so I dropped into a low curtsey, keeping my head bowed. "I'm sorry for speaking out, Your Majesty, but your younger son—"

"Is already betrothed. The bride is on her way."

I couldn't breathe as I jerked my head up to look at the king.

"We agreed upon the alliance. There is no going back," the king finished.

"Your Majesty, there are—"

"Silence, Orphus. Stop sniveling in my ear."

Orphus was trying to undermine the king's determination. I wasn't grateful for his help. I had foolishly opened my mind to him—a terrible mistake any of my sisters would never have made—and now he possibly knew my secrets.

Curiously, he spoke for me, not against me to the king. What could this mean for me? "Please, Your Majesty, I would like to ask for a word in private."

The sudden silence blew in like winds drawn by a storm, to be disturbed by a councilman, who stepped forward before the king and bowed. "The request is preposterous."

"Quiet," Henricus replied to the pompous man, then he looked at me. "These are members of my trusted council. What would you have to say that none present can't hear?"

I didn't want Orphus present but could think of no way of getting rid of him.

"Sire, I beg you to excuse my silence to your request. I assure you what I have to say in private will benefit you and Tarragona immensely."

"You can't possibly—"

"Thank you, Lord Arobet, but it's a matter I shall deliberate on without the guidance of the council." He returned his gaze to me. "I'm intrigued. First she wants to marry Andriet, and now she gives me secrets."

"The princess is not to be trusted, Sire." The nobleman continued with his fight.

"It's not a trick, Sire. You shall hear for yourself."

"And why is one so shy as to request a private audience is my question?"

"I can only say you'll be glad for the privacy when you hear what I have to say."

"By being mysterious, she is deliberately trying to seduce you to her will. Sire, please, do not—"

"Clear the room," the king announced with a wave of his hand.

"Sire—"

"That means you, Arobet."

The three lords glanced at each other, then reluctantly left the room, but Orphus stayed standing beside the king. It surprised me the king had agreed, but I doubted I could push Orphus from the room as well. While I loathed remaining in his presence, I knew he wasn't part of the treasonous plot, given the wizards' sole duty was to keep the Tannard line on the throne.

"It is as you wanted. I've cleared the room. Tell me, what secrets are so important that you would be so rude as to kick my council out?"

"Sire, I believe some of your trusted are plotting against you."

Moments passed, but the king's expression remained as if seized in stone. Then, slowly, his shrewd gaze cut deep inside of me as he gripped the armrests of his throne. "That is a treasonous claim."

"I have names."

"How has a stranger, who has not even spent a week within Emberfell, uncovered this plot?" Orphus asked, gliding forward on the dais.

The king didn't reprimand Orphus for speaking above him, instead, he glanced at Orphus as one would a superior. Here now, I was witnessing the true power of the wizards. Though they slunk in the shadows, Henricus knew they were the real power that kept him on his throne. He sat there like a servant awaiting his master's command.

"There is little that is hidden from those who remain in the shadows," I said.

The king looked to his wizard, seeking Orphus's judgement.

"Give us names?" Orphus said.

"There will be many more, but the people you want to question are The Duke of Eerlie, Earl of Vaelorin, and Lord Dowel."

The king's face drained pale.

Orphus took another step closer and stopped at the edge of the dais. "Do you understand what you're doing? These men are on the king's council. Very prominent and influential men. If it's proven you have lied, they will ask for your head."

"And if it's proven to be true, then I ask the king for a favor."

"And what may that be?" Orphus continued to speak for the king.

I focused on the king. "Allow me to think on my answer."

Orphus held his head at an angle, so I couldn't see his face, but I felt the probing of his mind, cautiously running across the surface of mine like a lutist's fingers light across the strings. In the king's presence, I tried to ignore his intrusion, hoping it was a subtle warning and nothing more, until the spear of his attack felt like a lance through my skull.

I groaned, pressing my hands to my temples.

"What is wrong with her?" the king demanded.

Eyes squeezed close, I tried to dredge up my soul word, but Orpheus's attack muddled my concentration.

"Is the woman mad?" The king's cry sounded faint.

This was a threat, or perhaps a lesson.

Discipline. A lesson I refused to heed. I abandoned trying to fight him, and instead focused on harnessing the wild thrash of my heart, the dizzying fear of being defeated and allowed my soul word to come to me.

Aetherius. It consumed my mind and poured into my veins like blood. *Aetherius!* My mental shout released the terrible force on my mind. I grunted with the shear effort it had taken to win free as Orphus staggered backward, clutching his head.

"Orphus," the king shouted.

"All is right, Your Majesty," Orphus intoned, holding up his hand to silence any more the king may say.

"Go," Henricus barked at me. "You there. Fetch my—"

"The king need not concern himself with me," Orphus said, keeping his eyes on me.

I curtsied and turned to flee.

"I won't spare your life if you have lied," the king shouted behind me, but I didn't stop.

CHAPTER

TWENTY-ONE

TAMAS

"You're either losing your touch, or you've grown weakhearted these past few days," the young nobleman said under his breath, nudging in close beside me.

I glanced over my shoulder briefly, then back to the procession moving inside the temple. "Who might you be?" What was Osmud doing here?

"I could ask the same. Your taste in fashion is terrible."

"At least you chose someone far more good-looking than yourself. It's a relief for all of us who have to look at you."

Osmud snorted. "He's lazy, lives on inherited privilege and spends like it too. I couldn't even find a butter knife on hand when I left my accommodation this morning. So I remedied that." Osmud opened his doublet to reveal a slew of small weapons tucked into various pockets. "He's a few

334

coins lighter, but he won't mind." He stuck out his hand. "Lord Angleton, at your service."

"Lord Bloodwyn."

Osmud took my hand in a firm grip and tugged me toward him. "We've made headway. Kaldor, Macrillion, and Giraldus have agreed to an alliance. Garrat is at this moment riding to meet with Thome. Once we have his allegiance, we've covered a half of the northeast."

I nodded. "I never doubted you, brother."

He quirked a brow at me, dropping my hand and focusing on the crowd. "The clans are questioning your ability to succeed."

"Don't tell me you came all this way to scold me?"

"I'm worried, Tamas. Many of us are. Garrat knows what you did."

I turned away, folding my arms across my chest. "You needn't be. One's dead."

"Not by your hand. Angleton filled me in on the rumors. Unless you've stooped to hiding in forests and jumping out to scare horses."

"It doesn't matter how it happened. One Tannard is dead."

He gave a long look before saying, "And two are very much still alive."

"The youngest Tannard prefers a man's bed." I knew the words didn't mean much, but in the brief moments I'd spent in Andriet's company, I'd grown to like the man. I hated the idea of ending the lives of good-hearted men; too few of those remained living long enough to have an impact on those around them. Unfortunately, his proclivity didn't stop his father from securing a marriage alliance.

"It makes no difference. The lad still has seed and will be required to spread it."

"The princess is very fond of him." I grimaced at letting that slip.

"What princess? Oh, you mean the one that we rowed for days in shitty weather, chilling ourselves to the bone to kill? The one you bit!" He didn't mean to raise his voice. We each glanced around, but the surrounding crowd was focused on the street. "Either tell me she pushed him onto his sword, or keep her out of this conversation."

I side-eyed him. "You're in a good mood."

"The winds were unfavorable, so I developed wing strain on my way down. And I'll remind you, I shouldn't have to be here."

"Why are you?"

"You told us of King Ricaud, what you felt, but you're still not making headway. We fear your telling yourself lies again."

I sighed, then dragged my hand down over my face. "You trust me, don't you, Osmud?"

In his new skin, it was hard for me to understand the subtle nuances of his expression, never having known Lord Angleton when he was alive.

"Well?" I prodded after he'd been staring at me for some time.

He rolled his eyes. "Of course I do."

"I'll do what needs doing. My way."

"The Tamas who took his father's throne balked at nothing to win."

I grimaced, then half-turned to him. "That Tamas paid a bitter price."

"A price that had to be paid. Tell me you have grand plans to end the young prince's life during the trials. It's the perfect opportunity to rid us of some of the nobility."

This time, I turned my body to him. "I have my plans."

"Here they are," cried a woman from my right. The crowd surrounding us surged forward, pressing against one another, each hoping to glimpse the royal family as their enclosed carriage churned to a stop in front of the temple doors.

I, too, positioned myself so I could see better. The King and his ailing Queen exited first, followed by his youngest son, Tressya, on his arm. Even though pale and sickly, the queen, in her deep purple gown shimmering with jewels along the hem that caught the fragile sun, outshone Tressya, whose fashion was little better than the noble women of lower birth, those whose titles would not gain them a place at court.

My attention stayed on her as she and Andriet made their way inside behind the king and queen. The rest of the nobility followed. Suddenly, Andriet broke from the line, taking Tressya with him, where they huddled in the gloom of the spiked arch over the entrance into the temple. If I were a gambling man, which I was from time to time, I would bet the princess was begging Andriet not to force her inside.

I'd seen the farce of a display she'd made beside Juel's body, and I knew she was relieved to be free from him. Even though she hadn't killed him—a sword through that part of the thigh would kill anyone in minutes—it had likely crossed her mind.

"I trust you, brother. You know I do. But I fear your attention is distracted."

"Never. My attention, as always, is on ending..."

Yes, it was as I thought; Tressya was bargaining with Andriet to aid her escape from the funeral. She stepped back, appearing as though she was on the verge of fleeing.

"Hey, Tamas." Osmud clicked his fingers in front of my face.

"What?" Feeling a shot of annoyance for the distraction, I turned my head to Osmud, before snapping it back to Tressya. If she was hoping to disappear, I wasn't about to miss it.

Osmud nudged me in the arm.

"What is it?" I snarled.

"It's as I feared. Thank the stars I arrived."

I kept my eyes on Tressya as I spoke. "She's no longer a threat now Juel's dead."

"She's a disciple. Any disciple's a threat to peace."

"Do you really believe that? I believe she'll play a vital part."

"For fuck's sake, Tamas. Listen to yourself." He glared ahead through the crowd at Tressya, stretching his neck around a very tall man to enable him a clear view. "What has that woman done to you? You're the one who's been adamant from the start. The disciples are never to be trusted."

I had to speak carefully here, knowing anything I said

Osmud would take as proof of my addled mind. But I longed to feel her sharp, slicing gaze on me again and subject myself once more to her astute mind, snappish tongue, and agile reflexes. Tressya was a far greater challenge than I thought I would encounter on my quest to end the House of Tannard.

"She's also a woman and that's your problem. I would say it's your greatest problem. Women are always at the heart of any great problem."

I glanced at him, knowing his meaning. I wasn't totally lost. Neither was I thinking with my cock, as I was sure he would mention soon enough.

"The disciples are never just women. You know that. And since the moment she stepped foot outside that carriage, your eyes have marked her."

"She's cunning, intelligent, and courageous, with a considerable amount of talent. She would be an excellent fighter, a valuable advantage on our side."

"You want to fuck her."

I knew that was coming. "I only have eyes for my goal."

"You have eyes for her tits and ass. What did she do to you down in that hold?"

I squeezed the bridge of my nose, tired of this conversation.

"The disciple is dangerous. Not to the Razohan, but there's no telling whose head she'll decide to twist. You're allowing the wrong body part to guide your decisions." He glanced down at my crotch. "Go find yourself a pretty little wench to shag. Thanks to your new skin, you're now a good-looking fellow. You shouldn't have any problems getting a lass to sit on your lap. A good fuck and you'll finally see straight."

"As usual, you've got it all wrong."

"Have I now? I'd say she's already half twisted you in her spell. The disciples are our enemy. They're everyone's enemy. There's no telling what their Mother Divine knows and what plans she's made by hoping to place one of her own on the throne."

He gripped my chin and wrenched my head to face him. "The disciple's presence within Emberfell will be your end if you're not careful."

I shifted my chin out of his hold. "Brother, where's your faith?"

He pulled a face, then folded his arms as he turned away, which was my cue to refocus my attention on the princess. The young prince had no choice but to desert her, leaving her outside the temple doors by herself. She looked anything but lost standing by herself, while the rest of the mourners—I would bet Ironhelm that not one of them will shed a tear—moved past her and inside. Instead, she looked purposeful, like she had a plan. When she moved away, I was ready, only for Osmud to grab my arm.

"Don't do it."

"You my guardian now?"

He ground out a frustrated breath. "I'm staying at Orbiteen House. I'm sure it won't take you long to find the place. I'll be expecting you."

"Doesn't Garrat need you in the north?"

"It was his idea I come keep an eye on you. You'll have

Bryra down here next if you're not careful. She's worried about you."

"What? No. You didn't tell her, did you?" I drove my hands through my hair. "She deserves to hear it from me. And she has no hope of crossing the Ashenlands by herself."

"If you care for her, you'll do what you need to do fast. Finish it, Tamas, then come home. The clans are hungry for victory. They want to get this done before the deep chill sets in."

I nodded. He was right. I patted him on the back, then pushed through the crowd, heading in the direction I'd watched Tressya disappear.

Yes, eliminating the House of Tannard was necessary, but it was equally crucial for me to seize every opportunity to sway Tressya to my side.

Now the royals had gone inside, the crowds lost interest and moved about with their day, and I seemed to head against the flow of people. I hurried to the temple entrance where the princess had stood moments before, then rounded the corner and skirted along the side wall of the massive building.

A stone wall, waist height, segregated the burial grounds from the rest of the city. Though a place for the wealthy, the graveyard was ill-kept. The white tombstones lost their luster now the sun had disappeared behind a gloomy cloud. Moss and age discolored many, but an array of purple and yellow-headed flowers, growing as weeds around the base of the gravesites, offered some color. Columns of giant mausoleums, the last resting place for generations of illustrious families, formed narrow walking trails around which one could stroll for hours.

I wasn't sure what led me to believe Tressya would be here. I doubted she would disappear into the city proper and risk being left behind when the royal party departed, so I buried myself further along the maze of tombstones, some standing taller than my head, expecting to stumble across Tressya ambling through the grassed walkways.

Hearing a noise to my left, like the scuff of shoes on stone, I smiled and diverted through the narrow gap between two mausoleums. I exited at the backend of the stone monoliths to the sudden scuffle of feet and found a blade at my throat.

"Is this your usual habit of greeting?" I looked over my shoulder, catching the princess in my periphery as she moved to stand behind me.

"For the untrustworthy. And those who weren't welcomed into my solitude."

"If you wanted me in a vulnerable position, you only had to ask. I know many more pleasant ways to—"

She pressed the blade against my throat. "I'm not interested in flirting with you, Razohan. I thought I made that clear on the hunt?"

"Before or after the death of your betrothed?"

She leaned in, so I felt the warmth of her breath under my ear and smelled the soft waft of lilac tickle my nose.

"Tell me what you're interested in. Name it, and we shall see if we have a deal," I said.

To my surprise, she lowered her dagger and stepped away, walking around to stand in front of me. She tapped the blade of her dagger on her palm as her gaze challenged me. The iron glare of her deep blue eyes tickled a thrum in my body, sending a thrill through my stomach. I felt the first stirrings of a fire burning through my veins. Too long it had been since I felt the exhilarating pulse of a challenge between worthy opponents.

It was damn well impossible not to slip within her again and soak in the exquisite wild flush of hunger I knew pulsed beneath her skin.

"I doubt you would disappear."

"You don't want that, Tressya. You know you don't. There's too much heat within you to be solely happy with the company you're currently forced to keep."

She snorted a laugh. "That's one weakness."

I dipped my head to her. "Please enlighten me. What weakness is that?"

"The Razohan are prideful and arrogant. Prideful and arrogant men are easy to topple and make the most noise when they fall."

"Spoken like a true disciple."

Her smug smile faltered. She paced around me, and I followed, turning my body in time with her steps, wishing she wore pants that outlined her figure rather than plumes of skirt. There would be no ballads about her beauty, but she beguiled me with her quick wit, sharp mind and the boldness lurking behind her eyes.

"Why didn't you kill me on the ship?"

"Perhaps I had more to gain by following and studying my enemy."

"At least you finally admit one truth."

"Which is?"

"We're enemies."

Damn. I shouldn't have said that. The worst she could be was my rival, but I thought of her more as my equal. Tressya was a woman worthy of gracing the halls of Ironhelm. The northern clan leaders were a tough breed, but she was a woman to gain their respect.

"Now it's my turn to ask a question. Why haven't you revealed me to the king? I don't believe your excuse."

"It's on the tip of my tongue whenever I'm in his presence. Besides, I need amusement to whittle the hours away, and you've proved quite the joke."

"With Juel dead, the hours must stretch before you."

She stopped pacing, no longer looking so assured of herself.

"What's your plan now, little princess? The king's running out of sons."

I regretted saying that as her sharp eyes lanced into me.

"What were you chasing in Emberforge?"

"The princess will have to give me something in return for such a vital piece of information."

"Okay, man of the north, tell me about the Razohan." She turned and walked away, expecting me to follow. I would, of course, and that probably revealed another weakness, hence the reason she decided to walk.

"Is this through genuine interest, or are you hoping to find another weakness?" I took larger steps to catch up with her.

"Knowledge is vital."

"You're right. It's power."

She quirked a brow. "Besides, I already know two of your weaknesses. And it's been minutes. As yet, you don't know the first thing about me beyond the fact I'm a disciple." She wove around a low tombstone, peering down at the inscription as if it interested her.

"Two?"

She glanced up at me. "You're male. That's flaw enough."

I had to stop and laugh. It came from deep in my heart and felt good. How long had it been since this feeling had swept through and washed the weight of the past and my impending destiny from my shoulders? Then when I glanced at her, the small spark of joy faded, and something else burned there instead. She looked confused, uncomfortable, and I wondered how many times she'd laughed since reaching Tarragona, since learning of her fate, since she became a disciple.

All that I knew of the Sistern came from the Nazeen: their rivals. The Mother Divine guided them, elected for her superior skill in soul voice. I knew they sought alliances through the realms, but their alliances were duplicitous, often birthed in secret to men of power. Because of the Nazeen's presence, they kept out of the north, and the Creed of Salmun restricted their ventures into Tarragona. Sending a disciple to the bed of Tarragona's crown prince was a bold move, perhaps a desperate one.

"Fine. Since we have formed our entire relationship around deals, let's make one now. I'll tell you one thing about the Razohan, then you share something about the Sistern."

She tilted her head to the side, her stern gaze fixing me in place. "Fine. But this is not a relationship. It's a test of endurance." She smirked. "And cunning."

"I like that." And damn if my voice purred. Because, dammit, I liked it. A lot. I was up for the challenge.

Her smirk dropped, then she glanced at her feet, as if uncomfortable. Was she feeling awkward that I would find her alluring? If I was a man to keep tally, I would notch a small engraving under my name. It was hardly a win, but something told me I would need to grab any win I could against her, no matter how small.

Then she was off walking again, this time leading me down a gap between two mausoleums, both grayed with age. As we walked, she ran the tip of her dagger along the stone with a dull scraping sound. Once out onto another path, she half spun to me. "You may start."

I splayed my arms, looking around where we stood. "Here? There are more comfortable—"

"Speak." And she turned and kept walking just to see how far I would follow her. Normally, I would refuse to allow anyone to drag me along by my shirt front. When she was the one doing the dragging, I found it... captivating.

I heaved a sigh as if she was being difficult because I couldn't allow myself to look the pathetic fool trailing after the princess. "The Razohan favor bravery and loyalty over all else."

She stopped, giving me a chance to catch up, then rolled her eyes and groaned. "I could mention a legion of men who claim the same. Give me something else. Something particular to the Razohan."

"Certainly, once you've had your turn."

She folded her arms, ran her tongue on the inside of her cheek, then unfolded her arms. "The Sistern focuses on the female line. They consider the males of no importance." She continued walking.

I chuckled. "Touché."

"That's particular to the Sistern," she said over her shoulder.

"And hardly a secret."

"You never asked for secrets."

She turned left at the next tombstone, a spike of a thing, with a wreath of multi-colored flowers growing around its base. Tressya bent to slash the stalks with her blade, then gathered the flowers and kept walking. I should've thought of that, but it never occurred to me the princess would like flowers.

"Okay. The Razohan can take the form of anything they choose, human or animal."

With the flowers at her nose, she spun. "But the Huun-gardred can't, or so I've been told. Why is it different for the Razohan? You're descendants, after all."

"It's your turn."

She huffed and buried her face in the flowers before rolling her eyes at my intense gaze. "Fine. Disciples are born into the Sistern."

"So you had no choice?"

"Don't make it sound like a prison, and I believe it's your turn."

My lips twitched, but I fought the urge to smile. "To become another, we must first take their soul."

She gasped. "That explains it."

"What?"

"What I felt when I entered you that night at—Well... Now I understand." Her eyes glinted with intelligence and curiosity as her mind latched onto what I'd revealed and worked it over. "To take a soul means you would have to kill them."

"True." I looked for condemnation, hatred, disgust, but saw none of those, just her mind alive with ideas. "What happens to the souls when you take them?"

The flowers were forgotten, hanging limp by her side, while she gazed at me as if her eyes alone would discover all my secrets. It was her turn, but I liked having her full attention, so I answered. "They remain within us." Osmud would knock me on the head if he were here.

"All the souls? Forever?"

"Yes."

She licked her lips, appearing to search for her next question, and I should insist she give me something in return. Instead, I waited.

"That sounds like a burden."

I quirked a half smile, then strolled up to the tombstone and bent to pick the only white flower amongst the colored array. I handed it to her. "It's very handy. But, yes, it's also a curse. It's not something we enjoy, or do at all if we can help it. Bloodwyn's is the first life I've assumed for a very long time. Then Petrulus; he was vital, but the wrong apostle. The new skin takes some getting used to. Most of the memories I can do without. Many do become a heavy cloak, but there is no way to shut them out. Bloodwyn here, thankfully, has spent his life in idle indulgence. Hasn't lifted a sword his entire life beyond the sport of blade-dueling, and he wasn't much good at that." I arched my head back and scratched my neck while I wondered why in the seven realms I had said all of that.

"Petrulus was the wrong apostle because he didn't give you what you wanted to know. But it explains how you knew so much about the goings on in Emberforge."

"Not everything."

"Would Selisimus have provided better information? You stole the key from him, didn't you? Rewas couldn't understand how you had it. Which has to mean only a certain few have access to the library, and Selisimus was one of them. He would've know more about the scrolls in the library than Petrulus."

Her quick mind impressed me, yet one more thing about her that did. It was time I stopped finding her attributes so impressive.

"What happened to you on the Bone Throne?"

The sincerity in her tone tempted me to confide in her. It was surprising I resisted, given how deeply she had already influenced me. I clung to this one secret, in case all my plans for us proved false, and in the end, we were no longer allies in the battle against the tyrants vying for control of the Etherweave.

"I'm not sure."

She hesitated a moment, as if trying to decide if that was the truth or a lie. Then finally she spoke. "Our soul word is our power."

I believed soul voice to be their true power, but then

again, what did I truly know about the inner workings of the Sistern?

"I only just discovered the truth." She half laughed, sounding more awkward than amused.

By her tone and the way the words rushed out of her mouth like a sudden revelation meant this was important to her, so it was important to me.

"They didn't teach you?"

"We're supposed to learn that truth for ourselves. It's taken me all this time. I'm so far from the Mother, she won't know I've finally learned the greatest lesson. Something all the other disciples already knew."

That one statement sounded filled with judgement and pain. I knew enough about those two afflictions to know their efficiency at eating away at your heart. Once again, I struggled with the urge to slip beneath the surface and seek what troubled emotions darkened her expression. The day I did such a thing was the day Tressya took my blood and formerly agreed to our union. Until then, that privilege would never be mine.

She blinked at me, opened her mouth as if to speak, then snapped it closed again before she said. "We're even."

"Not even half, princess."

Now the barriers were down, I wanted to know so much more. I couldn't give a damn about the Sistern, I just wanted to know about her. She wasn't my enemy, she was not a Levenian, rather a woman drawn into this age old fight.

"You know more than you deserve to know." She turned away from me.

I bent and picked a purple flower, this time stepping in

close to slip it behind her ear. "Then tell me how I become deserving so I may learn more about you."

Her eyes followed every movement I made. Disbelieving eyes, shocked eyes, and I understood why. Those living south of the Ashenlands favored beauty in a woman above all else.

"What else can I give you? I'm here to take back the throne for the Razohan. But you already know that."

At first she touched the flower I'd placed in her hair, then, with an expression I couldn't read, she turned and walked away.

"I was only a child when my mother died," I yelled at her back. "It killed my father to lose her."

She half turned, the blue of her eyes deeper than the warmest sky focused entirely on me, and my mouth was in freewill. "Then I..." I pressed my lips together clawing back the terrible truth. "Lost my father."

"My mother died birthing me." It was close to a whisper.

There was a quiet ache of loneliness in her voice. She looked confused, small and lonely, and I wanted to adorn her body with all the flowers in the graveyard just so she knew I'd heard her, beyond the words to the sentiment under-neath. And when she turned once more to leave me, I felt an inexplicable desperation to make her stay. I couldn't push her.

It was crucial I made no mistakes for the sake of my people, meaning I needed time to make my last decisive decision on my next move.

"You better go, princess. The funeral will be over soon, and the youngest Tannard may come searching for you. You don't want him wandering through these mausoleums all by himself. Not when I'm lurking."

I held up my hands in surrender when she glared at me. "Just jokes." Then backed up before spinning on my heels and walking away.

I wanted her trust—I needed it as much as I needed air—but the Tannards had to die.

What a fucking mess.

CHAPTER TWENTY-TWO

TRESSYA

RADNISA WAS a thorn embedded in my skin, but thorns could be removed. In Radnisa's case, it took silent patience before she grew bored of her own acid voice. She finally left me alone in my room, departing in a cloud of fury, robbed of her chance to gloat over my impending disgrace within my father's court on the return voyage to Merania.

I rose from my bureau once the sound of Radnisa's departing steps no longer echoed in the corridor. "Deliah, you can come out now." I'd seen her through my mirror, darting in and out of my bedroom during Radnisa's tirade, as if she feared Radnisa might see her and turn her vengeance onto the spirit.

"Thought she'd never leave," Deliah groused as she materialized before me.

"She's only poisonous to the living, so you needn't hide

from her. Radnisa is not one of the lucky few to possess my talent."

"I need to ask you a few questions." I crossed to my bed and patted a space beside me, which was ridiculous, but Deliah approached and settled down where I'd indicated, her body slipping beneath the cover, so her head was level with my shoulder.

"Glad you changed the king's mind. I was hopin' you'd do it."

"Thanks to a friendly trio of spirits, I had information that proved valuable to him. Though, Orphus played a part in persuading the king, which makes me uneasy."

"That prick. I don't understand why he'd help you. You need to shake him off."

"I agree. But he's not who I want to talk about. I'm interested in Queen Gusselan. Tell me everything you know about her."

"She hates the king."

"Common in royal marriages. Where's she from?"

"She came across the sea. Like you. Place called Avaloria. Home of the Levenians, or so I 'eard. Somewhere there anyhow."

I sucked in a breath. "She's Levenian?"

"So the story goes."

"You're aware she's being poisoned?"

Deliah nodded. "Not really my concern."

"Why aren't the Salmun doing something about that? I thought they were Levenian pets?"

She snorted a laugh. "Pets, sure." She nodded, appreciating my analogy. "They only care about protecting the throne."

"The queen has played her part in birthing two heirs, and now she's expendable." Despite her threats, I felt sympathy for her. It wasn't hard to see myself in her shoes, loathed by my husband, discarded once my duties were fulfilled.

"Do you know anything about the mark on her right wrist? What does it represent?"

"Didn't know there was one. I lived a long time ago," Deliah intoned, her interest in our conversation waning.

"Do the Levenians have any abilities, or is it just their pets, the Salmun?"

She shrugged. "Why you askin' this stuff? I dunno. The war was long old even when I was alive. I know nothin' 'bout them."

I swallowed my frustration. Deliah wasn't the right person for this conversation.

"What else can you tell me about the queen?"

"What does it matter? She'll be gone soon."

"That's the problem. I don't want her gone." As a disciple, I should end her life myself given I suspected she belonged to a secretive order. Why else would she have been made queen? But if the Levenians didn't have any special abilities, perhaps she wasn't a threat to the Mother's plans for the Tannard throne.

"You should. She's been makin' plans against you."

I couldn't mask my surprise. It wasn't the revelation of the queen's machinations that astounded me, but the fact Deliah waited until now to reveal them. I swallowed any retorts and instead inquired. "What are those plans?"

"She's been talkin' to that stuck-up bitch Juel favored."

"Lady Astaria?"

"Yeah, that one."

"What plots have they concocted?"

"Well, it ain't me who knew 'bout it. It's that dumbass Truett 'eard it all."

"And what did Truett tell you?"

"Nothin'. I try not to talk to 'em. I stay away from the three of 'em as best I can, but eternity is a long time. It ain't easy. I over 'eard him."

I took a breath before I spoke. "So what did Truett have to say."

"The heirs 'ave to be careful, you see. No spreading their seed. It's been like that forever 'cause they don't want bastards all over the place claiming a right to the throne."

"That would tip the scales to rebellion. But in all this time, there hasn't been any slip ups?"

She shrugged. "Who knows. I don't care what babies they 'ave. Got nothin' to do with me. Makes no difference to me if 'em lot are wiped from the throne. I'd be glad for it."

I rose from the bed and paced. "The queen wanted Lady Astaria to bear Juel a child."

"'Em Salmun would make sure that doesn't happen."

"But that was the plan, right?" I didn't wait for her to reply as I continued to pace, pouring through possible malicious schemes. "She either wanted to replace me with Lady Astaria—"

"Swap the babies."

I pivoted to face her. "Truly? That would require impeccable timing, which seems impossible." My curiosity regarding the queen's audacity overshadowed any anger I might have felt. As Juel was no longer alive, my position as wife and mother wasn't mine to defend any longer. I could thank my luck for that; hardly a loyal thought for a disciple, but it was the truth.

Once more, Deliah shrugged. I could see her attention drifting from our conversation.

"How would she achieve that under the Salmun's watchful gaze?"

Another shrug was her sole response.

"So, who's poisoning her? The king or the Salmun? I would think the Salmun would employ more direct methods."

"The Salmun are a secretive lot. Nothin' they do is understood. It's the king. I'm sure. The queen lost his love and protection a long time ago."

"Do you mean the king, or are you suggesting her family in Avaloria no longer provides protection?"

"What would I know or care?" She rose from the bed.

"Might the trio of spirits have more information about the queen?"

She shrugged, telling me it was time to stop my questioning. "Thanks. You've been helpful."

"Really?" She seemed taken aback.

"Was there something you wanted? Is that why you appeared?"

She shook her head. "Curious. That's all. Truett said you had some secret in your favor."

"It seems gossip amongst spirits is as widespread as it is amongst the living."

"He says you got the king to kick all his men from the throne room."

"He's been prying."

She snorted an unladylike laugh. "You're fascinating. We can't help it."

Just what I needed—a horde of pesky spirits shadowing me. It was time I honed my skill in the death arts to fend off their intrusiveness.

I headed for my door. "Thanks, Deliah." Without waiting for her reply I swept out of my room. Of course she followed me, popping through the wall beside me, keeping pace as I hurried off down the corridor.

"Where you goin'?"

She was becoming a little too familiar, gliding close so I felt the beginnings of the haunting ice chill I always felt when touched by spirits. My skin pebbled just thinking of the horrible feeling, but I didn't want to offend her by asking her to keep her distance. Instead, I picked up my pace, which was a useless endeavor.

"I need to speak with someone."

"Who?"

I turned the corner, ignoring the grand sweeping stairwell and strode onwards to the southern wing of Emberfell.

"'Ere. This is the king's side of the castle."

Staying silent, I picked up my pace. A race with a spirit felt ridiculous.

"What you doin' this side?"

Deliah left me behind when I stopped. She doubled back and wafted in front of me while I tried to find polite words to say. Pressing my palms together, I took one breath. "Please,

Deliah. I'm asking you for some privacy. Can you do that for me?"

"What for?"

"A private matter."

"What 'bout?"

I inhaled. "Nothing interesting or important."

"Why's it private then?"

Curses. Not even Radnisa could help me develop my new found skills in the death arts. Unfortunately, I had little time to dedicate to perfecting the skill.

"Didn't you ever want privacy when you were alive?"

She shrugged. "Don't remember."

"I'm sure you did. Everyone—"

Her eyes widened. "You gonna see her, ain't you?"

I pinched the bridge of my noise.

She gasped. "You gonna kill her."

I walked around her in a wide arc. "No."

"Yeah, you are. 'Em lot won't believe me."

"Deliah." I spun on her. "This is a private matter, remember?"

She nodded. "Yeah. Private." She pressed her lips together as she wafted backward, away from me.

I strode toward her, instinctively reaching out to grab her hand, then snapped it back when the ice tingles reminded me of what I would suffer if I dared touch her. "Deliah. Don't tell the others." I warned with my firmest tone, which failed to quell her smirk.

Curses to her. I focused inward, gathering my concentration, reaching for my soul word, thinking that would be the secret link to spiritweaving. But Deliah vanished before I could even graze the power of Aetherius.

"Damn it," I hissed, spinning on my heels and marching down the long corridor.

The echoing thud of my boots on the stone floor slowed my pace. The oppressive silence when I stopped felt like a vice grip on my shoulder. I refused to glance back. Instead, I picked up my pace, striding past the king's quarters. Gilded edges adorned the doors, and a faint scent of wood oil wafted from the gaps into the corridor.

Beyond Henricus's rooms, the corridor darkened. The intermittent flambeau, held by elaborate iron sconces on either side, cast an eerie glow, elongating and contorting my shadow behind me. Ahead, sporadic light created shadowy alcoves concealed behind massive stone arches.

The entrance to the queen's quarters lay ahead, the only door remaining in this hallway. My visit here was more out of curiosity than anything else. Given I no longer had a tie to the throne—traitorous as it was to my duties, I couldn't help but rejoice at the fact—I was no longer a threat to her, but I doubted she would surrender any of her secrets. Still, I had to try.

Upon reaching her door, I paused to collect myself. The woman had just lost her son; I wasn't seeking confrontation, but I was eager to learn anything I could about her. Her ancestry, her probable links to another order, all left me hungry to know the woman behind the title of queen.

"The little squirrel was right," Borrat said from beside me.

I jumped on hearing his voice so close to my ear.

"Is there to be another death in the House of Tannard?" Truett inquired.

I groaned, knowing there was little point telling them all to scram. I turned to face Truett and Borrat. "I'm new to the skill of spiritweaving, but once I get the hang of it, I'll send you two to the dungeons every time you interfere in my day without suitable warning."

"Is she threatening us?" Albert remark from behind.

I rolled my eyes on hearing his voice.

"The audacious little hoyden has the insolence to threaten us," he continued.

"Gentlemen, please," I implored.

"Now she wishes to be amicable,' Truett mocked. "Too late, my queen. Oh, pardon me, that is not your title yet, and it never will be."

Ignoring them, I grasped the door handle, deciding not to waste my time with the spirits, but before I could turn it, Borrat warned, "She spoke against you to the king the moment you arrived."

I stilled my hand on the handle. "Why would she do that? Our first meeting was in the carriage during the king's procession."

"She has an ally," he continued.

"Enough, fool! We agreed not to assist her," Albert interjected. "Like any woman, she possesses a duplicity of spirit. On one hand steadfast as a towering oak, on the other fickle as desert sands. We must remember all are born with a conniving soul."

"No," Borrat retorted. "You told us not to help her. Truett and I never agreed."

"Good gracious, man. Are you such an ignoramus—"

As their bickering persisted, I slipped into the dim room, gently closing the door behind me. Pressed against the wall, I inhaled the musty air of illness, thankful the spirits hadn't followed. After ensuring they'd left me be, I ventured deeper into the chamber.

A slither of light filtered through a gap in the drapes and ran along the rug and stretched across the bed, revealing the queen's form lying on her side.

"Merrilda?" a feeble voice inquired from the bed.

I approached the window and pulled the drapes further apart, casting more light into the room. Silhouetted against the backdrop of another cloudy day, I gazed down at the barren courtyard below. Emberfell had no beauty to offer. Only a few skeletal trees, long stripped of their leaves, stood as proof of life.

"You," the queen murmured weakly.

"You need more light, to begin with," I replied.

From the shadows, her muffled voice came. "Leave me be."

Ignoring her plea, I approached the bedside table. I poured and sniffed the contents from a pitcher. It reeked of cheap, sour wine. I promptly disposed of it out the window.

"From now on, you'll drink only what I provide: quality wine. But you can't survive on wine alone. I will ensure you're served water as well. The king shall never know."

"What are you doing?" she mumbled.

I returned to her bedside. "You'll be given wine worthy of the king's table and fresh water boiled to purity. Is Merrilda the one caring for you?"

The queen remained silent, her eyes hidden in the gloom.

"She'll be dismissed. Clearly, she's been feeding you poisoned food."

"No. Merrilda stays," she insisted.

Crossing my arms, I stared down at her. "Then it's neither the food nor drink."

Slowly, she rolled onto her back, exhaling wearily. "Why would a disciple concern herself with me? I have nothing to offer."

Straightening her bedding, I mused, "Maybe I'm driven by reasons more nuanced than duty."

"I find that hard to believe."

"Is Merrilda your ally?" I said.

"I don't know what you mean?"

I smoothed more of the bedcovers flat. "I mean did she travel with you from Levenia?"

She remained silent.

"I've been asking about you. Though my source wasn't as helpful as I'd hoped. Is Merrilda the one who revealed my identity?"

Again, she chose silence, so I eased myself down on the side of her bed. "I'm no longer your enemy. I have no claim to the throne. Andriet is to marry another."

And I had no choice but to kill his bride. Duty to the Mother came before all else. *If that's so, why are you protecting your greatest enemy?*

I rose from the bed, uncomfortable with how that thought made me feel.

"The serpent who arrived with you. Did she tell you?" She hesitated.

"Radnisa wouldn't tell me if I asked. Don't worry, I also struggle to find any nice words to describe her most of the time." For a moment I forgot about my self-appointed job of tidying her bed and took a moment before I next spoke. "I'm sorry about your son."

She inhaled sharply. "You don't mean that."

"While I won't mourn him, any mother's loss pains me. I played no part in his demise. The wound was such that even with the king and his men, he stood no chance."

I sucked in my cheeks. Bloodwyn, was another thorn in my skin, but one I was too weak to remove. Mostly because the thorn felt good lodged inside of me.

I closed my eyes and inhaled. Such traitorous thoughts for a disciple. Since when had I become so weak?

Queen Gusselan rolled her head away from me. When she next spoke her feeble voice was muffled by her pillow. "You used your voice power to make him slice his leg." I still heard every word.

It was a stunning accusation. Would I have dared come up with such a plan? It would mean a terrible betrayal to the Mother. I couldn't give a definitive answer, but deep down suspected I was capable of such a thing given he deserved no better end. "In all sincerity, I did no such thing. Marrying him was my duty."

She met my gaze once more. "And we can't deny our duty." Was that bitterness in her voice?

"You can't disagree you controlled the king with your voice. It's why you remain in Tarragona."

"No," I replied, resuming my task of tidying her bed. "I don't have that power. I have yet to master it." Secrecy and discretion, I disobeyed two of the Sistern's six pillars in one reply. Where was my head? Where was my loyalty? Lost along with my emotions in the graveyard. That bloody Razohan was twisting my devotion to the Sistern.

Only, right now I felt a strange connection with the queen. She too was a woman bowing to duty, and her remittance was her life.

Her laughter was a raspy cough.

She shifted her gaze to the bed canopy. "What more does your Mother want of you?"

"I chose not to question the Mother's motives. But I'm curious. You knew about me from the time of my arrival, why did you not reveal me to the king, or the Salmun?"

She continued to gaze up at the canopy as if she never heard me."Until my youngest's bride bears an heir you're still a threat."

"Not to him. Never. I'm very fond of Andriet."

The queen lowered her gaze and watched me while I made my way around the end of the bed, smoothing my hand across the top until it was crease free. Once I'd finished with that task, I cast a look around for something else I could fuss on, not willing to meet her gaze. Neither did I want to acknowledge my reasons for staying here. It amounted to another betrayal toward the Sistern. Befriending another from a different order. I obviously wasn't thinking straight. *Damn you Bloodwyn.*

"I find that hard to believe. Duty isn't a choice," she said.

"Spoken like a true disciple. Is that what you consider yourself or does your order have another name for its faithful?"

She closed her eyes as if to shut me out, which was the best she could do given her fragility.

"We are the same, you and I. Both sent from our homes to marry someone we didn't love."

She sighed. "It was a privilege to be chosen."

I slid down onto the end of the bed. "In all honestly, I struggled to feel the same. The Mother chose me above all my sisters. That was a privilege." *Not because she believed in me.* I unconsciously rubbed at the old wound on my chest. "It was hard to say goodbye."

"I don't believe it. A disciple claiming love."

"Attachment, maybe." It felt wrong to say so, like I was betraying Carlin and everything he had meant to me, but my life in Merania felt distant to me now.

I sucked in a breath when my thoughts drifted to Bloodwyn again. *Don't pollute Carlin's memory with him.*

"If you lack power, why did she choose you?"

"You need to offer me something in return if I'm to answer you." I fought against a smile at how familiar this exchange felt, then dropped my smile when I realized how much of our conversation led me to think of Bloodwyn because he was always in my head. I had to do something about that.

"I don't know why you're bothering," she whispered.

"Let's not take this conversation in circles. It's obvious why the mother sent me here. You've already guessed that."

"The king is not poisoning me."

That surprised me. "The Salmun?"

"It's not poison. You can't save me from my fate."

I rose and came around to stand beside her bed. "You're Levenian. I don't understand."

"You know nothing of Levenia. My order gives fealty to King Ushpia." She inhaled as she closed her eyes. "Enemy to King Bezhani."

I waited for her to catch her breath. When she didn't continue, I did it for her. "The Salmun give fealty to King Bezhani?" I knelt beside her bed. "They didn't realize your connection to the enemy monarch before you were sent across as bride to Henricus. But now the Salmun know."

She stared at me, her eyelids drooping, then she blinked herself alert again.

"Why did your order want you to marry the king of Tarragona?"

"Why did yours?"

I sucked in my bottom lip, holding back the words that would end my loyalty to the Mother. It was silly. Gusselan knew the reason. It was the same reason her order sent her. They wanted one of theirs connected to the Tarragona throne. "Why is everyone interested in the Tarragonan throne?"

"Not the Tarragonan throne. The Bone Throne."

I sat back on my heels.

"I fear the Salmun were behind Juel's death. I fear for Andriet," she said.

"It was an accident. It would leave the Tarragona throne without an heir. They wouldn't risk that."

She exhaled long and slow. "Yes. You're right." Her voice was weak.

"I should leave you to sleep."

Without thinking, I laid my hand on top of hers. Her eyes fluttered open.

"I want to find a way to help you. I'll try." Against the Salmun, I couldn't promise.

"Why?" she croaked.

"Because most of the men in power don't deserve to win."

CHAPTER

TWENTY-THREE

TRESSYA

THE NEWS CAME AS A RELIEF. The Duke, the Earl, and a select few of the peerage had lost their heads after weeks of trials in which each swore their innocence. It was Lord Dowel who'd broken down under torture and surrendered the names of all the conspirators in exchange for his life—which wasn't granted. The king would know I hadn't lied. And now he owed me a favor.

I stopped outside the king's favored rooms to steady my nerves, not caring the sentinels stared at me.

Here I was, fighting to stay within Emberfell, yet protecting the identity of the one man who could destroy the Mother's plans all because...he wanted to know me.

In the last few weeks, I'd seen Bloodwyn from afar, though I thought of him more times than I should. Able to disguise himself as anyone he chose, he was a far greater threat to the House of Tannard than any treason, but I couldn't bring myself to reveal him as a Razohan.

As a disciple, my duty was to obey, not feel. Emotions weakened a disciple, made us question, made us falter. The Mother had no use for such women. Bloodwyn was wrong; while I may not have chosen to join the Sistern, I gave my life to them, to the Mother.

Yet I had not tried to avenge Anderline's death, as I swore I would, when I had my blade at his throat in the graveyard? A quick flick of my wrist, some added pressure, and I would've sliced him from ear to ear as a loyal disciple should. Instead, I let him talk, I listened, I replied. I even revealed to him a very special secret: that I had found my soul word. The first person I'd shared my triumph with was my enemy.

I bunched my fists against my temples. *Curse you Bloodwyn.* He made me question myself; he made me falter. He made me *feel.* And it felt too good to deny. Because of him, my loyalty was divided.

I let my hands drop to my sides. I mustn't allow that to happen.

Juel was dead. I needed to marry Andriet to fulfilled my duty. His bride had to die.

I huffed out a breath. *Convince the king to allow me to stay, then kill the bride and take her place.*

Most of all, don't trust the Razohan just because he'd shown a smidgeon of interest in me as a person and a small dash of compassion, which was likely false. He traded faces as easily as I dressed. Maybe his emotions were as easily gained and lost.

He'd shared some of his fractured heart.

I slammed my palms to my thighs and groaned my humiliation, causing the sentinels to frown. Everything he said could've been a lie to lull my wounded heart. He could be playing me as deftly as I'd seen many courtiers in my father's court do repeatedly for their own amusement. From what I'd gleaned, the Razohan were masters of falsity. He was likely no different.

Except he hadn't ended the House of Tannard. He could do it anytime he wanted. Myself and the wizards would be powerless to stop him. The Salmun, for all I could see, didn't even know he walked amongst them.

I fisted my hair, then spun from the sentinels as I covered my mouth with my hands. *Stop it, you stupid fool.* He was playing with me, and now laughing at me, like so many had done before. I'd grown up accustomed to my plainness, feeling no jealousy toward Edilene for her beauty or any of the other exquisite women in father's court. In his court, a woman's worth was based on her beauty. All they ever won was an arrogant ass of a husband, and through her beauty he gained himself a favored place in society while remaining blind to her unique qualities. Besides, I'd expected no pleasure or love in my life. Until Carlin. He was the only man who seemed capable of overlooking my plainness to love the woman underneath.

But he'd never really known me. Carlin saw the wounded princess struggling to breathe amongst a court of vipers and not the killer underneath; not the woman sharpened by the Sistern to be the Mother's weapon. He thought he knew my heart, but the woman Carlin loved would not hold her hand over a dying man's mouth to silence his screams.

Unlike the Razohan. He knew me for what I was because I was as duplicitous as he. But what crazy, foolish mind I had grown to think for one moment, this Razohan would actually be interested in me? Was I that pitiable, that desperate to feel love again that I would dally with my enemy? That I would feel flattered? That I would feel a sudden thumping of my heart and a tiny flutter in my stomach because he wanted to know me?

"The princess is acting strange," Lord Truett said, flashing in front of me.

I jerked at his sudden arrival, conscious of the sentinels behind me.

"She is clearly quite mad with grief," Borrat said.

"It is an interesting turn of events. Did we not warn the princess not to meddle in the affairs of men? And now it would seem a handful of the king's council are dead. Heads off, the lot of them," Albert said.

"Go away," I hissed under my breath.

"What next does she plan to do? Strip the king of the rest of his council by claiming treason once again?" Albert continued as if I hadn't spoken.

It was time I made a serious effort to perfect my ability as a spiritweaver.

I glanced over my shoulder at the sentinels, seeing they were staring ahead and not at me. Then I focused on the spirits in front of me. *Go.* I mouthed the word, even dared give a small flick of my hands.

"I do not think we are welcome here, gentlemen," Truett said.

"But I very much want to see what the king has to say," Borrat said.

"The Salmun have intervened. The princess is to stay. What more is there to know? I for one have more important lives to drop in on." Albert turned and disappeared down the corridor.

I jerked my head at Albert's retreating form, then swept a hand through my bun to smooth my hair, spared one calming breath, then turned to face the doors. The sentinel's lips were twitching. I could imagine the stories they would share in the servants' quarters, but I doubted anyone mentioned me favorably, so I cared little.

This was an important moment for me. The king had to give me what I wanted now I'd proven my worth. But I had more to prove. I just hoped he wouldn't take my head, deciding I was more a danger than a useful aid. And while the Salmun's support of me was crucial for the king's ear, I'd been foolish in exposing my ability to Orphus. Uncomfortable tingles ran along my spine as I wondered what interest he now had in me.

The ever-present sentinels opened the doors onto a lush atrium, its ceiling soaring overhead and fashioned like shards of glass. Plants of varying sizes and color were tamed into beds either side of stone paths, and in the center, sat at a small iron table, was the king eating his breakfast.

He glanced at me as the doors closed behind. "Come, sit." He nodded to a servant partially obscured by the drooping branch of a large broad-leafed plant. The servant rushed forward at the king's silent command.

"Tea," Henricus ordered.

"Yes, Sire." The servant scampered away behind the dense greenery as the king motioned with a wave of his hand for me to sit next to him.

Henricus treated me like a friend, which felt weird and a little creepy. Even so, I slid into the seat that was already set, grateful he was not kicking me out. It was a good start to our conversation.

He didn't look at me, continuing to scoop out the runny yoke from his egg and slurping it into his mouth. Neither did he speak to me, so rather than watch him eat, I looked out of the glass wall across from me. The green of the lush plants inside the atrium grew stark against the dull day. From here, I could see the tops of the distant buildings and the spire of the Salmun's temple, the end spearing into the heavy clouds.

The servant returned and poured me a cup without asking if I wanted any. Once done, he slunk away between the foliage again. To my left, another place was set, and I wondered if the king was expecting his wife to join him.

"Eat," the king said around his mouthful.

The first day of my arrival, I'd been forced to endure an evening meal with the Tannard family. Since then, it was rare that the royal family ate as one. Juel had vanished most nights, likely to eat with one mistress or another. The queen was never well enough to join us, and the king, Andriet told me, liked to eat alone, or he endured an evening meal with his council men, leaving Andriet and I together, unless he snuck off to steal a night with Daelon, and I would disappear to my room with my meal.

I selected a large boiled egg and a thick piece of dark brown bread from the array of breakfast dishes in front of me. I had worked myself up over this conversation, so I had no appetite. The smells of the buttery pastries did nothing to improve it. Instead, they made me feel queasy.

"I've invited you here as a thank you."

"There's no need, Your Majesty."

He nodded as if he thought the same. "I give my thanks rarely, so it's advisable to accept it."

"Of course, Sire. I'm honored, but I was only doing my duty. My loyalty lies with the House of Tannard."

He stopped chewing and, for the first time, looked at me. He swiped up his napkin, wiped his hands on it, then he settled back in his seat as he threw the napkin onto his plate. He was done eating, and I'd yet to have a mouthful. I lowered my fork and sat back.

"Don't stop. You haven't even started."

Etiquette deemed I should stop when the king stopped, and I wanted to because my stomach still felt tight, but I did as he said and picked up my fork.

"You look little like your sister."

I swallowed, preparing myself for what was to come.

"Her portrait was very favorable. Juel was most pleased." He picked at his teeth. "But I more so with you."

I nearly choked on my bread and pretend a dainty cough to ease it down. There were many words I could say right now, praising the king, thanking the king, playing coy. Instead, I waited for him to speak.

"Beauty is a flaw. It disguises many truths and makes fools out of men." He sighed. "It's age that has taught me that."

He took a sip of his tea. "You're quiet. None of this

constant banter and frivolous chatter ringing in my ears. I find the quiet far more tolerable. Everything is more peaceful now the queen is keeping to her bed."

I took another mouthful of my bread dipped in egg, wondering where the king was going with this.

"Lady Astaria is most distraught. She won't be seen in court for some time. I believe she's fled to her father's estate to recover, which she'll do soon enough. Then she'll set her sights on the next young man of esteemed birth. No doubt, she'll be waiting to see the outcome of the trials, as will all the unmarried ladies of noble birth."

When the king granted the winners—those that survived—a favorable position at his court. This was why the young noblemen were willing to risk their lives. Recognition from the king, honors and titles and the pick of eligible women. Lady Astaria would be at the front of the queue.

I continued eating, knowing he wasn't interested in anything I could add to the conversation, neither would he be interested in hearing my view on the trials.

He threw down his napkin. "You may speak. I praised your silence, but too much of it makes you dull."

"Sire. I'm sorry for your loss." It was the first thing to come into my head.

He raised an eyebrow at me as he leaned back in his seat. "But you're not sorry to see him dead."

I pressed my lips firm but refused to drop my gaze from his.

"Don't think I was blind to my son's flaws. All young men have more vice than sense. He would've grown, matured, learned he wouldn't find greatness beneath a lady's skirts. Under the guidance of the Creed of Salmun, he would've become an excellent king. In time, his vices would've lost their grip, and he would have settled beside you."

I could only nod, not wanting to offend the king in contradicting him.

"Age is meant to humble us."

For a few, perhaps. The older men in father's court still found their ways to bicker, scheme, gamble, flirt, and make fools of themselves.

"You're an intelligent woman. I see it in your eyes. Your silence is a very handy trait to possess. In my experience those that say little, listen a lot. That's how you learned of the plot to dispose of me."

He leaned his elbows on the armrests of his chair, staring at me over his steepled fingers. "Tell me, how did you discover the plot?"

I took a breath before responding, wondering if this might be the right moment to ask the king for my favor. "The night of the ball, I stepped onto the balcony for some air. There was light coming from your library window, and when I moved closer, I overheard Lord Dowel among others discussing their plans inside."

He stared at me as he tapped his fingers against his lips. "I hated you."

Great. Definitely not the right moment.

"When I saw you there beside my dead son, I wanted to strike you down. They told me it wasn't your fault, that there was no hope with such a wound, but I wanted to blame you all the same."

I inhaled, feeling the fierce tug of his gaze, seeing the clench of his fists.

"You'll understand one day. When you have children of your own. One dead son and one I will have to order into his new bride's bed," he grumbled as he sat forward to grab his teacup.

Knowing he knew about Andriet and Daelon's love softened my view of him a little more.

"It was Orphus who spoke on your behalf. Something he's never done before."

"Sire." I could say little else, but the idea that Orphus showed any interest in me churned an uneasiness in my gut.

"It's curious. As are you." He set his cup down. "My plans for the marriage celebrations will continue. Only now the focus will be on Andriet and his new bride. She'll arrive on our shores any day."

"Sire, perhaps it's not wise to continue with the trials."

Someone hoping to topple the House of Tannard would find their perfect chance during the trials.

He harrumphed. "This is a tradition that dates back to the great war." He shook his head. "Impossible."

"You have taken care of one treasonous plot, but I think it's dangerous to assume that was the only—"

There was a rustle from the thick foliage and another servant appeared, hurrying to the king's side to whisper in his ear.

"Ah, excellent." He glanced at me as the servant moved away. "We have company."

I looked at the extra plate. Perhaps the queen had

arrived, though I wasn't sure he would act so pleased about that news.

At the sound of the doors swinging wide, I glanced over my shoulder to see Bloodwyn stride inside. I snapped my head around and stared at my bread and egg, gripping the sides of the table with my fingers. Curses that I should feel this way. My little self-talk did nothing to stop the sudden flush of flutters churning my stomach.

My body vibrated to the tune of his boots smacking on the stone floor as he pounded toward us. My heart climbed my throat and a fever burned low in my...

This wasn't me.

"Your Majesty." He halted behind me. "So kind of you to agree to see me, and in your private rooms."

I felt the softest presence at my left shoulder, the smallest hint of warmth, and I could almost feel his fingers brush at my shoulder. Tingles flared around my bite mark. I wouldn't look behind, no matter how painful the urge.

The king waved his hand to the third table setting. Not the queen, then.

"Obliged."

My eyes flittered closed on hearing his voice, full of arrogance. There could be no better time than now to reveal him...if I felt sure anyone would believe me. Which they wouldn't. I would have to reveal my talent in order to prove the truth, and the Razohan would never trip up and make an accidental mistake, given he carried Bloodwyn's soul. He would know exactly how to act and what to say to keep his identity a secret.

"Princess Tressya," he uttered in shock as he slid with agile grace into his seat. "What a great surprise."

I gave him a vexed look while my right hand twitched to rub against his bite mark. "Lord Bloodwyn."

I would imagine the real Razohan looked like a hunch-backed ogre and not someone with compelling amber eyes that never failed to ensnare me; not someone who made my heart beat painfully against my ribs.

"I wish to extend my utmost sympathies. The last time we met—"

"Thank you." I knew he spoke of the hunt and Juel's death, but my mind went to the actual last time. I wouldn't allow myself to think of that.

Surely Bloodwyn's soul infected the Razohan enough to give him decorum. A beast-man of the north, he'd be ripping meat from a carcass with his teeth otherwise. No way would a Razohan know how to give a woman pleasure.

I don't care. I don't care. I didn't care if he knew a woman's head from her toes. It meant nothing to me.

Looking far too pleased with himself, Bloodwyn leaned forward and grabbed himself a thick hunk of bread, then slathered it with an even thicker layer of butter.

"The princess eagerly awaits the trials," the king announced.

I sipped my tea, keeping my eyes on the table. I had yet to offer my proposition and this sounded as though the king had decided to let me stay in Tarragona.

"Does she now. I hope we can put on a good show for her."

"You're entering, Bloodwyn?"

"Of course, Your Majesty. Given I'm unlikely to get the chance again, I wouldn't dream of missing out."

I darted him a hard look, knowing the real reason he chose to join the trials. If they were as dangerous as Andriet claimed, then what better way to dispose of Andriet without raising suspicions. Though the Razohan would have a hard time, as I doubted the Creed of Salmun would let Andriet out of their sight.

"Huh. There, see, princess. Everyone loves the trials."

"It would seem, Sire."

"I hope the princess will be there to cheer me on?"

Our eyes locked. My gaze was combative, but Bloodwyn merely smiled and raised his tea to his lips, and curses that I watched his lips touch the side of his cup. The cup disappeared and those lips were suddenly on my skin.

I blinked, snapping my eyes to my plate. Seeing my half-eaten slice of bread and egg, I attacked the bread, sawing a large slice, then thought the better and cut it smaller before popping it into my mouth.

"Whether I'm to remain in Tarragona for the trials is up to the king to decide," I said once I swallowed my mouthful.

Damn that Bloodwyn was here, for I couldn't speak freely in front of him.

"Yes, I see," Bloodwyn murmured. "My reason for requesting an audience with Your Majesty is of grave importance." He glanced at me. "It's fitting the princess is here. I know she wouldn't wish me to mention her name in any of this, but I feel I must."

My heart climbed my throat. I turned the full force of my hatred toward him. If he dared reveal who I really was, I would do the same, regardless of how many believed me. I would make them believe me; I would find a way.

"I fear, Your Majesty..." Bloodwyn continued.

Curses that I was so pathetic to think he was genuine in anything he said to me when he used the ultimate subterfuge. That smidgeon of compassion he'd shown to me was false. I took another sip of my tea, only to feel the slight tremor in my hand.

"The treachery the princess revealed to you is only the beginning."

I hated him. From the depths of my heart, I hated him.

"What is this?" the king growled. "Tell me."

"There are others, Sire. Within the king's council."

What?

"What?" the king breathed.

"And, Sire..." Bloodwyn glanced at me.

I could feel the cold on my cheeks.

"It is once again the princess you have to thank for this knowledge."

What? I choked on my sip of tea. Whatever his plan, I loathed being part of it.

"Indeed. Tell me more," the king demanded.

Bloodwyn leaned over and offered me his napkin, even though mine was in easy reach. I ignored his and used mine, which was petty, but I wasn't about to take anything he offered, even something as insignificant as a table napkin.

"The princess came to me asking questions about Tarragona's trade relations with the north. She'd heard a discussion between Weselton and Leto regarding their strategy for moving merchandise through the Ashenlands.

The princess was unaware of any relations with the north or provision for moving trade between borders."

Damn, he was good.

"I therefore took it upon myself to investigate before I brought any claims before you. I called on Lord Weselton and when told to wait for his return, I rifled through his private papers, and found this."

He pulled some parchment from his jacket pocket. A servant rushed forward from behind a large broadleaf and took the parchment from Bloodwyn and gave it to the king.

I studied the king's face as he read the letter. His face paled as his lips pinched tight. Within moments, he scrunched the letter in his fist. "Do you have more proof?"

"For now, no. Sire. But I am sure there's plenty to be found in Lord Weselton's manor in the north. He likely keeps all his secret correspondence there, believing it would be safe."

Planted by Bloodwyn, perhaps, or did he have others here with him, within the king's court or his guard? The Razohan would aim for anyone close to the king. He was too good, too thorough, too cunning. Not only that, the Razohan was an adept liar, better than any I'd heard before; perfected by Bloodwyn's soul. How could I hope to protect Andriet and the House of Tannard? How could I win against people who could become anyone?

"It's my belief they hope to do more than benefit from opening a new trade route. I would say they hope to gain new allies."

The king threw down the letter and launched to his feet with such violence, his chair fell backward. The lush indoor garden absorbed the loud smack as his chair hit the floor. A servant appeared and scampered forward to right it.

"Is there no end to this treachery?" he snarled.

"Sire, I ask your permission to investigate. I'll make it my sole focus to discover any validity to the claims and see how deep the treachery runs. If there are culprits, then I shall bring them before you on their knees."

With the king's back toward us, I glared at Bloodwyn, only to receive a seductive smile and a wink. Ignoring the tingles that sparked in my belly, I intensified my glare, narrowing my eyes as if I could fashion them into spears.

What better way to undermine the king than strip his support? At this rate, Bloodwyn would have the king execute all of his noblemen.

Bloodwyn had told me he had to win. The deviousness of his plan made me fear he would. How could I outsmart him? Without enough time to think, killing him seemed my only solution. As a disciple, I shouldn't balk at the idea. I gritted my teeth, hating the uncomfortable weight lodging in my chest at the thought of slicing his throat.

I slipped my hand through the discreet slit in my skirts and into my pocket bag, feeling the dagger inside. The cold steel of its hilt cooled my palm. I tried not to show the relief in my expression.

The king spun around. "Andriet's bride arrives any day, and I won't allow anything to interfere with my plans. The trials and the marriage will go ahead."

"May I suggest a plan, Sire?"

When the king slumped down in his seat once more, Bloodwyn leaned forward and rested his palms on the table.

My body tensed as I watched him. Even that insignificant gesture reminded me of a predator, like those big hunting cats that lived in Merania's forests.

The king waved a finger, indicating Bloodwyn should continue.

"Let me send some of my men to search Lord Weselton's manor while he is in Tolum. Then we shall know for sure if and who the true traitors are. If it turns out, Sire, the rumors are true, then what better way to see their end during the trials. They need never finish the trials. If you know what I mean."

"They need to be made an example of."

"Your Majesty, if anyone knew there was a way to trade through the Ashenlands... Surely you would want that kept a secret."

"There isn't a way. There could be no way. The Levenians saw to that. The Ashenlands have existed for one thousand years and the north has never won their way through. If any of my councilmen have found a way, then it's with the help of the Salmun, and I cannot believe that."

"It's merely a suggestion, Sire."

The king blew out a hard breath and sunk back into his seat. "Your plan has merit. Let me think on it."

"Of course, we mustn't forget the role Princess Tressya played in uncovering yet another treasonous plot."

The two men focused on me. *Curse you, Bloodwyn.* I couldn't begin to imagine what he hope to gain by calling me out like this? I concentrated on the king, ignoring the urge to glare at Bloodwyn when I felt his eyes like the hot burning sun baring down on me. It was then I realized I would have to surrender some of my pretense if I hoped to gain some ground here.

"I am indebted to you again, Princess."

"Speak nothing of it, Your Majesty." I gripped the hilt of my dagger firm in my palm.

"Yes, it would seem the princess is conveniently placed once again. One would question what magical listening skills she possesses."

I kept my eyes on the king. No way would I let him see me squirm. And showing my fury would let him believe this was his win.

"Yes, she's quite an asset to the House of Tannard."

"It's a shame she no longer has a permanent place within your household...Forgive me, Sire, if that was insensitive..."

The King flicked his wrist to quieten Bloodwyn's concern. I released my hold on my dagger and stood, drawing both men's attention.

"Your Majesty, I thank you for your high praise." I tapped the tips of my fingers on the table and shifted my gaze to Bloodwyn. He drew his eyes from my fingers, dancing their little tune, and arched an eyebrow at me.

"Lord Bloodwyn is far too generous in what he says. I fear he may be not as sincere in his praise."

"The Princess questions my sincerity?" He locked his amber eyes on me. "I shall excuse her for that. She's new to Tolum and doesn't know me well."

"Perhaps the Princess knows you more than you know yourself," I said.

He smirked. "Impossible. I'm a complicated maze, Princess. Far too much dwells within me. You need only look inside of me to know that was true. If that was at all possible."

I gave a soft laugh as I strolled toward his chair. "Your Majesty, when we last met, I asked you to grant me a favor should the treasonous plot be true."

"I recall. And now you wish to ask for that favor?"

I strolled behind Bloodwyn's seat. This close I could smell warm leather mixed with a deep and heavy spice, rich in syrupy thickness. Once behind him, his seat obscuring my right hand, I delved through the slit at my side for my pocket bags and gently pulled my dagger from its sheath.

"I must warn you, Sire, making bargains with the princess—"

I whipped my dagger up and placed it hard against Bloodwyn's throat.

The king jerked to his feet, his chair again slamming to the floor. Once standing, he staggered away. The leaves rustled as the servants rushed for the exit, to alert the sentinels, no doubt.

"You have nothing to fear from me, Your Majesty."

"I would question that claim—" I pressed the blade harder to Bloodwyn's throat, not so it broke skin, but enough for him to know I was serious.

The doors burst open, and the sentinels rushed in.

"Wait," shouted the king, holding his hand up to the rushing guards.

"I meant every word when I told you I was loyal to the House of Tannard. But you must know something about me. While my sister perfected her needlework and singing, I learned a far more useful skill. A little deadly, you may say, but my father found me very useful."

The Razohan wasn't the only one who could spin a tale. I wasn't sure how much the King of Tarragona knew about the Sistern, but I wasn't taking any chances. I was sure I would lose my head were he to know.

"My sword skills equal any fighter, and I'm swift with a dagger. I can be a far greater asset to you as your blade than I ever would've been as a wife to your son."

"You're forgetting I have the Creed of Salmun."

"Who was it to discover the treasonous plots?" I might as well make use of the praise Bloodwyn won for me, even if the second treasonous plot was bound to be false. "Everyone within your court knows to keep secrets from the Salmun. No one will suspect a woman such as me."

"Sire, may I speak?" Bloodwyn croaked.

This time, I curled my fingers through his hair and gripped hard, pulling his head back so he looked up at me.

Keeping the pressure of my blade to his throat, I said, "The Lord is too fond of his voice."

"The Lord is even fonder of his neck," Bloodwyn replied, then coughed as if choking.

I quirked a brow.

"Let him go," the king commanded.

So I did, then strolled around the side of his chair, working my hand through the slit in my skirt to sheath my dagger. Bloodwyn kept his gaze fixed on my actions with a quizzical raise of his brow.

I sat back down, my back rigid with tension. After one calming breath, I turned to the king.

"Go," he barked to his sentinels, then eased himself into his chair. He steepled his fingers and eyed me while the sentinels retreated and closed the door with a clunk.

"Is this what has drawn Orphus's attention?"

"I wouldn't know what has interested Orphus, Sire. But you're the only man to know of my secret."

"Not so," Bloodwyn added.

"That can be remedied," I mumbled, keeping my gaze on the king.

"You have given me much to think about. It's quite extraordinary." Then his gaze narrowed. "How do I know your father did not send you to end Juel's life?"

"If it were true, he would've died long before he fell from his horse. My father would gain nothing from killing the Crown Prince. This alliance is very important to Merania. If anything, he wanted me to protect Juel."

"Which didn't go down so well," Bloodwyn said.

The king stayed quiet. His stare felt like thick nails hammered to the ground to keep me in place.

"We must remember after all the treasonous plots, the king—"

"Can think for himself." I interrupted Bloodwyn, keeping my voice and face deadpan.

"I was merely—"

"Interfering in something that doesn't concern you."

I turned from him as if dismissing him, yet was keenly aware of his eyes burrowing into my head. I loathed how much he stole my attention, even when I wasn't looking at him.

"Sire," I began, but he held up his hand to silence me. Curses to Bloodwyn for interfering.

Finally, he sat forward. "You have proved yourself loyal to the House of Tannard twice now." His gaze was slicing, but so far it sounded promising. "I'll grant you your wish. You shall become my eyes, my ears, my blade. But I warn you, princess, I'll be watching you."

"As will I," Bloodwyn murmured.

"Don't give me or the Salmun a reason to mistrust you," the king finished.

CHAPTER

TWENTY-FOUR

TAMAS

"ARE the letters where they need to be?" With the trials commencing in four days' time, we needed to move quickly. The better it was for us if more of the king's supporters died by his own hand.

"Why are you asking me?" Osmud grumbled.

"I hear the taverns in Burnside have excellent ale."

"They do, and Weselton's wife was very accommodating. I managed both without failing in my duty. Which is a lot more than I can say for you."

I sipped from my goblet and eyed the room, which was abuzz with excitement. "My plan's unfolding nicely."

Henricus sat within his seat at the center of the table, and for the first time since I'd arrived in Tolum, his wife sat at his side. She looked a sickly sight. A pale reminder of her beauty remained, her cheeks now gaunt, her hair losing its luster. I'd seen much sickness in my day, which made me suspicious of this one. The faint tinge of blue on her lips was telling, so too the ashen paste of her complexion, but no one seemed to notice. The king was a bastard for insisting she attend the festivities in celebration of Princess Cirro's arrival, though seeing her now, I wondered if he wanted to hasten her end. It was none of my business, but it spurred my interest in hastening his end.

"Your plan is to dance around the princess—"

"I've no interest in Princess Cirro."

"Dammit—Bloodwyn," Osmud hissed, anger peeling his mask aside such that he almost said my real name. "You know who I mean. Fuck the woman, then finish it."

I glanced at Osmud, standing to my right. "You're very eloquent tonight."

"I can get more eloquent if you like." He half turned to me, lowering his voice for just the two of us. "I didn't just stop in Burnside."

"That would explain your delay." I moved away from the pillar, leading Osmud to the back of the ballroom where the entire room was visible and no one could lurk behind pillars to hear conversations they shouldn't.

"I went north."

I suspected he would say such. "And?"

"The clans are making their way to the south. Kaldor has granted them leave to camp in Wilhelm. Aric has opened his lands to the south near the Lanrial River."

"And what of their passage through the Ashenlands?"

"Garrat believes it will work."

"How sure is he? He needs to be certain."

"Romelda has not been idle. Since leaving the augur, she's traveled the north, gathering the Nazeen—"

"Interesting—" I pushed off the wall and strolled, dipping my head to the couple coming our way. The lady smelt as though she'd tumbled into a patch of lilies and rolled around for hours.

Once they'd passed, Osmud came alongside me. We continued our stroll behind the crowds of onlookers, forming a curtain around the dancers in the center of the ballroom. My eyes were forever searching for one person, but I'd yet to find her.

At the far corner, where the chandelier of candlelight failed to reach, I settled against the wall once more.

"It seems she at least understood what that buffoon was saying, and now seems desperate to call the blood-eyed Nazeen to our cause. Unfortunately, she says the last thousand years have not been kind. There are fewer and fewer blooded."

"Any Nazeen by our side is a help. Henricus has agreed to death by trials for the traitors.

"Their focus will be on Andriet."

"And not the passage, or the king. Already a decree has gone out, enforcing his will. All Lords must take part in the trials. By the end, he'll have killed his own council and many of their sons. That shall distract the Creed of Salmun, who'll be busy ensuring their maligned creatures carry out his orders. It's the perfect opportunity for an invading force."

"And Andriet."

"Andriet is no soldier."

"He's a Tannard."

He was a significant friend of Tressya's in this House of Serpents. How would she feel if I killed him?

"I'll focus on the king first."

"What's that over there?" Osmud bit and jerked his head toward Princess Cirro.

She was shockingly young, a dark-haired beauty with a thick spiral of midnight black curls balanced on top of her head. Small and petite, two of my hands would span her waist; one hand would easily snap her neck. For one so young, she was full of grace and poise, her lush red lips pulling into a delicate smile at every introduction. A faint blush flared on her cheeks every time she glanced up at Andriet, who'd dutifully stayed by her side. It seemed the child bride was happy with her match, but Andriet looked stiff and awkward beside her.

At last, I finally caught sight of Tressya, moving toward us along the opposite side of the ballroom, though she'd yet to see us. I took her in with one look, overlooking the opulent gown and elaborate hair accessories to focus solely on her face.

As the king's blade, she remained in disguise.

"The young princess is one more innocent who should never have made it to shore... Are you listening to me?"

He jerked around to follow the line of my gaze. "Stars above, Tamas, you haven't listened to a word I've said. Have you?"

"Your voice is like insects buzzing in my ear."

He spun back to me, moving so he blocked my view of Tressya. "She was better when she was Juel's bride. Now we have trouble."

"Trouble I'm handling."

"Trouble you *want* to handle. Let me take care of the disciple. You focus on Andriet and the king."

I grabbed Osmud's elbow. "The princess is *my* responsibility," I said sharply, my tone brooking no argument.

The shock in his eyes almost made me release his arm and excuse my tone.

I had never spoken to Osmud this way. What was I doing? He was my brother, my best and truest alongside Garrat, and I treated him like this?

"I'm sorry, brother."

Osmud yanked his arm from my hold and leaned in, jabbing a finger at my face. "This is the problem." He bared his teeth as he spoke. "She is the problem."

"I don't disagree." *Perhaps not in the way you believe.* "But let me handle this my way."

I kept a watch on Tressya as she drifted closer, wishing she would confess why she kept me a secret from the king? It had to be because she felt something for me.

Osmud blew out a long breath and turned away from me to stare at the new princess. "She's a child. I can't touch a child."

"Forget Princess Cairo. The king grows impatient. The trials come before her marriage. By then, the bride will have no groom."

"Neither will there be a king," Osmud replied.

I searched out Tressya again to find a nobleman had cut off her path.

"You've done all you can do for now, Osmud. Go find

yourself a pretty lady and a tankard of ale. Enjoy yourself while you can."

I left Osmud cursing under his breath and headed straight toward Tressya. Her back was to me, but I wondered if she felt my approach through our link, the bite, and already knew I was here. Biting her removed my element of surprise. But the link between us would be more beneficial to me in the end.

"Princess." I came alongside her and bowed with a flourish as the musicians began another song. "I hope you haven't forgotten our dance." I held out my hand.

To my surprise, she placed her hand in mine. I led her to the center of the room before she could refuse or offer a snide remark. I had expected tension in her body as I brought her in close and resistance to my lead. I even thought she would insist on maintaining a certain distance between us and slap my hand away from her back. However, she did none of those things. Instead, she folded into me as if we were once molded into a single entity. She wasn't a great dancer. Within the first few minutes, she stepped on my feet twice, which made me want to enfold her close and lift her onto my toes, saving her from the hassle of the dance steps and keeping her attention solely on me.

At one point, I caught Osmud's glare, but I spun her away so my back faced him, concentrating on keeping our rhythm and guiding Tressya as best as I could. The room and everyone in it seemed to disappear when she leaned close, almost resting her chin on my chest. That simple gesture made me hold my breath, feeling like I balanced on a precipice, eager to fall. The way her eyes held me prisoner should have concerned me, as well as how staring at her lips obliterated every thought beyond us—her closeness in my arms, her lilac fragrance, warm against her skin, became the most intoxicating poison.

Tressya's head reached my shoulders. She wasn't broad and muscular like Bryra, yet she was already a serious headache for me, one I wanted to endure again and again. Never had a rival been so perilous and yet so enticing.

"I hope I haven't taken your attention from your task as King's blade by drawing you in to dance."

"I know who the real enemy is, Bloodwyn, and it's not the pathetic noblemen of the king's court. That was brilliant of you, by the way."

"I'm glad you think so." My gaze hadn't left her lips. She knew where my eyes lingered and made no effort to draw them away. Did she appreciate my gaze? "What is it that makes me clever?"

I was surprised by my sudden reaction as she pulled away from my suffocating hold. My arm stayed firm around her waist, muscles tensing at the thought of releasing her. The first threat of my claws tingled behind my nail beds. *Don't try it, my little princess.* I wasn't ready to let her go.

"The demesne of Lord Weselton and Lord Leto are in the north. They abut the Ashenlands."

"Is that so?"

"And your demesne, Lord Bloodwyn, is also far north. Tell me, how many more lords in this new plot we've discovered have lands bordering the Ashenlands?"

I glanced over her head, surveying the room, not

focusing on anyone in particular while pretending to ponder her question.

"Quite a few, I would say."

"And how many are also on the council?"

"Not all. I didn't want to be too obvious."

The dance called for a change in partner, so I pulled Tressya away from the circle, forcing the couples on either side of us to scramble in finding their new partners. It was a bold move that drew every eye to us, but by now I no longer cared. If he had them on hand, Osmud would throw rocks at my head, but not even the thought of his fury bothered me.

Tressya went with me, stumbling over my newly devised dance steps, but my strong hold prevented her from falling. Compared to any woman in the room, she was graceless, but in my arms, she became a queen, at least to me.

"I'll protect Andriet with my life," she declared solemnly and with force, a determination I admired, sending a fiery arrow into my loins. With seductive words like that, how could Osmud expect me to ignore this woman? Her mother was blind to think Tressya a compliant disciple. No one could tame this princess. I knew that the first moment I met her. Behind her plain face yet expressive eyes lay fire and a warrior's heart, making her the most beautiful woman in the room.

Yet, her adoration—dare I say love—of Andriet was evident. A man I had to kill.

"I know."

And I'd foolishly allowed myself to be lost in the feel of her in my arms, letting the familiar smell of her become a cherished memory. She felt otherwise. Her deep blue eyes penetrated mine like a lance. There were barbs and arrows in her heart, but I knew there were also flowers. In a spasm of hatred, I loathed Andriet for picking them all before I had the chance.

"What do you know of the Sistern?"

"I know enough to understand you'll fulfill the Mother Divine's command. If it suits you."

She took in what I said, keeping her intense blue eyes on me. Finally, she replied, "Then we have a problem." She leaned close. "Because Andriet will live." There was so much conviction in her words.

Like a fast-flowing river, a hopelessness swept through me. What if I couldn't make her trust me? What if I couldn't win her heart. The idea nearly crippled my restraint. The overwhelming urge to force my kiss upon her humbled me. I wouldn't be gentle. Rather, I'd punish her for the impossible emotions she sparked in me. It would be no kiss of desire. Instead, I would vent the anger boiling in my heart, along with the confusion in my head. I also tasted dread, burning the back of my mouth. It rose like an anvil, lodging heavily in my throat.

"A problem with no way out?" I tried to smile, but it only deepened her frown.

"It appears so. What do we do?"

"We improvise?" I was desperate to reverse the terrible turn this conversation had taken.

"What happens when we meet face to face during the fight?"

"I don't know, princess. You tell me."

My heart seethed with anger over the cruel twist of fate

that led me to a woman who captivated my soul, only to be fated to destroy those she cherished. If we were loyal to our fates, we should be mortal enemies, yet here we were, entwined in each other's arms. That had to mean something significant for our future.

When she dragged her eyes from mine, I finally took a breath. She had ceased to cooperate, turning to wood in my arms, so I spun her around, making her gasp. Not letting her catch her breath, and despite her punishing my feet and shins, I spun her again and again, until we were caught in a dizzy spiral. Her laughter washed the gloom from my heart.

It was Tressya who noticed the music had stopped. "Bloodwyn," she whispered, gasping for breath.

I slowed the spin and glanced around the room. "We've made a spectacle of ourselves." But I didn't stop dancing with her, fearing if I did, it would end our time together. Keeping the sway, we shuffled around on the spot.

The whole ballroom watched us, but she seemed immune to their stares, and I loved that about her.

I would spin her again the moment I saw her eyes lose their laughter. She had returned to the real world far quicker than I, which left me scrambling to think of another way to keep us locked in the fantastical dream I'd already created in my head.

"This is what we do," she said. "We each keep going. We do what's required of us. And then, when the time comes, and we find ourselves facing each other on the battlefield... Well, then I guess we decide."

"Are you making a deal with me?"

The twitch of her lips, the promise of a smile, and the

sudden heaviness inside of me, threatening to pull me down into a pit, released. A bright light pierced my darkness when her smile won through.

"Yes. It's the only deal I can make."

"Excuse me," came a male voice from our right.

"Lord Bothridge." As fast as a blink, his name came into my mind, so too the aged smell of dust and cluttered rooms.

"Lord Bloodwyn." He dabbed the tears from his rheumy eyes, then flittered a gaze to Tressya, his gray eyes dipping down her body. After a further wipe of his teary eyes, and a twitch of his nose, he turned his attention back to me. "This is rather indelicate of me—"

"No need to embarrass yourself, Bothridge." I patted him on the arm as I led Tressya from the floor.

Couples parted to form a path for our escape. Many of the ladies hid their mouths behind their fans, but not before I saw their smirks. Damn that I'd kept her out there on the dance floor in front of everyone, giving them the opportunity to mock her in their minds. I glanced at her, hoping to gain a glimpse of how she felt. She walked tall and proud, staring ahead as if there was a better horizon to look at.

We moved to the back of the room, further from the chandeliers and into the shadows. Everyone soon lost interest in us when the music started up again.

I turned her to face me. "I won't put you in that position again."

She huffed a laugh. "You really think something like that wounds me, Bloodwyn?"

I exhaled and, for a moment, closed my eyes, wishing it was my name she spoke and not some pompous moron who favored gambling and whoring more than honor and courage.

I opened my eyes to find her staring at me, her lips slightly parted, and damn if I forgot where my thoughts were going.

"What's your name?" she whispered.

My eyes flared. I almost staggered back with the uncanniness of her question. I shook my head.

"Will I ever see you? The real you?" Said with a hint of longing, I almost dropped my restraint and used my connection with her to peek inside her heart.

My eyes trailed up her body, understanding the gown she wore was her disguise. Beneath was the real Tressya—the woman who held me spellbound, the woman whose loyalty and courage had no equal within this room. Except against me. Which led to our greatest problem. Neither of us could relent on the path of our duty; I had to destroy the House of Tannard, and she had to save them.

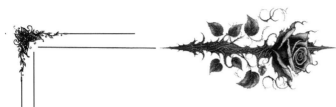

CHAPTER

TWENTY-FIVE

TRESSYA

WE TRAVELED for six days to arrive at the edge of a wasteland. There was nothing but blackened trees with twisted, leafless branches everywhere I looked. The forest floor, like baked clay parched from a sun that rarely broke through the heavy clouds, spread as far as the eye could see. A wind swept along the ground, eddying dust plumes and drifting the stench of decay. It was a desolate, forgotten place. However, I knew that if I were to step foot within the Ashenlands, the place would appear reborn.

Andriet had shown me a book with images drawn by noblemen who'd survived the trials over the last few centuries. Their drawings showed an abundant forest, gloomy and dark but as rich as any found in Merania. It was the Creed's curse, according to Andriet, that shielded the truth from our eyes. Similarly, the curse prevented anyone standing on the southern side of the Ashenlands from seeing beyond into the north.

They had erected a tent city on the edge of the Ashenlands, transforming the isolated pocket of land into a bustling hive of activity and excitement. Not only did noblemen from across the kingdom arrive with their entourage to take part in the trials, they also brought with them a household of staff and every conceivable luxury to make their time here as pleasurable as possible, given the great risk they faced during the trials. According to Andriet, the trials could take weeks or more to complete.

Following in the path of the nobles and the king's household came the smithies to sharpen blades and shoe horses, the market stalls for servants to gather their daily fare for their masters, the bakers, the minstrels, the entertainers, the healers. I even spied a clothier in case the ladies dirtied their gowns beyond repair.

I turned away from the low-slung clouds, hanging heavy like dirty cloth, and headed inside Andriet's tent. There I found Daelon on his knees, finishing the laces on Andriet's boots.

Unable to stay still, I paced across his fur rugs. Today the trials began, and regardless of my pleas to the king, Andriet was to ride out with the rest of the noblemen. Once they crossed the demarcation line, they would disappear from our view.

"Tradition is not to be altered," the king had claimed. And from then on, he'd closed his ears to me.

Given so many had plotted against the king, I had hoped he would see reason. The first any of us would know the outcome of each trial was when the winner crossed the demarcation line and returned into the lands of the living.

"Please, Tressya, you're giving me a headache. Come sit down, or you'll have me up and pacing with you." Andriet patted the bed beside him.

"Your father's the headache. Not me."

"Do you not trust the Salmun to keep me safe? I'm told they will ensure their pets steer clear of me."

"It's not their pets I'm worried about."

I surrendered my pacing and joined Andriet on his bed. He slung an arm around my shoulders and pulled me close beside him like a parent would do a child to soothe their fears.

"I simply need to ride in and reclaim each of the objects, then return. A fall from my horse is the worst that can happen. Lucky for me, I have impeccable horsemanship. Nothing will dislodge me from my seat." He winked at Daelon, who was busy with the laces on his other boot.

"I'm with the princess. You be careful out there," Daelon said, giving him a stern look.

"Is this the sort of encouragement I'm to expect from both of you the entire time?" Andriet cried in mock offense.

"If that's what's required to make you take this seriously," I said.

Andriet squeezed my shoulders. "Remember, I'm untouchable."

I wanted to bang my fists on his chest. It was the next best thing to punching him in the side of his head. It wasn't his fault I was irritated, though. As much as I wanted to, I couldn't even blame the king. I could blame only myself. I was the only one who knew Bloodwyn would attack him in the Ashenlands. I was the one who hadn't exposed the Razohan, and the one who woke most night from dreams of feeling his tongue on my skin, then lay awake devising ways of gutting him.

"This is foolish. Worse, it's dangerous. Andriet, you can't do it. Let the other noblemen risk their lives, not you. There's no need. You're already the crown prince. What more could your father grant you?"

Andriet turned incredulous eyes to me. "And have my name written in the legends as the prince too scared to enter the Ashenlands?"

"Do you really care about that? As king, you can forbid those legends from ever being told."

"Who would respect me if I never dared?"

I groaned at the stupidity of it all. "There are far better ways of proving your bravery."

"You don't live in this world as a man, so you don't understand," Andriet played with my hand. "As future king, I must prove myself worthy every day. My people must trust I'll have the fortitude to make the right decisions and do what I have to to protect Tarragona. No one willingly follows a coward."

"But you didn't want to be king."

He squeezed my hand. "I've found myself with no choice."

I should reveal Bloodwyn to the king before the trials began. That way, it wouldn't matter if Andriet competed.

"He has a point," Daelon added.

"Then it's a good thing I've entered too."

406

"What?" they shrieked in unison.

I shrugged Andriet's arm from my shoulders. "I've got to keep an eye on you."

"But you're a woman," Daelon stated.

"I am a woman, but that has no bearing on what I can and can't do."

"There's no tradition for—" Daelon continued.

"Has the king ever had a woman as his blade?"

Andriet shook his head. "I can't say any king has ever had his own personal assassin. That's what the Salmun are for."

"You're telling me there is no tradition for such a thing?" I insisted.

Andriet rolled his eyes. "This is different."

I rose from the bed. "It's simply one more tradition I intend to subvert."

"See." Andriet nudged Daelon. "She's wicked. That's why I love her."

"But the noblemen will be in uproar to see a woman amongst their ranks," Daelon said.

"Do you really think I'd get anywhere wearing this?" I held out the hem of my skirt.

"A disguise. This is excellent." Andriet clapped his hands.

At that moment, the tent flap parted and Princess Cirro entered, bringing with her the smell of sun-drenched days rolling in fields of flowers. Three lady's maids clambered after her, trying in vain to keep the hem of her long gown off the dirt floor.

I turned away, grinding my teeth. She was one more person proving my failure as a disciple. The princess shouldn't be alive, but Andriet had taken to her, rarely leaving her side at the ball.

My opinion from the night of the ball until now changed little. She was a beautiful young woman with a warm and generous smile. I bit my lip to stop myself from returning the smile. The wind's chill flushed her cheeks, so they matched her soft rose-colored gown, trimmed with lace and jewels embroidered into the bodice. Hardly the sort of dress for a place like this, and I wondered if she had a lady-in-waiting who insisted she dress like a doll. A fountain of black curls swept into a wooden clasp revealed her graceful long neck.

Daelon and Andriet jumped to their feet and bowed.

"Your Highness," Andriet began, but Cirro waved him silent.

"I hope I'm not intruding."

"Gracious, no," Andriet stammered.

Dear Mother, he really liked her, and I would be her killer.

"I couldn't let you go without... I came to wish you good luck." Her voice was small and high-pitched. The softness in her tone made it less irritating to hear.

"Thank you. It's appreciated, but there's no need for luck. I shall be the first to return every day."

Not everyone returned daily. Andriet told me each trial could be arduous and take many days to complete, forcing them to sleep rough in the dangerous Ashenlands and to forage for what they could to eat. There were four trials in all each nobleman had to complete. Then there was Bloodwyn's scheme to do away with some of Henricus's court during the trials. And I still kept my mouth shut about him. In this regard, I'd made myself complicit in his schemes; a betrayal to the Mother.

The Sistern always saw me as a failure.

Princess Cirro eyed his spacious tent as she moved further inside; her gaze settling first on his large bed, covered in blankets and furs. Then it shifted to the small wooden table beside his bed, already filled with books. There was a spacious table for his meals and two chairs. I was sure he insisted on the second chair for Daelon, who he made his second—the man to care for his horse, his blades, and his person, clothes, and the like. And no doubt more.

I had yet to ask him about his feelings toward his marriage. Nor had I spoken to Daelon alone. But like myself, both of them had always understood the fragility of their happiness.

After gazing around the room, the princess's eyes shifted to me. There was no condescendence, arrogance, or contempt in her gaze. Instead, Cirro stared at me with open curiosity. A valid emotion upon seeing the woman she was replacing on the throne.

She curtsied. "Princess Tressya, I believe."

I reciprocated.

"I'm sorry for your misfortune."

I'd spent a life learning the difference between platitudes and heartfelt words. I could see Cirro's sincerity in her expression and gentle gaze. Damn my soul, but I liked her straight away. It seemed there would be no end to my disloyalty as a disciple?

"Andriet has told me stories about you, especially about the first time he met you. How he found you brandishing a sword and tales of your success against the wild men of the north. I have no friends in Tarragona beyond my lady's maids. Perhaps we can talk sometime. You could tell me how a woman such as yourself became so accomplished."

Of all the women who could've ended up in Andriet's bed, the king had chosen someone impossible to hate.

Andriet clapped his hands. "Excellent. Best friends already."

"I would like that." My heart should be cold as iron, but I meant it. "But the trials will take all my attention for now."

"They assured me the trials weren't dangerous," Cirro said, her delicate brow furrowing as she looked to Andriet.

"They're not. Tressya's mothering me. And taking part in the trials herself."

"Oh!" Cirro's beautiful purple eyes widened, making her look even younger and more childish. "I thought the trials were a sport for men."

"Yes. But there is always time to create new traditions," Andriet said.

"Then I shall have two people to cheer for. Andriet." She smiled at him. His smile was equally unrestrained. "And how could I not cheer for a woman?"

"You must keep this to yourself," I said quickly. "If the noblemen were to know a woman has entered the trials, there would be an uproar."

"Of course," Cirro said with a nod of understanding. "Women mustn't be allowed to disrupt a man's place." And she winked at me.

Curse my luck, I liked her a lot.

"Well said," Andriet added.

Cirro's cheeks tinged pink as she gazed up at him through her eyelashes. I couldn't stop myself from glancing at Daelon, who'd slipped into the background, no doubt uncomfortable surrounded by those so far above his station. Cirro already adored Andriet. It was in her eyes, her smile, her body language as she leaned ever so slightly toward him. My heart ached for what Daelon was forced to witness. He diverted his gaze, then bent and scooped some clothing off the ground and walked away, folding it.

I already liked Cirro a lot, but I liked Daelon a great deal too. Unfortunately, someone was going to walk away holding the pieces of their heart.

"I must prepare," I said, and hurried out of the tent.

I had better things to concern myself with other than broken hearts; the trial for starters, and I also had to worry about how I had to force myself to kill the princess.

My insignificant tent stood alongside the king's grand palace of white fabric. His tent rose above the tent city like the top of a steeple with Tarragona's heraldic standard flapping in the breeze. Each nobleman hung their own banner atop poles erected at the front of their tents, giving the city a vibrant swathe of color.

I had hoped to duck inside and grab my extra dagger, but had only made it halfway there when Radnisa blocked my way.

"If we're lucky, you'll perish. It will save you from facing the Mother's displeasure."

"I don't have time for your poisonous words." I pushed past her, but Radnisa grabbed my arm.

"I don't know what you think you're doing." Her glare

drifted down my body, then glanced over my shoulder before looking behind her. Once she felt sure we were alone, she continued. "The Mother didn't send you here to run around in the shadows playing your silly games and doing the king's bidding."

"I'm aware of what I was sent here to do."

"I doubt that." She folded her arms. "As a disciple, you would know what to do. And it has nothing to do with dressing in costume."

"The king signed his alliance for Andriet's bride before I even arrived."

She quirked a brow. "And that's why she must die."

I snapped, grabbing her arm and dragging her further away from the tents. Once there, I released her and turned away, shielding my face and gave a sigh.

"Do you really need me to say it again? I can't be any clearer. There's only one son left."

"Leave me to make the decisions." My voice sounded strained.

She yanked me around to face her, leaning close so her breath tickled my face. "What are the six pillars?"

I shook my head.

She clasped my cheeks between her hands, squeezing them firm. "Tell me."

I wrenched my head away, grinding my teeth. "No."

"Loyalty," she spat. "Or have you already forgotten the primary pillar?"

"I'll find a way to make it work."

She eased back, folding her arms once again. "How? You had one task. Birth the next heir. You can't do that without a royal husband. The king would not survive such humiliation if he had to cancel the wedding for a second time because— oh my word—now there's no bride. He would be desperate to find a replacement. Any princess would do. And how convenient that he has one spare."

Loyalty. The Mother's will remained above all others. It was my duty: always my duty to the Sistern.

"I'll think of something." I'd thought the same thoughts, begun to plan how I would kill her. But now...

"Time is running out for your little schemes, princess. Or should I call you the King's Blade? How are you going to fix this mess while you're playing in the trials?"

This time it was me who stepped into her space. "Do not touch the princess. Do you hear me?"

Her eyes narrowed at me, and I could feel the venom in her gaze. "Is that a threat?"

"Take it how you want it."

"Careful." She smirked. "All it takes is one word."

I closed my eyes against the fear that slithered down my spine and breathed heavy through my nose. One day I would learn her soul word. Maybe now I had found the power of mine, it would become easier to master soul voice. But I had to actually start trying, something I'd not done since leaving Merania's shores.

"Just let me get through this first trial."

"Don't tell me you're going to seduce the King?"

My stomach churned at the thought.

"I'm not surprised. Call it a defect in your lineage."

Ice slid down my front, chilling me deep into my bones. "What did you say?" She was referring to my Mother. I'd suspected—and argued against the thought—my mother seduced my father on the Mother's command, gaining the Sistern a connection to the Merania throne. Only now—after what she'd done to me—I knew it wasn't the throne but a link to the death arts the Mother craved.

"Pay no attention to my ramblings," she said with a wave of her hand. "You better run along and finish preparing yourself. I think the trials are about to begin."

She turned from me and sauntered away. I huffed out a breath, not realizing I'd been holding it all that time. In my haste to get away from her poisonous words, I staggered over tent ropes, stumbling as I rushed for my tent. Inside, I howled and banged my fists to my temples. The burn of my hatred made it hard for me to swallow. If I met her out in the Ashenlands, I wouldn't hesitate. I would put a dagger straight through her cold heart.

Delirious with anger, I drew the dagger from my trunk and threw it with a harsh shout, aiming for the wood pole. Instead, it was caught moments before impaling the wood by Bloodwyn coming through my tent door.

I gasped, feeling nailed to the spot, before the flames fanned by Radnisa flared again. "What do you want?" I barked, spinning from him and pacing to the back of my tent. As it wasn't large, I didn't have far to go before I was staring at the tent fabric.

"Not a dagger thrown at my face, that's for sure."

"If I had known you were coming, I would've aimed a little lower."

"That's what makes you my favorite person."

Hands on hips, I slowly turned to face him. He wore a

baldric and multiple sheaths fashioned on his belt, hiding a selection of weapons I couldn't make out. He'd dressed in a sleek black coat, which stopped just below his waist and breeches. Even his leather riding boots looked shiny. The line of his breeches left no doubt to his muscular thighs. And the fit of his coat gave me an ample idea of his broad chest.

Great. What I didn't need right now was the added distraction his presence provided, especially when dressed like that. But this was not who the Razohan was, merely a skin he wore.

"I'm sure that outfit will impress the Salmun's creatures," I snapped, hating how much I enjoyed looking at him.

"I aim to please, always."

"Why are you here?"

He strolled toward me, holding my dagger hilt first toward me. "It's called getting to know your rivals."

I took the dagger and sheathed it, furious at how hypnotic he was when being so arrogantly annoying. "You've visited each tent this morning. I'm impressed. The sun has only just risen."

"I'm only bothering myself with my greatest rival."

I didn't have time for this frivolous conversation. I delved into my trunk once more, searching for my extra dagger. For a moment, I feared Radnisa had left it behind on purpose. There were only my clothes when I swore I packed my weapons last.

Bloodwyn was suddenly there beside me, and I'd not heard him approach. Curses, he could move with silence. And I would blame my argument with Radnisa for distracting me. No one should be able to creep up on me like that. If I hadn't let my guard down, no one would have.

"Is this what you're looking for?" He pulled my second dagger by the tip of the blade from beneath an item of clothing.

"Thank you." I held out my hand, but Bloodwyn made no effort to hand it over, preferring to stare down at me. And since I swore never to step back from anyone, he forced me to share my breathing space with him.

The tingle in my wrist flared. But I was growing accustomed to it and, dare I admit it to myself, found it a pleasurable feeling.

"What did that viper say to upset you?"

I arched a brow.

"You know my attention is always on you."

That shouldn't sound so good. "None of your concern."

"Trust me, it's my concern, because you're now my concern."

I shouldn't like hearing that. And now my heart was racing. I opened my mouth to huff some retort, then slammed it shut with a blink. Don't give him the satisfaction of replying.

"Whatever was said stays between the two of us." I held out my hand for my dagger.

"All you have to do is say the word, and I'll get rid of her. That will save you the guilt of doing it yourself."

"A tempting gesture. But if you dare touch her, you'll find one of my daggers in a place you won't like."

"You say the most erotic things." Bloodwyn returned my

dagger hilt first but refused to release the blade when I tugged for it.

The angrier I became with our pathetic little tug-of-war, the more salacious his smile grew, until I was ready to punch him in the face. Perhaps he read that thought in my expression because he suddenly yanked his end of the dagger hard, pulling me off balance, forcing me to tumble into him.

"What's our tactic today?" he asked in a low, slow, seductive voice, and I would be lying if I said I remained unaffected.

"We try to keep our weapons from each other's throats, for starters."

"And after our little game of fetch?"

He was still too close, and I was too weak to prevent my body from pulsing with an unfamiliar tune. This tune was gradually unraveling the knots in my heart, in my soul, and in my desire—that dark, feral beast which had lain dormant for far too long. My erratic heartbeat was the only sound I could hear, along with Bloodwyn's breathing. If I closed my eyes and concentrated right now, I could meld my heartbeat with his, aligning us so our hearts beat in rhythm.

"Tressya?" he crooned. The way my name rolled off his tongue sent tingles to all the right places.

"Afterward I'll be busy in my bath." Why did I say that?

"Excellent. What time do you want me? I'm known for my back scrubs." His nails grew into claws as he held up one hand.

"And I'm known for reacting badly to any breach in my solitude."

His leaning close was the first slash upon the cord's that

kept my hunger in. "You shouldn't tempt me, little princess." Then he turned and strolled across to my bed. "I've done it once and survived."

He eased himself down, stretching out and folding his arms behind his head. As I watched him, my insides screamed to climb out of my skin, savoring how good he looked lying on my bed. I was on the brink of surrender, almost ready to fall to my knees and crawl across the tent floor to reach him.

Discipline.

I blinked in a bid to drag my mind away from the precipice of a very bad idea. He was so sure of himself, of his ability to outsmart me and win, given any situation. In equal measure, I admired his confidence as much as I longed to show him just who he was playing with.

"Have they given you any hint of your first object?"

I'd spent a painful snippet of time enduring Orphus's presence in my tent this morning. He'd said little of worth but placed a hand on my head, as if anointing me, then stood in the center of my tent, head bowed in silence. I stayed alert to any invasion of his presence in my head, but felt none.

Afterward, Andriet informed me each competitor endured the same from a member of the Salmun. It was all part of the trials. The Salmun used their mind tricks to learn what objects in our lives had personal value, because the trials were a game of fetch.

The competitor was to retrieve four objects personally significant to themselves over four successive trials. With each trial, the significance of the object grew as the trial became more deadly. Hunting down one's object could take a day, a few days, or a week, depending on the individual's attachment to that object, their cunning, and their skill with weaponry; the latter in case they came upon some of the Salmun's vile creatures—along with many other traps and dangers in the Ashenlands.

I busied myself with shifting my clothes in my trunk once I realized my gaze had lingered too long on Bloodwyn stretched out in comfort. Would the real Razohan look equally as good stretched out on my bed? Curses. Why was I asking myself such a thing? "I'm not in the trials to chase objects around in circles."

"Andriet can't have told you."

"Told me what?"

"You must retrieve your object if you ever hope to return."

I dropped the tunic I was making a hash of folding. "That's not true."

In one swift motion, he slid off my bed, reminding me of how smooth a hunter he could be, and strolled toward me.

"It most definitely is. I have it on good authority."

"Whose?"

"Lord Bloodwyn's."

"Oh." I blinked. "How much of Lord Bloodwyn's life are you able to pick over?"

"Rather than think of it as picking over his life, I think of it as becoming his life...for the time it's useful."

"I see no difference."

He flashed a brief smile as he closed the distance between us, leaving little space for me to make a defensive move if the moment required. "Perhaps we should stick together during this first trial." He shrugged. "Help each other out."

I snorted. "Don't you have a malicious purpose for being here?"

He shifted his gaze to my hair. There was nothing pretty or elaborate about my plait, but his eyes seemed to suck in my hair style first before they returned to my face, like a man adoring his favorite horse, or...the woman who'd caught his attention across the ballroom. I was foolish to think it was the latter.

"I have many purposes, not all malicious."

He moved quickly, spinning me around and pressing my back firmly against his chest, while a palm splayed across my stomach anchored me in place. Instead of focusing on a defensive strike, my mind fixated on the feeling of his warm body against mine, and the way my body molded and curved into his. The smell of him infected me so thoroughly my head swam through a thick haze all because I longed for his hands to explore my body. I sucked in my breath when a small moan escaped from my lips. Curses for all the secrets of my soul that I was giving him.

I ached; a pain once buried deep, or so I thought. Loneliness or true desire, I couldn't tell. I wasn't this weak, but maybe I was a woman who needed more than what the Mother could give?

His other hand he brought around and held in front of my face. Slowly at the tip of one finger, a claw protruded, growing longer before my eyes, until it was the length of my finger. Dark, thick, and lethal. The end pointed into the sharp edge of an arrow.

He lowered his head, leaning close to my left side. I swear I felt the faintest tickle of his lips on my ear. "I can be very helpful," he whispered.

I wanted him to be helpful, in so many ways and none had anything to do with the trials. *Mercy.* I shook my head. These thoughts infected my head because I was a failed disciple with too many emotions running free through my heart.

For starters, his wintery spice and summery leather was a toxic combination that addled my senses. His body, solid, yet yielding, melded with mine like the perfect sword in its master's hand; the two together formed a powerful duo.

But, always, the disciple lurked underneath. I wasn't so lost as to surrender. Not entirely. I swiped my dagger from its sheath and sliced through his claw, halfway down to his finger.

He huffed. "It will grow back."

"Pity."

He released me, stepping away, and I stifled a whimper as my body cried in misery for losing the tantalizing hint of what he offered. It wasn't just my body crying in vain. Before I could stop, I pressed a hand firm against my chest, for the little comfort I could give myself, and felt Carlin's necklace, which only brought a fresh wave of emptiness and heartache.

"Is that your answer?"

I sheathed my dagger and turned to face him. "We're on opposing sides."

"Does that mean we have to abandon all feeling?"

"I trust few. You will never be one of them." As a disciple,

I couldn't, even if my heart cried on hearing me say the words.

He nodded slowly, as if struggling to absorb what I'd said. A flash of something that looked strangely like disappointment crossed his face, too quick for me to analyze. Then he bowed and spun on his heels, marching out the tent door while I bit back my overwhelming urge to make him stop. I would close my eyes with my own disappointment if not for the fact I couldn't draw them from his departure.

Before he disappeared outside, he looked back at me. "It would surprise you to know what I have surrendered from the moment I boarded your ship."

CHAPTER

TWENTY-SIX

TRESSYA

THE HORSES PAWED at the ground, jostling in the line, eager to be away. With a head covering pulled up across my face to disguise myself as a man, I'd maneuvered my horse alongside Andriet. Then, to my annoyance, Bloodwyn nudged the nobleman on the other side of me away and took his place. I had to stay close to Andriet, and if Bloodwyn hoped to trail me, then maybe it was a good thing. That way, I could keep an eye on them both.

Given the number competing in the trials, we were in a tight line with little room to move. Bloodwyn's leg press firm against mine, while Andriet's and my horse's rumps bumped together. We'd yet to begin and already the smell of horse sweat filled the air.

Behind us, on a makeshift wooden platform, sat the king. Beside him sat Princess Cirro. The queen remained absent, still sick in her bed, but alive, according to Andriet, who'd spent the night before the caravan departed for the Ashenlands, sitting by her side. Behind the royal party stood two Salmun, their presence as ominous and dark as the ladened sky. Orphus was not one of them. I craned my head along the line, thinking I may see him on a horse, ready to join us in the Ashenlands, but no.

My gaze landed on Radnisa, standing at the front of my tent. She'd been unusually happy this morning, and now she wore her smirk so wide it was hard to miss from this distance. Turning my attention from her, I inadvertently met Bloodwyn's gaze.

"She looks pleased with herself."

"She's thrilled to see me disappear into the Ashenlands."

He leaned over his horse. "My offer from this morning still stands, you know."

I cast a sly glance around me. "I don't want you killing anyone. Not even those who deserve it."

He sucked in a noisy breath. "You drive a hard bargain."

"It's a warning. Not a bargain."

Bloodwyn winked at me, but I said no more because a herald rode to the front of our line.

"If you stick with me, I'll see to it you return alive," Bloodwyn said as I strained to make out what the herald was shouting.

Bloodwyn leaned forward to catch a glance of Andriet. "I suppose you'll be sticking with him."

"Shut up. I can't hear what he's saying."

"He says we stand little chance of finding our first object

or even surviving our first trial. And if we were smart, we'd stay in our tents, drink ale, and fornicate."

"We'd all be happier if you took that advice."

"If you joined me in my tent, I'd knot the ties at the entrance tight and make sure no one could open them."

That distracted me, as did the instantaneous vision of being wrapped up in his bedsheets. I turned my head toward him, only to receive another of his winks. *Dammit.* That wink of his was growing on me.

"You wouldn't be disappointed, princess."

I snapped my head away before he caught the twitch of my smile. Right now the trial should take my full concentration. I had to make sure I never lost sight of Andriet once we were in the trial. But with Bloodwyn beside me, the constant urge to glance at him became as persistent as night and day.

In my periphery, I saw movement on the king's platform and turned to see the king rise from his seat.

"This looks like it. You sure you won't take me up on my offer?"

"Never." I kept my face turned away, so he wouldn't see that I'd lost the war with my smile.

"You realize if I'm occupied in my tent, I'm not chasing your darling little prince around the Ashenlands, and you have nothing to fear."

The king began his speech as I whipped my head around to face Bloodwyn. "You think I fear you?"

"No. I think I'm slowly succeeding in working my way under your skin."

I shook my head.

"Admit it. I make you smile, something you haven't done

in a long time. Am I right? Perhaps I make you think a lot of other things."

I tried to frown against the truth of his words. He would never know how many times I thought about him. Not one time were any of those thoughts pure. "You're right. I think of sharpening my blades." I turned away before he noticed how hard it was for me to keep my frown.

"At least I'm in your thoughts. I'm sure a lot of other men haven't even got that far."

Trumpets sounded, then a heavy thunder of hooves as the line of horses took flight, leaving me dazed, my horse prancing on the spot as I held her reins tight. Andriet was gone from my side. Curses, so was Bloodwyn. Both raced neck to neck, their horses' hooves nearing the death line demarcating the Ashenlands.

I dug my heels into my horse's flanks and let her have her head. She shot forward, but I was already far over her withers, urging her into a gallop. Ahead of me, dust billowed up, obscuring my view, as the line of horses galloped across the parched ground.

Damn you, Bloodwyn.

I urged my horse for more speed, and she gave me all she could. The death line drew near, and then my horse shot across it and onto the dead ground. Dust billowed around us, filling my nose, clogging the back of my throat, and even finding its way underneath my clothes to scratch against my skin. I coughed, then reached for the cloth I'd used to cover the lower half of my face.

I couldn't see where we were heading, or the surrounding riders, and neither could I hear the thunder of hooves from a hundred horses or more. I bent lower over my horse's withers as an itch tickled my nose. The itch grew and grew, and before I could stop myself, I sneezed.

One blink with the sneeze was all it took. I opened my eyes to find the Ashenlands had disappeared, so too the open ground upon which we'd raced. In her speed, my mare lost her footing on the dense roots and went down, sending me over her head. I landed on my side, my shoulder hitting the trailing end of a root.

My head spun, but my horse's gentle whinny brought me back to the present. Thankfully, the mare was on her feet, unharmed. My shoulder throbbed, my hip ached, and my head was in a total muddle, so I wasn't sure I was so lucky. Growling as I stood made me feel a smidgeon better.

"Damn, you, Orphus." He was but one of many who cursed this land, but he made the best target for my anger.

Surrounding me was dense forest with no end in sight. All around, roots rose like deadly snakes. Carpets of dull green creeper threatened to strangle the fat trunks of the trees, and moss turned the black loamy soil into a slippery floor. The canopy, knitted like a web, blocked most of the natural light, surrounding me in an eerie gloom. Not a sound penetrated the thick, warm air. Beads of sweat broke across my forehead, the moisture dribbling down into my eyes. I pulled at my collar, feeling a restrictive heat prickle against my skin.

"Andriet," I cried. Not even my echo returned to me.

I didn't know which way was forward and which way would get me out. Damn Salmun trickery. At least everyone would be stuck like me, meaning Bloodwyn would find it hard to hunt Andriet down.

"Easy girl." I doubled back and took my horse's reins, then encouraged her into a walk. She walked without a limp, which was one mercy I would be grateful for.

"It's on foot from here." I found speaking to my horse eased my nerves. Neither did I feel so alone.

Our objects were supposed to call to our subconscious. As long as we didn't oppose our instincts, we would be led toward them, or at least in the right direction. Apparently.

I stopped and inhaled deeply, allowing my eyes to drift closed. Andriet had said that a competitor needed cunning, but perhaps cunning began with starting slow and listening. I wasn't sure what I was listening for, but if my object was going to guide me, I needed to be attentive, whether to the sensations within my body or the sounds of the forest.

At first, I heard silence. Then a distant melody wafted through the trees. I opened my eyes and turned in a circle, confused about the direction it was coming from. I saw nothing but the gloomy darkness, thick trunked trees, and a creeping fog, sliding over the roots and crawling around my feet, which had not existed before. I held my breath, finding the strains of music over my heartbeat, going from my left.

I gathered the horse's reins and guided her around the trees toward the growing sound of the song, until the trees fell away, and I stood on the edge of a lake. In the center of the lake, dancing above the eddying fog, was the spirit of a young girl, glowing almost as bright as the sun. The fog glistened and glowed around her. She twirled in a circle, so the lower half of her ill-formed body twisted into a knot of bright glittering starlight.

When she spied me standing on the edge of the lake, she stopped.

"Oh my. It's a woman." Her voice was high and child-like.

She glided across the top of the lake toward me, trailing the dregs of her ill-formed legs behind her, then stopped in front of me.

"Poor thing, she must've lost her way."

"I kind of did."

Her eyes looked about to pop from her head. She pointed to her chest. "Me?" It was all she could say in her surprise.

"Yes, I see you. And hear you."

She gasped, her eyes growing impossibly wider as she attempted to slap her hands against her cheeks, only for them to sink through her skull. "You're speaking to me?"

I nodded.

"That's never happened." She spun up into the air, dizzying up into a spiral above my head, squealing in glee, before settling down in front of me again.

"You're my best friend," she declared. "We're going to have so much fun." She tried to grab her long plait, now falling over her shoulder, but her fingers kept missing and sinking through into her chest.

"What's your name?" I asked.

She stopped fussing with her plait. "We can make this into a game."

Great. I would have to stumble on the spirit of a child. "I don't have time for a game. I need to find my friend."

Her face brightened. "That's the game. You guess my name, and I'll tell you everything you want to know."

Frustration threatened to consume me, and I shook my head. "I want to know where my friend is and which way is out."

"But you're a woman. They don't allow women to join the trials."

"Good, you know about them."

"We all know about them."

"There's more of you?"

"There are many villages full of us."

How many villages were caught within the Salmun's curse? I frowned, wondering what these lands were like before. Shaking myself of the thoughts, I said, "If you know about the trials, then you must know about the objects and where the Salmun have placed them." Maybe that was an impossible ask, but I had to hope.

"You're silly. The Salmun don't put them anywhere."

"That makes little sense."

"Yes, it does. Now can we play my game?"

I blew a breath. "I have to find my friend. Maybe someone from your village—"

"No. You have to play my game." She shouted in her high-pitched voice. "That's what friends do." She folded her arms with a frown. "We're good friends now." Her brow smoothed. "We'll be better friends soon."

I couldn't help the feeling of unease that shot through me. Her words reminded me of Scregs. I had to lose this spirit.

"You can't go," she said as I gathered my horse's reins.

She shot forward, and I jerked my arm away before she could touch me.

"Wait. I'll give you three guesses."

What if there was a special reason I'd found her? "Three guesses for what?"

"My name. Three guesses for my name. If you get it, I'll tell you all about my village, and my family, and the things I've seen."

"Which way to find my friend, the object, and the way out. That's all I want."

She scrunched up her nose, tilting her head to the side and pressed her lips together as a smile spread across her face. "You're not playing."

"I can't guess it in three."

I wanted nothing more than to get away from the annoying little spirit, but I was now sure I'd ended up in this exact spot for a reason.

She tilted her head to the side again, her gaze focusing off beyond me, like she was listening for something. Maybe if I threatened to leave, she would give in and surrender her name, then perhaps I would get what I wanted.

"I have to go." I half turned.

"No. You can't. That will break the rules."

"Rules you've created."

"No. The rules of the trials."

"What rules?"

Her eyes flittered over my head. "Oh, just those rules," she said absentmindedly.

"Where is your village?" If I found an adult spirit, I may be in luck.

"You'll know soon enough."

Creepy tingles flared across the back of my neck. I spun to look behind me, following her gaze, but saw nothing. "I think it's time I left."

She smiled, and the tingles multiplied. "You could try."

My horse let out a whiny, then reared up beside me, and the reins slipped through my fingers. I grabbed for them, but the mare lurched forward and raced off through the trees, gliding over the exposed roots with speed.

"Dammit," I yelled.

"Don't worry. You don't need your horse anymore."

"What do you mean?" I growled at her, but she'd returned to staring over my shoulder.

I spun to see something large and black lurking in the distance. Its shape was indistinct, but the white glow of its eyes pierced through the gloomy forest.

"Now it's too late," giggled the spirit child.

She'd played me, all right. The game was a ruse to keep me here long enough for her pet to come.

"You'll be my friend forever."

Drawing my sword, I moved away from the edge of the lake to give myself room. The creature clambered through the canopy, jumping from tree to tree, its claws chipping bark and leaving deep slashes in its wake. Coat as dark as a starless night, slit-like holes for ears, four long limbs, it loomed above me, gums peeled back to reveal long, blade-sharp teeth. It was like nothing I had seen before.

It pounced, landing without noise where I'd been standing, but I had long danced away. A swipe with my sword met only air. It rose onto its back legs, and I ducked low as its blade-like claws tried to slice me in two.

With all those roots to trip on, the ground was my disadvantage. I couldn't take my eyes off the creature, but neither could I avoid looking where I stepped. Luckily, the creature's strike was slower than I expected, but the beast blended nicely into the gloom of the forest behind.

Discipline. One calming breath.

I jumped over a large gnarled root, looking for more space. In my periphery, I caught its next attack and ducked. Diverting left, I felt the breeze of its strike over my head. Before I took another breath, it brought its left arm down to gouge a chunk of exposed root on my right, then rumbled a frustrated sound deep in its throat.

The next root I missed and staggered, flailing to keep my feet with the sound of thumping stomps lumbering behind me. I glanced over my shoulder to see the spirit girl wafting from the lake to follow behind, but the beast soon obscured my view of her.

As I ran, I scanned the forest for a better position. I had no hope of wounding or killing it from here. The lumbering thumps of its heavy tread vibrated up through my feet as I dodged behind a thick trunked tree. Next came the sound of ripping bark and littering fine shavings upon me. Curses, it was climbing into the canopy.

I darted away from the tree, hopping over the roots. The glow of the girl rose over my shoulder, spreading its light into the forest in front of me. Overhead came a rustle of leaves, a snap of a branch.

Glancing up, I saw it leap to the tree I was rushing for. I

doubled back, but the spirit girl's glow blinded me, and I tripped. I fell hard, losing my sword, my stomach hitting an exposed root. With the jarring impact, I bit my tongue.

I scrambled to my knees. *My sword.* Thanks to the girl, I'd lost my night vision. I crawled on the ground, skimming my hands around for my sword, but a loud crack from behind sent me scurrying to my feet.

I needed another calming breath, but my training had not prepared me to fight a creature more than double my size, with claws and teeth for weapons, on treacherously uneven ground, half blinded by light. I gritted my teeth as I lunged away, abandoning my sword.

The crack was a fat branch, collapsing under the creature's weight. The spirit girl's light created shadows in the deep crevices of the roots as she wafted alongside us and spread out as shimmering ripples across the lake beyond.

I couldn't allow myself to be caged between the forest and the lake, and it was no help to me if it didn't know how to swim because neither did I.

A heavy stomp rattled the ground behind me. Dagger in hand, I darted forward, stumbling over more roots in my haste.

"Give up," the girl shrieked.

I growled, then foolishly glanced at her. "Never," I shouted.

The beast lumbered along behind, stripping up roots and tossing them aside as it came. In her excitement, the spirit girl wafted closer, brightening the forest floor around me. As the light hit it, the beast suddenly jerked right and took to the trees.

"Stop," the girl shrieked. "You'll love it here with me."

I didn't stop, but I couldn't keep running. I had to be smart.

Something hard hit me between my shoulder blades as I leaped clear of another root. I staggered, lost my footing and went to my knees. My pounding heart and will drove me to my feet again, but halfway up, I was hit in the back again. A sharp pain lanced my side as I was knocked to my stomach. The ring of a *chink* echoed through my head, but I was concerned more with my dagger as it skittered from my hold. I tried to roll right but found my left side pinned.

A looming darkness obscured the spirit's light as the beast reared overhead, its claw piercing my smock, nailing me where I lay. The beasts glowing white eyes leered over me. With my right hand, I reached for my other dagger, only to realize the chink I had heard was the beast's claw hitting the hilt of my other dagger as it severed the sheath from my belt. Miraculously, its claw had missed my skin.

"A short time. That's all. Then it will be over," the girl said, her voice coming from afar.

She'd retreated, drawing her light away. Because... Probably not. Maybe.

The beast lowered its head and roared. I turned my head away, as it breathed its rotten breath over me, and I drowned in a stench of sewers and decay.

This is not it. It's not. I won't let it be.

The beast lowered its head, releasing another roar, and I held my breath, turning my head.

Gritting my teeth, I tried to pull myself free of its claw. *Dammit.* I was wedged tight. Its mouth hovered close to my face. My attention caught on a sharp fang as it snorted and snuffled, sniffing me. My heart beat so fast it hurt my chest and strangled my lungs so I couldn't breathe. The pulse of my blood hammered through my ears. I wouldn't die.

Aetherius. My soul word surged into my mind. *Aetherius.* I shouted the word in my head, fearing the powerlessness of my impending death. The power of spiritweaving flowed within me. I funneled it outward, searching, seeking, until I latched onto the spirit girl.

"Come here," I demanded, but nothing happened.

My lungs released. I gulped in air. "Come. Here," I commanded again.

I felt the feeble struggle of her small and fragile mind as I pierced the veil dividing the living from the dead and slammed through her, destroying her free will.

"You're cruel," she whimpered, fighting against me and failing.

The forest grew brighter as she neared. The beast reared up, then roared, thrashing its head from side to side.

"Hurry," I shouted.

It was as though the sun had risen. A brilliant glow flooded over the beast, transforming its outline into a silhouette. It rose high on its hunches, releasing a deafening howl, then launched up into the trees and lumbered away.

"You're mean, and cruel, and no longer my friend," the girl yelled, folding her arms across her chest.

I slowly rolled to my side, wincing at the pain, and sat up. "Now you'll tell me where I can find my object."

"I don't know. I'm not telling."

"I'll command you again. I think you'd prefer to do it willingly."

"You can't. You can't. It's wrong."

Pressing my lips tight, keeping the groan inside, I rose to my feet. "I'm not staying in this cursed place any more than I have to, so you'd better tell me."

The girl floated backward until she was out over the lake once more. I followed her, about to call on my soul word to command her, when I spied a rippling glow from beneath the water. I stepped up to the water's edge and peered in.

It was a dagger. Of course. Something significant to me.

"There. It's yours. Take it." She pouted.

"I can't swim."

She smirked. "That's a problem."

"You'll have to get it for me."

She giggled, but the sound was more evil than nice. "I'm a spirit. How can I do that?"

The same way Truett had touched me. He'd pierced the ethereal divide long enough to touch me lightly on the arm. Spirits couldn't do that on their own, so I must've done it for him unconsciously. Pulling the dead through the veil into the realm of the living was the greatest of a spiritweaver's power. It wasn't a true life we gave them, or a true body they gained, simply a poor semblance of what they once had, the ability to touch and feel again, but there were still many limitations. Death was death, it could never be evaded.

If I could pull her through long enough to retrieve the dagger, I was out of the Ashenlands.

"I need it. And you'll get it for me."

"Shan't."

"Shall I enslave you to my command again?"

She shook her head.

"Then do it." After her prank, I struggled to feel any compassion toward her.

She dived, not a ripple or splash in her wake. I closed my eyes, allowing my soul word to surface. *Aetherius.* It rose, splintering the boundaries and expanding my mind beyond the limitations of this earthly realm. This time, I cradled her mind like an infant and gradually pulled her toward me. Her presence brushed alongside me, her awareness a tickle in my mind. She didn't fight what I was doing, even though I felt her anger.

I opened my eyes and watched the wavering glow below the water grow ever closer to the surface. She broke through, this time with a splash. Blade held high, water brimming at her chest, she came toward me, wading on the bottom of the lake because...she now had legs.

Slowly the water receded down her body, then finally she stopped in the shallows, a broad smile splitting her face. "It's oozy and squishy," she giggled.

I held out my hand. "My dagger."

Her eyes blew wide. "I can feel everything."

I tried to grab the dagger as she waved her arms in a wide circle.

"Sorry. It won't last. You can't stay on this side."

"But...You can't. No. I don't want to go back."

I released my hold on her, feeling her essence shrink in my mind like sinking sand.

"No. Stop! You can't."

As the young girl became a spirit once more, the dagger

plopped into the shallows. I swiped it up as she cursed me using words someone so young should never speak.

The moment the dagger was in my hands, I felt a tug in my stomach and the forest swirled around me, its gloomy hues melding into one stream. My stomach roiled as I was jerked off my feet, then thrown onto them again, but I lost my balance and tumbled onto my aching side. I rolled and lifted my head to see the tent city rising in front of me.

The dagger had disappeared.

CHAPTER

TWENTY-SEVEN

TAMAS

I LANDED on the soft loamy soil, talons tangling in the thick bed of creeper. Once I folded my wings, I loosened my hold on the feathered form and surrendered to the aching feeling of transforming bone. What once took tens of minutes to achieve, now took seconds and the pain was over. In the soft glow of Garrat's flaming torch, I bent and retrieved the handful of black feathers I'd lost during the process, then held them up into the flame until they caught alight.

"You took your time," Osmud grumbled, while rotating his shoulder.

"That arm still bothering you?"

"I haven't had time to rest it with all the trips I'm forced to make back and forth—"

"Maybe you should ride rather than fly next time." I

patted his arm and strolled past him, not ready for a lengthy diatribe about my failings so far. "Garrat."

Garrat's flaming torch cast ghoulish shadows across his face. "Tamas."

We embraced.

"All is well?" I asked, stepping back.

"We've made camp on the southern border of Wilhelm, and on the banks of the Lanrial River. We're in position, waiting your signal. Romelda has gathered five of the blooded."

"Five?" I repeated. "I had hoped for more."

"Many have passed. Fewer choose to be blooded anymore. One thousand years, Tamas," Garrat said. "Many of the Nazeen gave up hope."

"I plan on restoring that hope."

"Huh," snorted Osmud from behind me.

I rolled my eyes. "Ignore him."

"Ignore," snapped Osmud, coming up beside me. "There's plenty that needs ignoring, and it's not up to Garrat to do it."

"What's going on with you two?" Garrat's gaze darted between us.

"Osmud's developed wing strain, and it's put him in a foul mood."

"Tamas is panting like a dog, and it's robbed him of his senses."

"Perhaps Osmud needs some relief of his own to take the edge of—"

"Osmud can't spare the time because he's forced to babysit—"

"Shut up or I'll cuff you both. We're planning a war in case that insignificant detail evaded you."

"My mind's on the mark," Osmud said. "Always has been. Which I can't—"

I sighed. "Leave up. I have my plans—"

Osmud turned to me. "And what are those, exactly? So far the only plans I see involve bedding a certain—"

The scrape of a sword leaving its scabbard preceded the blade at my throat by a breath. It was no surprise, and I could've maneuvered myself away in time, but I relented to Garrat's frustration.

"I don't want to hear another word." He glared at Osmud. "We have an army on the other side of the Ashenlands, and you two are scuffing like littluns."

As usual, Garrat was the sense in our threesome. The cold of his blade at my throat snapped my focus back to the task. "Is Romelda sure the Nazeen's spells will work?"

"The spells Romelda thought to conjure proved of little use to most of the Salmun's vile creatures. Nothing new there. We've done three incursions into the Ashenlands since arriving in Wilhelm and made an interesting discovery."

"What might that be?"

A thousand years of lore regarding the impenetrability of the Ashenlands and the might of its vile beasts meant centuries had passed with no northerners daring to venture this deep within. My father took a handful of strong followers and skirted the perimeter a few times and brought back stories, but there was little that could be said about the dark depths.

"There are two types of creatures inhabiting the Ashenlands. We're calling them the source and its manifestations. Romelda says there's powerful magic behind it.

"The source has dull eyes, its manifestations, nasty creatures made corporeal have glowing eyes. It was Romelda who discovered the trick. If you want to kill the horde, you find the source. Otherwise you're fighting an unwinnable war against a deathless army."

"Kill the source—" I said.

"Kill its spawn," finished Osmud.

"Romelda believes the manifestations are never far from the source. Which is handy. She also believes they lure the source to the prey. All you have to do is hold out long enough for it to arrive."

I clapped Garrat on the back. "You have been busy."

"That's not all. We've also discovered the manifestations shy away from light. They'll keep their distance as long as we pass through with enough torches to last the distance."

"That's a lot of torches."

"Plus some help from the Nazeen."

"What about if we set fire to the forest and move through in its wake?" Osmud said.

"We tried. It won't take. Everyone is set to work making torches. Each will carry their own and the Nazeen will add their spells to ensure they glow brighter than is natural and remain lit for the passage."

"This is good," I said. "The king's court has gathered to the south of here. We give the trials time to play out and the king to have eliminated most of his councilmen."

I nodded to Osmud. He'd played his part in planting the

treasonous letters within Weselton's Manor for the king's men to retrieve.

"I shall take care of the king and his son while you march the army through the Ashenlands. Then we take out the rest of the noble families."

"And when all the Tannard line are dead, the Salmun will have no choice but to recognize you as heir to the throne."

Before they crossed into the northern realm, the Nazeen combined their power in one last stand against the Levenian, and encased the Etherweave within stone and bound it to the House of Tannard. None but an heir of the Tannard line could unite with the Etherweave and take the Bone Throne; the seat of the Etherweave's power. But unbeknownst to the Nazeen, a soft-hearted Levenian warrior spared King Ricaud's sister from slaughter, which proved their boon, for now they had a Tannard. She was forced into marriage with one of their own, creating a Tannard with Levenian blood links: the new House of Tannard.

A strange melancholic sound rippled through the night air.

"How about we pat ourselves on the back for making good plans somewhere else?" Osmud said.

"We're finished." I rested my hand on Garrat's shoulder. "How long do you think it will take you to cross the Ashenlands?"

"We hope to do it in a day with the Nazeen's help."

"Osmud will send word of when to start your journey."

Garrat nodded, then turned and disappeared through the trees.

"My shoulder won't like this," Osmud grumbled.

But already his words were fading as I took the form of a eagle once more.

****

I left Osmud grouching on the edge of the tent city and headed for my tent. Somewhere behind the tents, a bonfire had been lit, music played, and the smells of roast meat wafted on the gentle breeze. For one moment, I stood outside my tent, contemplating joining the festival to have my fill of ale and spiced meat, but thought the better of it when a wave of weariness sunk in. I'd not slept for days and had spent far too much time as something else other than human form. It was taking its toll.

I felt the disturbance in the air the moment I entered my tent and jerked my upper body away from the attacker's swipe, blocking their strike and flipping them over my shoulder. I intended to pin them to the ground with my weight, but instead I crumpled in a heap with a groan when something slammed into my groin.

"Asshole," Tressya grouched, pushing at my shoulders so I fell to my side on the ground, still nursing my screaming balls.

"Next time..." I inhaled. "Don't surprise..." I huffed. "A Razohan." I cupped my hands delicately between my legs. "My fucking balls."

"I saw you head into the Ashenlands." She coughed. "What's this? A feather."

I opened my eyes and looked up at her, seeing her hold the black feather up to the thin ray of moonlight that had found a gap in the tent flap. I found the strength to release one hand from my balls. "That's mine." And I snatched it out of her hold.

"You can change into a bird?"

"I'm a shape-shifter, Tressya. I can be what I want."

"Not only do you have the souls of people inside of you, you have animals as well?"

"A boon and a curse, remember?"

I eased myself back onto my knees. "Are you going to help me up?"

Tressya stood and walked further into the tent and out of the moonlight. At least she was walking in and not out of my tent, though I doubted there would be any stirring down below since it felt like I was wearing my balls inside.

I heard the rasping of flint in my iron bowl, followed by a small flame as the dandelion seeds caught alight. Tressya lit my candle from the small flames, then set it aside on the same wood table beside my bed.

It took some effort, but I climbed to my feet and hobbled across the tent. Once at my bed, I collapsed onto my back and gently stretched myself out, covering my face with my arm to hide my smile. The smile was because she stayed perched next to me rather than leaving my bed for the other side of the room.

"You haven't bothered to change back into one of your gowns?"

"It's dark. Who's going to see. Besides, everyone's at the festival, and this outfit is far more comfortable." She settled herself better. "Why the Ashenlands? What evil schemes are you making?"

"I'll tell all once you reveal how you were the first out of the trials today."

"Yesterday. The midnight hour has past."

"No wonder I feel exhausted."

"I have my skills, Razohan. If you get in my way, end what is mine to protect or annoy me, you will find out what they are."

"Another promise I'm sure you'll keep. Though I still have my heart."

I felt the movement of the bed and peeked out from under my arm to watch her stroll around my tent. She took the candle with her, leaving me in the shadows, but casting a warm glow upon her face. Her plain features had never looked so beautiful, her unadorned attire now irresistibly alluring. Though grace had never been her ally, tonight, each of her movements flowed like an elegant dance, and I was unequivocally entranced.

From her expression, I could tell she was deep in thought, seeming far away from our conversation. That I didn't like. I had never been a jealous bastard, but at this moment, believing she wasn't thinking of us, made me nearly grow claws and shred my blanket to pieces.

"You lost your sword and daggers, I noticed, but you seem to have another. Do you need any more weapons? I've got plenty to share." Crazy of me, but I wanted her to own something of mine, even if it was a weapon she could use against me.

"The king is generous with his gifts."

I bet the wanker is. "Can't have his blade without one, now can he?"

447

Was that a small smile I spied struggling to break free of her expressionless face? Good. I had her back where I wanted her. Focused on us.

"What was your object?"

"Some trinket of Bloodwyn's. I barely noticed it."

I didn't need to find any such objects to escape the Ashenlands. I simply transformed into a bird and soared out. Instead of hunting down pathetic novelties, I'd hunted down Andriet. At least I tried to, but the Salmun's magic was more powerful than any of us in the north had thought. Somehow, the moment the competitors crossed into the Ashenlands, not only did we plunge into a thick gloomy forest, but all signs of life disappeared, except the wizards' vile beasts.

"How about yours?"

"A dagger."

"That's fitting."

"Did you come across any of their creatures while you were there?" She tried to keep her voice disinterested, but I knew that game only too well.

I rose to sit on the edge of my bed and watched her as she stopped at my trunk and had the audacity to pick through my things. She was welcome to do so, for I had nothing in there to hide. It was all Bloodwyn's possessions.

"You mean the creepy glowing eyed creatures?"

She froze, bent over my trunk, and glanced back at me. "You saw them too?"

"I'm impressed. How did you get away?"

She straightened. "How did you?"

"Agility and skill with a blade."

"Same."

Liar. Already I was adept at reading her body language and facial expressions, a result of studying her so closely. "It's the dull eyed ones you really have to watch."

She turned to face me. "Oh?"

I enjoyed having more knowledge than her. It gave me leverage.

"You know, the source." I shrugged like it was no big deal.

Dark shadows fell under her eyes and nose because of the candlelight, obscuring her gaze, but I bet she fixed it on me.

"Don't play with me, Razohan." *Oh, I want to play with you little princess. I want that very much.*

I huffed a laugh as I stood, then stretched slowly, testing the extent of my aches. Finding them bearable, I crossed to the trunk. "There's the source, and there's its manifestations. If you want to rid yourself of the manifestations, you have to kill the source." She was going to describe me as an arrogant ass again for the way I sounded. The thought made me smile.

"So the manifestations are the ones with the glowing eyes. That's the creature I fought. But you say the source has dull eyes. I never came upon one of those."

"You fought only one?"

She frowned. Yep, the word arrogant would definitely come up soon.

"The manifestations can't die. Kill the source if you hope to get rid of them. Lucky for us, the manifestations rarely venture far from the source. Perhaps they can't. Eventually, the source will turn up. If you can hang out that long."

"They're afraid of light. The manifestations are, at least."

I quirked a brow, then smiled at her sharing secrets again, even if I already knew that secret. "See, that wasn't hard."

The candlelight accentuated the deep grooves in her brow, then her lips twitched against a smile and my heart fluttered a beat. My hand twitched to reach out for hers, but perhaps that was moving too fast. But dammit, I was ready for everything and anything with her. "There's much we can do to help each other."

I wanted her to survive the trials, something I would never admit to my most trusted. I'd never wanted anything as much as that truth. No. That wasn't true. I wanted her. I wanted her smile and her fight. I wanted to hear my real name on her lips as much as I wanted to feel yet another of her daggers at my throat. I would take her wit and sarcasm any day just to hear her voice and dare sleep with one eye open just to lay by her side every night. Above all, I yearned to hear her beg me to ceaselessly please her body and soul.

"There's much we can do to hurt each other as well," she added.

I bowed my head, unable to face that truth. It was like a punch to my gut.

"We're on opposing sides, Bloodwyn."

The name Bloodwyn was a discordant note on her lips. I opened my mouth to give her my real name, then slammed it shut. The two of us alone in this tent, the candlelight drawing the night close around us... Osmud's constant warnings rang like an alarm in my head, but I ignored them. I wanted her to say my real name, not tirelessly repeating the name of a noble unworthy of her attention; I should know, I lived in the guy, and he'd achieved nothing of honor in his life.

"We don't have to be—"

"So, you're choosing to give up your goal and return to the north?"

"I didn't say that."

What was I saying? I didn't know myself.

"Then we're enemies, and there's no way around it."

"Perhaps we can find a way we both achieve our goals while accommodating the other."

"Mine is to save the Tannard line, and yours is to destroy it. In what way are you proposing we accommodate each other?"

What way, indeed? I had no solution, yet, but I was desperately trying to work one out. All I knew was I couldn't let her go. At some point I'd taken her small hands and wrapped them around my heart, folding them in close and hoping she'd never let go. I was in deep, deep shit.

I stepped away from the intensity rising within me. It felt like grabbing hands, clawing to seize her, steal her away and hide her somewhere only I knew.

What did I want to do more right now? Shake her for being so obstinate or kiss her for being so...fearless, bold, confident, resilient, resourceful, perseverant. The list was long and contained everything I adored and desired in another, in a life mate.

I paced, rubbing my hand across my forehead, trying to straighten my thoughts.

"Do you even understand who you're protecting?"

"It's the Mother's will." She responded fast, then blinked as if surprised she spoke the words.

"And you always do as the Mother asks? Without question? Without knowing why she asks it of you? Not caring about the risks to yourself?"

She inhaled, then turned back to the trunk and set the candle beside it. Then, surprisingly, grabbed a shirt and folded it, none too kindly.

"Do I get an answer?"

She threw the shirt back into the trunk and spun on me, hands jabbed to her hips. "Why is my goal any less important than yours, Razohan? Answer me that?"

"Because I know exactly what's at risk, whose fates are being decided, and whose will be destroyed by keeping the House of Tannard alive."

"I've met my share of seers in my day to learn most of them are fakes. What I have learned is fates are many, each as true as the other, depending on who is the one believing."

I'd closed the distance toward her without realizing. We stood close enough everything around us disappeared and the strains of lively music and merriment grew faint. The frustration that had drawn me close to her eased now I was here, to be replaced by a sudden shaming feeling of defeat. I had little I could say to refute her claim, because no matter the fervor of the Nazeen, no matter that the augur's departing words drove my new found conviction, no matter our lore, spanning a thousand years and passed down through the generations, or King Ricaud's possession, I could only follow what I believed.

I bowed my head so she couldn't read my conflict. The

north learned to despise the south, loathe and fear the House of Tannard and their evil wizards, but I could well ask what did the south learn of us? I'd spent my youth shunning everything Romelda told me, a rejection born from my fear. As my father's murderer, perhaps I wasn't worthy. Maybe I would be the next tyrant.

"No answer, Razohan?"

"I must do what I have to," I replied.

"As I."

My heart was neither honest nor innocent. My past actions were a testament to what I could and would do. Perhaps Andriet was more worthy of the Etherweave than I.

"We've sorted that out," she replied with a clipped voice.

"I wish it wasn't so."

"I guess I'll leave." She pressed her lips together.

I could only stare at her.

"Fine." She fiddled with her belt in an awkward gesture.

"I'll think of something that will solve our problem."

Her eyes widened. "You would?" Then she blinked, ducking her head. "Fine." She repeated herself, this time rubbing her palms down her sides, while her eyes darted from me to our surroundings, then back to me again, undecided where to look. And that gave me hope. Dare I believe she wanted me to find a way to free ourselves of this divide. She'd kept me a her secret for all this time and that gave me the greatest hope we'd find a way through this so we could be together. We had to. From the very beginning, I'd gambled everything on there being an us.

"I'll..." She picked at her fingers. "I'll..."

"Stay alive in the meantime."

"I intend to. Thank you for telling me about the...source."

"And thank you for telling me about their fear of light."

"We're even then."

"Perhaps."

"Then...I shall go."

I nodded.

She pressed her lips into her mouth, then after one inhale, she moved around me for the exit. Once there, she stopped and turned to me. "Good luck tomorrow, Razohan."

"One day you'll say my real name. I promise you."

I wanted to gather her close for the way she stared at me.

"Goodnight, Tressya... Oh, by the way."

She stopped halfway out of the tent flap.

"Those berries won't work on me."

Her eyes widened, so I winked at her. "The ones you slipped inside your pocket while you were rifling through my trunk. Just make sure to keep them away from anything you eat or drink. They're quite lethal."

CHAPTER

TWENTY-EIGHT

TRESSYA

WHILE I PREPARED MY HORSE, I listened to the soft tread of the approaching footsteps.

"Good luck," came the soft, delicate voice.

Detailed embroidery adorned Princess Cirro's bodice of the palest lavender on a gown not fit for the fields. A light rain soaked the already damp ground. The continual passage of horses and tramping boots churned the green fields to mud, which now clung to her discolored hem. Her lady's maids had seen to her hair, twisting it into an elaborate style fit for a ball, which now hung limp to her head. Though she didn't seem to mind. Her eyes were lit with a child's eagerness.

I was starting to despise myself for my lack of conviction in carrying out the Mother's will.

"Thank you. Perhaps you should walk the fields and wish the men more luck than me. I feel they need it."

She giggled. "You were tremendous. Winning the first round of the trials. There is much talk around the fire of the mysterious young nobleman who dazzled the king with his prowess. Can you imagine how they would react if they knew a woman beat them?"

Her enthusiasm was infectious. "That's why you must keep it a secret. There'll be an uproar if they found out my true identity. The king would have no choice but to withdraw me."

Please, Mother, forgive my failure.

"Don't worry, I'll not say one word. I don't gossip. And I don't want the king to make you leave the trials."

She came closer, running her hand along the horse's side.

"Have you seen Andriet this morning?" I asked. "He would appreciate some well wishes, too."

"I went there first. But there was a guard at the entrance of his tent. They didn't permit me to enter. His valet was preparing him for the day ahead."

I cast a sideways glance, curious of the tone in her voice, and saw the blush in her checks before she flicked a glance at me. Then she sighed and clasped her hands in front of her. "I don't gossip, but that doesn't stop my lady's maids from doing it. I can't help but hear."

"You can tell me if it's about me. Don't feel shy. I care little about what the court thinks of me."

"I wish I was like you. I care too much. But it wasn't about you, and I won't say anymore because it's gossip after all. Nothing to be trusted."

I stopped checking my saddle bags and turned to face Cirro. "It was about Andriet, wasn't it?"

"Envy makes people say wicked things. That's all it is. Because he'll be king."

I walked around her for the horse's head and checked the tension on the buckle under the horse's chin.

Cirro hesitated slightly, then said, "He's very fond of his valet."

"Is that a question?"

She turned her attention to the horse, soothing her hand down its neck. "He just seems to be."

"They've known each other since they were boys."

"And are still very close."

"Is that another question?"

She dropped her hand and huffed a breath. "I'm sorry. I'm being stupid."

This time, I gave her my attention. "I think I know what you're trying to say. I can imagine the gossip your lady's maids have picked up."

"So it's just gossip."

This was not my secret to tell. I averted my eyes while I tried to decide what to say that would respect both of them.

She stepped toward me, and in her eagerness, took my hand. "I don't mind." Then, seeming to remember herself, she let me go. "He's kind and gentle and funny. Not at all like I expected. He'll make me happy. I know he will. I think I already love him. It doesn't matter if I have to share him. I know I'll grow to care a great deal for Daelon as well."

I couldn't end her life, and not because Andriet adored

her. She was genuine, compassionate and innocent. I adored her too.

"Maybe that is a conversation you can have with Andriet."

Her cheeks flushed, so I squeezed her hand. "I'm glad. You two...three will be very happy."

I went to let her go, but she grabbed my hand with both of hers. "I don't want you to hate me."

"Why would I hate you?"

"I'm..." She dipped her gaze to her feet. "I'm taking your place so soon after you lost Juel. I'll be queen."

I snorted a laugh. "Believe me, I don't hold that against you."

Mother, I've failed you.

"You'll make a much better queen," I said. "I'm content with the place I have found for myself. I'm much better living beneath everyone's notice, moving in the shadows."

"But you'll never be beneath my notice." She glanced over her shoulder, then leaned close. "No woman in Acravia could ever hope to aspire to your position." Andriet had sworn her to secrecy regarding my new position with the king.

"Is it common in Merania?"

It was surely impossible, but I now adored her even more.

"No. I got lucky."

"I was never a ward. Father insisted I was brought up within his household and court. This is the first time I've left his side. King Henricus's court frightens me." She cast a glance over her shoulder, then moved closer. "The Creed of Salmun frightens me even more. They appear out of the shadows. You never hear them sneaking around in the corridors."

"They take some getting used to. And they're definitely creepy, but you don't have to worry about them. They're loyal to the Tannard throne."

"But we'll be friends, won't we?"

"Always. You never have to worry about that."

I could no longer call myself a disciple. The first and greatest of the pillars was no longer in my heart.

From over Cirro's shoulder, I spied Andriet and Daelon approaching.

"I hope you do't lose this horse today. Father didn't bring an endless supply of them." As always, Andriet's lively voice matched his warm smile.

"I'll try my hardest to keep this one."

Andriet leaned against my horse's side, resting his elbow on its rump. "I wish you wouldn't do this. The Salmun are protecting me. No creature of the Ashenlands can touch me. Whereas you're vulnerable."

"Are you forgetting my win?"

"I would never forget that. More so, I'll never forget the expressions on the nobles' faces when they learned some young lad with unknown titles beat them all." He dropped his arm, his smile fading as well. "Seriously. Each new trial grows more dangerous."

"I have a few tricks for dealing with the Ashenlands' beasts."

"I don't doubt you. And I long to see the faces of the

king's court when they discover at the end that a woman beat them all."

"Because it will be Tressya. Of course it will," Cirro said, becoming swept up in Andriet's enthusiasm.

"There is no doubt of that," Daelon added.

The three of them surrounded me now, three people offering me genuine praise, each assured of my skill and ability. That was three people more than had ever believed in me before. And for one traitorous moment, I was glad Juel was dead, glad I would never birth the heir to Tarragona's throne. I would rather be the assassin in the shadows than the queen upon the throne. *Mother, please forgive my traitorous, weak heart.*

I pressed on my lips, unable to reply and glanced away, only to spy Radnisa stomping through the muddy ground toward me. I should've known my brief spark of happiness would be ruined in an instant.

"There you are, Your Highness," Radnisa gave the faintest curtsey. "Prince Andriet."

I gritted my teeth as her eyes grazed over Cirro, which seemed all she was prepared to do in acknowledgment to the young princess.

"I have things to do before the trial begins," Andriet announced, holding out his arm to Cirro. "Come, Cirro, let me tell you all about yesterday's fun."

Cirro threaded her arm through Andriet's, but her eyes lingered on Radnisa as her smooth brow developed deep grooves.

"Come, Daelon. There is still much to prepare." Andriet

spared me a slight smile with a subtle shrug as if to say he was sorry for deserting me.

I glared at Radnisa as they departed, then moved to the horse's girth strap. I'd already checked the buckle was fastened tight, but it was something to do to help me ignore her.

"It seems you learned something during your years of training."

I stopped what I was doing. "I don't believe it. You're impressed that I won yesterday."

She snorted. "I wouldn't say impressed. Many others survived. There are three more, each harder than the first."

"And the king will lose many more of his noblemen before it's over. But you're right, today's trial will be harder. I need to prepare my horse, then I need to change out of this dress and into something more appropriate for a man." I turned my back on her and walked around to the other side of my horse, for no other reason than to get away from her.

Radnisa was determined to have her say because she stayed on my heels. "It's pathetic what you're doing. The Salmun are protecting Andriet. And far more adept at the task. You couldn't even find him in the Ashenlands."

"They weren't there to protect Juel. And now he's dead."

"If the boy is going to be so stupid as to fall from his horse and die the same way his brother did, then I say he deserves his inglorious death. Meanwhile, you're running off and playing the savior, leaving me to take care of things at home."

I spun to face her. "What do you mean?"

She dusted invisible flecks from her sleeve. "You're no

closer to sitting on the throne, and even further from birthing the next heir to the House of Tannard. Why keep the second alive if he's not your husband? Instead, you're wearing men's clothes and pretending to be a hero."

I knew where this conversation was going. I took a step toward her, but like me, Radnisa never stepped back from anyone. This drew us uncomfortably close. "Don't you dare. I've already told you I'll take care of it."

"Oh really, I don't see how. She never sent you here to be the king's blade. If that's what she wanted, she would've used someone far more accomplished. You were meant to sit on the throne alongside Juel and birth out his children one by one until you were too fat to be of use anymore."

I initially joined these trials for Andriet's sake. But after the fleeting yet exhilarating rush of power that surged through me during my first trial, leaving a profound sense of emptiness once it dissipated, my motivation altered. I found myself yearning to recapture that intense sensation, to feel that extraordinary energy coursing through me once again. While protecting Andriet remained my primary focus, an additional allure now drew me to participate in these trials.

None of this, I would share with Romelda. Instead, I said. "Leave the princess alone."

"Is that a threat, dear Tressya?"

I spun from her, scrunching my eyes up to stem my fury. When I opened them, I noticed her pull something small from her pocket. I turned to see what she held, and saw her drop one of Bloodwyn's berries into her palm, then another, and then another as if she was counting out coin.

I lunged for them, but Radnisa moved her hand away.

"Give them back."

"They must be important to match the fire in your voice. I've never seen them before. Tell me, what are they called and what do they do?"

"Just give them to me. It's none of your business. How dare you search through my personal belongings."

"I'm your lady-in-waiting. It's my job to go through your trunks and ready your clothes for the day."

"They weren't in my trunk."

"Does it matter?" Her mockery stopped, her expression turning dark as she leaned in, filling my vision with only her needle sharp eyes. "Tell me what they do."

"No."

It was as though I'd slapped her. "Do I need to make you?"

"Yes" lingered on the tip of my tongue, as I had not yet disclosed my defense against my soul word being used as a weapon against me.

It was forbidden to hold secrets amongst disciples. We were told secrets between disciples were like a disease that slowly killed the strength of the group, the unity of the Sistern. But nothing would make me reveal the truth. I had already grown disloyal and committed the forbidden by disobeying the Mother's directive. And now I wielded the blade again, slicing once more through the fabric that tied me to the Mother.

"They're poisonous. I found them in a nobleman's belongings. So I took them. He was a traitor to the king. I was going to present them to the king as more proof of his treason."

Secrets and lies, both a canker growing in my heart.

"One of the dead, I assume?"

"Yes." I held out my hand. "Give them back."

"I think I'll keep them for now. You don't need them while you're in the Ashenlands. I'll keep them safe. I wouldn't want anyone to accidentally swallow them."

"Don't you dare, Radnisa. Leave the princess alone."

"Honestly. Another threat?"

I turned from her, unable to look at her face any longer.

"Perhaps you need to list the six pillars. It seems you've forgotten your place and who owns your soul."

I closed my eyes, inhaling deep to find my calm place and failed. Instead, I listened to Radnisa's tread as she stalked up behind me.

"Go on then. Recite them for me."

My blade sheathed in my saddle was in my hand as I spun. I'd faced Radnisa so many times, I knew exactly how far I had to raise my arm to reach her throat. But once around, my blade finding its way to her neck, I felt the cold steel of her blade pressing at my throat.

"Precision." I smirked. "Never miss."

"That's one. But you were never good at that one."

I felt the pressure of her blade indent my skin and waited for the sharp sting of its piercing. We remained like this, staring at each other while my heart climbed up my throat. It seemed there was no way out, neither of us willing to withdraw first.

I was a disciple. These actions were not the way of the Sistern; not sister against sister. I would truly curse my soul if I was to strike her down. Only she would likely strike me first.

"The mother is very disappointed." Her remark broke the spell.

In my periphery, I saw her fidget with her pocket using her free hand.

"I took the liberty of writing to her. It was most important she knew what was happening here."

She held up a folded letter, already opened. "It's for you."

I snatched the letter and shoved it into the pocket of my dress.

"You're not going to read it?" She smirked.

"Shall we remove our blades?"

She pressed hers one more time into my neck, then released it from my throat and sheathed it through the slit in her skirt.

"I'll read it later. I need to prepare for the trials, which means I need to focus on the task ahead."

A large part of me feared reading the letter. It was one thing knowing how much I disappointed her; it was a different and painful experience to read the words as if hearing them, as if kneeling before the Mother and suffering her barbed gaze while she recited all the ways I'd failed her.

And then, traitorously, a small part of me wondered who I would be without the Sistern, a thought I never would have dared contemplate weeks ago. Free from the Sistern's hold, free from the Mother's will, free to direct my life as I chose: an impossible thought. I was nothing without the Sistern, or the Mother who gave me my life as I knew it.

I returned my dagger to its sheath on my saddle and took the letter from my pocket. Radnisa was keen for me to read it in her presence, which meant the letter contained nothing good.

There was no point in shying from the inevitable. If the Mother had decided to abandon me, I might as well know now. I opened it. Scrawled across the page were three words.

Kill the Princess.

CHAPTER

TWENTY-NINE

TRESSYA

An arm snagged my waist, wrenching me from my saddle. My gasp disappeared on the wind as we raced across the barren Ashenlands. Before I knew it, he slung me across the front of his horse, a large hand pressing down on my shoulder blades.

"Don't struggle," Bloodwyn barked. "Easy girl." He calmed his horse with a soothing voice.

With his hand now removed from my back and the horse slowing to a walk, I reared up, twisting my torso, and punched him in the face. The accuracy of my aim hit him square in the nose. The force snapped his head back, then his body followed, toppling backward over his horse's rump.

I slid off the horse's neck and marched toward him, dagger already in hand. Bloodwyn lay on his back, blood pouring from his nose, watching me approach. He made no attempt to defend himself, merely lying there with a smile on his face, raising his hands in surrender.

"Well, look at that. It worked."

"I just lost another horse. And my sword," I growled, pointing the tip of my dagger at his chest.

He was breathing heavy, and damn if I couldn't stop my gaze from wandering down to his chest. I rather liked him on his back.

"Yes, but I managed to keep us together on the cross over."

"You're the last person I want to be stuck with in the Ashenlands." This was a terrible time for divided focus, and Bloodwyn was the one person who could steal the entirety of my attention just by his proximity.

"Not so, little princess. Otherwise, that dagger would already be through my heart. You're warming to me."

I hated that he saw right through me. I hated that his voice soothed over my body like a gentle caress, and made me weave dreams of magic in my head, dreams about us, impossible dreams about two enemies being together. "Did the punch to your nose give it away?"

"That and the fact I'm still breathing. Now, if you'd sheath your dagger and let me get up, we could discuss our plans to make the second trial a success."

He rolled to his side and slowly pushed himself up to a sitting position.

"I'm not interested in forming a partnership with you."

Bloodwyn undid the buttons on his jacket and used the hem of his shirt to clean his nose, then pinched the bridge to stem the flow. In doing so, he revealed a tantalizing patch of his stomach. I licked my lips and swallowed the saliva from my mouth, then got lost in pleasant thoughts, wondering how smooth his skin would feel beneath my tongue. All those ridges of muscle, forming grooves I could slide my tongue between.

"Too late. We're stuck with each other now. We best make the most of it."

"Hmm..." I said, not really paying any attention to what he said. My gaze still lingered on the glimpse of his luscious skin. Would it taste like he smelt?

"Hey, princess. You with me here?" And he clicked his fingers.

I snapped my gaze to his face. Damn, I could feel the flush in my cheeks, so I sheathed my dagger, ignoring his smirk. "Why did you do it?"

"Curiosity."

"I'm to believe you're taking part in these trials for fun?"

He removed the hem of his shirt from his nose, and I nearly groaned at losing the view. "I do admit I'm distracted." He lifted his head. "Is it still bleeding?"

"This is not a game to me." He'd diverted my attention, forced me to reveal how hungry I was for a taste of him. He wouldn't do it again.

"I'm making it easy for you to keep an eye on me."

"The trials are deadly serious."

"I would argue the accuracy of that statement."

"Many noblemen will die in these trials because of you."

"Will you mourn them?"

"What're your plans?" I demanded.

"I thought if we—"

"I mean for the Razohan," I interrupted. "The border to the northern lands isn't far. We're ideally located for an invasion."

"Don't forget the Ashenlands." Bloodwyn rose to his feet. I wasn't sure if his slow movement was for my benefit or if he was feeling the effects of his fall—though I doubted the latter.

"They've been a formidable wall for the last millennium."

"Then why have you come south now? And where is the rest of your force? If they're all shape-shifters, they could be amongst us like a plague of mice." These were worries I should've concerned myself with earlier. Instead I allowed his presence to fill my head with thoughts that were undeniably delicious but should never be there. It seemed I was destined to be plagued with my failures forever more.

He pinched the bridge of his nose. "I might have a concussion. That's too many questions."

I spun on my heels and walked over to his horse, nosing through the ground creepers for something to eat. With reins in hand, I swung up into the saddle. Without securing my feet in the stirrups, I nudged the horse into a walk.

"Hey! You're not going to leave me."

"You can shift into a dog and trot beside me." Then I nudged the horse forward. I had to admit, I fought hard not to look over my shoulder when I heard no complaint from Bloodwyn.

Finally, after a short time, my mental fight dissolved, and I glanced behind. He wasn't there. Given the canopy strangled most of the light, and I didn't have the eyes of a night creature, he was likely still there somewhere, silently watching.

Fine. I wasn't here to babysit him. He'd have to find his own way out. I nudged the horse onward, already wishing I was free of this place.

I gave the horse its head, allowing the creature to amble where it chose for now, while I tried to remain alert to any hint that my object was near.

Reining in the horse, a realization hit me: this was Bloodwyn's horse. Had he trapped me in his trial instead of my own? I shifted in the saddle, turning to look behind. "Bloodwyn!" I shouted as I slid off the horse. I couldn't have gone too far. He should still be within earshot.

"Damn you, Bloodwyn! I know you can hear me."

The only sounds were those of the Salmun's creatures, hunters adapted for silent movement.

"Stop sulking," I shouted.

"I never sulk."

I jumped when his voice sounded close behind me.

He reached for my waist as I toppled. As if on instinct, my body surrendered and softened into his touch. I gasped, lips parting and looked up at him, for one desirous moment falling under some spell, and in my mind, I saw his mouth coming closer to mine. Before I knew what I was doing, I was on tiptoes, snaking my arm around his neck, anchoring his head in place.

"Just making sure you don't trip over your feet."

I blinked, each breath pressing my breasts into his chest and tickling my nipples erect, which sent shards of pleasure between my legs.

Bloodwyn stared down at me with a look to peel my clothes from my body. Igniting under his gaze, I was on the verge of doing just that to his, shredding them with my teeth if that was the way I'd get them off quicker.

Mercy to the Mother. I'd lost my mind. I pushed him away.

"How... You..." I closed my eyes and swallowed to reel my lust deep inside of me. "You were in front of me?"

"Trotting's beneath me. I flew." He pulled a loose black feather from between the buttons of his blood-smeared shirt. "What made you change your mind about me?"

How could he behave so nonchalantly, seemingly unaffected by the intense, sizzling nerves that were consuming me? "I think I'm in your trial." *Keep your head on the trials and nothing else.*

"How interesting." He flashed a smile. "That means we'll have to stick together if you want to get out."

"That was your plan?"

"Honestly, I hadn't thought of it. But it works in my favor."

I still didn't know how these trials worked, so he could be telling the truth. "Sniff away, Razohan. I'm weary of this trial."

I wasn't going to last with him so close beside me. If the asshole so much as showed a whisper of interest in engaging in pursuits other than hunting for his object, I'd... I'd...make sure he failed to leave the Ashenlands with clothes intact, sanity intact and with claw marks covering his body. He may flirt and dally around me with teasing, amorous words but it seemed I was the only one with a voracious appetite, and he was on my menu. *Bad girl,*

Tressya. Really bad disciple. This really wasn't me. What had the Razohan done to me?

"You realize the object could be personal to Bloodwyn. He might not want witnesses."

Maybe I could bed him, then kill him.

"Bloodwyn's dead." I gave his conversation little attention.

Who're you fooling? This was more than just lust because I never did *just* lust. I didn't know how. I knew how to lose my heart. That was all. I'd done it once before despite the Mother's training, but my emotions and desires had not felt so raw, so feral, like the survival of my heart depended on us being united.

"I might choose to be embarrassed on his behalf."

Oh wow. That couldn't be true. I was not losing my heart to my enemy. I didn't even know his real face or name. How could I lose my heart to a stranger? But he wasn't a stranger anymore. He was infuriating, obnoxious, and bullheaded, yet he had saved my life and had been honest with me from the start—the only one in this twisted game to show such candor.

He had wanted to know me.

And yet, he bit me, choosing me as his lifelong mate, without my consent. I should gut him for that alone, but he exuded an aura of undeniable power and influence I found compelling. Like a supreme hunter prowling, he moved with strength, agility, and grace. These traits combined were mesmerizing. His swordsmanship was unquestionable, stemming from breathtaking confidence in his skill.

He could have had his pick of courtiers in the north.

Yet, he had chosen me. For no other reason, it seemed, than to save my plain self, the failed disciple, from his blade.

"Hey, you're doing it again," he said, waving his hand in front of my face.

"No, I'm not," I snapped. *I'm not falling in love with you.*

"It's hard to say when your eyes get that faraway look, like your thoughts have shifted away from us... Us in the trials, that is. Helping plan our escape from here."

"You're right. I'm not thinking of us. Not in the least."

"Fine. But we need to work together if we want to get out of here, so perhaps your thoughts could stray a little to us for a while."

I rolled my eyes, then couldn't help falling into his. For too long. Bloodwyn made it easy by staying quiet and returning my stare. The oppressive darkness of the Ashenlands enveloped us like a cocoon. It should concern me that I felt no want to cut this moment. *Kiss me. Like I'm your last meal.*

I pushed him away—but he didn't budge—shocked at how forceful the thought had come to me. So much so I almost complied and kissed him first, savagely.

The slow creep of his smile snapped me out of his seductive trance. I placed my hands on my hips and glared at him. Waiting.

"I'm not feeling anything at the moment. Let's walk." Bloodwyn gathered the horse's reins, then hesitated before he moved off, his hands twitching by his side, like his first instinct was to take mine.

If only he would, like he did in Emberforge.

"I wonder why nothing's attacked us yet." I stepped over a root, leading the way.

"Don't hurry the inevitable."

"I'm curious how you knew about the difference between the source and the manifestations."

"I'm more interested in your past. Illegitimacy isn't even a term in the northern realm. The Razohan don't use it. Every child is cherished."

I held my breath, focusing on where I walked rather than on him because those few words were a promise. He couldn't know what they meant to me.

"It wasn't hard to find out," he continued, sounding defensive, as if I'd accused him of prying into my history.

"Do you really think you will win against the Salmun?" Steering the questions was my best way to keep him from the secret ruin of my soul.

He exhaled slowly, and I stole fleeting glances at his profile, which was not the way to keep my head focused on winning the trial and out of the turbulent mix of my emotions regarding him.

"Did the Mother ever make up for the absence of your birth mother?"

I hesitated in my steps, but Bloodwyn kept walking, seemingly unfazed.

"What about the others in the northern realm? The Huungardrerd? How many will follow you south?"

"Do you trust the Mother?"

I halted. Bloodwyn turned to face me. "In the graveyard, you mentioned learning the power of your soul word."

"A lapse I won't repeat." Curses that he remembered.

This conversation was bound to unravel me into loose threads, so he could rewind me into knots and twist them around his finger. Only, I was starting to dream again, because I didn't believe he would. *Look where all those dreams have gotten me.*

"Your Mother dumped you in Tarragona, surrounded by a court of serpents when you were vulnerable and powerless to use soul voice."

How dare he? "Have I ever appeared vulnerable to you?"

He stepped closer, his presence overwhelming. "I'm curious about the other special talents hiding within you, princess?"

"I'd guess fewer than you. You're rather crowded in there, I would say."

He chuckled. "Well said."

Unexpectedly, a tingle spread through my stomach, flooding me in warmth on hearing his laugh. I clenched my fists. I should be irritated, not charmed.

"Loyalty is one of our six pillars," I stated.

"I asked how you felt about the Mother, not the specifics of your training."

"The Mother is devoted to the Sistern. She's chosen for—"

"I'm not interested in the Sistern's propaganda. I'm interested in what you feel in your heart."

"My loyalty is to the Mother—"

Bloodwyn silenced me with a finger on my lips, and I was unprepared for the violent punch of lust.

"No more rehearsed responses, Tressya. Speak your heart."

He couldn't know what his words did to me. They were spells of the sweetest kind. I found clarity in silence, but everything inside of me was either at war or on fire. My emotions raged against each other, one side wanting my surrender, the other charging in for the kill. His touch, that singular gesture of his finger lightly pressed to my lips destroyed my carefully practiced restraint. Discipline would never be mine to master again as long as I was with him. I closed my eyes and thought of that finger trailing all the way down my neck.

"You'd probably say or do anything to come out on top," I whispered.

Regret was a bitter taste. It poured into my mouth like stomach acid when he withdrew his touch.

Bloodwyn moved on with the horse. Staring at his back, I felt the vicious stab of rejection, and the blade remained lodged between my ribs.

"It made no sense." I stomped after him, not paying attention to where I put my feet and tripped over a hidden root.

Bloodwyn caught me. My skin overly sensitive to his touch, I stayed in his arms. I *wanted* to stay in his arms. What would it be like if I surrendered completely to him? Gave him what he wanted, the end of the Tannard line, and his ass on the throne?

Mercy, what was I thinking? I could never betray Andriet.

I pulled myself from his hold. "I wondered so many times. But it's not my place to question. It opens the way to disloyalty." I spat the words out in a jumble. I disobeyed the pillars everyday. I'm no longer worthy of the Mother's respect.

"Your heart already seems heavy with guilt." His soothing words were calming. I turned away, unable to handle the intimacy.

"There it is."

"What?" His words jolted me. I glanced around. Had he found his object?

"That spirit."

I was taken aback. *He can see spirits too?* "Where?"

He gripped my wrist, gently directing my attention to him and touched my chest. "Right here. It's never far, thankfully. And no, you've never appeared weak or vulnerable to me. Neither I find alluring."

His words left me breathless.

"Listen," he whispered, attention on the woods. "Do you hear that?"

Right now, we could be drowning in the sea, and I wouldn't care.

As he gathered the horse's reins, his hand engulfed mine. It felt right. It felt like I had come home.

"No," I played along, letting our hands remain intertwined, comforted by his warmth.

"This might be what we've awaited."

"What is it?"

"A woman's moan."

"Maybe you were right. This could be embarrassing."

He smirked. "Bloodwyn was quite the rogue."

"It's unsettling he's inside you."

"But helpful. The Salmun would've recognized me instantly without Bloodwyn's memories."

"It's still creepy."

Unfazed, he pointed out. "The sound comes from over there."

We moved stealthily, even the horse being discreet. Still, I heard nothing and wondered if Bloodwyn was simply finding an excuse to hold my hand, which he didn't need to find.

"Are we getting closer?"

"The sounds are sporadic. I can't tell if she's in ecstasy or distress."

"Are you telling me you don't know the difference?"

"You can't hear her?"

"Sensitive subject, I see."

He yanked me to a stop. "I thought you wanted to be serious about this trial?"

"You wasted a fair amount of time back there asking me private questions. I'm just returning the favor. And no, I can't hear a thing. Remember, this is your trial?"

He nodded. "Good. Then you won't see her either."

"Why? Is she going to be naked?"

"I wouldn't know?"

I reached up and poked his temple. "His life's in there."

"It's a possibility."

"I'm not surprised."

Rather than reply, Bloodwyn led me through the trees. I glanced over my shoulder once, feeling a few eerie tingles, but saw nothing. Thankfully, the creatures of the Ashenlands had stayed away so far.

When he stopped abruptly, I bumped into him. "I see her."

I rubbed the tip of my nose as I came to stand beside him. "That seemed suspiciously easy."

"It's far from easy. She's on a small island in the middle of a marsh, which is probably deadly."

"I don't see a marsh."

"An illusion. That's alright then."

"Illusions can be just as dangerous in this forest."

He squeezed my hand, looking down at me. "I'd suggest you stay here, but once I touch her, I'll vanish back to tent city."

"I can handle myself. I don't need your protection."

"Tressya," he growled. "Do you want me to leave you alone?"

"No. I'm just in the habit of antagonizing you."

"I've never wanted a woman that rolls over for me, but this isn't the place to start arguing."

There went another punishing flare of tingles. Only this time they started lower than my belly.

"Actually, there are situations where a woman rolling over—"

I fought with my smile. "Any minute we're going to be attacked."

Bloodwyn winked and stepped forward, then groaned.

"What happened?"

"My foot's sunk to my ankle."

I stared at the ground, seeing his boot. "No, it hasn't."

He closed his eyes and shook his head. "It's a potent illusion."

"But I can guide you. There's no marsh." What other deceptive tricks would we face?

He inhaled sharply and took another step. "My other foot just sunk."

"It's all in your mind."

"It feels like ice."

"Release the horse. We don't need it. Concentrate."

Bloodwyn did as I said, but the creature remained still.

"Come on," I urged, pulling his hand. "Straight ahead, right?"

"Get behind me, Tressya. We're uncertain of what lies ahead."

"I thought you said you never saw me as vulnerable or powerless."

"I can't help wanting to protect you."

If only my enemy would stop being so nice. I never needed a man to save me, but that he wanted to melted my heart.

I grunted, tugging his hand, but Bloodwyn resisted. "My feet are stuck."

"They're not." Yet, I could see the illusion overpowering his mind.

He clenched his teeth, a muscle twitching under his left eye as he tried to pull his feet free.

"There's no marsh, Bloodwyn. Your feet aren't stuck. Trust me." I pulled his hand again, and he stumbled into me.

I stumbled backward, but Bloodwyn caught his balance in time to prevent me from falling.

"Let's keep moving." This time he pulled me along.

Walking with exaggerated strides, it seemed as though

he battled to lift each foot. I held his hand tightly, hoping my touch would remind him the illusion wasn't real. Until he fell to one knee.

He pounded the ground and growled. "It's not real."

"What happened?"

"I've sunk to my knee."

"You're kneeling. Get up." I looked over his head to the dark forest beyond. We were going too slow, and with this illusion consuming Bloodwyn's concentration any attack would be deadly.

"Come on, Bloodwyn." I tried to pull him up, but he growled in frustration.

His cheeks between my palms, I leaned close, then covered his eyelids with my fingers. "Close your eyes and listen to my voice. Get. Up. You're kneeling not sinking."

"The cold's paralyzing my leg," he admitted through gritted teeth.

I shook my head, as if it was I that needed convincing, then I crouched and grabbed the back of his calf. "Do you feel my hand?"

He shook his head. "No."

"Can't you? I'm squeezing your calf. You must be able to feel that."

"If I could I would say. I'm not pretending."

"I don't want to do this." I went for my dagger sheathed at my belt. "But we're in deep trouble if I don't."

Bloodwyn gently pushed me away. "Find your object and get out."

"Too late. You ruined my chances there." And I slashed a shallow cut across his calf, ensuring he felt it.

"Arrh! Did you just cut me?"

"If you were submerged, you wouldn't have felt that. Stand up."

He collapsed forward, using the ground to push up. "My hands are sinking through. It's like they're in a vice." He tried to lift them, but they remained grounded. Squeezing his eyes closed, he huffed. "It's an illusion."

I pressed my hand to the wound at his calf, smearing the slippery warmth of his blood. He jerked.

"You feel that, don't you? That's not an illusion."

Bloodwyn nodded, so I sheathed my dagger, grabbed his arm and yanked, leaving smears of his blood on his sleeve. "I'm sorry." Despite my efforts, he remained immobile.

"No you're not."

"I might have enjoyed it a tad. But if you can't break free from these illusions, I'll have to cut you again."

"You could've tried a kiss."

"That's your reward for freeing yourself and reaching the woman."

"A challenge I can't decline."

He sunk his head. I let him go and sat back and watched, but he remained on his hands and knee. As far as I could see, he wasn't doing anything or making a sound. The wait became an agony, but I pressed my lips tight not wanting to disturb him.

The thrash of my blood through my ears drowned out the forest noises, and the gloom cloaked anything creeping in close. That we'd not been attacked already seemed too convenient. Right now was the perfect time for one of the Salmun's creatures to appear, which made me think what

Bloodwyn faced was his trial. Marshlands? Even marshlands that paralyzed were tame. There had to be more.

"I'm done being patient. You need to fight."

He stayed like a perfectly carved statue.

"Bloodwyn?"

I received no response. "Bloodwyn?" I crawled toward him and tapped him on the head. When he remained still, I gently lifted his head using a finger under his chin, then recoiled upon seeing the whites of his eyes. His head dropped, as though he'd fallen into a deep sleep.

Maybe another cut from my blade would break him out of the trance he seemed to be caught in. Before I could even draw it, Bloodwyn let out a cry. His right arm gave way, collapsing him onto his elbow.

"Let go of me," he snarled.

With his elbow and arm pinned to the ground, he tried to thrash about.

"Curses, Bloodwyn!" I lunged at him, striking his arm. "Fight!" Yet, he was unreachable. It was like an invisible wall had descended between us, severing us apart.

He cried out again, dropping onto his left elbow. I could only imagine the horrors he perceived in his mind. He continued to struggle in vain, battling the unseen forces dragging him down. This was his trial, a mental challenge that seemingly not even a mighty Razohan could break free from.

Acting on impulse, I slipped onto my ass and shuffled underneath him before he fell flat on his face. For whatever reason, I felt sure once he was flat on the ground, I would lose him. Perhaps the illusion would make him believe he was drowning until he ran out of air.

Grains of dirt and sharp twigs burrowed under my clothes, and my dagger got ensnared in some creepers. I strained, shimmying down his body's length, all the while he wildly shook his head and continued his loud protestations.

Grasping his face, I yelled. "Bloodwyn!" trying to be heard over his own outbursts.

His features, twisted in fury, betrayed his torment. "No!" he bellowed, spitting over my face in the process.

With his eyes a haunting shade of white, the illusion seemed to have completely taken over. Perhaps he believed his only way out was death—a thought I couldn't bear.

I wrapped my arms around his neck, my legs around his waist, pressing myself flush against him, wanting to become his anchor, hoping to bring him back, unable to let him go. When he roared again, I seized the moment to kiss him, silently pleading this would be enough; I would be enough.

Driven by desperation, I drove my tongue into his mouth, kissed him like I'd never kissed before; like a savage, hoping to connect with him in a way words couldn't.

I had wondered what it would be like to kiss him, but never dreamed it would happen in the middle of the Ashenlands. And it would be better, amazing even, if Bloodwyn responded. He didn't. Instead he remained like wood. My kiss didn't work. The disappointment burned like red glowing metal, and I sobbed into his mouth, a wounded sound that ripped at my heart. *I wasn't enough.*

What he did do was bite my lip. I yelped and recoiled.

The surprise made me release my grip, causing me to tumble to the ground.

"Asshole," I snapped, regaining my composure to deliver a swift right hook to his jaw.

His head snapped right at the same time he collapsed on top of me, shunting the air from my chest. I didn't have time to take in breaths before he kissed me back with ferocity, such that I thought he wanted to suck my lungs up my throat. For a breath, I allowed him. I did what I dreamed of doing and gave in, opened myself to the powerful wave of arousal shooting through my body like arrows, the most pleasurable way to be wounded.

My moan was my wake up. Or a combination of his and mine. But the united sound of our budding bliss reminded me of our fates. I fisted his hair and pulled, peeling his lips away.

You had your chance.

"Is that your blood or mine?" were the first two sane words he'd spoken since believing he was stuck in the marsh.

I wanted to punch him again. Even so, my relief that he was back overpowered me. And now I was caught between wanting to punch him or kiss him again. The next best thing was to growl. "Get off me."

"Seriously, is that your blood or mine?"

"It's yours. Please, I can't breathe."

Bloodwyn pushed to his knees, grabbing my hand as he went and helped me to sit. "Why were we on the ground?"

"You don't remember?"

"No."

"Nothing?"

"Thinking I had sunk up to my ankles."

"Fine," I snapped and went to get up, but Bloodwyn snagged my elbow and reeled me toward him.

Holding me close to his chest, his eyes dropped to my lips. Using his thumb to slowly swipe at the blood, he whispered. "Liar."

When I pushed at his chest, he reluctantly relinquished me, but continued to frown. "What happened?"

"Do you still see the woman?"

He gave a small shake of his head, telling me he was annoyed at my persistent habit of never answering him, and glanced over the top of me. "Yes."

"What about the marsh?"

"We're sitting in it."

"But you don't feel trapped?"

"No. I seem to have freed myself from that part of the illusion."

"I guess it shows the force of your will."

"I guess it does." He worked his jaw as he rubbed it.

I would feel smug if I didn't feel mad. Or was this disappointed? Violence worked better than a kiss.

I turned my back on him and climbed to my feet. "Don't you dare start believing you're sinking again."

"Your ass is soaked," he quipped and scooped me up into his arms. I gasped and, despite myself, tried not to laugh.

"Let me spare your boots from getting muddy. She's not far."

"We're still in the Ashenlands. You've got no excuse for being in a good mood."

"It's not every day you discover your mind's an iron cage."

"The invincible Razohan."

Bloodwyn carried me the rest of the way. He continued to hold me in his arms when he reached the woman, but the weird tug and pull effect of returning to tent city wrenched us apart and we both landed face down on the edge of the Ashenlands.

CHAPTER

THIRTY

TAMAS

I RUBBED my jaw as I watched Tressya from across the bonfire. Holding a bone of meat, she laughed with Andriet's lover. It seemed decorum was lost during the revelry, and most of the courtiers indulged themselves in ways they wouldn't dare in Tolum.

My jaw had continued to bother me since returning from the trial. My nose wasn't much better, but I remembered how that came about. It was unsettling having no memory of what happened during the trial, and I worried about how I acted in front of Tressya. She seemed a little distant on our return.

Andriet sat beside the king, with Cirro at his side. The north were yet to give me a signal, which meant all three would stay alive for tonight. The timing needed to be perfect.

Daelon had held Tressya's attention too long for my

liking. There was that rare and unfamiliar jealousy rearing up again. And since I didn't want to add him to my list of kills, I made my way around the bonfire, weaving through the dancers until I stood in front of them.

Daelon saw me first. Tressya turned, following his gaze.

"Your Highness," I dipped my head.

"I see the Salmun's creatures haven't tried hard enough," she said.

I smirked. "It's hard to stop a man with a mind like an iron cage."

"I could name a few ways, swamps for one, a fist to the jaw maybe another."

I touched my jaw. "'Er what?"

"Never mind." It was close to sounding like a sigh.

"I'm needed elsewhere," Daelon announced, then ducked away into the crowd as quickly as he could. Smart man.

A dog pounced on Tressya's discarded bone, then she wiped her hands on the kerchief she'd tucked inside the belt, cinching her dress to hug her waist, and slid off the large barrel. "I'm going in search of a drink." She strolled off toward the myriad of stalls erected as a side alley away from the bonfire and dancing. Knowing my little princess like I did, I took that as my invitation to follow.

Flaming torches on long poles staked in the ground provided the light for the crowds gathered to peruse the stalls, from herbs, trinkets, oils, and soaps to hot, spicy food. The peasantry from Tolum made good money on these rare occasions.

"I can only guess I embarrassed myself out there today."

"You can't be embarrassed if you don't remember. But who was the woman?"

"No one special to me. I do remember one thing, which ties into the provocative position I found us in."

She turned her head away, pretending to inspect posies of herbs. "Lots of weird things happened," she mumbled, seemingly uninterested in our conversation, and that only set my determination not to let her escape from my questions.

"You call a kiss weird?"

"That was the weirdest of the lot."

I moved in close beside her and leaned down, speaking in a low voice. "It did happen?"

When she turned, our faces were close enough it wouldn't take much for me to lean forward and dare another kiss. I was sorely tempted, but I wouldn't put it past her to punch me in the nose, again.

Large washing troughs were our only means of bathing out here, and Tressya had made the most of it. Her fragrance was delicate. Her usual lilac was replaced with an earthier scent tinged with a mild dash of spice, which suited her better. My feral little princess was better wearing a fragrance reminiscent of the wilds and not the perfume of cloistered courtiers.

I plucked a posy of dried herbs and sniffed the sweet woodruff and anise.

"A perfect complement," I said and slipped it into the belt at her waist, then flicked the stall owner a gowl.

"It happened, but it was poorly performed." Then, with a

quirk of her lips, she tried to get away from me, but I slipped a finger into her belt and hauled her back.

"I demand a second chance."

"You had a second chance. It was much like the first."

In my surprise, I released her. "What?"

Tressya backed away. "Don't believe I would be so foolish as to allow a third attempt. The second was how you got your sore jaw. Or was that the first?" She turned and strolled away.

I marched after her, then jumped in front to cut her off, but she spoke first. "Was a bloody nose and sore jaw not enough?"

"Not even—"

She held up a finger, her face solemn. "Let's not turn this into something."

"I have to. There's a distinct cooling between us, and I want to know why."

"We never burned, Bloodwyn."

She attempted to escape, but I wouldn't let her go. I burned. I burned so bad I was surprised everything I touched didn't incinerate. And I wanted to make her burn. We both deserved to be in flames. Besides, I'd done something unforgivable during the trial to erect her walls. That I wouldn't tolerate. There would be no walls between us.

Hitching a finger in her belt again, I flushed her against me. "There were sparks. Sparks need time to catch alight."

"You had your chance—"

I seized her chin, her cheeks caught between my fingers and thumb, and tilted her head up. "No. I was caught in an illusion. That's not a fair chance." Before she could argue, I silenced her with a kiss filled with a brutality and longing that savaged even me. Everything in my heart that I couldn't voice aloud, I unleashed into my kiss, a kiss to seal hearts, a kiss to join souls.

I had severely underestimated how perfect she would kiss; how delicious she would taste; how wonderful she would feel. She came with me, folded into me, fell with me, responded with her own style of savagery. And for a wicked moment, I lost my shield of strength and opened myself to the flow of her emotions to find they were united with my own, fiercer and wilder than the Ashenlands beasts.

It startled me when I realized what I'd done, so much so I almost wrenched us apart. A shout nearby did that for me. The throb of my fury when she pulled away, released a claw, which I struggled to force back inside.

"We shouldn't have," she whispered, her face flushed. She glanced around us.

"We most definitely should've." I loved hearing her small feverish pants.

Any doubts I once harbored about Tressya's significance to me, to my path—to our *shared* journey—had long since been demolished.

"My lady," came a voice from beside us.

She was dressed in well-worn robes with a weave of thick gray hair tangled into long braids then knotted at her nape, her face harshly lined with age. The woman believed herself to be an augur. I knew their look only too well.

I took Tressya's elbow intent on steering her away, in no mood for prophetic nonsense. But Tressya resisted me and turned to the woman, whose head reached Tressya's shoulders.

"Do you want something?" Tressya said.

"It's you, my dear, in need of something. Come, let me show you."

"She's not interested in anything you have to say," I said, and took Tressya's hand.

Her eyebrows shot up. "That kiss doesn't give you privileges."

I groaned and leaned to speak in her ear. "She claims to be a seer. They're crazy at best."

"I've had to endure crazy since meeting you. I think she'll be much easier to take." She turned back to the woman. "I'm ready."

I rolled my eyes, silently cursing and followed them as the augur wound us through the stalls, the frustration still humming through me from our interruption. My body had yet to cool down, and I felt close to clawing someone down their middle, so when we ended up in a dimly lit tent behind the stalls, which smelt of burning oils, I wanted to growl, then laugh, then claw my way through the back of the tent.

I huffed and snorted through most of what the woman said as she instructed Tressya to take a seat on a low wood stool that looked fashioned by a blind man.

"Hold out your hand, my dear." The old woman had seated herself close to Tressya and pulled the single candle flame from the middle of the table close.

"Wouldn't one require good light if one wishes to see the lines on the hands more clearly." Palm readers were charlatans.

"Experienced seers, perhaps not," countered Tressya, frowning at me.

"Palm readers are hardly seers," I scoffed.

"All that you say is true, young man. But I have no intention of reading her palm. I don't know how."

Tressya smirked at me.

"I'm far more interested in this mark." And she exposed Tressya's inner wrist by pulling back her lace sleeve to run a finger over the bite mark.

I stifled my gasp. There was no way she could've known it was there. Tressya was no longer smirking.

"I was bitten by a savage animal," she remarked.

"An animal that has left a lasting mark," the old woman said. "Both inside and out." She shifted her eyes to Tressya. "But you already know that."

Tressya glanced at me. "And is there a way to remove what's inside?"

"Hmm..." The old woman continued to inspect the mark, seeming to genuinely pondered Tressya's question.

If I could explain how she'd even known the mark was there, I would throw a few gowl on the table and lead Tressya away, but a weird and uncomfortable feeling had settled across my chest.

"I would say yes...but it would only work if it was truly desired."

"It is desired. I do want to be free of it," Tressya snapped, avoiding my gaze.

The old woman closed her eyes as she patted Tressya's arm. I expected Tressya to pull her arm away, claiming the old woman a fake, but she waited, seeming hypnotized to the woman's next words.

"There is a silent war raging within." The woman murmured; her eyes still closed. Here came the crazy babbling and weird prophetic announcements.

"A dormant hunger yearning to be free. A wildness yet to be known. A spirit long forgotten."

I rolled my eyes when Tressya glanced my way. If Garrat were here, he'd laugh, then perhaps bare some sharp teeth at the woman.

"I think you've said enough," I rose, offering my hand to Tressya.

"The same wilderness roams within you, northerner."

A chill froze my heart. Beside me, Tressya gasped.

The old woman's gaze returned to Tressya. "You're losing, my child. But perhaps that's the way it's supposed to be."

CHAPTER

THIRTY-ONE

TRESSYA

Surrounded by a deep and dreary gloom, where the dense canopy suffocated the sun, there was no way of knowing if I had returned to the anywhere familiar. Even if I had, I wouldn't know which way I should head to reach the lake I'd stumbled upon. From every direction, the blackened trees rose over me like the vile beasts that roamed this forest.

I brought my horse to a halt, then rummaged around in my saddlebag for the fat candle Bloodwyn had brought to me this morning. There was a small pouch of flint and an iron rod for lighting, and he followed them up with a half-smile as he told me he hoped they would be enough to light my way.

My panic reared on discovering the small pouch wasn't with the candle in my saddlebag. I must've left it behind. I searched my jacket pockets and found it there, along with something else. I pulled out the small round object and held it up. It was a berry, one Radnisa had missed when she searched through my belongings. I slipped it and the pouch back inside my pocket. The candle was likely too small to be of any use, and I had a better way of finding my path in this deadly forest.

In a small clearing, I stopped my horse and focused on my breathing; best I get myself a guide before any of those foul creatures found me again.

I closed my eyes, using my calming breaths to harness my concentration, then gathered the edges of my awareness and dragged it all the way inside my mind, then deeper into the depths of the void. It felt like I was pouring sand inside my throat as a weight to hold me down. My body grew so heavy I felt anchored in place. The barriers of my mind shattered like fractured glass and out of the chaos flowed my soul word. *Aetherius.* It came to me easily now, as if eager to be free.

With my mind quietened, the forest grew noisy. Moving through it with my eyes open, I'd not realized the small creaks and groans from the boughs and the occasional rustle of leaves from the gentle breeze that tickled the fine hairs across my face. It all made concentrating hard, and I struggled to keep my thoughts from thinking of creeping beasts.

Discipline. To steady my racing heart, I fisted my hands, digging my nails into my palms. My building panic was slowing me down. All I needed was one look to convince myself nothing was there.

I cracked an eyelid, then both, and glanced around.

Nothing. So I closed my eyes again and focused on my soul word. This time, when my mind's barrier fell, I spanned my awareness outward and felt nothing but my own beating heart. Still I released the call.

A faint male voice reached me through the trees. I stood on tiptoes and craned over the horse's rump to the forest beyond, and spied a dim glow.

"Come on." I gathered the horse's reins and led it toward the distant light.

It felt like I'd traveled a suitable distance, weaving the horse around the dense foliage when I came upon the spirit of an old man sitting, in the weird way spirits did, on a large, fat tree root. Half of him had sunken through. Even though the spirits were dead, in the Ashenlands, I began to see them as life, the light my savior.

His head was bent, his body slumped, as he mumbled to himself.

"Hello," I said.

He lifted his head. On seeing me, his eyes grew wide. "Ah, it is you."

Sitting, he looked a short man of middling age—wearing peasant clothes, hanging loose around his body and dirty from hard work—with thin, wispy hair that exposed most of his scalp.

"I see my little friend has been talking about me."

"Most laughed at her. Me included. She was a funny one alive." He tapped the side of his head. "And a pain in the ass dead. If there was some way I could make her alive again just to get rid of her, I would. But"—he spread his arms outward to me—"this is a miracle."

His light glowed less brightly than the young girl's.

"I'm Tressya."

"An interesting name for an interesting woman who ventures into the cursed land dressed as a man. Never heard of it."

"Times have changed outside the Ashenlands."

"So I see, but maybe not as much as you say. The kings of Tarragona still send their noblemen to prove themselves or die. And now it seems there are not enough men left and so the king sends a woman in their place. Or are they all cowards? And me name's Tulin."

He rose from his seat and drifted toward me. Beside me, my horse whinnied and shifted sideways, perhaps sensing something strange in the air.

"You don't look strong. But the lass says you did good against the rotspine. That's what we call them. That type, at least. We've made names for plenty more. There's a long list. You'd be looking for a special thing, I'd say."

"Firstly, I need to know if there is a way to reach the other competitors while they're in the Ashenlands?"

He slowly nodded his head as if in thought. "Ruthless. Sabotage you'd be thinking then. Remove your competitors from the trials."

"It's not that. I'm worried someone else involved in the trials is thinking that very thought."

He shook his head. "It's impossible."

"I have to protect my friend."

He guffawed. "You're a strange creature. I believe some things have changed since my day." He chuckled for longer, then pulled himself together. "Ain't never seen it done. You're all on your own journeys."

"This place is an illusion, but you're not. You're not governed by the same rules as the living. I don't believe you're caught in the same illusion."

He stroked his chin, fingers slipping through his jaw. "You got me there," he chuckled. "You're right. I see both the illusion and the dead lands. Each of you is trapped in your own little fantasy. No two ever end up in the same place. The Salmun make sure of that. Otherwise, you might end up working together."

"If you can see the people, then you can guide me to the man I want to protect."

"Bullheaded woman. The Ashenlands stretch for eternity. You do know that, right? Once they enter the Ashenlands, they're sent anywhere. There's no telling where your friend may be. That you've ended up here is for a reason. This friend of yours could be a long way away."

Curses, I had thought my plan would work. The distance would mean nothing to Bloodwyn, since he could transform into a bird of prey. My only hope was he'd ended up so far away it would take him forever to soar the skies in search of his quarry. That's even if his keen eagle eyes could see below the canopy.

"Fine," I huffed. "Where is the thing I must find?"

"Ah, now we're getting to the important part. So here's the deal. I'll lead you where you need to go to find what you need to find, but don't go telling me what to do. No woman ever told me what to do when I was alive, and none shall do so now I'm dead. Especially no woman who seems to control the dead."

"The little fibber told you that as well? Fine. It's a deal, as long as you don't plan to trick me. Your light and your guidance, give me both for the time I need them, and I'll promise not to bend you to my will."

His bottom lip protruded as he thought. "I don't know if your word is worth much, but I guess I've got no choice. Come on then."

He moved faster than I could pace while leading my horse, simply passing through the fat-trunked trees when I had to weave around them.

"Wait up," I shouted.

He floated back toward me, popping out of a tree trunk right in front of me. "Was that a command?"

"No. But in case you haven't noticed, I can't go through trees, and my horse isn't nimble over these roots."

"Slow is it, then? We'll be walking through the night at this rate."

"I never imagined there would be such a thing as an impatient spirit. Haven't you got eternity?"

"Ah..." He chuckled. "I've got that for sure. But I'm thinking of you, love. The Ashenlands isn't the best place to be at nighttime if you're flesh and blood."

"You made your point. Let's get moving."

"Thought you'd see it my way. Over here." And he popped through the tree again.

We weren't walking long before he started moaning. "Can't the beast move any faster? It's like watching someone die in quicksand. This is what my cursed existence has come to? Waiting for beasts to find their way around roots. What would my Reta think of me now?"

It seemed I had a knack for attracting the less agreeable spirits. "Who's Reta?" I asked, hoping that would distract him.

"My wife. Died peacefully in my arms during the great war. Thank the great god Carthius for that mercy. She's beyond this place. If only I were with her. I would choose to be with my Reta rather than chained to this doomed existence. I can't smell, touch or taste. I might as well be vapors."

Not all spirits remained tethered to this world on death. Only those whose death's violated their souls. The lucky passed through to the ever after while the unlucky lingered with a thin fabric separating them from the living.

My horse shied, refusing to step over a large root when Tulin ventured too close. I placed a hand on her neck to soothe her until he slipped further away, then coaxed her forward once more. Suddenly, she jerked her head high, forcing the reins through my hands so they burned across my palm. I kept hold of her, determined I would not lose another this time, and tried to calm her, but she pranced about, snorting and making anxious sounds.

Tulin came beside me. "Best stick with me. Those foul beasts are lurking."

I glanced around, catching glowing eyes peering around trees, then darting behind as we passed by.

"It's just ahead."

"Where're we going?"

A dark shape reared up through the trees. In the gloom, it

was hard to define, but as we neared, I realized they were massive rock pillars.

"In here," Tulin said, moving ahead between the two pillars.

My horse had yet to calm down, prancing beside me and throwing her head. When I tried to lead her between the gap in the rocks, she reared over me, forcing me to release the reins. Free, she turned and bolted into the trees.

"Curses. That's the third I've lost."

"She wouldn't be able to follow where we're going anyhow."

Seeing a flash of glowing eyes peering out from behind a trunk, I turned and hurried after Tulin. The narrow vein between the rocks led us further into a maze of twists and turns. In places, the rocks leaned on each other, forming a natural ceiling overhead. Further ahead, the corridor opened out so I could look up and see that small shrub-like trees perched atop the rocks.

Ahead, Tulin disappeared inside a cave, his glow brightening the small entrance, revealing etchings in the rock. The patterns stretched across the low ceiling.

"What is this place?"

"It was once a sacred place, a place before my time. The ancients did those carvings, practicing dark magic and evil conjurings. They were the first to create the great magic. It was said whatever they made lived within these caves. We stayed away from this place out of fear."

"Who were these people?"

"No one knows. On death, when no one or thing could harm me any longer, I entered these caves and realized that's all they were. Caves. There was nothing here but darkness and insects."

"You think my object is in here?"

"Yes."

We continued on, Tulin as my light, until the cave floor sloped downward and a cold, stale air rose to meet us. Further still we went, following the patterns etched upon the roof and along the walls with only my footsteps as noise.

Finally, we stepped out into a cavernous chamber, cold and dank and smelling of ages lost. The ceiling spired high above us, and a shaft of natural light cut down through a thin crack in the rock. It was coming on to dusk, the light from above seeping to blue gray, casting a dull hue across the rock-strewn dirt floor.

Thanks to Tulin, I saw the expanse of the cave, his glow reaching the walls on all sides and revealing another passage diverging to the left. From that direction came a gentle, chilled breeze and the smell of long forgotten paths.

Etchings and drawings of forms I couldn't make out adorned the walls. Some were far up the cave wall, too high for an ordinary person to reach.

"As you see. It's nothing but rock," Tulin said.

"What is it I'm supposed to find down here?"

"I'm not rightly sure if this has anything to do with you, to be honest."

I glanced over my shoulder, already feeling the first tingles of caution creeping into my gut. "This better not be a trick."

"I promise. It's no trick. But I was thinking it weird. You entering the trials and being able to talk to us spirits and all.

And then appearing in the Ashenlands so close to this place. It seems mighty suspicious. That's all."

"That's why you brought me here?" Had I just wasted valuable time?

"The Salmun claimed this place as theirs."

"They did?"

"In the decades after the war. Or somewhere thereabouts."

I glanced around me, expecting to see evidence of their presence. "Why would they do that? It doesn't look like they use it for anything. Unless they wanted to hide something in here."

"Indeed."

I turned toward him. "Tulin?"

"Is there nothing unusual you see? Or maybe it's a feeling. I often thought that's what led a person to their special thing. Maybe some guiding force inside their mind that led them in a certain direction, yet they don't know why."

Against my better judgment, I followed his advice and looked around, yet nothing stuck out to me. I sighed. This had been a waste of my time.

Gritting my teeth, I spun in a circle. "I don't see anything. Why did you bring me here?"

"There it is. I knew it would be in there somewhere."

"What?" I barked.

"A temper. Women are fire. Sometimes no amount of water will put it out."

"Will you just tell me what it is you want me to see?"

"There." And he pointed to the right of me. "Over there by that large overhang of rock."

Taking a calming breath, I headed over to where he pointed while pressing my lips together to stop myself from yelling a commanding word, something that would make him disappear.

"I see rocks," I said through gritted teeth, looking at the shadowy edge of the cave.

"You're in the circle."

I looked down at my feet to see the cave floor cleared around me. Tulin was right. Someone had stacked the rocks into small uprights, making a circle around a large boulder, which had fallen from the ceiling, forming the crack that allowed the light from outside to filter through into the cave. The boulder sat at an angle, strewn with sharp chips and edging.

About to make another frustrated comment, I felt a sudden pulse ripple through my chest.

"What was that? I was right. You felt something, didn't you? I saw it in your expression. This is it. This is what you're meant to find. After all this time."

Turning my back on Tulin, I faced the rock, and the pulse grew stronger. Two cautious steps forward and the pulse expanded beyond my chest, beating down into my stomach and tingling out through my fingers.

"What is it?" I breathed, not looking for an answer.

"The Salmun placed it here long, long ago. Thought it would be important given they hid it in the Ashenlands. Only a handful of the living have stumbled in here during the trials, but none ever found it."

I wasn't sure what I was looking at, but if this mysterious object had something to do with the Salmun and was causing this weird sensation in my chest, I wasn't leaving until I uncovered its secrets. I surrendered to the tug, guiding my feet along an invisible path until I stood at the highest point of the rock.

"That's it. You're there."

A shiver rushed up my back on hearing Tulin speak.

A gentle warmth touched my cheek, like someone's palm held just above my skin. I slowly reached out my hand toward a jutting edge of the rock, drawn by the warmth. The moment my hand touched it, the shard glowed a light blue and came away in my palm.

Beside me, Tulin gasped. "I ain't never seen it glow like that. Not even those Salmun can make it do that. I knew it. I was right. Just wait till I tell that donkey Petro. He laughed in my face. Now I get to laugh in his."

I raised the glowing shard up before my eyes. "This isn't the object I have to find. I'm still here. I should've returned."

"Don't worry about that. You can come back to my village and speak to Petro. Show him I was right, and he's an ass. The beasts won't get you there. You'll be surrounded by curious, friendly faces. We'll look after you."

Catching a blur of light in my periphery, I turned from Tulin. The air seemed to shimmer above the jutting rock. Occasionally, flashes of dull greenish and brown light appeared in a swirling haze before blinking out. Slowly, the color stopped its crazy swirl and took on a shape that reminded me of an eye.

"Never seen that," Tulin said.

A crunching sound echoed down from up the sloping passage. Creeping tingles like spider legs, danced across my neck at the thought of being discovered. I had no idea what the Salmun could do. So far, they were nothing more than ominous cloaked figures floating in the shadows. But to create the Ashenlands took serious magic.

Forgetting the weird illusion in front of my face, I shoved the shard of rock into my pocket, then withdrew my sword. It was likely a beast, not the Salmun.

"They were sneaking upon us and we didn't notice," Tulin shouted. "But I'm here...unless it's one of those originals."

Sword at the ready, I faced the passage. "Why is that a problem?" I had no idea what he meant by an original?

"Because the originals have no fear of the light."

"Why didn't you tell me that before now?"

"It would've changed nothing," Tulin said as he slowly backed away.

A horrible howl rushed down the passage like a gale. The ferocity of it, the beast was furious, and sounded huge.

"What're you doing? Nothing can hurt you. Go and have a look," I said.

"It sounds like an abyssal hound."

That didn't sound good. I positioned myself away from where I may trip over debris on the ground in a fight.

"Those in particular give me the creeps," he continued.

Great. For all his bluster, I was stuck with a scaredy-cat spirit. How was that possible? "If you won't help, there's no point in you sticking around."

A thunderous vibration shook the rock walls, bringing down dust and grit from the ceiling. While the rock formation had looked sturdy before, I now questioned if it would tumble down around us.

"Everything I've done for you, and you're repaying me like this? I led you here. I—"

"Get out of here!" I shouted in frustration. A heat rushed out of my chest and up my throat. The sound of my voice reverberated off the walls.

Tulin stiffened, his eyes bulging as if a giant's hand had squeezed his middle. Then he was gone. Oops. I didn't mean to command him away.

Another shuddering noise sent more dust and grit flaking down around me. I huffed out a breath at the next agonizing roar and strengthened the grip on my sword. If it was that big, surely it wouldn't be able to fit through the passage. Even so, I couldn't stay stuck down here forever.

More sounds came from the passage, scuffles, then a chink, like metal—or perhaps claws—dragged along rock. I pressed my hand against my pocket. The heat from the rock flared to life, sinking through the fabric to warm my hand. If only that was my object.

I braced myself, my dagger making it into one hand, while I held my sword with the other.

Any minute, something would loom into view. I gripped both weapons tight, so my knuckles turned white as my heart raged against my rib cage. There was limited space in this cavern, which benefited me as a large beast would find it hard to move.

At the first glimpse of movement, I threw my dagger.

"Damn, woman. That was close." Bloodwyn straightened, the blade tip pinched between his fingers. "You nearly had my heart."

"Bloodwyn?" I gasped. A heady jumble of relief, thrill and desire ate at my focus. "How... The bite mark?" Was that how he found me down in a cave?

"There's an ugly bitch on my tail. You might want to save the questions until later." In the dull light from the crack in the ceiling, I watched him skip the rocks toward me.

"Bloodwyn," I cried, my throat tightening as he misjudged the last rock and tripped, staggering into me, but caught himself—and me, by my waist—before he had us both over.

"Why are you here?

"To rescue you."

I pushed him in the chest with everything I had, but he didn't budge. "I don't believe you. You were hunting down Andriet, weren't you?"

He blew out a breath as he handed me my dagger, hilt first. "Your dagger, princess. You're going to need it."

I sheathed it as I seethed. "What Razohan magic have you wielded to get here?" My gaze flittered his body for feathers.

"The Razohan aren't magic wielders," he said as he looked around us, taking in the cavernous cave in one full slow glance.

I said nothing, wondering if he was looking out of fascination or if his object had drawn him here. Perhaps the rock in my pocket was his object.

Snapping out of whatever trance he'd fallen into, he grabbed my hand and then paused for a moment, turning toward me with his head tilting downward. Was he staring at my pocket? In the terrible light, I couldn't decide where his eyes had strayed. Then seeming to think the better of speaking, Bloodwyn continued guiding me along the rock strewn ground, back toward the passage. "We should get going before we're trapped," he said as we went.

I tugged on his hand. "Why are you here?"

"To rescue you, princess."

"Liar. You were led here." I yanked my hand from his grasp. "Your object's here."

"Not mine. You're here. Maybe it's yours."

I dove my hand into my pocket. The moment I touched the rock, I felt its warmth. A bluish glow shone through the fabric. I pulled it out and held it up in front of Bloodwyn, watching his face take on a bluish tinge.

He stared at the stone as if caught in a snare. I swear it was like he wasn't even breathing. From ages gone until now, the rock remained important to the Salmun. I couldn't fathom why, or any reason for the blue glow, but perhaps it had something to do with Bloodwyn's desire to take the throne.

"If it was mine, I wouldn't still be standing here."

"It's not mine," he repeated in a low voice, as if shielding our conversation from others. His eyes shifted up to meet mine.

I was not mistaken. There had been a flash of something in his eyes the first instant he'd seen the rock. Was it recognition or hunger?

"You'll return the victor of this round if you take it."

His eyes dropped to the rock once more before shifting

back to me. Then his lips quirked. "You'd miss me too much if I returned."

I wasn't expecting him to tap me on the nose. "Besides, this is me being heroic."

I frowned.

"Rescuing the princess. I can hardly return and leave you stranded."

Just then, a loud boom shook the ceiling.

CHAPTER

THIRTY-TWO

TAMAS

OUR ESCAPE REQUIRED my full concentration, but I was unable to focus on where I led Tressya. My mind remained stuck on the rock. Mercy on our souls. The Etherweave.

The Salmun's fury on learning what the Nazeen had done with the Etherweave was legendary. The Nazeen hoped to take the rock with them when they fled, but the Salmun attacked with brutal efficiency, wanting to secure the rock for themselves. During the battle, a piece broke off. What Tressya had in her pocket was that piece of rock.

This close to it, the call that had steadily grown stronger these last weeks, vibrated through my head and heart, messing with my attention for the task at hand; calling to me as bloodborn, one born from amongst the beast children of the north, as an augur had foretold many centuries ago.

The third day of the trials, and I intended to find Tressya, not Andriet. Knowing the manifestations were undefeatable on their own, I couldn't rid my concern for her safety. She was smart and bloody good with a sword, but I couldn't let go of the fear knowing she would face these beasts alone. Then, the moment I'd entered the Ashenlands, the pull of the Etherweave was so great, I felt I would lose my mind if I ignored it. I'd transformed into a bird and flown across the vast stretch of the forest, guided by the Etherweave's lure, to reach this point.

Only to find Tressya.

Perhaps I'd lost my sanity. Osmud was right. My attention was no longer primarily on my goal. For the first time in ever, something else came before duty. And that something else had a warm little hand, fitting inside mine like they were one.

And now she possessed a small fragment of the Etherweave. Still bound within the rock—waiting for the moment to rise—it had responded to her touch—I wouldn't dwell on the reason for that.

The noise above fell away, and a sudden quiet rang down the cave passage as a deafening silence.

"Not on my life do I believe it's left," I whispered.

"It's laying a trap."

She tried to slide her hand from my hold, but I instinctually gripped her hand tight, not letting her escape. She was mine to protect.

"It's a source," I said.

"Good. Then we can eliminate it."

Always courageous. I adored that about her.

"There's no telling how intelligent they are. I'll go

first since it knows I'm here, though it might know you're here as well. They'll have a keen sense of smell and excellent eyesight in this gloom. Surprises likely won't work."

"If you distract it, I'll deal the killing blow."

I quirked a brow and smiled, which she would miss now we'd moved away from the filter of light in the cave. The darkness held us close, with the faintest glow from outside making its way this far in, but not enough to see each other's faces.

"The things a monster, so there's no need to get bold. It's probably best to aim for a wounding strike. It's likely all you'll get in first. I'll do my best to keep its attention. Go for the legs."

"Are you telling me how to win this fight?"

"I'm offering advice...that I really hope you accept."

There was silence for a heartbeat.

"Make sure you keep it confined. If it's a monster, then it'll have trouble moving around in those entrance alleys. That's our advantage, so don't draw it out into the open," she replied.

"Now who's telling who how to win the fight?"

"Are we doing this, or arguing?"

I'd kiss her silent if we weren't nudging death in the shoulder. Instead, I snapped my head away and increased my pace through the passage.

Annoyingly, I couldn't get the idea of kissing her out of my head. Especially after last night's spectacular kiss. Not even the sudden cascade of small rocks into the entrance of the passage drew all my attention away from the thought of pushing her against the cave wall and giving her something to really argue about.

What in the seven realms was I thinking?

Concentrate, Tamas.

I needed my wits on one task for now. Our survival. The kiss, well...maybe that would be her thank you at the end.

Stars above. I gritted my teeth.

"Stay on task." Meaning it as an admonishment to myself, it slipped out as a whisper.

"I am."

"Good. Quietly now."

She came up behind me, a light touch on my arm as she tried to whisper in my ear. "You're the one talking."

My thoughts lingered on the warm feeling of her small body touching my side as she leaned in. She would be standing on toes to reach up as far as she could so she didn't have to raise her voice. It was instinct, not of survival but another undeniable instinct that turned me toward her, so our bodies faced each other, so her face, her lips, would hover close to mine. But on feeling me turn, she moved away.

My mind floundering, I said nothing.

"What?" she hissed.

I mentally slapped myself. "It's likely planning to ambush us from overhead," I whispered. Not what I was going to say, but it worked to cover the awkwardness.

"I thought the same."

"Wait until I'm out—"

Her hand pressed over my mouth, ripping my focus from the impending fight. "Don't tell me how to fight smart."

My lips tickled as they brushed against her palm while I

spoke. "Best not to manhandle me before a fight, little princess."

I heard her gasp, and just when I was about to kiss her hand—without conscious thought of what I was doing—she snatched it away.

I leaned in so her warm breath tickled my lips. "You're very distracting."

"I believe the fight's that way." She pressed her finger into my cheek and turned my face to the entrance of the cave. Was she not even a little distracted? Rather than continue to make a fool of myself, I moved forward, feeling Tressya slip behind.

For a desperate moment, I wanted her to stay in the cave's safety while I dealt with the beast, but no way would I dare say such a thing aloud. I trusted her ability with a sword, her skill in a fight, but there was always that risk, that one moment when you made a mistake.

This time I did slap myself because I needed my head right here and now, not on the woman behind me. I ignored her small gasp and leaped out of the cave entrance, sprinting as far as I could to the wall of the giant pillar opposite as a heavy thud shook the ground at my feet.

I dodged left as a funnel of wind whipped past me, followed by the sound of cracking rock. I spun to see the long lash of its tail and the sharp spike of its tip pulling free from the rock. A tail like a mace. That made things tricky.

"Tail," I shouted, though I'm sure Tressya had seen it. "Not yet," was all I managed to get out, hoping she would listen and stay where she was a little longer.

The dusky gloom made it tricky to see the beast clearly,

but there was no missing the tail. Without its glowing eyes, it was difficult to know where it was looking. Did it know Tressya was there?

It was massive, at least five times my height as a Huun-gardred beast, with enough clearance from the ground that I could slip through its muscular haunches.

Just not yet. I ducked as its tail, thick as a tree trunk, soared over my head, and swiped upward with one slice. To lop its tail off, I would have to land a blow closer to the end, but its roar of pain-laced fury was satisfaction for now.

With its tail caught on its sweeping arc, I dove forward, dodged the swipe of one arm, and aimed for its knee. Not stopping, I rolled out of the way as the beast lashed out with its leg. A claw the length of my arm flitted past my eyes.

"Lethal claws on its feet," I yelled. I didn't need to keep with the running narration, but I couldn't stop myself. "That tail's nasty."

In a fight, I remained silent, my focus entirely on the individual, attempting to preempt every move they made. However, this recital, though seemingly useless, calmed me. I didn't know Tressya's whereabouts, but it felt like my talking somehow connected us, keeping her safe. "I've landed a blow to its knee."

I raced across the small enclosure, hemmed in by the pillars, intent on keeping the beast's eyes on me. "Looks like I'll need to land a few more blows." It moved as if I had missed. But I don't miss—or at least rarely.

At a full sprint, I sprang towards the rock pillar, leaping up and using it as a base to launch myself, twisting mid-air as a stiff wind brushed past me, followed by the sound of claws grinding across rock.

I stabbed out with my sword, spearing the beast in the arm just below the elbow, then curled up, bracing for my landing. Rolling with the momentum, I was back on my feet, evading a stomp from its foot. Not missing the opportunity, I lashed out, swiping my sword across the back of its ankle.

The air filled with its vengeful howls, masking Tressya's movements, wherever she was. For that, I was grateful. I continued moving, darting and dodging. A creature of that size had half my agility and a slower response time. Nonetheless, its thick hide meant that any blows I landed were shallower than I would have liked. And being so massive, there was little hope of inflicting a lethal blow.

I stood my ground against its next swipe until the last moment, bringing my sword down on its finger as I dived away, severing the claw. A spray of black blood gushed from the tip, and the creature arched back, raising its arm into the air with a furious roar. I considered attacking its leg while it was distracted, but it swiped its arm down too quickly for me to close the distance. Instead, I dived sideways, only to be knocked off my feet by a heavy blow to my back. I crashed into the ground, shoulder first.

This was a dangerous position to be in. I tried to roll away and found myself pinned by my jacket on my side.

Fuck.

Over my shoulder was nothing but darkness, the creature blotting out the gloom of dusk. The killing blow would come anytime. Thank the stars, I held onto my sword as I jarred into the ground.

I turned as best I could and sunk all my force into my downward stroke, slicing it across its finger. A pump of blood coated my jacket, and I loosened from its hold. I rolled with the beast's roar in my ears and kept rolling across the ground a few more turns before springing to my feet to see it thrashing about, swiping its arm across its torso. Then it fell to one knee, punching an arm down to where I had lain only seconds ago.

Not missing an opportunity, I lunged forward and struck again. This time going for a more lethal place, only for the beast to crash forward, forcing me to dodge left or be squashed under its massive body. Not wanting to see it rise again, I speared my sword into its head, pulled it out and speared again. Repeatedly, until I collapsed beside it, panting.

Tressya. In seconds, I was on my feet.

She suddenly appeared beside me. "Are you hurt?"

"I was going to ask you that."

"Are you?" she demanded.

"My pride. I thought I'd be the one to kill it."

"Does that upset you?"

"I'm glad it's over." I wiped my blade along its pelt to clean the blood.

"You fought well," she said.

"*Well.* Is that the strongest word you could find?"

She sighed, so I knew it was time to shut up. "Are you often that noisy when you fight?"

"I find it adds a flourish to an otherwise grim moment."

"It's very distracting... But helpful." She mumbled the last.

If only I could see her face because I was sure, right now, she would fight another one of her smiles.

"I knew we'd work well as a team."

"Don't get too comfortable, Razohan, we're stuck together because you crashed in on my hunt."

I sheathed my sword. "We should get going. Staying in one spot only encourages the beasts."

I turned and headed for the passage that began the winding path out of this rock contortion.

"It was the bite, wasn't it? That's how you found me."

I stomped off down the passage. "Is this really important?"

"This is going to be a real problem. I won't have you tracking me down like this whenever you want."

The path wound back on itself, and I found myself desperate to escape the hemmed in walls of the rock pillars either side.

"Even after I rescued you?"

"I killed it, remember?"

"I seem to remember someone else there, running around like a man without a brain, shouting nonsensical warnings to aid you."

"Oh him," she sighed, which she was doing a bit of late. "He was more a hindrance than a help. But I don't want to mention it. I fear it will upset his ego."

I couldn't help but chuckle, which was wiped short when I spied the end of the labyrinth. "Things are going to get tricky. It's night-time. Who knows how active the Salmun's creatures are at night."

The glow of the Etherweave broke the dark as Tressya came up beside me and took my hand.

"I want to know, Bloodwyn. Is this your object? There could be no other explanation for you appearing here."

I avoided looking at the rock. Instead, I gazed at Tressya, her face alight with a blue glow, all the while the stirrings in my chest drove a wild desire to touch the rock.

Romelda, backed by the augur, declared the day it would rise free from its cage. That was not today, but it would glow blue under my hand as much as hers, and I wasn't prepared to deal with her persistent questions why that was so. I would keep my hands to myself for now. And try to ignore the fact it glowed blue for her.

"It's not. Bloodwyn has never seen the likes of that before."

Her expression remained challenging.

"Perhaps you have secrets to tell me. Why were you drawn to the rock?" I countered.

"I wasn't."

"Then why is it in your hand?"

There, I caught it. A flash of awkwardness, a shadow of desperation in her expression, swiftly concealed by straightening her features into a bland mask. "I stumbled on it by chance. And why would I need to tell you any of my secrets? If I had any to tell."

I decided it was best to ignore that question since I detected a hint of defensiveness in her tone. "Anything magical is precious. If I were you, I would keep it hidden from the Salmun."

I would thieve it at the next convenient moment or

convince her to leave it behind. It wasn't much good to me now as it was, and Tressya was safer without it. The Salmun would do anything to keep the rock in their hands.

"I would say they already know."

I didn't doubt it. They were hardly going to bury something that precious all the way out here and not keep an eye on it. "Then I would advise you to leave it in the Ashenlands. Don't make the Salmun's eyes turn on you. Come, we should get moving." Before thinking better of it, I took her hand and led her away from the pillar of rocks and the cave. She didn't draw her hand from mine. And that made me smile.

If the Salmun had buried the fragment of the Etherweave in the Ashenlands, what else had they hidden here? It made me uncomfortable that Tressya continued to carry the rock in her hand, but it lit our way, and was a good deterrent to the many evil creatures using the night as a cloak.

Her next question pierced the quiet of the night. "Why did you come after me?"

"We're enemies, remember? I can't trust you." I guided her toward the thinner end of a large root, snaking its way from the base of a fat gnarled tree.

"Why not Andriet?"

"What're you hoping to hear me say?" *That I couldn't bare the thought of you being hurt; that I wanted to be your hero.*

She didn't reply, so I cast a sideways glance to see she was staring at the rock.

"You keep staring at that. and you'll—" Trip, which was what she did, losing the rock. Its light blinked out the moment it left her hand, leaving us stranded in a veil of darkness. I swiped an arm around her waist and hauled her to her feet.

"Thanks," she breathed. "But I lost the rock."

She struggled out of my hold and lowered to the ground. "We can't go anywhere without it."

The thought of the Salmun descending on Tressya for possessing the rock made me shudder. I'd rather see the rock left behind. Who knows what they would do, but the moon's glow failed to penetrate beneath the canopy, so I joined her, crouching down and running my hands across the ground.

"We have no hope against the beasts without it." I heard the tinge of urgency in her voice.

"It can't have gone far."

"Wait." She grabbed my arm. "Can you see that?"

I raised my head, looking ahead, and, sure enough, spied a dim light in the distance, its glow reflecting off the trunks of the surrounding trees.

"Now that's an interesting coincidence. Let's go see what this new find has in stall for us."

She held onto my arm as I went to rise. "We have to find the rock."

I hauled her to her feet. "We're going to be a lot safer over there than crawling around on our hands and knees in the dark."

"But the rock's special. The Salmun wouldn't hide it there and keep a magical eye on it, otherwise."

I froze. "Wait. What? A magical eye?"

"It doesn't matter. We need to find it."

"You saw a magical eye? In what form?" It didn't surprise me to hear it, but I was alarmed all the same. I loathed the idea the Salmun would know who had taken the rock. Tressya wasn't safe now.

The darkness swallowed her expression. "It's of no consequence. The rock matters. Help me find it."

Hearing her breathing close beside me, I feathered my hands through the darkness until I found her, then gripped her waist, making sure she didn't drop to the ground and continue her search. "It's too dangerous for you to keep. Don't think you're smarter or stronger than the wizards. You'll live longer that way. Let's get to the light. That's our safety."

She huffed, then said. "You're right."

I blew out a silent, relieved breath as I heard her running her hand over the root in front of her, feeling her way forward in the darkness.

About to follow her, I kicked something with my foot. A muffled *thunk* followed as it hit the root in front of me. Tressya was already on her way, so I bent and felt around the base of the root. The moment my fingers touched the solid edge of the rock, the blue glow flared to life. I snatched my hand away and glanced ahead. Tressya was indiscernible in the darkness, but I could hear her fumbling her way forward, so I swiped the rock up and buried it in my jacket pocket, then hurried as best I could after her.

"It feels like it's getting warmer," Tressya said from up ahead.

I quickened my pace, catching her up. "My guess is we're about to stumble on your object."

"What about you? I suppose you'll transform into a bird and fly out of here."

"Don't worry about me. Let's see what this is."

What we found was a giant gaping hole in the ground. It was as if someone had come along with a pale and scooped the floor of the forest away to reveal a deep pit. Standing at its edge, looking over, heat washed our faces, radiating upward from the swirling pool of liquid flames bubbling at its base. Every so often, a spurt of liquid fire shot skyward from the boiling pit.

"What in the seven realms?" Tressya said.

"It's as true as the Ashenlands and beast manifestations. Nothing but wizard conjurings."

"And both are deadly, conjured or not." After a moment, she said, "It smells real, not like burning wood...but it's weird. I can't describe the smell."

"We have no choice but to descend. See the path spiraling along the wall? I'd say that cave halfway down it is where we need to head."

"I can't wait to see what they give me for my third trial."

"Aren't you glad I found you?" I took her hand and headed to the start of the path.

It turned out to be a narrow, treacherous descent. I led the way, using the exposed roots jutting from the sides of the pit's walls as an anchor. Some were so large, they blocked our path, forcing us to duck beneath or clamber over. All the while, waves of heat baked the sides of our faces.

It was a long descent to reach the cave. The thin path wound around the side of the gaping pit as it spiraled down-ward. Halfway down, I questioned our sanity. But I was sure this was Tressya's only way out of the Ashenlands. I could transform into a bird and guide her out once I soared above the tree canopy and learned the direction, but that would mean wandering the Ashenlands in the oily black of night... or we could use the rock. I shied from that thought; the questions it would raise should she find out I'd secretly pocketed it. Her sharp mind would dig until she discovered the answer —or got it out of me.

I failed to miss the irony of what I was doing. If Osmud were in my place, he'd push her over the edge. Garrat would've taken Bloodwyn's object and disappeared back to the tent city. Romelda would've stabbed Tressya long ago. Yet I was sticking close to ensure she made it out alive. The idea of Tressya dead...I couldn't contemplate it.

I shook my head at my failings moments before Tressya shrieked. The sound of falling rocks seized my heart. I spun to catch her going over the edge, a small black creature, its spiked tail lashing like a whip, clinging to her hip.

Before I breathed, I leaped the short distance and snagged her wrist, suspending her mid-air as I anchored myself on another root jutting from the wall. She banged against the side of the ravine wall with an *oomph*, but I'd saved her fall into the boiling liquid fire below.

Her smashing into the wall dislodged whatever disgusting creature had clung to her hip by its teeth, which was a boon, but already, I could see the blood discoloring her jacket.

Osmud's voice rose in my head as if he was whispering in my ear. 'Let her go,' it said. The same words I would find echoed from all my men if they were here as witnesses.

Tressya arched her head and looked up at me. She made no plea for help, even though the fear was real. Instead, her eyes locked with mine, and she waited to see what I would do. Grabbing her arm was instinctual, but now my wits had caught up, whatever I did going forward would be a conscious decision. For the north, I should let her go.

For my heart, I couldn't.

A sharp pain speared through my wrist. I glanced over my shoulder to see another small creature clung onto my skin. Small it may be, with ribs jutting through its leathery hide, its wide mouth contained ample blade-like teeth, capable of gouging me to pieces. Glowing eyes. Dammit. This was not the source.

I growled, feeling my grip on the root weakened through the agony of its bite. I gritted my teeth and hauled Tressya up the side and back onto the path. The moment she was secure, she pulled her dagger and deftly sliced the creature's head from his body, avoiding my wrist.

"Obliged," I panted.

Then the wall beside us erupted. Nasty black creatures poured out of the crevices made by the exposed roots. In no time, they swarmed over both of us until we were nothing more than a wriggling black mass, swamping our hands, covering our weapons, eating us alive. Then, just as fast as they'd appeared, they vanished, leaving us oozing our blood through marks left by their sharp spiked teeth.

"I would say the source reached the end of its fall," I said, and we both looked down into the pit.

I caught Tressya wavering in my periphery and reached her just in time before she pitched over the edge once again and caged her body against the wall of the ravine.

"My head," she groaned. "I can't see straight."

"Dammit," I hissed. "The source had a poisonous bite." I swept her off her feet, cradling her close to my chest, and hurried my best along the path without throwing us both over the edge. "I swear, Tressya, if you die on me, I'm going to kill you."

CHAPTER
THIRTY-THREE

TAMAS

I'D DARED NOT MOVE us far into the cave. Tressya needed the warmth from the liquid fire below, and I needed the light. In a hurry to undress, I'd torn the buttons on my jacket and shirt, using them as makeshift bedding for her. It wasn't enough, but at least it kept her upper body away from the cold cave floor.

By the time I'd reached the cave, her body hung limp, her head lolling over my arm. My heart beat a savage tune and my breaths came labored, as though a hand plunged through my ribs and seized my lungs. I had thought the moment I'd seen her fall over the edge of the pit was the worst moment of my life, but I'd been wrong. This was.

Her hair clung limp to her forehead, damp with fever, and I was helpless against it. I wasn't a healer. I didn't even have water and cloth to clean her wounds. There was nowhere I could touch her and not coat my fingers in her sweat and blood.

I couldn't think straight. *Dammit.* Fisting my tremoring hand, I punched the ground beside her with as much force as I could muster, welcoming the pain. "Think, damn you." Fear had never gripped me so tight. I felt useless.

I wiped the blood from my eyes before feathering a finger across her brow. "Tressya." It came out as a lament, and I sucked in a horrified sigh on hearing it, as I wiped the blood from her eyes.

"Don't you dare die. You hear me?"

I held my hand close to her mouth and nose, relieved when her moist breath tickled my palm. The poison acted so suddenly, there was no telling how much further it would run. I swiped my hand through my hair, feeling a ruthless rage inside of me at my helplessness. I'd felt something similar to this once before, but I made it through with the blend of vengeance in my veins, hardening my heart while it slowly cracked in two. This time there was no vengeful fury to counter the looming agony now bound to my fear.

"You can't die," I growled to her through gritted teeth, then sat back on my heels, fisting my hair.

"Fucckkk," I yelled to the sky, knowing my refusal to let her die wouldn't save her.

I would see the end of the Creed of Salmun. A promise I would keep no matter the cost, and if Tressya died, a result of their vile beasts, I would ensure their deaths were their biggest torment. The Etherweave was my only hope of ever reaching that goal.

I touched my pocket, then slipped my hand inside. The

Etherweave responded, pulsing a warmth through the rock like it was a living being. I pulled it from my pocket and held it before me.

"What magic will you give me?" I whispered, then closed my eyes. "Please, enough to save her life."

Night lit as day, the augur's words, the foreseen day when the Etherweave freed itself from its cage. Not on a night as black as a tar pit. I would find no help in the essence lingering within this rock. It was outside of my reach no matter how much it called to me, itched my skin with prickles, or basked my face in its blue glow.

If I could harness its magic, would I be able to save Tressya's life?

I kept my eyes closed to better steel my focus. *I will do this.* Fuck the night as day horseshit. I would free the Etherweave, no matter how inconsequential this small amount may be to what I needed. It was all I had.

Come to me, I commanded in my panic, then pressed the rock between my palms as if I could squeeze the Etherweave from its prison.

When nothing happened, I growled in frustration. "If the blooded are right, and I really am the bloodborn, then you are mine to command." With a deep, prolonged exhale, I pressed the rock between my palms again, this time to the point of pain, its sharp edges cutting through my skin.

"Give me the power." My voice lingered in the air, a weighty presence within the silence.

It came into me, a flood so great I felt as though I rose off the ground. I sucked in air, arching my head back with the overwhelming intensity, the sheer pleasure of its power funneling through my veins. Every gasp of air was like tasting the sweetest syrup. It was more pleasure than pain, but the pain was a real and throbbing entity, searing through my body as the Etherweave flowed, seeming without end, until I felt sure my skin could no longer contain it.

When it was done, I collapsed forward onto my hands, dropping the dull rock to the cave floor. My fingers seized into a fist, pleasurable pain lancing across my shoulders and down my spine. I stared at my hands, forcing them to relax, then groaned a breath, releasing the tension as I rolled my neck. My body tingled. I felt reborn, powerfully alive and ready to fight. The wounds over the backs of my hands, my arms, and torso had healed. Where once my body was covered in deep lacerations and seeping blood, it was now miraculously smooth and clean. I stared at my healed hands, held in front of me. Healing magic.

I shuffled to Tressya's side and placed my hands over her chest, feeling it rise and fall. If I couldn't make the Etherweave work to heal Tressya, then I didn't want it.

"Come," I breathed and closed my eyes once more, concentrating on funneling the power through my fingers and into her, not knowing if it would work. I was prepared to try anything.

It rushed like water. I opened my eyes and watched in awe as her wounds sealed, as the blood dried and vanished from her skin. It was working, but she'd yet to stir from the poison, so I pushed harder, forcing more of the Etherweave's power inside of her, amazed at how easily it bent to my will. But there was only so much stored in the rock. I could only hope it was enough to rid her of the poison. I clenched my teeth, determined to drain myself dry if I had to.

Feeling the power wane, I let out a sob of desperation. Tressya had yet to stir. "No, damn you. That can't be it." I focused hard, clenching my jaw and gritting my teeth so hard it felt like they would shatter.

All the heightened bliss, the searing heat of the Etherweave's power, poured from me into her, leaving me drained and weak. I slumped forward, my hands still pressing hard on her chest, and growled my frustration when she didn't stir. My only chance of saving her.

My eyes roamed over her, and I felt panic begin to claw its way, a ferocious beast rampaging through my heart. Though I didn't feel the Etherweave's power in me anymore, I was about to try one more time when, through her torn jacket, I glimpsed the bone carving she wore as a necklace. Only now it was glowing a bright blue.

My gaze shot from the necklace to her face, and I huffed an exhausted, relieved breath when I saw her eyelids flutter. Unable to keep myself upright any longer, I hunched forward to rest my head on her chest. My strength had gone. So too the Etherweave. Feeling Tressya stir, I pushed myself up and slumped onto my ass beside her and ran my hand across my forehead. If anything attacked us now, we were dead. I had no energy to defend us.

"Bloodwyn." Her voice was weak, confused.

All I wanted to hear was my name on her lips, not his.

"It's all right." I gathered her hand in mine. "We're safe." For now. Or not. Given the adventure we'd had so far, that could be a lie. But I wasn't about to be honest.

"What...happened?" She tried to sit up.

I placed a light touch on her shoulder. "Relax. It's still dark out. We're not going anywhere for now." I wasn't sure I could move even if we had to. Using the Etherweave to heal Tressya took everything from me. I was battling to stay upright.

"I don't...remember."

"You're lucky. I'd like to wipe everything from my memory, too."

"Wait... There was... Then... You were..."

"Yeah." All I wanted to do was close my eyes and sleep.

She tried to sit up again.

"Easy, Tressya."

"We're in danger?"

"Not anymore."

"Bloodwyn," she gasped and gripped my hand. "Those things."

"Gone."

She was determined to get up, so I relented and helped her sit, finding nothing left in me strong enough to deter her. I kept a hold of her hand. "How do you feel?"

"You look terrible."

"Thanks."

"No really. You're so pale." She touched my lips. Through my exhaustion, a flame lit inside of me.

"Your lips. They've lost their color." She moved her fingers from my lips just as I thought to kiss them and ran a finger under my left eye. "There's dark smudging under your eyes."

"I feel a little rough." That was an understatement

"You're the one that needs to lie down." She placed her hand on my chest and gently pushed. On my bare skin, her warm palm felt like a branding iron, and I was too tired to resist her. "Oh, wait." Then she grabbed my arm to stop me. "Not on the ground."

She gathered the clothes I'd used as her bed and pushed them underneath me. Once laying flat, the extent of my exhaustion rode over me like a caravan of bullocks. My eyelids grew too heavy. Sleep tickled at the edges of my mind, but the sudden feel of her hands running over my skin pulled me back.

"You must be hurt somewhere."

"No," I mumbled. Then I changed my mind. "Yes." If that would keep her hands on me.

"You are? Where?"

I huffed a laugh that never came and tried to lift my hand so I could touch my lips, but my hand felt weighted under a boulder. I groaned inwardly. This was my chance for sympathy, maybe even a kiss, and I couldn't muster the energy to ask for it.

"I can't find any wounds. On you or me. That's weird." Then she gasped. "The rock."

Curses. I should've hidden it, which I would've done had I not felt like the Etherweave sucked my life from me. I cracked an eyelid to see Tressya frowning at the rock in her palm.

According to the legends, bone captured, harnessed and magnified the power of the Etherweave, but not just any bone, only that belonging to the Bone Throne. And only the rightful king, born from King Ricaud's line, could wield it without consequence. That I had drawn the small shard of Etherweave from the rock before the right time confirmed I was the bloodborn, but without the Bone Throne, it nearly killed me. And now it was gone without the Bone Throne to stabilize it. I was too weary to contemplate what I had seen when I funneled the Etherweave into Tressya.

"There's nothing there now."

"For the better," I mumbled as I closed my eyes once more.

"Why didn't you tell me you found it?"

"Can't answer right now."

"A good feed and some water will replace your strength. There's probably nothing to find around here, but I'll see what—"

"Don't," I croaked, finding the strength to grab her hand. "No. Not safe. I need sleep. We go together."

"You'll feel much better—"

"Promise."

She didn't reply.

"Promise. To stay put." My words slurred.

"Okay." She sounded far from compliant.

I wanted to growl at her but sleep finally rolled over me.
****

I jerked awake, lurching upright. Where was she?

On seeing Tressya sitting beside me, her back resting against the cave wall, I slumped to the ground.

"Feels like someone's stuck me with a lance, straight through my head," I groaned, covering my eyes.

I heard Tressya shuffle closer beside me. "You have some color back in your face." She lifted my arm and leaned over to look down at me. I would bear never seeing the sky again if I could gaze into her eyes each day. Their color, richer than the bluest sky.

It appeared the Etherweave not only sucked most of my life away, but my brain, replacing it with that of a bard spouting romantic verse, because I could only think of this perfect moment, the two of us surrounded by the silence of the cave with no commitments, no promises or duty. We were equals, surviving only because of the other. In this suspended breath, there was no space for adversaries, only allies. Our pasts vanished, so too our judgements, and those who made us enemies. I would hold us in this moment forever if I could.

"How long did I sleep?"

"Enough to rest you, it would seem."

I sat up, feeling stronger. "How're you feeling?"

"I'm good."

"How much do you remember?"

"The climb down. The creatures. They burst from the wall and covered us. I remember the pain. It was everywhere. Their teeth." She glanced down at her body. "And then...It was weird. I...remember nothing else."

"It's for the best. Bad memories aren't worth holding."

"What happened to you? Your clothes?" Her eyes moved over my torso before flicking to my face, then darting away to the pile of clothes crumbled behind me. And damn that I couldn't tell what thoughts lay behind her expression. I wanted desire, but thought I saw awkwardness. Hopefully, I was wrong. I wished it was my body those deep blue eyes caressed and not Bloodwyn's. He was in good shape, considering the lazy ass did little with his life. At least that was something. The last thing I wanted to read in her eyes was revulsion.

"It wouldn't look good for me if I simply dumped you on the dirt."

Her lips twitched. The smile won. That's when I noticed the faint dimples in her cheeks.

"You looked close to death. What happened to you?"

"It was a stressful time."

Deep grooves formed between her eyes as she stared at me, her mind working to decipher what I wasn't saying. "I can't even remember what happened to those creatures."

"The source was the one to bite you first. When you fell—"

"I fell?"

"Kind of. You didn't go far. Your fall dislodged the vile little beast. Then they attacked us, which didn't last long once the source disappeared into the pit." I blew air from my mouth. "*Pffft.* Gone. The lot of them."

"I remember so little. I must've fainted. I've never done that before."

"The source's bite was poisonous. Nothing lethal, so it would seem, since you're awake and healthy now."

"You must've carried me down here."

"Weird, huh? I could hardly let you go over the edge. I don't think I'd ever get out of here in one piece on my own. You're handy to keep around."

"Liar, you could fly out."

I rubbed my hands down my thighs to rid the dirt. "There's no challenge in that."

"Why aren't we injured? I felt their teeth piercing my skin. All over me. I'm sure they spared none of me."

I shrugged. "Perhaps our injuries were illusional, and when the source died, so too the illusion."

She held my eyes, believing nothing I said. Her eyes were too penetrating for me to hold any longer, so I turned around and grabbed my crumpled shirt.

"We should get out of here," she said as I slipped my shirt over my head.

"You need to find your object. It was the reason we came down here." I lifted one flap of my torn shirt.

She frowned. "How did that happen?"

"I forgot how to undress it seems." I slipped on my jacket, unable to button the front to hold my shirt on my shoulders because I'd busted those. "Do you feel anything? A tug in any direction?"

She shook her head. "Nothing. It's not how it happened the first time, either."

"How did you find your first object?"

"I stumbled on it by chance."

She replied too fast. After everything we'd been through and she continued to hold her secrets; to be fair, she remembered little of the actual events, so I would excuse her for that. And how many secrets did I continue to keep?

"I wouldn't advise stumbling around this place until you find your third object." I stood, glad to see I didn't waver.

Tressya stayed put, half-turned from me, her head bowed.

"Are you all right?"

She shuffled around to face me and looked up with glistening eyes. In her hand, she held the metal chain around her neck. "It's gone."

I crouched in front of her. "The bone carving?" Rather than the chain, I looked into her eyes, then wiped the few tears from her cheek. "It was that special?" Perhaps the bone attracted it, but given it was ordinary bone the might of the Etherweave destroyed it.

"The person who made it was." She squeezed her eyes shut as she vigorously shook her head. "It's silly. That part of my life is over. It's nothing but the past."

"The past is you, Tressya. Every decision you've made and will ever make is guided by your past. You should never deny it, nor the people in it. They played the biggest part in creating who you are. Your past is as important as your future." I nursed the necklace in my palm, the back of my hand touching her skin. "This moment will also become your past. I hope you never try to forget it, or who shared it with you."

My form of wisdom delivered, I should look away. I couldn't.

"Thank you."

"Hold on to that thanks. We must make it out of here first." I took her hand to help her up, but she pulled her hand from mine and sprung to her knees, then into my arms, locking hers around my neck so tight it felt like she wanted to wrench my head from my neck.

I closed my eyes, sinking into the feeling of her body pressed against mine, my arms folding her in and holding her like she was the only thing keeping me alive. Unable to believe what was happening, but not willing to question it, I buried my head in her nape and breathed deep, taking in the scent of her sweat, the deeper scent of her body, wanting to remember both, always.

"No one ever sees me," she whispered against my skin.

"I haven't stopped seeing you."

She shook her head. "Not me," she breathed. "Not the real me. Not deep inside."

"I know what that's like. Only I don't allow anyone to see what's really underneath. It's not pretty."

She pulled back and looked into my eyes. "I'm not talking about appearances."

"Neither am I." Feeling the beat of her heart pounding in rhythm with my own, I wanted to believe she would accept me no matter what I'd done. She wouldn't hate me, judge me as evil as I did myself.

She dipped her gaze briefly before searching my eyes again. "I would like to think my mother loved me. She was a disciple. So probably not. It's not one of the six pillars."

"I've spent too long trying to avoid life's rules."

"If that were true, you wouldn't be here."

I saw the shift in her eyes, the moment she remembered why we were here and what we were meant to be to each other. She moved out of my hold. "You're right. We need to go before something else finds us." Then, spying the rock, she snatched it up. "It looks like we won't have any help from this anymore."

"We should find your object."

I stood and held out my hand, eased her to her feet, then guided her to the mouth of the cave. There we stood, staring down into the pit of liquid fire.

"How could I not remember this?"

"Because it's not a sight to remember. Is your object calling to you? Do you feel anything?"

She shook her head, then made to touch her necklace, but stopped at the last, remembering it wasn't there. "Nothing."

I arched my head, seeing for the first time since entering the Ashenlands, the sky, and the first glow of morning light.

"Maybe it doesn't matter if you never find it. Between the two of us, we'll get ourselves out once I fly up there and work out the direction we need to take." I nodded skyward.

She followed my gaze, then, after a while, said, "Do you see that?"

I squinted, saying nothing, then after a pause. "I'd say it's something we don't want to meet."

CHAPTER

THIRTY-FOUR

TAMAS

It didn't take long for the shape to take form. I'd never seen something so large able to take to the sky. Another beast with a lethal tail, which it dragged behind it like an enormous snake. Beating its massive wings with a lethargic rhythm, it closed the distance with good speed. I couldn't make out the color of its eyes yet, but hoped they were dull. The last thing we needed was to face both the manifestation and the source.

Tressya tugged on my hand. "We could use the cave as a barrier. It looks large enough not to fit."

I dragged her toward the path. "The cave will trap us. It'll struggle to get beneath the canopy. And if it did, it won't be able to maneuver amongst the trees."

"We'll risk getting lost in the Ashenlands."

"Never. I'll get through and find our way." I increased our pace, sparing one more glance skyward. It was coming fast.

"Will we make it?" Tressya said.

"We have to." My legs felt weighed by rocks. The remnants of my near death lingered.

In my haste, I wasn't watching where I trod. The sound of rocks hitting the exposed roots in the pit as they crumbled from the edge tightened my throat. One glance to the sky and I stopped worrying about the path, instead tightened my hold on Tressya's hand as if she was about to be ripped from me at any moment, then increased my pace.

This time it wasn't just a few rocks tumbling that tightened my throat. The ground under my left boot fell away completely, and I lurched sideways, pulling Tressya with me and into a jutting root. Tressya's hand slipped from mine with the impact. I fumbled for her, feeling her name well in my throat as I staggered forward, tripping over a lower root laid as a trap at my feet. If I wasn't still recovering from death, I would've been agile enough to stay on my feet.

"Bloodwyn." Tressya wrenched my arm. "We'll never make it in time climbing over all these exposed roots, and you're not strong enough. You'll exhaust yourself climbing out and have nothing left for the fight."

"You're wasting time." My back ached, my head spun me in circles.

She helped me straighten, then shoved me in the chest. "And you're being stubborn."

Rather than fight her and waste more time, I relented and allowed her to pull me back down toward the cave.

She moved too fast.

"Watch the edging. It's loose."

My warning came too late. The path gave way under her feet, taking her with it, leaving her shriek behind. This time, I was too slow to reach for her. Seeing her disappear, I didn't think. I leaped through the gaping hole and plummeted.

The heat of the liquid fire burned my skin as I released my hold on Bloodwyn's form and became the Huungardred beast. Moments were all it took before the thick pelt of the beast smothered the fire's burn. The smell from below became overwhelming, searing my now sensitive nostrils, but in this form, I felt my vitality and strength return.

Large and heavy, I overtook Tressya's fall. Spying a small ledge protruding from the pit wall, I swiped out and hooked Tressya on my large claw, then flipped, changing the path of our fall to line up with the ledge as I pulled her in and cradled her to my belly.

I'd maneuvered myself around onto my back, sparing Tressya the brunt of the fall, so when we hit, it felt as though every bone in my body broke. Not only that, my size was too large for the ledge. My big rump hung over the edge. This close to the pit, not even my thick pelt could keep the scorch of the fire from reaching my skin.

I growled, wanting to ask if Tressya was all right, but as a Huungardred, I couldn't form the words.

"Bloodwyn," she sobbed as she slid from me.

I growled the question in my mind, but more useless beast noises came out. It had to result from my pain, but hearing her use his name, I wanted to shout my own. And that should be the last thing worrying me right now.

The weight of her leaving me wasn't a relief. When she

lay on me, I knew she was safe. Now she was moving around on this tiny ledge. What if she fell off again? My panic eased when her small hands soothed through my fur. *Stay close, Tressya.* Feeling her was the only thing that corralled the wild rampage of my thoughts and made the pain bearable.

"Bloodwyn," she cried, running her hands down my snout and tangling them with my chest fur.

The fear in her voice triggered my beast's instincts. Before I could stop myself, I released a roar. She needed me on my haunches, ready to fight, not on my back, belly exposed like a coward.

No, dammit. I wasn't thinking straight. The ledge was too small for a Huungardred beast, and Tressya needed a man, not the beast. Just a few more breaths as I was, then I would loosen my hold on this form and transition back into a man. For now, I needed the Huungardred's fast healing ability to strengthen me again.

"I wish there was something I could do."

I wanted to tell her she was doing just fine, running her hands through my fur. It felt luxurious, harmonizing my body like nothing had ever done before. I took deep beast breaths and moaned them out slowly, tilting my head back to encourage her hands to glide up my throat. I couldn't fathom the pleasure I would feel with them soothing over my bare skin once I was a man. But I'd wallowed enough in this desirous dream. A fight was coming. We had to be prepared.

If only I could warn her of the change, so she wouldn't jerk away and risk falling off the ledge. I placed my paw over her hand, still tangled in the thick pelt at my chest, to keep her close to me, and let go of the beast. Both forms were as natural to me as breathing, so I could take one or the other with little thought.

Tressya gasped and slid her hand from mine, but I squeezed her hand to stop her. "Don't." My voice croaked, which wasn't unusual. It usually took a while for the voice to return to normal after a transformation.

I cracked an eyelid when Tressya stayed silent, to see her beautiful blue eyes wide in disbelief.

"Witnessing a shift can be a shock for anyone. I didn't let your hand go because I was afraid you'd pitch yourself over again in horror."

She shook her head, denying her shock.

"It's all right. You don't have to pretend even if it repulsed you. It will take more than that to shame me." I pulled at my open shirt, feeling the heat this close to the pit.

"No," she whispered. "Look." She lifted my hand, the one holding hers tight, and held it up in front of my face, and I realized why she was staring at me like she'd never seen me before.

"Oh." I sighed.

The olive complexion of my skin was a testament to my mess-up. Worried about Tressya, I wasn't thinking straight and shifted back into my true self. Tamas.

"Curses," I hissed when I tried to sit up.

Tressya did her best to help me, but I tried my damnedest to do it on my own, unwilling to accept how feeble I still felt because I'd not given myself long enough as a Huungardred to heal all my aches.

"We'll have to climb," I mumbled, scouring my face with

my hands, not willing to accept the fact I'd screwed up and revealed what I really looked like.

"And into the jaws of whatever is waiting for us up there?"

"We'll cook if we stay here any longer."

"Then we lure it down, and it can cook as well."

"We may cook first. I don't know about you, but I'm ready to peel off my clothes."

Her eyes widened a fraction, her lips parted, and damn my weak-willed male blood for staring at her lips and forgetting for one precious moment we were in a life and death situation. There my eyes stayed, and this time, I felt my own lips part, my pulse thump through my veins. The touch of her lips... The feeling, I knew from experience was as good as the touch of her hands.

"What's your name?"

I rubbed at the scratchy bristle of an early beard. "I guess there's no point hiding now." I met her gaze. "Tamas Savant."

She smiled, and it was like someone had brought the sun down and aimed its radiant beams into my eyes. Then she held out her hand. "Please to meet you, Tamas Savant."

I didn't shake her hand. I held it and continued to hold it long after it was natural or polite to hold a woman's hand.

She blinked, then her lips twitched. "We have a problem to deal with. Remember?"

I scrunched my eyes closed. "Lethal creatures that want us dead. Right." My mind played tricks when I tried to stand, dizzying my head, almost pitching me over the ledge. It was thanks to Tressya, hauling me backward, that I was saved from that disaster, only to trap me in another. I tumbled back and into her, pinning her against the wall with my body. And while this was not a disaster right now, it could soon turn into one because my weak-willed male blood betrayed me again. My mind faulted. Flush against me, her wild heart beat with mine.

I saw her blue eyes first, before my eyes trailed down to her small slim nose, down to the slight indents in her cheeks, then settling on those lips. Her head craned back as she looked up at me, as if she was asking for...which she wasn't. *Dammit.* Yet I savored the length of her body against mine, craved the feeling of her skin, salivated with the need to taste her.

Curses, Tamas. I was crushing her small body against the root strewn wall.

The screech from the creature above sent me stumbling backward and almost over the edge again.

"Tamas," Tressya shrieked.

I stilled as my eyes fluttered closed, feeling my name spoken from her lips feather over me, a wondrous and captivating treat.

Another shriek from above was the punch in the face I needed. I wrapped an arm around Tressya's waist, hauling her against me while I pressed myself back against the wall and looked up.

A large beaked head peered over the rim of the pit.

"Stars above, it's massive," Tressya breathed.

"That beak looks a weapon all on its own." Perhaps the length of my body, if not longer, and pointed as any blade. It had an enormous scaly head, to lift its enormous sharp beak.

Our only consolation was its eyes. It was the source. "As much as I hate to say it. You were right. We should've stayed in the cave, narrowing the breadth of its attack."

"Apology accepted. Now, how're we going to get ourselves out of this?"

I shifted Tressya behind me and leaned out to look back up the face of the wall. "We could climb back up to the cave. The creature seems hesitant to enter the pit. I don't think it likes the heat."

"I'm calling this one nightmare," she mumbled.

"More a challenge than a nightmare. There's so many exposed roots, the climb should be relatively easy."

"I was meaning the creature."

"You're naming them now?"

She shrugged. "It's a recent thing."

"Okay, but before the nightmare decides it will brave the heat, we should start climbing. You go first."

She narrowed her eyes for a moment, then quirked a brief smile. "So you can look at my ass."

"Weirdly, that didn't cross my mind, but now you've mentioned it..."

She rolled her eyes.

"I'm stronger. I'm better able to support you if you fall." I spun her around and gave her a light tap on the ass. "Up, princess."

Without another word, she gripped hold of a fat root and hauled herself up to mid-waist with a little help from my hand on her ass, pushing her upward. She didn't need my help, but I couldn't resist. I anchored her boot on another root. "Keep going," I encouraged her.

She needed no encouragement from me, and I should shut up before I broke her concentration. I leaned out for a better view of the monster above us.

"Damn." I gripped hold of Tressya's foot and yanked her down.

She shrieked as I peeled her off the wall, a small root coming away in her hand as she tumbled down on top of me. I caught her fall and fell backward against the wall.

"Change of plans," I said, setting her down and drawing my sword.

"Curses," she hissed.

We both watched as the beast clambered its way over the rim and down into the pit. The thick leathery hide of its wings formed a web from its body to its powerful forearms, adapted for gripping. Large claws pulled chumps of dirt and root as it scaled its way down.

"We can't defend ourselves here." She glanced around us.

"We can." Because we had to. I leaped, pressing her against the pit wall, covering her body with mine as a large clod of earth and rock sailed past us.

"Close." I looked over my shoulder to ensure nothing else was coming down, then released Tressya.

"What's our plan?" she asked, pulling her sword from her belt.

"I'm going to get on its back."

"What? That's ludicrous."

"If I can make it fly out of here—"

"No." She yanked me around to face her. "You're not invincible, Tamas. You'll be killed."

I loved how easily she swapped my name for Bloodwyn's.

It was like he never existed. "You're only saying that because you don't know what I'm capable of."

I pushed her backward again, using my body as a shield as the nightmare dislodged more debris.

"Bullheaded, egotistical stupidity, it would seem," she snapped, picking up where our conversation had been cut short.

"How about a powerful instinct to survive and determination to win?"

She harrumphed. By now, the nightmare had clambered halfway down into the pit. Soon it would be upon us. "Fighting while it's directly overhead will be awkward. At some point, I'll need you to distract it."

"We're standing side by side. You won't be able to take it by surprise."

"Then we'll blind it in one eye."

"Good idea." She announced with false gaiety. "That's easy enough." She glared at me as she drew her dagger.

I swiped a scattering of rocks away from the ledge with my blade, then caught Tressya in my periphery, wave her arm. When I turned to her, I noticed she had lost her dagger and was only holding her sword. The deafening screech of the nightmare's fury filled my ears as it rebounded off the pit walls. Wings now spread, I saw the large hooked barbs growing from the end of the veining in each wing as they blotted out the sky above.

The nightmare took flight, scraping its barbs down the walls on either side of the pit as it tried to maneuver in the confined space. The heat from below was no doubt the reason it seemed hesitant to drop lower and remained hovering above us. The ledge shielded us from the worst of the heat, but even I was feeling like my insides slowly cooked.

It wavered, then tilted left, allowing the sun above to glint off the small protrusion on its chest. Tressya's dagger.

"As always, your accuracy astounds me."

"An insignificant threat," she growled.

The nightmare reached the wall on the opposite side of the pit, then scrambled down, safe from anymore weapons for now.

"Are you still set on that plan of yours?" Tressya kept her eyes on the nightmare.

"Trust me. It's a good plan."

Tressya pulled her second dagger from its sheath, then closed her eyes for a breath as she nodded, as if she couldn't believe what she was agreeing to. "I'm crazy, but I trust you. I'll blind it, you get yourself onboard. And if either of us fail, it was...interesting knowing you."

Taking my eyes off the nightmare, I glanced at her. "Interesting?"

She shrugged.

"Fuck that." I wrapped an arm around her waist and hauled her into me, smashing my lips against hers with no restraint and slipping my tongue inside her mouth. Seconds it took for her to overcome her shock and soften against me. But Tressya didn't just soften, she opened, she surrendered, thankfully, avoiding stabbing me with her weapons as she locked her arms around my neck and devoured me as hungrily as I did her. I groaned into her mouth, my control slipping with our desperate kiss. The feel of her, the taste of her, filled my head, pushing the nightmare away.

Too soon, Tressya left my head spinning, my hunger bereft, when she released her hold and pushed me away.

"Get ready," she snapped.

How did she do that? My mind remained hazy, unwilling to leave the kiss behind. I shook my head. *Survive.* I breathed the thought deep inside, then drew my second sword and turned to face the nightmare.

Tressya jumped up and down, waving her arms about, and yelling, being careful to avoid slashing me as she did so.

"I figured I could tease it over," she said as if she needed to explain.

Thanks to Tressya, my attention was on task now. I stared ahead to the creature, which had lowered itself to the height of our ledge but remained on the other side of the pit wall. If it stretched its head and body out, it could attempt to spear us on the tip of its sharp beak.

"Once it's halfway across, I'll throw."

"And I'll leap. I trust you not to miss. Climb underneath the ledge if you can handle the heat."

"It's going to do it," I said, noting the way it shook its head, eyed us, lifted a forelimb from the wall. It was as though it was judging the distance, the heat it would be exposed to as it leaped across and where it would grip once here.

I tightened my hold on the hilts of my swords, waiting.

"Any moment now," I said.

"Come on," Tressya muttered, then wiped her brow with the back of her hand.

Sweat dripped into my eyes, but I dared not move a muscle.

When it launched, my heart tightened, my breath stalled. In a blink, it covered half the distance across the pit to our side. In my periphery, I saw Tressya release her weapons. Less than a heartbeat later, the nightmare's head jerked left, which was my signal.

I leaped, loosening my hold on my form so I could tap into the Huungardred's might to power my leap. I crossed the distance, aiming for the thick hide on the nightmare's neck. We collided mid-air, but I was so insignificant, the nightmare reached our side of the pit wall, digging its claws in tight. I stabbed my swords into its neck and used them as pickaxes to help me climb up onto the back of its neck. From here, I could see the black blood seeping from its eye.

The irritant Tressya's blades created caused the beast to thrash its head from side to side, before it bashed its eye against the wall of the pit, intent on ridding the blades. Rubble tumbled loose and rained down onto the ledge below, but Tressya was already gone, taking my advice and climbing off the ledge.

Now it was up to me. I speared my blades into its neck as I climbed up to its head. The nightmare thrashed, screeching in fury, and I lost my footing, hanging by my grip on my blades.

I curled my legs up, hitching one over its neck again, then pressed myself flat to its body and stabbed repeatedly high on its neck with one blade, using the other as my anchor. The nightmare screeched, releasing one forearm from the side of the wall and attempted to swipe at its head, missing me with each swipe. I continued to stab, hoping I would make it mad with desperation to dislodge me.

It worked. The nightmare pushed off from the pit wall, beating its massive wings to lift it up and out of the pit. Once out, it climbed up ever higher into the sky. The ice wind raced over its body and over me. In seconds, I felt chilled in place. I pressed myself as close as I could to stay on and avoid the worst of the wind. If it continued to climb, I would freeze to death. Already I could feel my fingers aching in their grip.

Teeth clenched, I pulled one blade after the other, stabbing them in one at a time as I worked my way up its body. In the distance, a mountain range loomed into view, its peak hidden in clouds. Was there no end to the Salmun's magic? No mountain range was visible outside the Ashenlands. How far did the illusion extend? Could one be stuck inside forever and never cover the same ground?

Whatever the answers were, I didn't want to end up on that mountain. Tressya needed me.

As I continued working my way to the top of the nightmare's head, a black blur to the side of me caught my eye. I turned to see a manifestation keeping speed with us. Every so often it darted its beak toward us, swiping across the top of the source's head and forcing me to flatten myself once again or risk being knocked off. It was as I suspected. The source created and controlled the manifestations as and when it needed them.

I climbed downed from the nightmare's head, easing my way, using my blades to prevent me from sliding off. Sheltering close to its ear from the harsh, bitter wind, I devised a new deadly plan. Then blew a heavy breath at the thought of what I had to do. Tressya would strip my hide if she knew.

It wasn't easy climbing downward, skirting the side of its beak, especially when a second manifestation appeared on the other side. The new manifestation speared its beak toward me, skimming close to the source's face. I almost laughed at the possibility. Maybe my plan would work.

I kept going down with the added challenge of avoiding being plucked from the source's body by the beak of one of its protectors. Once I'd reached as low as I dared, I stilled, steadying my breath.

Come on, Tamas. Now or never.

I released one sword from the nightmare's leathery skin and hung on with one arm. One more deep breath, and I again tapped into my ancestral strength, this time growing claws. With the Huungardred's might, I pulled out the other weapon and fell. Swords raised, I gave myself the seconds I needed to fall as far as I dared before I stabbed out, weapons and claws piercing deep into the underneath of its throat.

Legs dangling in mid-air, I clung on for my life fueled by the Huungardred in my veins. A manifestation appeared beneath me, the other keeping pace at my side. Neither made a move, so I pulled the blade and released my claws, then stabbed it in again, driving it so deep with my added strength, the hilt disappeared into its flesh. Then I repeated my vicious stab using the other weapon, again, puncturing holes in its throat, as insignificant as they may be. This was not the way to kill the beast, but the way to drive it insane with fury.

When the manifestation veered toward us, screeching in

fury, I was ready, curling my legs up out of reach. Its beak jabbed at me, shaving close to my ass. When it swerved away, I lowered my legs and continued to irritate the source with my unrelenting stabs, until another manifestation appeared. Now four of them shadowed us.

Again I made ready, curling my legs up at the last to evade another ferocious beak stab. As it missed, the manifestation screeched so loud it felt as though my ears blew. I released another blade and stabbed again and watched as the manifestation shook its head, responding to my attack.

One last stab sent the source into the raging fury I needed. The manifestation beside me dived in, rearing its head back and stabbing blind, straight through the neck of the source. Black blood poured over me as the manifestations disappeared. I growled, my hands growing wet and slipping from the hilt.

As the source's wings collapsed, the enormous beast plunged out of the sky.

Huungardred strength was not endless, but I called on more as I crawled one hand up the hilt of one sword to touch the source's leathery skin. On contact, I shifted my focus and plummet inside the source's body, searching for its soul.

Tressya was right in saying this was a terrible risk, but I figured we were dead if I didn't try. In learning of the difference between the manifestation and the source, I figured the latter was an animal whose soul I could plunder. I knew my father had tried this trick once before and failed when he'd traveled the Ashenlands, as well as a few ancestors before him. But no one knew of the distinction between the two back then.

The beast's inner life was a complicated labyrinth, like nothing I'd searched within before. And the forest's canopy was fast approaching.

You can do it. My slick hands ached from their savage grip, forever threatening to slip from my hold on the hilt.

A messy twist of confusion stretched before my mind's eye. So many paths for me to follow, so many dark and endless places with no end. The source would bust through the canopy before I found what I was looking for. I roared my fury and tunneled all I had, feeling myself fall into the abyss, searching for my salvation. What spread before me was blinding, confusing, and utterly consuming.

I won't end like this. No way would I give in now when Tressya waited for me to return, when I was possibly her only hope out of the Ashenlands. I remembered her blue eyes, the first thing I saw when I woke in the cave. I wanted that as my first sight every time I woke.

I roared, then slammed into the nightmare's essence.

You won't defeat me.

Its animalistic mindset burrowed its way through my consciences, fighting for supremacy, but as a shape-shifter, my mind had greater mastery.

It took no time to bend the creature to my will as I assumed its form. When done, I punched out my wings and soared upward into the sky.

CHAPTER

THIRTY-FIVE

TRESSYA

I'D BEEN HALFWAY up the pit wall, climbing myself out of that torturous place, when the nightmare appeared. I'd no longer carried any of my weapons, having lost them all to the beast. I was powerless against it.

It wasn't fear that gouged away at my strength and made me want to weep as I stared up at the enormous creature blotting out the fading sun. It was devastation. Tamas had not survived. That was the single thought running through my head as I clung to a fat root, not that I was weaponless, helplessly stuck halfway up the pit wall, with no hope of defending myself.

Tamas had not survived.

Heaviness sunk into my limbs and belly, and I closed my eyes, pressing my forehead into the dirt. I'd wondered if there would ever come a day when I remembered this exact moment without feeling as though I was falling apart.

When the nightmare came closer, I opened my eyes, ready for a warrior's death. It hadn't taken me long to realize that what looked out at me from behind those black eyes was not an unintelligible void of violence, but someone who'd risked all to save us.

He had survived.

And he'd come back for me. There were two choices he could've made. Abandoning me ensured he won, as he said he would. Rescuing me led him down a different path, and I was too confused to work out which direction that now sent him...sent me. Sent us both. Neither would I give it any thought. I couldn't, at least not yet. Tamas was the most beguiling and enigmatic man I'd ever met, the only person who could make me fear and desire him in one breath; the only person who could make me question my duty; my fate.

I sighed. There were too many questions I had to ask, too many obligations in my path conflicting with the emotions in my heart. Discipline ensured no disciple lack certainty. The Mother's will kept the disciples together, gave us a foundation, fed us strength, but I felt beyond her now.

Tamas was a man of many lives, lies, and complexities, yet I felt drawn to him in a way I never have before. Not with Carlin, not with the Sistern.

And now I stood at the edge of the demarcation line between the Ashenlands and the tent city, empty of my weapons, empty of my object, and wearing a simple peasant's dress—forgoing my princess clothes—but feeling the aches underneath. I watched Tamas stride out of the Ashenlands, like the victor of a long battle, like a king. He'd transformed back into Bloodwyn. All I saw striding toward me was the true man underneath.

He stopped when he spied me waiting for him at the edge, my toes peeking over into the dust, my heels remaining on the green grass. I wondered if I ever stood any hope of winning against him, against a man who could be anyone and anything at anytime of his choosing. I also wondered, in the far depths of my traitorous heart, if I wanted to.

He glanced down at himself, then back at me, and held his hands out either side of himself as if offering an apologetic smile. I preferred his real self.

"You haven't joined in the celebrations?" he said as he came closer.

"They've got no reason to celebrate." I'd had time to return to my tent before Tamas reappeared after he'd left me safe on the edge of the Ashenlands, time enough to change my clothes and wash my skin as best I could of grime and blood. I also had time to hear the gossip from the last two days of the trials. Some had yet to return, most of those likely never to return if the king had his way. Those who had returned thought they were the lucky ones, spared from facing their death, but neither had they faced themselves. Not like I had done. Having never questioned myself before, I did now. I questioned everything. Was it possible for me to survive alone without the Sistern?

Tamas reached me, aligning his toes with mine. Only he stayed on the side of death, remaining in the Ashenlands as if he was an illusion created by the Salmun to bring me to my knees.

"But you have," he told me, staring down at me with Bloodwyn's unusual amber-colored eyes. Tamas's were a deep purple tinging to black, dark and mysterious, much like the man himself.

"I question that."

Tamas was taller, broader, darker, and dangerous. He was too arrogant, stubborn and wild to be contained; too forthright, cunning and deceptive to be dismissed; too courageous, resilient, and loyal to be ignored. I'd never forgotten my purpose, or my fealty, because of my hunger. Never. Until him.

He frowned, and I fought the urge to run my thumb across his brow to smooth the creases away, or simply to touch him. Dark eyes, dark hair, dark skin, he was the embodiment of night, a man who could draw in the shadows and command their mystique. It was as though the Ashenlands were made for him.

"You don't believe you deserve to survive?"

"I'm not faithful." I'd dishonored my vow to the one person who had protected me from a disgraced life. I dishonored that vow the moment I met Bloodwyn, and continued to do so in every decision I made and action I took. Perhaps I had cursed myself when I silenced Juel's dying screams.

"That is a heavy burden to carry on your heart."

"You went to your people." It wasn't a question. When he left me on the edge of the Ashenlands, then took to the sky again, I knew what he was doing. His goal was to win. Just as he promised he would. And I couldn't make myself stop him. I didn't know who this person was, this woman who fell for the enemy. This woman who balked at doing what was best for the Sistern and the Mother.

"Yes."

"They're coming."

"Yes."

I wouldn't ask him if he was still faithful to every oath he made to his people, just as I couldn't ask if he would willingly sacrifice his success for me.

"Then we're at war with each—" I couldn't finish what I had to say. A thickness in my throat and the sting at the corner of my eyes prevented me from uttering another word. Dare I show how much he'd crippled my heart?

Who was I?

He trailed a finger down my temple, the touch gentle, barely perceptible, as if he and this moment were my imagination, then his fingers made their way to my lips, covering them to prevent me from speaking.

"No."

"Tamas," I whispered against his fingers.

He smiled as he pulled them away and rested them on my chin, tilting my head up. "You can say that word, but nothing else." His eyes fell to my lips, like they'd done in the pit.

My breath wouldn't come. I shook my head, pulling my chin from his fingers. "It's not me, Tamas. I'm not a courtier. I don't swoon or faint or falsify my emotions. And I definitely don't surrender." Like I had, like I was doing at this moment.

"That's why you're special, why you're still alive."

He stroked the side of my face, but it didn't take long for me to realize it wasn't his finger, but his claw, now drawn in front of my eyes. He seized my chin in his hand, miraculously keeping his long, sharp claws from touching my skin. "When I boarded that ship, my sole purpose was to kill you. Every moment we've met since then was another chance for me to do it."

"Because I'm a disciple?"

"Because another Tannard heir within the line of the Levenian must never be born. That you are a disciple makes it all the more dangerous, makes you all the more dangerous. And to me, all the more desirable."

I sucked in a breath, drawing Tamas's eyes once again to my lips.

"We're enemies," I whispered.

Tamas seized my wrist and tugged me across the demarcation line that kept me safe. Further, he dragged me until we were both plunged into the gloom of the forest.

I opened my mouth to protest, but he yanked me close and kissed me instead. Kissed me like we faced death. And if we did, I didn't care because I could no longer restrain my hunger. I clawed at his hair, his shirt, his skin. I bit his lip, his throat, his neck. I moaned, cried his name, begged, with no idea what I was begging for. Never had I abandoned myself so completely. Never had it felt so sublime to be out of my head and floating far from the ground. So easily I'd pushed my mind aside and opened myself to simply feeling.

The illegitimate princess, the disgraced disciple, the almost queen, I had to escape all three. I was simply the woman who had all but crawled on her knees to the altar of her enemy.

The heavy thud of a looming threat broke us apart.

Tamas groaned as he dragged his mouth from mine and looked over my shoulder. Using his unmatchable speed, he spun me around, shielding me with his body.

"It's time you left," he said, facing down the large snake-like creature.

"What? You think you're invincible now?"

He looked over his shoulder and winked. "It's not far. Just retrace your steps. Make sure you go straight ahead."

"Tamas," I growled, as if speaking to an imbecile.

"As much as I love hearing you speak my name, you're a distraction I don't need right now." He pushed me away as the snake-like beast reared up and wavered its head back and forth, as if trying to decide the best moment to strike. "Please, Tressya. You've got no weapons. You can't help. Go."

"You want me to worry about you?" I voiced it as an accusation, but it was true; it was the moment in the pit when I thought he'd died.

"Sorry, but I can't help feeling flattered knowing you would." He glanced over his shoulder and winked. "I'm the nightmare, little princess. Remember that. You have nothing to worry about. Please, go."

I did as he asked, knowing he was right. If Tamas could defeat the nightmare, who was I to think I could do better?

I turned and ran through the gloomy forest, clearing exposed roots, refusing to deviate from my path. One turn and I would find myself lost in this cursed place once again, running blind, weaponless. One last leap and my legs buckled as I hit the dusty ground of the dead land, landing me flat on my belly. The last few feet I crawled until I sank onto the green grass.

"I thought you were gone," came the venomous voice in front of me.

I pushed to my knees and dusted myself off. Great. The last person I wanted to see when I was feeling raw. My lips still hummed from our kiss, and my body still vibrated from the savagery of our combined desire. If I closed my eyes, I could still be in his arms.

"Glad to disappoint you." I took my time reaching my feet, attempting to compose myself. But there was no getting the last two days out of my head, especially the last few minutes. Those would take a lifetime to erase, if ever.

Tamas and I had stumbled back into the Ashenlands with dusk falling as a curtain to shield my glorious disgrace. In that time, the murky blue had turned to gray. Our kiss had been more consuming and enduring than I'd thought.

"You seem satisfied with yourself."

I arched my head back and stared up at the first stars, not ready to face Radnisa. My skin was like peeled overripe fruit. I touched my lips, then, realizing I had done so, pulled them away as I ducked my head. I didn't need her eagle eyes noticing and gathering yet another thing to use against me. The ache in my arms for someone to hold became an ache in my heart. I wanted to run back into the Ashenlands to be with him rather than face what was in front of me, yet I knew I was fooling myself. No matter how much it felt true, we weren't as one.

She huffed. "That's interesting."

"I don't care." And I walked away, pushing past her. Anything of interest to her would be the last thing to intrigue me.

"It looks like you had help."

I stopped. "What would you know?"

"That you arrived on the edge of the Ashenlands with nothing in your possession and wearing that?"

I glanced at my dirty dress.

"It's a dress fit for the gutter. Where are your weapons?"

After escaping the Ashenlands for the first time today, I'd avoided Radnisa on my return to my tent. I'd chosen the simple outfit as it made dressing myself easy. She didn't know this was the second time today I'd stepped out of the cursed lands. Telling her would give her ammunition.

"You don't get to question, since you've never crossed that line." I jerked my head toward the demarcation line. "I need to eat and drink. Not talk." And I marched away.

"You're just in time," she yelled after me. "There's plenty of that at the king's table. Make sure you pay a visit. Soon."

Behind my tent, the bonfire lit the dusky sky. I paused in the doorway, having pulled the tent flap aside, thinking I could hide within. Truth was, in solitude I couldn't escape my thoughts, so I released the flap and headed toward the festivities. The music and revelry would force all my confusion and my exhaustion out of my head. I was smelly, my dress dusty, my hair likely a tangled mess because I'd never bothered tiding anything beyond the grime and blood. One grouch from my stomach, I forgot about the way I looked and headed over to the festivities.

I wound my way through the maze of tents, aiming for the glowing orange light of the bonfire. Almost there and a shadowy figure appeared in front of me. I nearly tripped on the tent rope.

"Orphus," I gasped, pressing a hand to my chest as my heartbeat turned to spikes, threatening to pierce my skin.

"Princess. A successful return. A day later than everyone expected."

With the light from the bonfire behind him, Orphus was an ominous silhouette, a predator.

"There were challenges."

"I never doubted you for a moment. You have a remarkable gift for surviving. One would almost think you had help."

There was something in his tone, a knowing, that put me on edge. My thoughts went first to Tamas, and then the rock. "I do. My skill with a weapon, my ability to think, my refusal to lose, and my stamina."

"Yes. You're quite the mystery." He moved closer, dropping his voice. "Arriving from the Ashenlands empty handed, I see."

He was definitely talking about the rock.

"One of your foul creations is lying dead in your cursed lands with my blades staked through its eye."

The resin and smoke stench on his cloak roiled my stomach for what it signified.

"You're a remarkable creature. Such a shame Juel had to die."

"We can all be grateful for Princess Cirro."

"Yes," he hissed, taking one more step closer. "A weak fool rules the throne. An even weaker fool will replace him. Weak fools breed weak fools in perpetuity."

An icy cold sensation pressed itself into my heart. "What're you saying?"

"Our talents grant the Salmun extended lives. Did you know that?"

I shook my head.

"I have lived through generations of rule. Ushered each Tannard king to the throne. As supreme prelate of the Creed of Salmun, my duties are clear. The House of Tannard must survive."

Why was he saying this? "I've been told as much."

He drew closer, challenging my unrelenting promise to never step back.

"Yet," his voice was almost a whisper. "I question if this line of Tannard is the line the Salmun wish to nurture and protect."

A sickly feeling bloomed in my gut. "I don't understand you."

"A very special time draws near." He moved alongside me so he could whisper in my ear. "The Salmun have waited too long."

"What time is that?"

A heavy breath tickling my ear was his reply. In my periphery, I saw him raise his hand. A thousand insects crawled across my skin as I waited for his touch. If only I still had a dagger.

"This moment could not be more perfect. And now the Salmun's eyes have opened."

Unable to stay still any longer, I stepped away from him.

"I'm hungry and in need of ale."

He bowed. "Of course, princess, of course. The king and Andriet are at the feast. Eat and be merry." Fingers spread, he made as if to drag his hand down my face, never quite touching. "Princess."

I walked away, keeping my footsteps even and calm while inside my heart raced and my mind admonished me to run. Now I knew the mysterious formation of light I'd seen in the cave the moment I held the rock was the Salmun's warning. Orphus knew I had taken it. That's what he was referring to in saying the Salmun's eyes were open.

His talk was treasonous, and I feared to think why he would dare. I picked up my pace, desperate to see Andriet and assure myself he was all right.

In the center of the revelry, flames licked skyward. In the open fields, modesty, decorum, and hierarchy were forgotten, the music no longer the restrained instrumentals accompanying the formal dances, containing a rigid set of rules for interaction. Maid mingled with nobleman, butcher with heiress, inhibitions forgotten, each couple dancing a dance of their own, wantonly, scandalously, to the gay tunes of the lute and shawm.

I heaved a sigh at spying Andriet sitting at the king's table dressed in his finest, Cirro by his side. He leaned over and whispered something in her ear, making her laugh. They looked in love, but I knew better.

My mouth salivated at the smell of richly spiced meat, but after my weird conversation with Orphus, I stayed on the edge of the festival, ignoring my hunger. The king sat in his seat, laughing with the nobleman to his left. There were many vacant spaces at his table, many seats that would be filled with councilman if and when they returned from their trial.

"You don't choose to join the festivities, princess?" I found Daelon on my right.

"I never do. I'm better watching from afar."

"I don't believe for a moment that's what you really choose. It's what you do out of habit, and what you think everyone expects of you."

I folded my arms. "Oh, really?"

He tugged one hand free and pulled me along behind him.

"Daelon, I'm a mess. I've not long returned from my trial."

"And you probably had a terrible time of it. You need some fun to make you forget." He dragged me into the center of the dancers and twirled me around his hand before grabbing my waist and settling me in front of him.

I chuckled. "I could easily mistake you for Andriet. You both think alike."

He smiled, his gray eyes sparkling with joy as he drew me around the bonfire in time with the tune. We moved out of step with the rest of the dancers, but that was the point, and no one cared. "Andriet will be overjoyed to see you back. He arrived yesterday. It didn't take him long, but then no one expected it would."

"Is that why you're acting like an excited child?"

He tilted his head back and laughed. "I can't help being spirited away by the music."

"And something else. I don't believe it's music alone."

He settled his eyes on me, then bit his bottom lip as if trying to subdue his smile. "Cirro and I have spoken."

"Have you now?"

He twirled me around on the spot until I became dizzy. "Daelon, stop," I laughed.

Then he gathered me in his arms. "I adore her. She's added another light to our lives."

"Oh, what did she say to make you sing her praise?"

"She adores me back. She adores Andriet. She accepts that Andriet's first and true love is me, but she hopes we can both love her, too."

He pinched me on the chin the moment he caught my smile. "See, I knew my happiness would infect you."

I wrapped my arms around Daelon's neck and drew him close, closing my eyes against the sting. Strange I could be genuinely happy while feeling my heart break. Tamas and I would never find a future where we were one. "I want there to be nothing but love and joy in your life."

"There is," Daelon spoke into my hair. "I never dreamed it would happen like this. How is it I, a lowly servant, can be so fortunate? How is this my fate?"

"For once, something good comes to those who deserve it."

The scream rattled through the night air, halting the dancers and the music in an instant. I pulled from Daelon's hold and rushed past the dancers, around the bonfire, heading for the king's table.

Everyone at the table had risen to their feet, others gathering closer. Andriet was there. Alive. Thank the Mother. He remained in his seat, cradling Cirro in his arms, her lifeless eyes staring up at him.

CHAPTER

THIRTY-SIX

TRESSYA

Orphus? I glanced around, searching for him. Weak fools breed weak fools. Was this what he alluded to during our conversation?

Rather than Orphus, my eyes settled on Radnisa, the one person the screams failed to draw close. The second culprit. She quirked a brow at me, then turned and strode away. The bitch.

I was torn between comforting Andriet, consulting with the king, or going after Radnisa. My fury decided for me.

The onlookers slowed me down, and by the time I'd cleared the crowd, Radnisa had disappeared from sight. There were likely two places she would go. I headed for her small tent first.

Rage shuddered through my body at the sight of her silhouette as she moved around inside her tent. She didn't even turn to face me when I threw the tent flap aside and stomped inside.

"How dare you."

"How dare I?" She slowly turned. "On the sacred order of the Mother. That's how I dare."

"I told you not to touch her. I told you I had..." I sucked back the words with the threatening tears—not for sadness —that would surely come, but right now my fury suppressed all other emotions.

"I heard you." She turned back to the small table placed close to her bed. On it sat a bronze carafe and goblets. After pouring herself a drink, she faced me once again.

"Unlike you, I haven't forgotten what I am. I know what the Mother said in your letter."

"And I had a plan," I forced through gritted teeth. Liar. I didn't have any such thing. All I knew was that I couldn't kill Cirro.

"The Mother didn't ask for your plan. She gave you an order." She took a sip of her goblet, then strolled toward me. "I have done you a favor. The Mother need not know you failed her. I promise to keep the secret."

"I don't want your promise."

"She sent me a letter too, you know?" Radnisa delved into the pocket of her skirt and revealed a neatly folded piece of parchment. "Here. You may read it. After all, there are no secrets between sisters."

I shook my head. "I know what it says. Complete the task if I fail." It's what the Mother would say. She never communicated with any of us unless it was to give further orders.

"You can't be angry with me, Tressya. I was merely doing the Mother's will. As a good disciple should."

She turned on her heels and strolled away. I stared at the back of her head, imagining slicing my blade across her neck. Had I come armed, it's what I would've done first before hearing her confession.

"I'm protecting you. A shock, I know. I've never pretended to like you. But I see there's something to be gained for both of us in this situation. The chance to benefit myself is what motivates me. You'd find that more believable, wouldn't you?"

I took a step toward her. "You would've gained nothing from my position as queen. I would've dismissed you the moment that crown was on my head."

She returned her goblet to the table, then replaced the letter inside her pocket. "I find it amusing that you believe you can. I feel embarrassed for you, thinking the Tannards have accepted you into their family. You'll never be one of them, no matter how many babies you have. Not even the younger one cares for you. You're a convenience." She looked up from what she was doing. "You're a disciple. Always. You surrendered your soul to the Mother. Do not forget that." She turned to face me, placing her hands on her hips. "The Mother is your family. We're your sisters."

I closed the distance between us, coming to stand alongside her. "You wish to claim a familial connection with me after all this time and everything you've done?"

She sighed, staring ahead, as if I exasperated her. That's all I needed her to do.

"You don't know how much I've helped you over the years, Tressya. Benevolent cruelty was necessary. But it seems both the Mother and I were far too lenient. Otherwise, you wouldn't have held back for one moment. The princess would've died with her first step on Tarragona's soil, and you would now be queen."

Radnisa always held a chilling beauty. Even now, looking over her shoulder at me, she looked like an ice queen. She turned to her drinks table and poured out another goblet of wine, then handed it to me. "I'll be beside you when you're queen. I'll always be at your side."

I reciprocated, swiping her goblet off the table and handing it to her. She didn't even smile before she took a drink. I mirrored her. "Is that so?"

"The Mother gave me permission to use your soul word to make you obey. The forbidden. Imagine." She'd hinted as much before. "But I didn't. However, it's at my command if I feel it necessary; if you act rebellious, or grow a little too proud on your throne."

"Am I to thank you for not using my soul word?"

"I still could."

I shook my head. "No. You couldn't."

She turned her narrow-eyed glare on me. "You think you could stop me?"

Raising my eyebrows, I watched her dispassionately. "I already have."

Her glare disappeared, replaced by surprise, then slowly, horror. "No," she gasped, her eyes going wide, and clutched at her throat.

"I found one berry left in my pocket."

She staggered away from me, hitting the side of her bed, and crumbled to her knees.

"You shouldn't have accepted that drink." I followed her, then sank to kneel beside her.

"Loyalty," she gasped again, then made small sounds in her throat.

"Why should you deserve my loyalty?" How fast the poison worked surprised me.

She slid down the side of her bed and fell backward onto her ass, then further onto an elbow, reaching out one arm, clawing the air as if wanting to gouge out my eyes.

I felt no pleasure in watching her die. There was no victory to feel. I slumped down, leaning against the bed, resting my head back, feeling two days of no sleep and nothing to eat pull me under. Betrayal of the utmost cored me out. There was no returning from this, no lies that would conceal or places to hide from what I'd done.

Sensing her presence before me, I dragged my tired body to my feet.

"This is your home now." I avoided looking at her spirit.

"I...you...are you talking to me?"

"The edge of the Ashenlands is now your home." I looked at the ground rather than at her.

"You're—"

"Yes. I betrayed my oath to the Mother many times over. And this isn't the only secret I've kept."

"Tressya, you—"

"You'll remain here when the king's party leaves." I walked toward the tent flap.

"Please, you can't—"

I spun back, looking at her spirit for the first time. "You should've left Cirro alone." My voice held iron I didn't feel as a perverse guilt racked my body.

"You can't do this."

"I can bend you to my will, but I can't give your life back. No one can."

I hurried away, leaving my crime behind. A few tents along, I stopped to cover my mouth with my hands as I sucked in air. What had I done? Lying to the Mother, failing to follow her orders, keeping secrets from my sisters, was nothing compared to killing another disciple. Would I be able to forgive myself?

I'd always hated Radnisa, yet it was a hate tempered with perseverance, knowing she would always be in my life. For so long, I'd thought I needed her.

My hands shook as the trembling coursed through the rest of my body and the tears flowed free, but I wasn't sure who the tears were for, my dead sister, or my cursed soul.

I staggered forward, tripping over ropes staked into the ground as I moved blindly around the tents with the vision of Andriet's horrified expression caught in my head. I should go comfort him, tell him how sorry I was for bringing Radnisa into the court and into his life. I sobbed as I stumbled, unable to deny the truth. Cirro was dead because of me.

The pandemonium raged behind me, everyone drawn to the bonfire and Cirro's dead body. With Andriet in my head, I found my feet and ran, winding my way through the tents devoid of people, not thinking of where I would end up, until I slammed into the solid arms and chest of Tamas. Bloodwyn, not Tamas.

"You're back," I gasped. Through my dazed stupor, my gaze traveled the length of him, searching for injuries. This far from the bonfire, the tents cast too many shadows to conceal us from suspicious eyes, but it also meant I couldn't see his injuries.

"Only just. What's happened?"

"Cirro's dead."

He seized my shoulders and stared down at me. "Did you do that?"

"No," I snapped. "Never. But the murderer's already dead." The confession spilled from my mouth before I could stop it.

His eyes roamed my face, reading everything I couldn't say. Even in the shadows, I felt I couldn't hide from his eyes. He nodded and took my hand, leading me further into the darkness. I went, no longer feeling like my body was my own. Neither did I ask Tamas where he was leading me.

We ended up at his tent. I hurried inside, blowing out my held breath when he dropped my hand and moved around the tent. Alone, I pressed my palms into my cheeks, suffering the thrum of my heartbeat while listening to the excited babble of voices outside and the soft noises of Tamas moving about.

Sparks burst, then the wick took. His silhouette came to life in the gentle flicker of the candle light. Tamas's silhouette, not Bloodwyn's. It seemed in the short time I'd known him as the man he truly was, I'd unconsciously memorized every part of his body.

In the soft glow, he looked bigger, an overgrown predator. His snug pants outlined his muscular thighs, his hair a dark shaggy mess to his nape.

I crossed the distance, approaching him from behind, unafraid of this man who, only hours ago, was the biggest threat in my nightmares. I wrapped my arms around his waist and pressed my cheek against his back, needing a solid, warm body to cuddle against and the sound of a beating heart other than my own.

Flush against him, I listened to his breaths move through his lungs, and closed my eyes. It felt as though my body had been reaching for someone to hold for so long, and now it cried with relief. The tense coil of my muscles unraveled. Finally, I could breathe. Surrounded by a raging flood, he was my anchor.

Tamas pressed his hands over mine and arched his head back, taking in a deep breath. To me, it sounded like the sigh a man makes after a good meal, stretched out in front of a warm fire with a large ale in hand, but that could only be my dreams.

Because of his tattered shirt, my hands were on his warm skin, flattened by his palms. If they weren't held in place, I would dare explore the ridges and grooves on his stomach, savoring skin that felt like a courtier's expensive silks.

He squeezed my hands, then slowly turned in my embrace. My eyes gobbled up the sight of his dark nipples, his broad shoulders, and the taunt striations of his muscles. But mostly, I wanted to rest my cheek on the plane of his smooth skin and listen to his heartbeat.

As if sensing my desire, he wrapped me in his arms,

nestling me in close. I willingly caved, inhaling the smell of his skin.

"Give me two guesses. Radnisa killed the princess. And in retaliation, you killed her."

I'd almost forgotten our conversation. The physical sensations of our proximity took up all the space in my head.

This was the first time he'd made it out of the Ashenlands in two days. Regardless, I inhaled deep because underneath the sweat he smelt of power, compassion and...home.

"I hope for your sake the viper didn't make it gruesome?"

"She used the berries." My tongue was loose. Tamas stole my ability to hide anything.

"You gave her the berries?"

I wriggled out of his embrace, but he refused to relinquish me. "You really think I would give any to her?"

"It was stupid of me to say. I know you didn't trust her."

"You knew nothing about us."

Using his strength, he wound me back in, sealing me against him. I gave in, needing his comfort too much. It was unhealthy and dangerous.

"That's better," He sighed again, and I felt the echo of his voice rumbling in his chest. "I hate to contradict you, but my gaze has rarely wandered from you. I don't need it said aloud to know how it went between the two of you."

A treacherous thrill coursed through my body upon hearing his confession.

"She missed one berry." His muscles muffled my voice. My mind wanted to prove what the last few hours had done to my sanity by urging me to kiss his chest.

"Convenient." His fingers massaged the muscles close to my spine. I wished his hands were on my skin.

I really had gone insane. It seemed my constraints unraveled as fast as my loyalty to the Mother.

"Is your pain for Cirro?"

"I was meant to kill her. I thought I would do it."

His tone softened. "But you'd grown fond of her. So the viper did it for you. Now you carry her death as if you killed her."

"There's no denying she's dead because of me. I liked her very much, but it's Andriet that makes this hurt. His attachment to her grew out of nowhere. She would've given him a perfect life. One he deserved. Until I took it away from him."

I'd never shed tears or bared my pain to anyone. Not even Carlin. I always had to protect him from the Sistern, not to mention my father's wrath were he ever to find out we were lovers. Tamas was my first true confidante.

"I know the agonizing experience of suffering guilt for circumstances beyond your control, so I won't diminish your anguish by offering feeble clichés. But I do want to say one thing."

"Go on."

"Don't take on the guilt of others. It will end up crushing you. There's a thousand shoulds and ifs that you can twist all manner of ways that will dig the blade deeper if you really want to feel the pain."

I bit my lip and kept my eyes closed. Sometimes silence was better than words.

"Killing one of your own must also be hard."

Did we still have to continue talking about this? I shook

my head, then sagged into him because, yes, what he said was significant—my body told me so, and I would likely struggle with this for time to come. "She's been a blade in my back from day one. I've thought of killing her, figuratively, for years. But...I'm a disciple."

"Ah, yes. I know that feeling all too well. Honor and duty. I live by them. And sometimes they've crippled me."

I nodded.

With a finger at my chin, he tilted my head up as he lowered his head as if to kiss me. My heart stopped as a fire sparked deep below.

"And now you're free. Tonight, it may not seem like it. Tomorrow, and days after, you'll struggle, but in the end you'll spread your wings because you were always meant to fly. You can be what you want to be. You can make your own rules."

Mesmerizing and achingly slow, Tamas trailed his thumb across my lower lip as he spoke. I would reply, tell him I was never meant to fly, not a woman like me, illegitimate, plain, a failure in all ways, but I couldn't find the strength to disturb the hypnotic pull of his touch.

His words were poisonous to a faithful heart, addictive to the traitorous and to any hoping for a glimpse of a future no longer bound by duty.

When he finally released my lower lip, I buried my face in his chest, inhaling deep the aromas on his skin, feeling desperately needy. This is where I wanted to be.

"I can only think of how much I've failed."

I didn't want to be the King's blade for Henricus, but for Andriet, I would gladly wield my sword. Where did that leave Tamas and me? I couldn't ask. My pulse quickened at the thought of hearing what he would say. He wanted me, like I wanted him, but at the end of the night, what would he choose? I'd seen how far desire led two people; it was a short path, lasting the time it took the man to empty his seed and little further.

I would be stupid to think Tamas was any better. Did it change the way I felt at this moment? No. Because he was right about one thing, tonight was for making my own rules —at least for now. Tomorrow was too far away, and I'd denied myself too many times to find any strength tonight to do the same.

I lifted my head, pressing my chin on his chest and gazed up at him. "It's a good thing you're Tamas."

He quirked a brow.

Cirro was dead in Andriet's arms, Radnisa lay dead in her tent, all around us chaos reigned. It was wicked that this moment felt so right, but it was time I spread my wings. "Because I don't want to kiss Bloodwyn."

"You don't have to do this right now, Tressya. That's probably shock talking. So many terrible events have happened this day."

I straightened. "Are you turning me down?"

"Stars, no. I've endlessly rehearsed this day in my head. I mean, that's assuming the kiss is the start of a deeper, more exquisite pleasure. But you should only do this because it's what you truly desire and not a way to hide from guilt or pain."

"Wow, I did a better job than I thought." I nestled my chin back on his chest, pressing my body against his, an invitation for him to continue those slow mesmeric swirls on my back.

"You've been brilliant all along, but what job is this?"

"Making you believe I saw you as nothing more than a curse from the north."

"That didn't even occur to me. Did you really think that?"

I chuckled. "From the very beginning. But..." I smiled. "Things have changed." Then I tilted my head down and inhaled his scent once more.

There was a seriousness about his expression that made me uncomfortable.

"There's never a perfect time. I know, We're enemies—"

He pressed a finger over my lips as he shook his head, so I sucked his finger into my mouth. His eyes flared a fraction as he inhaled.

I bit his finger gently, then moved my head away. "I truly desire it, and I want to forget. I want to pretend I govern my own life. We're two people wanting competing outcomes. How can that end, Tamas?" I closed my eyes. "But tonight I ask something for myself, as selfish as that may be. And I want you to do the same. Be no one else but a man who wants nothing more than to be with me."

I dared reveal my heart. I wasn't even breathing.

He wrapped me in a tight embrace. "I don't have to pretend to be that."

"Then shut up and take your clothes off."

"Now that's an invitation a man can't refuse."

I didn't wait for him to do it. Instead, I slid his useless jacket from his shoulders, then gripped the hem of his tattered shirt and dragged it off so I could savor all of him in the candlelight. I smoothed a hand across the expanse of his skin, swallowing the satisfied smirk at seeing his stomach muscles quiver under my touch and hearing him suck in a breath.

"You play an unfair game. Why don't I get to put my hands all over your bare skin?"

I huffed a laugh. "Because you're impatient."

"For you, yes." His voice purred just above a whisper.

Now I knew the true reason I'd chosen this simple dress. I unfastened the lace at my bodice, then let it slip to the floor.

His eyes went immediately to the outline of my breasts under my thin cotton chemise. I gasped as he glided his hand over my peaked nipples, and a pulse stabbed through my veins, making me ache. The feeling sent shards of pleasure between my legs. He smirked, looking way too smug at my reaction, but I didn't care as long as he kept touching me.

"We've both waited too long for this," he whispered, his voice a deep groan that flowed out like syrup. Then, capturing my eyes with a stare to turn my clothes to cinders, he pinched both my nipples.

"I said, take off your clothes," I demanded.

"I rarely take orders from anyone."

"In that case." I pushed him in the chest, wanting space, but he refused to budge. Instead, he quirked a brow.

Why was I not surprised he would resist being shoved around? His sword was on his right hip, his dagger sheathed to the front of it. I wrapped my hands around the dagger's hilt and drew it out, then feathered it across the skin of his chest.

"I'll have to take matters into my own hands." Slowly, as

not to make him jerk, I trailed it gently down his torso until I reached the laces on his pants. Like any good warrior, he kept his blade sharp. It took no time for me to cut the laces away. As each lace broke, the muscles in his stomach rippled.

"That's better." I arched around him and threw the dagger, embedding it into a tent pole.

"I thought you were going to geld me."

"That comes later if you don't give me what I want."

He kissed me with as much violence as a raging storm. I matched him, my hunger just as great, our kiss as desperate as the first time.

No one had kissed me like this. Never had I kissed as voraciously in return. We were tongues clashing, hands clawing across skin. He matched my whimper with a groan that set a fire burning down to my core. My whole body throbbed as my hands found their way into his hair, tugging, then across his shoulders, gouging my nails along his smooth skin. Freeing my mind from thought, I surrendered to my body, wallowing in the sensations, the smells, the emotions.

Tamas gently ended his kiss, withdrawing his lips from mine and brushed light nips along my jaw, down my throat, and onto my shoulder. A smoldering desire within me grew hotter than the Ashenlands's pit, evoking a primal scream within my mind. Tamas's kisses brought me to the edge, and then he daringly released me. An unfamiliar savagery surged through my body at being denied. I wasn't ready for his gentle touch, so I fell to my knees, yanking down his pants as I went, freeing his hard cock, and it bounced up to slap against his stomach.

"Stars, Tressya," he hissed. "You don't have to—"

I grasped his cock firm, splaying my fingers over its girth as I licked my lips, arched my head back and stared up into his dark eyes. The dim light from the candle cast shadows across one side of him, hugging his face and body in all the right places, making him appear the lethal creature I knew he was, but his expression had slackened, his eyes hooded and hungry, as a faint tremor rippled through him and into my hand. The powerful Razohan was a man brought down, and all I had to do was put my hand on his cock.

As if that's all I'd do. I shifted my gaze to his shaft, ran my thumb over the tip, pressing down to splay the slit open, and leaned forward to lick the first bead of dew. Salty deliciousness.

Something inside of me snapped, some earthy desire festering for too long clawed its way out of its cage and rampaged through my body like a demented bullock. Tamas's soft groan didn't help, neither did his hand smothering my grip on his cock.

"I wanted to be the first one to do the tasting."

"Shut up," I barked, shaking off his smothering hand. And I shut him up from saying anything else coherent by running my tongue along the seam underneath his shaft, right up to the ridge of its fat head. Despite his cock being hard as a blade, the skin under my tongue was silky smooth, and tasted better than the sweetest syrup.

"Delicious," I whispered, then dived back in to lather the silken skin with my tongue, ensuring my saliva coated its entire length.

"Please, Tressya. I want to—"

My greedy suck drowned his voice, with lips stretched taunt, as I swallowed him all the way to the back of my throat until I almost gagged.

"Hmm," I moaned on imagining how stretched and filled I would feel after this night was over.

He groaned. "You're killing me."

I pressed my thumb over his slit. "I haven't even started." Then went right back to enjoying my meal, holding his gaze with mine as I trailed my lips over his cock, savoring what passion did to his features, making him appear greedy and more animalistic.

I'd never taken control like this, never acted so aggressively hungry, but this new thirst in me, unbound and inflamed by whatever fire burned through my veins, meant I would do anything to claim this male.

Claim him. The two words punched through my chest like a mace. A passion I would never normally feel, a thought I would never normally think. I was so out of my head at this moment, and I didn't care. Instead, I increased my rhythm, my head bobbing back and forth as I pressed my lips tight around his shaft.

Tamas arched his head back, a guttural, feral noise rising through his throat. His hips spasmed forward, but I anchored him in place with a firm hand on one hip, not willing to let him take the lead. This was my time for power, my time to bring him down.

The tremor started under my fingers, splayed across his hips, then moved down his shaft and into my mouth. He rumbled deep, gruff noises, grumbles of tortured pleasure, as the spasms took hold of his entire body.

"I surrender," he cried.

I joined my mouth strokes with my hand.

"Fuck. You've won," he uttered in a hoarse voice.

I didn't relent, this time gripping his heavy sacks with my other hand.

"You're my queen." His body vibrated uncontrollably.

A snarl ripped from his lips. "You're mine."

And he jerked his hips back, then pushed me backward. I landed on the makeshift bed, Tamas descending on top of me.

"You're cruel. You didn't let me—"

He kissed me while his feverish hands ripped at my clothes, tearing them away from my body, revealing my pebbled flesh to the cool breeze and his wet, desperate tongue.

"It's my turn," he growled, lashing his mouth over my nipples.

Desire unfurled like a poisonous flower below my skin. My breasts felt heavy, my nipples ached. I had no idea how much of me had died since leaving Carlin until Tamas kissed me, and my whole body woke, screaming in hunger.

I'd never felt so alive. My body, sensitive to the slightest touch, shivered at the caress of his hands and tease of his tongue. I felt free, just as he'd told me to be.

He reared back. "Fuck, you're gorgeous," he whispered.

"Don't," I groaned in return, turning my face away from him.

He seized my chin between his fingers and drew my head back, forced me to stare up at him. "Never look away from me." Then he gently brushed a strand from my cheek. "You're the most beautiful woman I've ever met."

I shook my head, but he pressed his fingers into my cheeks to still me. "I know what you're going to say," he growled, a low thundering noise that sent shards like daggers straight to my core.

I shuddered as his fingers found my clit, giving a light tease as he told me off. "I've lied before, but never about this."

"You're honestly going to keep talking," I groaned and rocked my hips into his palm as he continued to stroke me in the perfect place, using the perfect pressure and the perfect pace like he was inside my body feeling the sensations and reading my mind, knowing exactly what I needed.

He lowered, dusting his lips on the shell of my ear. "I saw your beauty the moment I met you." His warm breath tickled inside my ear.

He slipped a finger inside of me, then dragged it out with a lazy stroke. Then in again. "It's deep inside that I search. It's deep inside I saw your worth. A woman with no equal."

He'd replaced his one finger with two or was that three. I wasn't sure, but the stretch was turning my head, the gentle strokes building a slow release.

I felt the sting in my eyes and bit my lip, desperate to keep my tears inside. Happy tears, joyous tears, I'd never truly felt. Carlin was my first love, but my feelings for him turned to shadows against the power of what I felt for Tamas. This was a dream. It had to be a dream because something like this never happened to disgraced illegitimates.

Shut up. Let this moment be what it is.

"I've never stopped seeing you, Tressya. I never will."

I touched his cheek, swallowing the thickening in my throat. Face to face like this, we were exposed to each other, leaving us open, honest, and raw. The moment was powerfully intimate.

"I don't understand you." I couldn't accept what he was saying. "It frightens me." What would happen to us after tonight?

"It shouldn't. There's no fear in my heart for the way I feel."

"Tamas—"

He gave one hard kiss to shut me up, then he pulled away. "Don't let your mind ruin anything. Let your body tell you what to believe."

He wrapped an arm under my thigh and hitched my leg over his shoulder as he rose above me. "And now you're mine."

I gasped, arching my head back, pressing into his unmade bed as he slipped inside in one long, slick slide until I was sure he reached my throat.

I grabbed his hips, barely able to speak, and held him firm while I adjusted to the stretch. Finally, I breathed. "You're not what I'm used to."

His smug smile told me I shouldn't have confessed that. He winked at me, as deep in my core, I felt his cock jerk.

"How you feeling?"

"Deliciously stretched and starving for something other than food."

He seized both my wrists and dragged my arms over my head.

"Tonight is the start, Tressya." He withdrew, then plunged deep. "We're going to change everything. United, that's our power."

Then he let go. He fucked me hard, staring down into my eyes and capturing every expression on my face, as I did with him. My body turned to fire. Hot shards of molten iron poured through my veins. I couldn't look away from him, even if the Ashenlands beasts were to come crashing in, my eyes would be stuck on the raw and savage look on his face.

He kept his relentless pace until I turned dizzy from lack of breath and stars flashed before my eyes. When the exquisite tension broke, wave upon wave of pleasure crashed over me. His curses and groans filled my ears, and when his own climax broke, he cried my name as if in worship. Then with one last, deep thrust, we broke the makeshift bed.

We clung together, laughed, kissed, then laughed some more, and all the while I couldn't shake the thought I had never been so happy nor as deeply in trouble.

CHAPTER

THIRTY-SEVEN

TRESSYA

SHE LAY in my arms as I watched her sleep. My beautiful queen. I traced a finger in the air above her brow, not wanting to disturb her. How had all the luck fallen to me? I honestly thought I would never have her, yet here she was, in my arms, having surrendered to me as I'd surrendered to her.

Talk was the last thing on my mind before she fell asleep. Not that sort of talk, at least, so I had yet to tell her all of my plans. By morning, when all was decided, she would be happy with what I had to tell her. Her Mother wanted her to be a queen, and that's exactly what I would give her. Once I was crowned king, she would be my queen. Queen to the Tannard throne, but of the Savant line.

The lethargy of our sex lingered in me still, but there were many tasks I had to complete before the sun rose, even though I loathed to leave her side. There were endless nights before us, endless mornings we could refuse to see because we were too tired, too sore, too consumed with each other. I longed for that time.

Which was not now. I eased my arm from under her head and slowly, ever so gently, moved myself away. It was imperative she stayed asleep. Too many breaths it took before I was off the bed and on my knees, feeling around for new clothes. Still buttoning up my jacket, I slipped outside as Bloodwyn.

After the princess's death, the king sent everyone to their tents, leaving his guard to enforce his command. The night was full of rowdy gossip from all the tents, as everyone discussed the surprising event. Their heated debates disguised my passing, making my job easy.

Two guards waited outside the king's tent. More guards patrolled the grounds, ensuring everyone continued to obey the king's orders, also likely on the lookout for anyone hoping to slip away into the night.

I straightened my jacket, then left the blanket of the two tents and strode across the clearing toward the king's guard. They reacted instantly, drawing their swords.

"Halt," commanded the man on the left.

"Inform the king Lord Bloodwyn seeks an audience. Tell him I have important news."

The dimwits glanced at each other.

"Hurry now. The king is waiting to hear what I have to say."

One of them ducked inside. I went to follow him through, but his companion blocked my path. A spark of annoyance speared through my gut on seeing the blade barring my way, but I would accomplish little if I got into an argument now.

I gritted my teeth and waited. In my periphery, I noticed two more guards approaching. Damn, the fewer people around, the better. When the guard ducked back through the flap, I pushed past him and headed inside, already knowing the king had granted me an audience.

Henricus slouched in his seat, half pulled away from the table. Andriet sat opposite him. Which was unfortunate because he was here and because I couldn't touch him. Tressya would never forgive me if I killed him. And I had long given up berating myself for all the ways I betrayed my trusted and my people for leaving Andriet alive. Yes, there would be those influential noblemen who would rally behind Andriet and refuse my claim to the throne. However, the king had seen to the death of some during the first few days of the trials and my force would see to the others. Some might survive, but I doubted enough to create a credible threat against me.

Then there was the Salmun. They were a problem I couldn't control. Between Andriet and me, I was gambling on them accepting my claim. Andriet was weak. I suspected the Salmun, along with the Levenian, would desire a stronger leader. Though, there was the problem of my inheritance. I was not of the Levenian line, with no oath to keep me faithful to their masters. I could only hope we would prevail, that the might of the Nazeen and the Razohan would match the Salmun's magic.

Thanks to their creations, I was now a nightmare, and my men would arrive from the Ashenlands a myriad of other malicious and deadly creatures now we knew what souls we could take.

"Your Majesty." I bowed, then shifted my attention to Andriet. "My condolences, Your Highness." Curses, that he was present. I needed to be smart. "I have news." I flicked my gaze across to Andriet.

A man who preferred the bed of other men, who'd known the princess less than a week, he looked heartsick. Giving one's heart away too easily was the fastest way to pain. I should know, for it's happened to me. I pitied him, knowing if Tressya had been the one to die, I would've turned into a nightmare and razed this encampment to the ground, killing everyone in my path.

"What news is this?"

"Your majesty," I glanced at Andriet. "The matter is private."

"This is about Cirro, isn't it? You're to tell me as well. I have as much right to hear what you have to say. She was my betrothed."

Good men never deserved to die, but life didn't work like that. If not for Tressya, I would kill the son as surely as I would kill the father. That she cared for him spared his life and made my task difficult. I had to remove him from this tent, but the little bastard had fallen for his betrothed in whatever way a man who loves men could do, which meant he grieved as sorely as any lover. I would find sympathy for him if he wasn't in my way. "I understand, Your Highness. Forgive me. What I have to say has nothing to do with tonight's unfortunate events."

I'd caught both unawares. By now, Andriet was on his

feet, pacing back and forth behind the table, agitation bleeding from his every step.

"Juel first. Your councilmen conspiring. Now Cirro. There's no coincidence. It's a foul plot to undermine the throne. To bring the House of Tannard down."

His mind moved down the wrong path, though he was spot on with his assertion.

"Sit down, Andriet, your mood helps no one."

Andriet turned on his father, his face flushing red with anger. "Whatever you're doing to eradicate our enemies has failed. Who will be next? Me?" He stopped his pacing. "You?"

The king snorted. "I would like to see them try. The Salmun are on our side."

"They weren't on Juel's side," Andriet counted.

"They can't save a man from his own stupidity. As for plots to kill the Tannard line, the Salmun will never allow it. How do you suppose our ancestors have survived these last one thousand years and kept their might upon the throne?"

I averted my gazed for a moment to straighten my features and fight off my smirk. Though I was curious about one thing. Henricus was right in saying the House of Tannard owed their power to the Salmun alone, so where were they? Why were they conspicuously absent, given my lies of treasonous plots and Cirro's sudden death?

The time it took me to reach the king's tent, I'd devised several lies to gain an audience without raising the Salmun's suspicion. I had expected to find the king surrounded by the Levenian's pets, yet I found him with his son, who probably didn't even know the difference between the hilt of his sword and the tip of his blade. Still, I wasn't about to question my luck.

Andriet glared at his father, finding nothing he said matched Henricus's argument.

I strode forward, keeping my movements methodical, and picked up Andriet's goblet from the table and filled it from the carafe. "I can assure you, Your Highness, I will bring the culprit before you, minus his ears. And perhaps his tongue unless you have questions for him." I handed him his goblet. "Completing your third trial, and then this terrible shock, may I suggest you should rest, assured the king's guards patrol the borders of the encampment. The murderer will never escape, and I shall work tirelessly through the night hunting him, or them, down."

I needed to complete this task as quick as possible. The northerners would have cleared the Ashenlands by now and using the blanket of darkness to creep upon the encampment. I needed to hunt down Romelda before they attacked and take her back to my tent. She'd agreed to spare Tressya's life by placing her in a suspended sleep state. While she slept, I planned to take her far from here, leaving her somewhere safe. Miraculously, Romelda agreed to do the same for Andriet. The two would wake together once we won the war. I could only hope that was enough to prevent her from hating me.

"Them? You think there is more than one? Of course. There must be." Andriet took the goblet and paced again. "How many conspirators have returned from their third trial?" It wasn't really a question. And if it was, he didn't wait for an answer. "Arrest them first. Bring them before me. No. Throw them at the feet of the Salmun."

I inclined my head. "I shall do my utmost to defend the throne."

"Good." Andriet took deep gulps of his wine, not once glancing at me.

I ground my teeth, feeling the tension at the slow movement of time. My men awaited my signal, but unforeseen events may trigger their early attack. "There is nothing you can do at this moment," I told Andriet. "I ask you to trust your loyal servant to seek justice."

"All will be done," the king announced. "As Bloodwyn says. Rest, son. He and the Salmun will see we get our revenge."

Andriet took the last of his wine, then slammed his goblet down on the table. "You're right, father." He came around the table to me, stopping to place a hand on my shoulder. "Your part in this won't be forgotten."

It certainly wouldn't. Though, not for the reasons he supposed.

"When all of this is done, you'll be rewarded for your loyalty to the Tannard throne."

I intend to be.

I stared at the ground as Andriet strode from the tent, slumping my shoulders as if I was taking on Andriet's burden.

The king sighed and sat back in his seat. Concern aged his features. Lucky for me, he trusted the Salmun implicitly "A troublesome outcome. Indeed." He ran a hand across his brow. "My leniency is my flaw. Too many traitors made it through their trials. I had not thought them as resourceful or resilient. Perhaps I should've instructed the Salmun to kill them all on the first day. Better still, I should've taken their heads before we left Tolum."

I poured a goblet for myself and took a gulp. I had to say this for Tarragona; they produced an excellent wine.

"You couldn't have foreseen this." I took another drink.

How close I was to achieving success, it was strange I felt little. Divided focus was dangerous, and mine was on Tressya. Everything had to unfold as I planned, or she was at risk. Our one night together was enough for me; I was prepared to risk our success to ensure her safety, but I wasn't confident of how she felt, especially since I was about to betray her trust by deserting our bed to kill the king. I couldn't even contemplate how she would react in waking to find us the victors.

For a moment, I turned from the king and rubbed my hand through my stubble.

"It's good we have loyal men like yourself," the king continued.

She will hate me for this. Knowing that, I almost dumped my goblet back on the table and marched out of the tent. I should've told her I loved her. I should've voiced it.

"Now I have to find another bride. It took me long enough to negotiate the last two. I'll send Andriet back to Emberfell under the escort of the Salmun. He must be protected. Even if I have to confine him to his quarters. Until there is an heir, the Salmun will shadow that boy everywhere."

I inhaled, slowly seeping the breath out through my

nose. I never thought I would feel like this toward anyone. Incessant thoughts, urgent cravings, insatiable hunger and above all a dwelling torment entombing my body at the thought of losing her.

"You're quiet, Bloodwyn. What did you come here to tell me?"

"We're close, Sire." Why had I not told her my thoughts before the storm began? As a disciple, she would fulfill her promise to her Mother Divine as queen upon my throne. I would surrender it all to her. That had to be enough.

"Make yourself clear?"

I returned my goblet and strolled toward him. "Dawn will see the final judgement. All traitors will perish."

One day, I hoped to unveil Tressya's eyes to the terrible secrets her maleficent Mother Divine festered within the Sistern.

"So soon. Then you know who they are?"

"I've known all along, Your Majesty. It's taken time for me to prepare."

"This is good news. Tell me who they are. I shall alert the Salmun. I'll have their heads."

Standing beside him, I looked down at him. "And so will I."

Long, thick, and sharp was my claw that stabbed through the side of his throat, piercing straight through to puncture out the other side. I swiped my hand forward, slicing my claw free, as well as the sinewy flesh attached, including his windpipe.

The king failed to make enough noise to alert the guards to his predicament. Instead, he gurgled on his blood as it spurted to his knees and onto the grass at his feet. I grabbed him under the arms as his body slumped forward in death and dragged him to the floor so that I may perform my work.

Both my hands upon his torso, I dove deep within, spearing inside with the speed of a diving bird, needing to rip out his soul as soon as I could. I'd lingered too long in his tent, playing the risk while my mind was, yet again, distracted with thoughts of Tressya.

His was a frustrating maze of confused and mixed pathways, but, once inside, I always found what I wanted in the end.

"Let the king know Lord Everhart wishes a word," came the high, demanding voice.

Curses on high. This was an unforeseen disturbance while I was on the verge of consuming his soul. I sensed I was close, though it remained out of reach.

I pulled my concentration back and darted a look behind me. The fabric of the tent was strides behind me. I glanced at the entrance flap. Dammit, I'd run out of time.

Abandoning the king, I darted to the back of the tent and slid underneath the fabric, rolled once, then sprang to my feet, and rushed away as the shout rang out behind me. They'd found the dead king. I bared my teeth in fury as I wove through the tents, at the same time loosening my hold on my human shield and taking on the form of an eagle. Two flaps and I took to the sky.

More shouts heralded the chaos about to unfold. Panic screamed through my head. This was not the outcome I planned. Dammit, I needed to find Romelda. She had a task to perform. I needed to steal Tressya away, make her safe before the violence began.

Too late, the encampment erupted into chaotic cries from the guards and those early arrivers to the king's tent. With my bird's sight, I caught the flare of torches and the scourer of magic as Salmun brought down the sun's own rays to flush out the murderer. Too late, the king's murderer had already passed the border guards from up high and made his way west to where the northerners waited.

I let out a squawk of anger for what had unfolded because of my stupidity. Had I killed him swift, rather than pacing around, enjoying the splendid wine and savoring my fallen victory, the supposed king would be issuing orders for the heads of many innocents right now, namely his best bows men and strongest fighters and any with an ounce of sense that would make a decent foe against the northerners. I had hoped to take as many from within before my men entered the camp.

She would wake finding my side of the bed cold. My wings faltered their beat, and I fell from my height thinking about the fear she would feel believing I'd already killed Andriet.

I hit the ground as a man and curled into a ball, racked with the pain she would feel with the slow and horrible yet undeniable realization that I had slipped from our bed to betray her while my seed lay warm inside of her.

I staggered to my feet, then found my pace and raced across the fields, aiming for the dark patch of trees ahead, until something hit me in the back and sent me sprawling onto my belly, my face smashing into the grass.

"Fleeing without your swords, you ass," came Osmud's voice out of the dark. In the moon's silhouette, he held out his hand to me.

Our hands clasped, he hauled me to my feet. "You've royally fucked our plans."

"What's done is done," I growled, turning around to look back at the encampment, shining like day. Tressya was caught in the mayhem.

"It's not a creep now. We'll have to storm with brute force."

"The Nazeen will give those to come across the fields a shield that will get them right to the edge of the Salmun's door."

"A plan we didn't need until now." And he smacked me across the head.

I took it without a word. I deserved more than that. "The Razohan are in position?"

"A pretty bunch we are awaiting your signal."

The rest of the northerners would attack across the fields, but the Razohan took to the false forest, using the power of light enhanced by the Nazeen to defend against the manifestations as they hunted for as many of the source as they could find. An arsenal of the Salmun's maligned creatures, torn straight from the bounds of the Ashenlands and sent to prey upon their masters, should distract the wizards from defending the encampment, allowing the Nazeen time to defeat their magic.

"Tressya's protected. And that ass of a prince," I reiterated again, as I had done many times already during our preparations.

"Hey, brother, according to your plans, Romelda was supposed to get her and the prince out by now, both sleeping peacefully like babies. You know how it goes in the thick of battle. It's not easy holding your claws from anyone's throat."

"She'll take your hand before you get a chance. Remember that. And I'll take your other hand if you dare."

"You're a grumpy bastard before a fight."

"Spread the word."

"It won't be a simple task in beast form, or do you propose I shadow the woman, admonishing any who threaten her?"

I dragged my hand through my hair. "Let's just get this over with. Leave her protection up to me."

"And who's going to watch your ass while you play nurse maid?"

I growled at Osmud. "Your responsibility is the prince. See to it he's safe."

"That nightmare's sucked your brains dry," he retorted.

Ignoring his remark, I gave my final warning. "I'm suspicious of how easy it was for me to kill the king."

"Easy! Easy would not have started that firestorm."

I huffed a frustrated sigh. "I was careless."

"Understatement."

"The Salmun should've reacted to Princess Cirro's death by shielding the king and his son."

"Wait. You killed the princess?"

"It wasn't my doing."

"Treason within his own ranks. I like it."

"Tressya's lady-in-waiting was responsible."

"Never thought I would offer thanks to one of those bitches for furthering our cause."

"Be wary. Okay. The Salmun aren't acting as they should. Warn the Nazeen."

He patted my shoulder. "By morning, it will all be over." Then he turned into a bird, spraying black feathers as he disappeared up into the sky, heading for the Ashenlands.

I spared one more look at the bedlam, then released my form, becoming a bird once more and headed toward the forest and northern forces.

CHAPTER

THIRTY-EIGHT

TRESSYA

IT WAS STILL DARK when I lurched up in bed, then fell backward, groggy, not ready to be awake, feeling sore, confused, and sure something had woken me. There was a reason my heart raced.

Perhaps it was a bad dream, though I remembered nothing. Then a scream ripped through the darkness, followed by furious shouts. I lurched half off the bed and felt for my weapons on the tent's floor, where I always left them; at easy reach. They weren't there. Dammit, why wouldn't I put them there?

Then I remembered. I had no weapons; they remained in the Ashenlands, lodged in the nightmare's eye. The slick feeling between my legs brought the rest of my glorious memories back into my head. I also wasn't in my tent.

"Tamas." I flopped backward onto the bed, reaching

across for him. After last night, I should've felt content to roll over and snuggle in close to him, but the cries and shouts from outside wouldn't let me savor anything.

I patted his side of the bed, and felt a subtle warmth where he would've been. A fierce stab went through my heart. He wasn't there. Because he'd heard the first screams and leapt up to see what had happened? Or he... I couldn't stop the panic welling in my chest. I didn't want to think the worst, which was weird because I was never one to think the best. My heart favored denial.

More shouts drove me out of bed and onto the floor, scouring on my knees for my clothes. This wasn't what I thought it was. It wasn't. Tamas wouldn't do that to me. Not after last night.

I stopped to sit back on my knees. *You really think that?* I knew his people were coming because I'd asked him before he'd dragged me into the Ashenlands and made me forget which side I was on. He told me the truth. No lies, no twisted omissions, just the plain truth. And I accepted it, swallowed it, and kissed him.

My heart kicked into a fast gallop. How could I have been so wretched as to fall for his soothing words and hungry kisses?

"Sweet Mother," I groaned and covered my face. Last night's memory became a palpable agony for everything we'd done to each other when, in his head, he planned this very moment.

"You knew all along," I growled to myself.

I fell to my knees and resumed searching for my clothes. Finding my underthings, I sat on my ass and fumbled with them all the while cursing Tamas, then cursing myself. This was on me. The downfall of the Tannard line was on me. All for what? For a kiss? For a tumble? For a traitor who manipulated me and played me for a fool.

In the dark, I couldn't find the holes in the underthings for my legs. "Dammit," I shouted. "Curses to you, Tamas." I would stake him. That was the first thing I would do once I saw him.

I fell on my back. "Curses to the seven realms!" I yelled to no one.

Had I really thought he would stop because of me? Had I thought he would march up to the king and negotiate favorable terms that left him on the throne? Because he cared for me? I'd allowed him to play me like a fool. Everything that had happened between us from the day I met him meant nothing to him. It was all a cleverly orchestrated sham.

And I'd honestly thought I'd given up on fantasies.

At last, I was able to slip my underthings on.

It had been days since I last ate, and my stomach ached with hunger. As the aches cored out my gut, a slight tremor shuddered through my body from the lack of sustenance. Dismissing my needs so I could tumble into bed with Tamas, that's the pitiable disciple I'd become.

But I wasn't a disciple. I slowed before slipping my chemise over my head. I scrunched my eyes closed. No. Those were his words, the lying ass. He knew exactly what to say. And in keeping everything I knew quiet, I'd committed a worse sin than whoring myself to my enemy.

"You bastard," I growled to the man who'd deserted me.

Once I'd found all my clothes and dressed myself, I

rushed from the tent and into a soldier running by. The impact knocked me backward as the soldier kept on his way, hurrying to wherever he was needed. I gathered myself and ran in the opposite direction. I needed weapons first before I confronted this war.

I stomped off toward Radnisa's tent. Why? Why had I not said a word the moment I knew his people were coming? *Because you're a desperate, pathetic fool.* Because I'd thought he felt the same as me. Why go to all that trouble to rescue me? Many times over. Why? It made no sense when he was simply going to march into this camp with his army and kill us all.

I slowed, balling my fists to my forehead. Sweet Mother, he must have laughed at himself when he told me the truth, and all I did was pant for him. I fell all over him with one kiss.

Two people rushed past me, startling me into motion again.

"You're a weak, bloody fool," I moaned, then wiped the first tear from my eye.

That done, I stomped on. *One sign of affection and you think it's genuine.* One sign of hope that someone understood me. That someone sees me. He'd said that to me.

"He knew exactly what to say," I snarled.

At the entrance of Radnisa's tent, I steadied myself, pressing my palm to my stomach. Considering Tamas's betrayal, my guilt redoubled at what I'd done, enhanced by the callousness I'd shown my former sister by leaving her body in the tent unattended while I spent hours in... No, dammit. I wasn't going to think of his sublime touch.

I pushed the flap aside and rushed in. The candle flame flickered with the sudden gust of wind rushing in beside me. By now, the candle had burned low in its holder, shadowing Radnisa's turned face. I avoided looking at her body and hurried across to the trunk she'd placed at the bottom of her bed.

Inside, I found the weapons I needed, already sheathed and hitched to her baldric.

"This is all on you."

Hearing her voice didn't slow me as I slipped her baldric over my shoulder.

"It shouldn't matter to you anymore."

"The only thing that matters to me is your death. Which is coming soon. The two of us. Imagine it. Eternity together."

I heaved a breath, then turned to face her. "You won't believe this, but I'm sorry for killing you, even if you brought it on yourself."

She clenched her teeth and fisted her palms. "The Mother will make you suffer. Even beyond death."

Ignoring her fury, I had to ask. "What did the Mother put inside of me?"

"You think I'd tell you?"

"I guess not." I headed for the exit, the erupting chaos outside calling me.

"Wait," she yelled in desperation. "How should I know? Since when did the Mother ever tell any of us more beyond what we needed to know?"

"Whatever it was, it turned me into a spiritweaver."

"So it would seem." She folded her arms.

"You have no idea why?"

She rolled her eyes. "What disciple would not know the reason?"

"She wanted a spiritweaver sitting on the Tannard throne. But she knows how it works. There are no guarantees any children of mine will carry the talent. It's not readily passed down through the generations."

"And you were a handy convenience more than anything."

"One who had no defenses against her soul word."

"You really should've taken the time to learn Tarragona's full history and not relied on the fables that reached our shores. Maybe that would've enlightened you. A thousand years of oral history and the truth grows faint as quickly as its embellished. What's left is a heady tale, even if hard to believe."

"Tell me."

"Now you want to listen to me. It's as you said, none of this matters to me anymore, so why should I say anything?"

I ground my teeth. "Fine." And marched toward the exit.

"If you really want to know."

I stopped but kept my back to her.

"There was some mention of a power beyond measure now lost. It's said the power will one day be inherited through the Tannard line."

I slowly turned, caught up in the tale. "The Mother wants a loyal disciple of the Tannard line because of this power."

As Andriet had told me in the carriage ride. The power of the Bone Throne. And that was why Tamas was in Emberforge. He was searching for something that would help him succeed in taking the power for himself.

I bit my lip to repress my bitter laugh. How could I compete for his attention against the return of a prophesied power? Dammit. Why was that the first thought to come to my mind? I didn't want his attention any longer. Actually, that wasn't true. I would happily have him stare at me while I put my dagger through his eye.

A chorus of shouts erupted, followed by a dazzling light, making the night appear as though it was day.

"I have to go."

"No. Tressya, you can't condemn me to this place."

"There's nothing I can do for you now."

"You vicious liar. You know there is. You're a spiritweaver."

"I'm bound by the laws of life and death."

She rushed forward. "Shut up. Stop lying. You know you're not. Call me forth. Give me some semblance of existence back."

I shook my head. "You know I can't do that." With the power of the spiritweaver, I could—I had once with the girl spirit, but not for long. Disturbing something as fundamental as life and death came with terrible consequences. No one bothered to teach a lot about the death arts anymore because spiritweaving was so rare and growing rarer every decade, but that was one truth all in Merania knew.

"You filthy whore," she growled. "How much do you really know of spiritweaving?"

I didn't have time to listen to her.

"Perhaps you never learned the part about possession."

That stopped me. I spun to face her.

"That's right." She glided toward me. "You're like a baby, so new and vulnerable." She crooned. "The inexperienced are susceptible to possession by the very people they try to tame."

Maybe that was true; maybe she was trying to scare me. But right now I didn't have time to think about it. I turned and fled out of the tent. The sight that met me made me stumble in shock. I stopped, awestruck at the fabric of magic rippling around the encampment.

Someone bumped me on passing, jolting me back to the fight. Worry shot through me again, and I turned and ran toward the king's tent, surrounded by guards and a handful of Salmun. Nobleman milled out the front in close groups talking. Courtiers, servants, musicians, all wandered around in stunned silence, gazing up at the magical curtain overhead while more dashed about in madness, driven by their fear.

I picked up my steps, making straight for the king's tent, until two guards strode forward and barred my way.

"Let me pass."

"On orders of the Salmun, all are to return to their tents."

I glanced around at the chaotic jumble of people far from their tents. "Maybe you should deal with them first."

One guard glanced at my baldric.

"You know who I am. Let me pass."

"Stand aside," barked the order from behind.

Daelon strode alongside me, taking my hand with no care to who watched. "Come with me."

The two guards didn't budge. "We have our orders."

"Your orders were to calm this disorder and send all those unable to fight to their tents. Now do it." He yelled the last with such ferocity and authority, they jerked. After sharing a look, they rushed away.

Daelon pulled me toward the king's tent. "Thank god you're here. I was worried about you."

"Never be worried about me."

"You won't say that once you see this."

Ice rode over my shoulders. "Andriet?"

"Is inside. He'll want to see you."

The coiled tension in my gut eased on hearing he was all right.

Daelon ripped the tent flap aside and ushered me in. I made three steps forward, then shuddered to a stop. Andriet looked up from his crouch beside his father, with an expression so harrowing it speared me like arrows to my chest. His father's blood covered the floor. The tent was full of the iron tang of it. He covered his father's eyes with his hand, and when he took it away, he left blood smeared across his father's forehead. I swallowed, stuffing my sob deep down and crossed to him, stumbling as the spirit of King Henricus rose behind his son.

I averted my gaze from the spirit as Andriet rushed toward me and swept me into his arms. He held me tight for breaths, saying nothing. Neither did he cry. Only his tight embrace gave his emotions away, that and his expression.

"A blade to the throat. The coward," he whispered into my neck, his moist, hot breath on my skin.

"A claw," I mumbled before I could stop myself.

"What?"

"I'm so sorry, Andriet." It was genuine. I knew this would happen, and instead, I slept the enemy.

I unraveled myself from his tight hold. "They're coming for you next." I spun back to Daelon. "Take him to the Salmun. They must protect him."

"No," Andriet spat. "I'll fight these cowards."

"You can't, Andriet."

"You don't think I have the skill?" His grief and fury blinded him.

"You don't know what you face."

He stepped away. "Neither do you."

"You're the last heir to the Tannard line."

"I don't give a damn what I am. I'll not hide like a coward while those murdering bastards scheme to take my father's throne."

I grabbed Andriet by the elbows, paying little attention to the three councilmen inside the tent. "It's your throne now. Think like a king. If you die, who's left?"

He leaned in close and spoke through gritted teeth. "I told you, I don't give—"

"Andriet," Daelon said, placing a hand on Andriet's arm. "Remember who your friends are. Tressya says these things because she cares a great deal for you. She also speaks sense."

Andriet huffed as he staggered back, but I snagged his hand. "I know this feels unbearable right now. But remember, your enemy wins if you die."

His shoulders slumped as his head sunk sideways and onto Daelon's shoulder, who slipped an arm around his waist. With Cirro and the king dead and war upon us, the time for pretense was long gone. And I was responsible for Andriet's pain twice over, once for Cirro and once for his father. "Take Andriet to his tent. Only the Salmun are to guard him."

I breathed a sigh as Andriet allowed Daelon to guide him away. With them gone, I turned to the king's dead body, avoiding looking the spirit right in the eye, lest he think I could see him. There was little I would learn from questioning him I didn't already know. I spun and marched for the exit, not wanting to think how Tamas had not considered what would happen to me or those I cared for once he unleashed the nightmare. Also not thinking how he'd spared Andriet the same gruesome death, when he could have easily slipped through the campsite and murdered them both.

Outside, I grabbed the first soldier rushing past. "Where's Orphus?"

"The Prelate? I don't know."

I released him and ran on, not knowing where I was heading. That he wasn't at the king's tent drained a horrible feeling through my chest, down into my stomach. I staggered on remembering his ominous words of hours ago. Weak fools breed weak fools. It was the reason Tamas could get so close to the king. The Salmun had already withdrawn their protection? No. It couldn't be true. I glanced up at the magical ripple above our heads. Andriet still had their protection. He was a Tannard. And if what Radnisa said was true, he was the sole survivor under the Salmun's protection capable of inheriting this prophesied power. That was his value to them.

"Keep an eye on the sky," I yelled as I ran, but everyone I

passed stared at me as though I'd gone mad. "The worst will come from the sky," I added, but no one believed me. And why should they? Since when was a war fought in the sky?

A thundering shudder echoed around us. A chorus of shouts and screams followed as I instinctually ducked, looking up to see the ripple of energy above bowing and warping before settling back into place.

Magic. The Razohan weren't magic wielders, but they'd arrived with help. I marched on, continuing my hunt for Orphus as I seethed on all the ways I'd surrendered to my enemy. Disemboweling him was the only way to ease my fury.

I sat with him across from the king as he told lies about the king's councilmen, and I let it happen, knowing his intention was to remove all those faithful to the king, preparing for when he took the king's place.

How clever of him to wait for this moment. The king arrived at the Ashenlands with guards and a few soldiers for show, also missing valuable fighters lost in the trials, but minus his army because he believed the Salmun would protect him. And only a handful of those arrived with the king because a thousand years of peace had made even them complacent it would seem.

"You knew everything," I hissed to myself, but no one was bothered by my curses. I needed to get out of my head, or risk losing my concentration.

With the Salmun's attention on maintaining the magic shield, and the king dead, the hierarchy of power was scrambled. No one seemed capable of preparing a coordinated defense.

The king put all his trust in the Salmun. Had I foolishly done the same?

No, you bloody idiot. I had fallen for him. And thought he'd done the same for me. That's the reason I often found myself lost in my own thoughts, crafting imaginative dreams. Radnisa probably should have given me a stab or two just to bring me back to reality.

"You," I bellowed in my rage at a guard still gaping up at the shield. "Gather some of your men, form a defense around the perimeter of the tents, just inside the shield."

Not recognizing my authority, he frowned at me. Dammit. Where was Daelon? I pushed him in the shoulder. "Are you dumb?"

I spied another guard and hailed him over. "Go to each of the tents and gather everyone with a weapon. There still should be some of those. And don't shy from asking the women to join in."

"But the Salmun—"

"You're going to act as though the shield's not there. I doubt it will last until morning."

To make a prophecy of what I'd said, the thunderous sound raked the shield again, rippling the magic. This time, its color changed from shimmering white to a dirty gray in pockets along its arc.

"See," I bellowed at the men before me.

That seemed to do the trick as they rushed off in different directions, and I could only hope it was to do my bidding and not to go hide somewhere.

"Orphus," I shouted at the top of my lungs, fed up with his absence. Where were the Salmun?

Legends spoke of magic. I'd grown on the stories, but Merania had no magic wielders, so I knew nothing of the craft. I tried to think how it would be used. Perhaps to form a shield, they would need four wizards, each standing at the four quadrants: north, south, east, west. That made sense.

I didn't know which way to head, but the edge of the tent city was the best place to start. I'd made three steps when another attack hit the shield. This time the shield took longer to recover its shimmering brilliance, and I saw glimpses of the stars through the pockets of gray. Staring for longer, I realized the pockets of gray weren't discoloration, but places were the shield thinned.

When dawn broke, I doubted any of us would be alive. I'd faced death numerous times since leaving Merania, but this time, I had enough hatred in my veins to burn any fear away. I headed for the edge of the tents, armed with enough fury to bring down the nightmare if I had to.

When I reached my destination, I froze in horror. Through the milky haze of the Salmun's shield, I spied an approaching army. Dear Mother, none of us were going to see the dawn.

Overhead, another attack released a thunderous clap that crippled the shield. It bowed and warped, shimmering a dullish gray in too many places. It seemed with every relentless attack, our enemies' power grew. How much longer would it hold?

Men now gathered along the perimeter, armed with swords but no shields, because they'd not come here for war. Only the guards and soldiers were suitably attired, but there were not enough of those against the approaching army. I slowed as I neared them, seeing peasant folk amongst them, those who had come to feed and entertain the gathered masses. They brought to the line kitchen knives and hammers and any manner of simple tools they used in their daily lives.

I wanted to stride before them like a good general would, rousing them with encouraging words, but looking at their faces, I didn't have the heart to lie. The pitiable sight they were, I knew for certain we were going to die.

Another raucous noise rose overhead. Everyone gasped and looked to the sky. I counted the pockets of gray where the shield thinned, seeing many more than had arisen the last time I looked. I searched beyond the shield to the stars, and for one horrifying moment, they blinked out. Breaths it took before they reappeared. They didn't disappear, of course. The massive black shape flying above the shield hid them, waiting for its moment to strike.

CHAPTER

THIRTY-NINE

TRESSYA

TAMAS. I rested my hand on the hilt of my sword. This one was for him. The Salmun were the only people capable of dealing with the nightmare, but I would make sure I got my share of his flesh.

I had to find Orphus.

"Hold your ground no matter what. You're Tarragona's only defense if the shield breaks," I yelled at the fearful faces staring out beyond the shield. None of them appeared roused by my brief speech. They were twigs in the wind for the nightmare to pick off once the shield broke. And what manner of other Ashenlands beasts lurked out there, for I was sure the rest of the Razohan would take a form of their choosing now they knew how.

I left our weak defensive line and rushed along the perimeter of the tent city. As I raced, I tried not to look out at

626

the fields beyond the shield to the gathering army. It seemed with every breath I took, more warriors moved to the frontline until they spread across the field. Had the entire north left their lands to fight this war?

Thunderclaps rained overhead as the shield was attacked repeatedly, the reverberating booms making me stumble and lose my footing on the uneven ground. I fell to my knees as the skies turned into a fierce flash of firelight. Laying close to the shield where it reached the ground, I recoiled every time it waved like fabric billowing in the wind from the unrelenting attack, its ends skirting close to my body.

I felt sweaty and weak as my hands tremored and my stomach growled. I would be useless if I didn't hunt down something to eat soon. Already, my body ran on the last of my reserves.

Pushing to my feet, I felt a vibration run through the ground, then up into my body as a weird noise burst across the sky. I looked up to see a ring of clear starlight above my head, no longer hidden above the shield. It took moments for me to realize they'd broken through the shield.

In awe-struck horror, I gaped up at the warping ends of the torn shield until the stars disappeared, covered by a blackness as dense as tar. The nightmare soared through the opening, its massive wings punching outward once it was through. Its span was such that the barb tips of its wings seared across the shield at either end.

My sword will end up in your heart. I would never achieve that while he remained the nightmare. But I doubted he would stay the beast for long. He was the kind of man who would want his enemy to see his face when he made the last strike. It would be my face he looked at when that moment came.

The erupting screams from those around me drove me forward. Andriet. He was all I could think about. I also needed to find Orphus, the only person capable of helping us prevail. For one stricken moment, I didn't know which way to run. It was the nightmare who decided for me. Extending its huge taloned legs, it swiped up the king's tent and shredded it.

I ran like I was the one with wings, abandoning my hunt for Orphus and heading straight for Andriet's tent. It felt like I was running in quicksand, slowed by the bedlam of terrorized people screaming in all directions.

One glance up and I cried in horror when I spied small specks of black pouring in through the hole in the shield. Small as they were, they reminded me of the creature that had latched onto my hip in the pit.

"Mercy on us all," I muttered, then sprinted on. "To the Ashenlands," I bellowed as I ran.

The words sprang from my mouth with no conscious thought. But it was the only rational solution left for us. The beasts were already inside the shield. An army awaited beyond. The Salmun's cursed lands were our only remaining stronghold.

"Flee to the Ashenlands," I yelled, pushing people out of my way as I ran. No one could hear me above the deafening chorus of shouts and screams.

A man rushed past, cutting off my path. A scaly beast clung to his head, covering his entire face. I pulled my sword, but at that moment, someone else crashed into me and sent me stumbling sideways and into someone else.

Behind me came a scream of agony. I spun to find another creature smothering a hapless man on the ground, and for one wasted breath, I froze, thinking of Andriet, then rushed forward and sliced the creature's head clean from its body. To my horror, it transformed back into a man.

One less Razohan to face.

I raced on toward Andriet's tent, but it wasn't long before I noticed the nightmare had disappeared. Which meant one thing. Tamas was here somewhere amongst all of this chaos.

An arc of white flew overhead like a lightning strike, capturing one creature in a brilliant glow of light. Salmun retaliation. At last. The creature ripped through the top of a tent as it fell from the sky. Soon the sky filled with streaks of white crisscrossing through the sky as the Salmun launched their attacks.

Andriet. I forgot the fight and hurried to his tent. Bursting inside, I also found Orphus. And Daelon. Thank the Mother.

"Tressya." Andriet rushed forward and swept me into his arms.

I hugged him back, then pulled from his arms. "We must get to the Ashenlands."

"That's suicide," Daelon said.

"We're dead if we stay here." I turned to Orphus. "I don't know how many of your beasts are now under the control of the Razohan. If we're lucky, they've emptied the Ashenlands. But if we could reach there before we're slaughtered, perhaps we may survive."

"A wise decision, young princess," Orphus replied.

I wanted to shout at him, blaming this chaos on him and his pathetic protection. "They've outsmarted you," I snapped instead, unable to think of fitting words in my haste.

"But not you, it would seem." He continued to cover his face with the hood of his gray cloak.

His reply left me gaping. What did he know?

"Creatures have already penetrated the shield. We need to spread the word. Get everyone to the Ashenlands." I kept my glare on Orphus, hoping it would distract from my guilt. "I believe that's a task for your wizards."

"I'm here for the prince and him alone."

My eyes narrowed at him. "What about the king? Were you there for him?"

"I won't abandon my people," Andriet interrupted.

I dragged my glare from Orphus. "You won't have to. Daelon, alert the guards." What's left of them. But I wouldn't repeat that aloud. "Spread the word. Everyone must make for the Ashenlands."

As Daelon left, I focused on the prince. "Andriet, you stay with me."

"Don't treat me like a child," Andriet snapped.

"I'm not. But you're important."

"What sort of king am I if I leave my people defenseless?"

"An alive king. Don't be heroic, Andriet. Please."

"You must do as the princess asks." Orphus glided up behind him. "I will escort you both."

My gaze flicked over Andriet's shoulder. "No, thanks. Go gather with your kind and work out a way to end this fight."

Orphus allowed the king's death. I was sure of it. Perhaps

the legends were wrong. Maybe the Salmun no longer needed the Tannard line to control whatever this power was.

"I will not abandon you, princess."

"You will do as she says," Andriet snapped.

"The prince has no authority over the Salmun."

Showing more courage than Juel would've shown, I was sure, Andriet spun to face Orphus. "How dare—"

"Stop this," I shouted. "We've got to get away before he finds you," I snapped, then slammed my mouth shut on realizing what had come out.

Both men looked at me.

"Who?"

Ignoring Andriet's question, I grabbed his hand and dragged him toward the tent opening. "Anyone. The Razohan. Your enemy," I babbled.

"And you. Find a way to save our asses," I ordered Orphus over my shoulder. I wasn't sure why I thought he would listen to me, and there was no time to slow and find out if he did.

"And don't make us fight too long in your bloody cursed land," I barked as I tried to drag Andriet away.

"Princess," Orphus said as I was about to disappear out of the tent. "You know where to hide."

I held his gaze; the cave. It *was* his bloody eye that spied me.

"What's he talking about?"

"It doesn't matter."

Andriet tugged on my hand. "I can't leave without Daelon."

I almost growled in frustration. I didn't want Daelon to

die, but Andriet was my priority. Unfortunately, he was going to be a stubborn ass and refuse to come with me.

"Look around you, Andriet," I yelled.

Seeing the carnage for the first time, Andriet stared in wide-eyed horror. It was amazing there were still people alive, equally amazing the shield held—mostly. The winged beasts had found a way in, but the remaining shield kept the army at bay. Should the shield fall, it was our end.

I made the mistake of taking my eyes off Andriet. Too late, I realized the sound I heard beside me was Andriet pulling his sword from its sheath. He raced away before I could grab him.

"Andriet," I shouted, but my voice was lost in the surrounding chaos.

I ran after him, watching in horror as he threw himself on top of a creature mauling a fallen man.

"Andriet," I yelled, pulling my sword. By the time I reached him, his sword sat in the belly of a dead man.

Andriet clutched at his temple. "Do you see that?" he said to no one, staring down at the dead Razohan. "What cursed magic is this?"

"It's no cursed magic. Come." I tried to grab his hand, but he reared forward and yanked his sword from the belly of the man.

"They're men," he shouted. "They're nothing but men. Men we can kill."

"No," I growled, catching hold of his arm and using all my strength to pull him away. "They're more than just men."

Andriet fought against me. Though not Tamas in size

and strength, he was a man all the same, one able to stand against me no matter how hard I tried to yank him away.

"This is where I need to be. I'll not flee to the Ashenlands and leave my people to be slaughtered."

"Noble, Andriet, but it's not smart. The Salmun will defend them."

I caught sight of Daelon's head, bobbing about amongst the fighting.

"Daelon," I yelled.

"Where is he?" Andriet shrieked and ripped himself from my hold.

Curses upon him. He was a bull-headed fool. I rushed after him but skidded to a halt when a shadowed shape loomed in my periphery. I turned in time to see one of those scaly winged beasts flying low above the mayhem, talons extended.

I withdrew my dagger, spared one moment to learn its path, then threw. It impaled deep in the beast's chest. I didn't stop to watch it fall, but sprinted after Andriet, who was already fighting a beast alongside Daelon. By the time I reached them, the creature was dead.

"Daelon," I panted, exhaustion hanging on the fringes of my awareness. "Please, help me."

He nodded, then grabbed Andriet's arm. "Andriet, we have to go."

"The rest of them?"

"I've given the instructions. Everyone will make for the Ashenlands."

"What's left of them," Andriet spat in fury.

I took Andriet's other hand, and between us, Daelon and

I dragged him through the tent city toward the Ashenlands. Of those alive, many were already heading in the same direction. Orphus was nowhere to be seen. The shield remained, but the white streaks of light overhead were gone. That's because the winged were now on the ground. And thankfully, I'd not run into Tamas.

We ran as straight a line as we could toward the Ashenlands. To my relief, everyone we passed did the same, until we had a swarm of people racing after us. I didn't look back, despite the screams and shouts. My goal was to get Andriet inside the Ashenlands. From there, I would work out what to do.

"What do we do?" Andriet panted as we neared the shield.

I had no idea. "Just keep running." The Salmun would protect us. As the only alternative, I had to believe it for now.

Feeling Andriet and Daelon falter beside me, fearful of touching the shield, I increased my pace. And sure enough, within feet of touching the shield, it shimmered, then winked out, clearing our path. In the starlight, I could see the stalks of the dead trees only paces away. Overhead, I heard the flapping of wings.

"Run," I shouted, even though I felt lethargy tug at my legs. "Take my hand," I yelled at Andriet. "Hold Daelon's hand. We can't be separated."

I wasn't sure if this would work.

We broke the line, billowing dust into our throat as we charged forward. "Keep going," I cried, gripping tight to Andriet's hand. "Don't let go of Daelon." Panic was making me speak.

I slammed through the invisible illusion of the Ashen-lands and stumbled over the soft loamy ground to smack into a tree. Hearing the *oomph* beside me, I almost laughed. It had worked.

"Andriet," I gasped, pulling myself to my knees. "Is Daelon with you?"

"I'm here," came a voice a little way off.

We did it. There were others around us. Some had made it through without slamming into trunks, tripping over roots or their own feet.

"Is everyone all right?" I shouted as I dragged myself to my feet, then swayed once and hit the tree with my shoulder.

Give me strength to last until morning.

Andriet steadied me. "Are you all right?"

I nodded.

"I thought we'd end up split," Andriet said, steadying me with his hand.

"We're not in the trials now."

"Wow," Daelon breathed as he came over. "This is what it looks like."

"It's a deadly place, so don't sound so impressed. Those creatures we've been fighting in camp, there's more of those and they're much worse."

"Are we any safer in here?" a woman asked to my left.

I glanced around me, struggling to see anyone in the darkness. I couldn't count all the groans and whimpers, but it sounded less than I would've liked, but better than none. "How many of you have weapons?"

"I do," came a male voice from further away. "It's not

much, but I'll put it through the head of anything that comes at me."

"We stay together." *Curses*, I didn't have a plan beyond this. Hiding here would not win us a war, but it gave us a better chance than being picked off in the open. Maybe now we'd simply be picked off in the dark.

"And then what?" came another voice from the gloom.

"The Salmun are dealing with it. We just need to endure until they arrive." If they arrive. Which they would. And hopefully before Tamas and his lethal beasts did.

"I know the two of you have only entered three times, but did you come across anywhere we could hide? You know, some place that forms a natural defense?" Daelon asked.

"It all looks like this," Andriet said.

In the darkness, our voices sounded dismembered. I never saw the next man to speak. "I ended up on the side of a mountain the second time around. I couldn't tell you where that was. Fought something so ugly my heart came close to seizing."

I turned around and stepped away from the group, dredging up my soul word and harnessing the power it gave me.

"We should stick close to each other," Andriet said.

"Just give me a minute. I'm not going far," I said.

Inhaling deeply, I exhaled slowly through my nose, calming the erratic thoughts in my head as I walked away. I projected the call, the strength of my soul word amplifying it. The sound of my heart filled my ears, but with another deep breath, it slowed. I dredged up my soul word and harnessed its power to amplify the call.

On a gentle breeze filled with the smell of fresh earth and a hint of decay came a grumpy voice. "You're a filthy liar and a cheat."

I cracked an eye, then whispered. "Hello, Tulin."

"Here you are again, dragging a scraggly band behind you. You're a sorry lot, by the looks of you. So what's it this time, girlie? You promised me you wouldn't—"

"Tulin." I tried to keep my voice to a whisper. Behind me, everyone was arguing over what we should do next, which helped drown out Tulin's and my conversation. "Please, I need you to guide us to the cave. Remember the one with the special rock?"

"Fickle. That's what you are. You would promise me my life back only to take it the moment you granted it. And here I am again. I didn't ask to come here."

"I'm sorry, I really am."

"I got my own things to do, woman. I ain't interested in—"

"You're a spirit, Tulin. You've got nothing to do."

He folded his arms, lifting his chin as he turned away.

"Tressya," Andriet called.

"Give me a minute," I replied, not looking over my shoulder. I took a step closer to Tulin. "I need you to guide us to the cave."

"Of course you do. And that's the start. You'll have me—"

"Tulin. Please, the king's dead. The armies of the north have overrun us. That man behind me is the prince. The last of the Tannard line. We need the shelter of the cave."

Tulin craned his head, as though he were trying to look over my shoulder to glimpse the prince. "War's a bloody horrible business, but what's it got to do with me? The kings of the south did nothing good for my people. We're stuck here because of their bloody wizard pets. Why should I help you?"

"Tulin, please. Prince Andriet is my friend."

"Do you know how many friends I watched die at the hand of the king's men? How many of our wives and daughters they took for themselves? How many they slaughtered for fun? Perhaps the northerners would do a better job. And if they don't, why does a spirit of the Ashenlands care?"

I fisted my hands, my only outward sign of my anger. "You know what I'll do."

"We're hoping for some guidance here, Tressya," came Andriet again.

"Yes. I'm almost done."

"Aye. Why would I think you'd be any different from them southerners?"

I groaned. "I don't want to make you do this, but you'll leave me with no choice."

A woman screamed, followed swiftly by a man's cry. I spun, seeing only faint movement in the darkness. Tulin's glow ruined my night vision.

I pulled out my sword and rushed back to join everyone. "Andriet."

"Tressya, here."

"*Aetherius*," I breathed, feeling a rush of power flow through my body. "Give me light, Tulin," I shouted, not caring how crazy I sounded to everyone else.

Tulin appeared beside me, illuminating the forest and revealing the terrible creatures that had found us. No one else could see Tulin's light; each was floundering helplessly in the dark as the human-sized creatures fell from the canopy above, slaughtering people without hesitation. Frantic cries filled the air.

I shouted for everyone to follow my voice as I hurried to reach Andriet's side and pushed him behind the tree.

"Please, Tulin, you have to help us."

"What's going on, Tressya?" Andriet shouted, trying to be heard over the frantic, frightened cries. "Who's Tulin?"

"There are six of them." I pushed Andriet behind the tree. "Stay close to the tree," I commanded him. "Daelon, stay with him."

Andriet squeezed my hand so tightly I thought my bones would break. "Where are you going? What are you doing?"

I wrenched my hand from his. "Just stay there."

None of them could see their enemy. There were six of them, none with bright glowing eyes, so Tulin's light would not save us.

When I looked around, I saw carnage. With so few of us still standing, a rage swelled in my chest.

I called on my soul word, then shouted, "Come forth," and dragged Tulin across the veil, his glowing body and all.

The wisps of his lower half took the form of short, stubby legs, bowing at the knees. His eyes glistened with a burning fury as he glared at me.

"Stars above, what's that?" Andriet gasped, shielding his eyes from the sudden glow.

"Destroy them." I was too desperate to feel even a twinge of guilt for betraying Tulin by taking away his free will.

Tulin descended on the creatures. He had no weapons to

defend himself, but the dead couldn't die. Blade-sharp teeth, arrow-strong claws, nothing they used on Tulin worked. But he had enough of a corporeal body to fight back. It was the perfect distraction.

"Follow me," I yelled to those still alive. Orphus had said I knew where to hide, meaning my desire to find the cave would lead me there. At least, I hoped that's what he meant.

"Hey," someone yelled. "There are others."

I followed his gaze to find more survivors stumbling toward us through the forest, drawn by Tulin's light, more helpless joining our surviving few. To my relief, there were soldiers and guards among them, bringing valuable weapons.

"Hurry," I shouted, waving the new arrivals forward, but they remained dazed by the sight of Tulin tussling with the creatures, defying what was real as he floated up into the trees to reach those trying to escape.

I grabbed Andriet's hand and dragged him away. "There's a cave further in," I told everyone. "We'll use it as a fortress."

To my relief, Andriet kept pace with me. I dared one glance over my shoulder to see the band of survivors and our new arrivals hurrying along behind.

I felt nothing within, no tug, no sense of familiarity; nor was I confident this was the right way. But I had to believe Orphus said what he said because he believed I would find the cave, and that soon the Salmun would come. And if we survived this, I would have to send Tulin back across the divide. But right now, it was more important that we escaped, leaving him to fight the beasts.

Our pace slowed as we left Tulin's guiding light behind and were plunged back into darkness. With every jarring tread of my feet, my body screamed in exhaustion. After a while, I found I was leaning on Andriet more than I should. He said nothing about it but slung his arm around my waist and supported me over most of the exposed roots.

"What was that thing?" he said after a time. "I encountered nothing like that when I entered."

"Luck was on my side. He turned up and guided me to the cave."

"I don't understand how you know where you're going," Daelon said from the other side of Andriet. "I can barely see my feet. All around us, it looks the same."

"Luck will be on our side," was all I could say.

I wasn't confident about that but refused to give in to my fearful thoughts. Then something hit me in the back of the shoulders, ripping me from Andriet's hold and sending me to my knees.

Madness erupted. And this time it wasn't beasts we faced, but men.

CHAPTER

FORTY

TRESSYA

IT WAS as though the darkness birthed our enemy. They had sneaked upon us, using our noisy, frantic escape to conceal their approach. The only warning was a sharp war cry as they attacked from the rear.

Some distance behind us came a strangled cry followed by the sounds of a struggle. Then, silence. I reached for Andriet and found his hands searching for me in the darkness. The air filled with whimpers of fear. Facing the enemy blind was a poison to my sanity. Fear seeped from the survivors and hung over my shoulders like a wool cloak. In my mind's eye, hands with fingers like spears dug into my neck. I resisted the urge to swat away the phantom hands. So, when Andriet touched my arm, I jerked with a gasp, then fell backward over roots.

"It's all right," he leaned over me.

I grasped his offered hand, and he pulled me to my feet. Once upright, I drew Andriet close and reached up on tiptoes to pull his head down, so I could whisper in his ear, "No one can see who you are," as long as the Razohan stayed in human form. "I'm going to call you Melak."

"I hate that you're treating me any more special than—"

"Listen to her," Daelon snapped, having moved close beside us.

Another cry tore through the night behind us, then fell silent. They were picking us off one by one, like a predator toying with its prey. The darkness was near absolute. We stood no chance against an invisible enemy.

I kept a firm hand on Andriet's neck, wanting to convey more in secret. With people crying, babbling in fear, and talking incoherently to themselves, it was unlikely anyone would overhear even if I yelled. Using my free hand, I drew Daelon close, including him in my plan. "We have to separate from the rest and make our way to the cave."

"No," Andriet's response was fierce. "Not everyone here are fighters, which makes them vulnerable."

"Our enemy doesn't care about the vulnerable. They only care about you."

He clamped a heavy hand on my shoulder. "You want to use them as a distraction while we escape?" His tone was indignant.

"I don't claim to be noble," I replied with equal force. "We need to win by outsmarting them."

"There's no victory if my people die."

While such sentiment made him the perfect king, I wanted to kick this honorable side of him into the night.

"There's definitely no victory if you're dead," my voice cut through the air like a blade.

"She's right, Andriet."

This time, Andriet shouted when the next cry rang out. I jumped, losing my grip on him as I stumbled back, nearly losing my footing in the dark again. With the gentle eddy of wind beside me, I knew what Andriet planned, but I was too slow to stop him. The frustrating ass, who deserved to be king more than anyone else I'd ever known, launched away.

"Daelon," I cried, hoping he would be swifter than me at restraining Andriet.

"Andriet," Daelon cried out, and I cringed at the sound of his name.

Our shouts unleashed a torrent of fighters. I was sure most of northerners we'd seen in the fields had now also joined the fight. We were no longer battling only the Razohan. The night thickened with the bellowing of madmen and the sounds of battle. Metal clashed, women screamed, and the gruesome sounds of slow, agonizing deaths made my heart pound so hard, I struggled to breathe.

Daelon disappeared, charging back toward the fight, crying Andriet's name, and I swallowed a lump of frustration. Now our enemy would know their prize was among our pitiful party.

Sweet Mother, we didn't stand a chance.

I dove into my mind, wrenching my soul word forth, knowing our survival hinged on the dead. Damn the consequences; I would summon all the dead of the Ashenlands if it secured our victory.

Aetherius. With just one thought, the might of my soul

word surged through my chest, infusing me with power so immense I felt on the verge of splintering apart.

Discipline. Clenching my fists, my hands trembled under the force of my spiritweaver power. Closing my eyes to find my calming breaths, I focused inward into the abyss where my calm resided. There, I commanded death itself to rise. With ferocity, I shouted my command. The power coursed through my chest with a burning intensity, leaving a throbbing ache behind.

Upon opening my eyes, a vast stream of spirits illuminated the forest, piercing the veil. Scores of them, an invincible army, emerged through the trees. However, summoning the dead to walk among the living was deeply wrong, yet I had no choice. I vowed to restore the balance once victorious. In the meantime, I could only hope I hadn't unleashed a terrible curse.

"It's time to seek your revenge," I shouted, gesturing towards the battle. "Save Prince Andriet. Destroy your enemy. We must win."

Forcing the spirits to fight my war, against those not responsible for their deaths, was a grievous act. I pushed the thought aside. Guilt could wait until after our victory.

They advanced, unable to resist my command, illuminating their path. Soon, the fighters were overwhelmed, while overhead, bright lights flared. The Ashenlands now blazed with streaks of white, filling the air with a strange, sweet smell. Magic. The Salmun had arrived. Curse their late arrival. I wouldn't have summoned the dead had they come sooner.

Amidst streaks of white, I glimpsed the chaos of battle.

The forest floor, a perilous battlefield, saw fighters colliding with trees and stumbling over uneven terrain, entangled by thick undergrowth. The dead swarmed over them like ants. I searched for Andriet amid the tumult, but too many combatants cluttered the scene.

A shimmering haze of white-blue rose like a barricade, sparking where the Salmun's white magic clashed. I inhaled sharply. The Razohan's magic wielders.

Mercy on our souls, where was Andriet?

About to join the fray, an unseen force sent me tumbling over a root, crashing onto my back, the impact driving the breath from my lungs. I screamed in sudden agony, then groaned as I rolled onto my knees, my left arm throbbing painfully from shoulder to fingertips. Despite the pain, I foolishly tried to use it to rise, but it collapsed beneath me. Agony flared as I fell forward, face meeting dirt.

Vulnerable on the ground, I managed to rise to my knees, then froze, feeling a prickling sensation across my shoulders. I sprang up, sword ready, only to face a tall, willowy woman in a dark cloak, thick woven jacket, pants, and long leather boots. Her black hair, streaked with white like the Salmun's magic, flowed loosely over her shoulders, framing a still-beautiful aged face. Her eyes, blood-colored, held no visible threat except their hue.

"I had expected someone else." Power laced each word she spoke. "I should've known he wouldn't risk so much for something so fleeting as a beautiful face. That you're nothing special makes me believe the worst. I fear this is deeper than lust."

I braced for more.

"So young," she advanced, and I gripped my sword tighter, useless as it was against magic. "I would spare you, if not for your allegiance to my enemy and the Sistern blood running through your veins."

"I hope to see you suffer for yours," I countered, relying on the dead as my only hope, but spiritweaving took all my concentration. I couldn't deal with her and call the dead to my aid.

"Yes, I see why he's lost his senses for you, but to risk the fates of so many for one woman."

"Tamas?"

Her mouth tightened. "He revealed his name?"

"I also know his face. Easier to find my enemy."

"If only he thought the same. Kinder to have ended you on the ship. Tamas is a naïve fool, led by his heart."

I had thought I understood his mercy, but betrayal twisted everything. "I'm sure he regrets it now. Once I land a dagger through his eye, he'll regret it even more."

"You wouldn't have lasted this long if he regretted it."

"You say that because you don't know me," I tightened my grip. "He bit me, you know?"

She sighed, pressing fingers to her brow. "The fool. But things have turned out as they have."

Dropping her hand, she sighed. "I hold no ill will towards you, disciple, but I can't let you live." She raised her arms, and a spark of bluish light formed between her palms.

"Wait." Dear Mother. I had no defense against magic. "Will you at least tell me why I have to die?"

Aetherius. My soul word surfaced beneath my skin as if eager to do my bidding.

"Because you're a disciple, child. I would bear any other, but the Sistern are our enemies, as much as the Razohan are yours."

"I'm an unfaithful disciple." I loathed to plead for my life, but if I could trick, beg, or fight my way out of this, for Andriet's sake, I would.

"There's no such thing."

"Oh really, then you know less about the Sistern than you think."

The hard lines around her mouth softened. "Such courage. Yes, that trait in a woman is his greatest weakness. I say from my heart it's a shame you must die."

Distracted by the clash of swords close by, I glanced over my shoulder. I knew better than to take my eyes off my enemy, but I couldn't shrug my fear for Andriet.

A sharp pain pierced my side, propelling me backward to crash against the trunk of a tree. In the process, I lost my sword. I rolled to the side in search of my weapon, when suddenly, tingles erupted around the bite mark. Then, a different sensation burgeoned deep within, akin to a pull on my heart. This feeling intensified, transforming into a heavy burden. A cry welled up in my throat as immense fear gripped me, and a sense of desperation seized my throat.

"Romelda," came a sharp shout. And for a moment I thought I'd yelled the name.

Hearing his voice split me in two. My heart should burn with fury, not weep. I tried to pick myself up from my position slumped at the foot of the tree, but whatever magic Romelda had thrown at me smarted worse than a blade through my gut.

Tamas landed in front of me, sparing me one look. When our eyes met, I saw his silent plea. I also saw his sorrow and felt the pain of his heart, coring straight through me. His gaze then raked my body. On seeing the wound at my side, his eyes blazed like fire. I felt on fire, an unexplainable fury boiling within me. He turned back to Romelda, using his body as a shield against her attack.

"Stand aside, Tamas. You know it must be done."

"You made me a promise," he growled.

"Don't be a fool, young Razohan. She must die along with the last of the Tannard line."

"You promised me." His voice faltered.

"I bear the mark of one who swore the oath. You know where my allegiance lies. My life is in service to the Bone Throne. I won't turn from my duty because you have grown weak."

"You were never going to save her." Betrayal hardened his voice.

He made her promise to spare me. The understanding embraced my heart. No. I clenched my fists and teeth, forcing iron into my will. Don't be this weak. Love had no part in any war.

"You bit her, Tamas. There's no greater show of stupidity than that."

"Don't make me choose, Romelda. You won't like my choice."

"After all my years of servitude, you think I would allow you to ruin everything when we are so close?" Her voice thrummed with the power in her veins.

"There's another way."

"There is no other way, Tamas," she shouted.

"Please, just listen to me."

In his voice, I heard his respect for her. But this was a plea. Maybe not even a nightmare could withstand her power.

"There is too much at risk. Now stand aside."

For long moments Tamas remained like stone, saying nothing. From behind, I watched his head sink, dragging his shoulders into a slump. I could imagine the betrayal he felt, the fight he would have to win in his mind before he could speak.

"I won't move. I can't." The last sentence fractured my heart. I squeezed my eyes closed, feeling the moisture on my eyelashes dampening my cheeks.

"You know what she is?" Romelda growled.

"I do. I heard what the augur said, as did you. I asked if you still believed in me."

With a frown, I looked from Romelda to him and back.

"What are you talking about?" Romelda said. Her eyes widened, then she stared at me. "Then she has to die."

"No," Tamas shouted. "There's another—"

I let out a cry as his body stiffened. His voice caught in his throat, and his sword slipped from his grasp, plunging into the ground beside his feet.

"You'll rage. But in the end, young Razohan, you'll see my wisdom."

Slowly, Tamas sank to his knees before me. Dear Mother, this was it. My soul word fled me. I spun, searching for my sword, and spied it wedged in the groove of a large root. I would have to climb over too many obstacles to reach it.

"Please, Romelda," Tamas forced through whatever seizure of magic Romelda placed upon him. "I beg you. Don't kill her. I can't lose her."

"This moment is too vital to risk on something as fragile and unpredictable as love."

My side screamed as I heaved myself over the root I leaned against, then I dragged my exhausted, wounded body across the ground, reaching for my sword while searching for the power inside of me.

"Don't take this personally, child. But you're too dangerous to keep alive."

Romelda pursued me. She had left Tamas on his knees, his back to me, sparing him the sight of my impending demise. The small shudders of his body were the only resistance he could muster against her crippling magic.

"Please, Romelda, I beg you," he cried, thrashing his head from side to side. "I've pledged my life to her."

Romelda paused a moment, closing her eyes as she gently shook her head. "I know about that, young fool." She returned her attention to me. "Time will heal that wound. When she's dead, you'll be free again."

Tamas roared, but Romelda ignored him.

"Come to me," I cried, near delirious with a conflicting mix of fear and fury. The two emotions seamed together, infusing my pain-soaked body with the clarity of mind I needed to abandon my sword and dive for my dagger, still sheathed at my baldric.

"Spirits," I yelled as I threw the dagger.

To my horror, a bright blaze of blue light flowed from Romelda's palms and seized the dagger mid-air. I shielded my eyes with my forearm. Then as the brilliance faded, I pulled my arm away and uttered a cry, seeing Romelda untouched.

"For Tamas's sake, and your own, I'll make this fast," she said, already readying her next strike. The glow of her magic reflected off her face, sharpening her features into cruel looking arrows and tainting her bloodstained eyes a deep purple.

I tensed, preparing for the impact as a streak of white arced overhead, striking the light in Romelda's hands. The force of the collision hurled her backward. Not pausing to check if she remained down, I lunged for my sword, resolved to drive it through her heart before she had the chance to incinerate me. When I spun around, I saw Tamas on his feet, freed from her magic.

We stared at each other, my sword ready to strike while Tamas remained still and weaponless, his arms splayed to either side as if offering himself up to my attack. Too many moments passed with neither of us speaking while the surrounding forest filled with the cries of the dying and magic marred the night sky with lethal brilliance.

The thought of Andriet was never far from my head, but Tamas was the one to cast a spell. Not even the pain at my side could draw my attention from him. An ache greater than any physical pain destroyed my strength to keep fighting. My body had yet to forget our moment together. It never would. Neither would my heart. How could I hold my conflicting desires and stay sane?

"It wasn't meant to go like this," he said.

"I want to believe you." More than anything, I wanted to believe in Tamas. I wanted there to be an us.

But his people and my people were killing each other in a war of beliefs and ideals. How could there be unity?

"We can decide what we are to each other. Enemies or allies. It's up to us, Tressya. No one else."

My feet moved the same time his did, cautiously closing the distance between us.

"Andriet," Daelon cried.

The shrill cry rushed up my spine. I spun. What I saw turned me to stone. In that moment, the Mother's training failed me. Daelon fell to his knees beside Andriet, placing his hands around the sword embedded in Andriet's stomach.

"Andriet," I screamed. No.

My will was strong, but not strong enough to hold back death. Freed from the horror that had seized my body, I tried to rush to Andriet's side, but Tamas wrapped an arm around my waist and held me firm against him.

"No, Tressya. There's too many fighters. They'll cut you down."

"No," I whimpered, seeing the truth in what he said. They swarmed over us like ants. Some had even turned to beasts. But the spirits were equally devastating. The war was not won. We did have a chance.

I struggled in his arms. "Let me go." I funneled all my fury into my shout.

"I can't let you go." He buried his face in my neck. "You should know that."

"No." This time my voice held venom. "Let me go, Tamas,"

I screamed, kicking out with my legs and failing in his arms. "Andriet," I cried, feeling my powerlessness in Tamas's arms, feeling his iron grip and knowing he would never let me go.

There was an eddy of wind, a wet sound I knew too well. Then Tamas jerked backward, taking me with him as he fell. I landed across his torso, my legs tangled at a painful angle, my wounded side screaming. Half on my side, I felt a slippery wetness ooze across my cheek and smelt the iron tang of blood.

"Tamas?" I jerked up, ignoring my screaming side.

A dagger lodged in his chest, dangerously close to his heart.

"No! Tamas." I placed my palm over the wound, trying to stem the flow. In no time, the slimy warmth of his blood coated my hands.

"Tressya, come on." Daelon's words were an echo, bouncing off the walls in my head. "The Salmun are here. They'll guide us to the cave."

No! This was my curse for what I'd done: my fate was to lose the man I had abandoned my duty to be with—the man I loved.

I shook my head as I stared into eyes I'd first seen less than two days ago, but already they were my most cherished sight. He reached up and pressed his hand to my cheek. "You should go." His voice was strong, determined.

"Tressya. Andriet needs us."

"I can't," I whispered, my voice wobbling through my tears. "You wouldn't leave me, so why expect me to leave you?"

"Tressya," Daelon shouted.

"Go," I yelled over my shoulder, anger searing up my throat. "I'll catch you up."

"Leave with the Salmun. Let them protect you," Tamas said.

I shook my head. Now he was slipping from me, I knew without a doubt what I wanted.

"Andriet needs you."

"You need me more." *I need you more.*

"Shh," Tamas crooned, patting my hair. "I promise not to die."

"I don't trust your promises. You're saying it to make me leave. You've manipulated me from the start. This time I don't believe you." I wiped a tear. "You bit me because you wanted to always find me. But did you ever think about me. That I may want to always find you." *Always want to be with you.*

He huffed a laugh, then grimaced in pain.

"Don't do that," I barked. "You'll make the blood flow faster."

I pulled his hand from my cheek and clasped it tight in mine.

"I never dreamed I would be privileged enough to deserve your tears." He wiped one from my cheek with his thumb. "I wish it had turned out differently. I had so many plans for us."

"Shut up. You still have plans. You can still make them happen. With me, Tamas. We can make them happen together. You said so yourself."

He smiled, but it failed to convince me. "I'll see."

I dropped his hand and seized his cheeks between my

palms. "Don't you dare give in. You said we could choose what we would be to each other. I choose allies. Do you hear me?"

"Only allies. I had hoped for more."

I could feel my panic slipping through my vicious grip. I closed my eyes, fighting surrender. Then I opened them and stared down at him. "Of course we're more. We're so much more it hurts."

The long cry of agony sounded close. I looked up, facing the devastation both the spirits and northerners wrought on each other. So much death for power.

"Tressya." The feather light touch of Tamas's fingers tickled my chin. "I want you to go."

"And leave you to die alone," I sobbed.

"Listen." He gently tugged on my braid that had fallen over my shoulder. "I need to change into the Huungardred beast. I must do it before I'm too weak. It's the only way. I want you to be long gone before then."

I closed my eyes as I kissed the finger he ran across my lips. This simple touch, I wanted to remember the most. "You stupid fool, I've seen your beast, and I'm not afraid."

"That's not it." He grimaced as talking turned to pain.

Because you don't want me to see you die. "I won't leave you alone."

"Stubborn, little princess."

I pressed my fingers against his lips. "Don't talk." My fate was to sit helplessly beside him and watch him die. "Promise me you'll live."

"The Nazeen won't let me die."

"If you do, I'll drag your spirit back from the veil and

make you my slave."

His chuckle made him cough, which oozed more blood from his wound.

I bit back a sob. "Don't do that."

"Tressya, you need to do as I say. You need to survive."

"So do you."

"Listen." He snaked a hand around my neck pulling me closer. "It's time I told you the reason I spared you. I didn't kill you because I suspected you were more than you seemed."

I feathered my fingers over his lips. "Don't talk."

He pulled them away. "Your bloodborn, Tressya. I don't know how, but I'm certain you are. We're the same, you and I. We're more than partners. We are one."

"I don't understand you."

"You will soon enough." He feebly pushed me away. "Go, now. You're the only one who can prevent the Salmun from winning."

I shook my head.

"You're killing me by staying."

If there were words to make me leave, that was it.

"Andriet needs you."

At this moment, Andriet was far from my mind. But he was my dear friend, and I couldn't abandon him too. War gave us nothing but grief. At the end, would I care who was the victor when everyone I loved had died?

I kissed him gently, fearful of hurting him, but he seized my wrists, pulling me closer and driving our kiss with a suffocating fever. We swallowed my tears, then he broke our kiss and licked the tears on my chin.

"Is there a word stronger than love?" he asked.

I didn't hesitate. "Yes. It's lodged in here." I pressed one hand over my heart, my other hand gently over his, my fingers oozing through his blood. "It doesn't need a name, neither does it need to be spoken."

I closed my eyes. "Promise me. Promise me I'll see you again."

"I promise," he said.

I desperately required the Mother's teachings, needing discipline more than ever to force my legs to run. Leaving Tamas lying in his own blood, I fled, trailing my devastation behind me. I'd left a piece of my heart in Merania, but now, it felt as though I'd torn out the entire thing, leaving it to bleed out over Tamas. My streaming tears blinded my path. I staggered, stumbled, and fell to my knees three times, finding it harder to rise with each fall.

It didn't take me long to leave the spirits' light behind. At that point, I thought I would plunge into darkness and run aimlessly in circles looking for the cave, but it seemed the Salmun had anticipated my need. A faint shimmering light appeared through the trees ahead, showing me the way.

I ran until my legs felt like stone. Then I spied the looming pillars of the outer rocks, rising like Ashenlands beasts to guard the entrance to the cave. I hurried through, thinking I would stumble into darkness, but the light continued, guiding me through the maze to the cave entrance.

When I heard a low moanful wail, I staggered to a halt. I swallowed and pushed forward, marching, then running on the downward slope of the cave floor until I stumbled out into the cavernous chamber, alight with a mysterious glow of the Salmun's magic. Atop stakes of wood blazed balls of light, casting an eerie glow on the ancient etchings around the chamber.

Five Salmun were present, as well as a group of soldiers and noblemen. My gaze flittered over them before settling on Daelon and Andriet. It had been Daclon's cry I heard at the entrance. He was kneeling beside Andriet, imploring the Salmun to save his life. His pleas filled the chamber, resonating like a chorus of a thousand voices.

Lethargy weighed on my body, turning my legs to lead. The burden of my tortured heart, which I'd dragged along since leaving Tamas, prevented me from moving closer. No agony was greater than that which cleaved the soul. I was convinced my heart had ceased beating, overwhelmed by all the death.

I expelled hard breaths through my nose, then compelled my feet to move toward Daelon. Crouching down, I avoided looking at Andriet because, for once, I wasn't strong enough to confront the truth. Soon, his spirit would rise, and I wasn't prepared to witness it.

I snatched my hands back from touching Daelon, on spying Tamas's blood, turning my hands red.

"The last Tarragona heir is dead," said a nobleman from beside me.

"What does that mean for the prophecy?" said another.

"It means no Tannard will inherit the Etherweave. Those bloody northerners have seen to it. We should've stayed in the battle. Let them slaughter us as fighters, not cowards hiding in a cave." The man's voice rose in panic.

"You fled with the rest of us. No one made you come," grouched another.

No women or common folk stood amongst them. Did this mean all the women and common folk had already died, or did these noblemen and soldiers flee to save their own lives, leaving the more vulnerable behind? Not one of them knew how hard Andriet fought to save them all.

"All is well." Orphus's voice rang out in the cave.

Upon hearing his voice, I glanced up. His face was hooded, concealing where his gaze lingered as the crowd of survivors parted, allowing him to pass through.

"The northerners are defeated," he intoned with a finality that made everyone present murmur in confusion and doubt. "The spirits of the Ashenlands saw to our victory."

Even concealed beneath his hood, I knew he was looking at me. Flanking the survivors, the rest of the Salmun moved to circle Andriet, Daelon, and me.

"But we've lost the last Tannard heir to the throne and no way of claiming the Etherweave. We're as good as dead without an heir. The northerners will simply regroup and attack with more force, and we'll have nothing to defend ourselves with now."

"The Salmun have proved themselves weak in defense of Tarragona."

Fear bred dissent.

"Calm yourselves," Orphus intoned, showing no impatience toward the noblemen's accusations. "Everything has transpired as it should. We have lost nothing."

"How can you say that?"

Gradually rising to my feet, I eyed the hooded figures of the Salmun, feeling a sickness churn in my battered stomach that stemmed from something other than hunger.

"Because an heir to the Tannard line still lives."

"What?" A man surged forward. "Who?"

In unison, the Salmun pulled back their hoods. Gasps wove through the cave like ripples on a pond. There was little distinguishing each of them, except the weird ink markings on their faces and scalps.

Daelon stood up beside me and took my hand. In his eyes, I saw trepidation; in mine, he would've seen fear. My heart thudded so loudly, it surprised me that the cave ceiling remained intact.

"The Etherweave within the rock responded to her touch," Orphus continued, not taking his eyes from me.

"How can that be?" one cried.

"A bloodborn," snapped someone.

"No, she is not bloodborn, but of our line — a sole surviving heir of the Levenian line." He scanned the cavern, deliberately meeting each gaze before refocusing on me. "I command you all to bow before your queen," he declared, then raised his arms high. "This marks a new beginning for the House of Tannard."

In shock, I watched as the Salmun knelt before me. A ripple of unease emanated from the other survivors. Then, exchanging looks with one another, they gradually followed the Salmun's lead, bowing down one by one.

'You are of my making'. The words of the Mother echoed through my head.

Mother, what have you done to me?

661

Author's' Note

The idea for this book began with a history podcast about Katherine of Aragon. For those who may not know, she was the first wife of Henry VIII, sent from Spain to marry his brother, Arthur. However, Arthur died shortly after their marriage, leaving Katherine in a state of limbo. She then became an ambassador for England before eventually marrying Henry.

Becoming an ambassador in the 1500s was quite an achievement for a woman, but naturally, I wasn't going to construct a story around something as tame as that.

Tressya had to be more than just an ambassador; her betrothed had to be an ass, and magic was an absolute necessity. The Unbroken Queen was born.

If you'd like to stay ahead of everyone else and keep up-to-date with my new releases, as well as receive bonus good-ies, you can sign up for my newsletter here.

About the Author

When I wasn't riding a camel through the Rajasthani desert, white water rafting the rapids on the Zambezi, bungee jumping off the Victoria Falls bridge or hiking the peeks in Pakistan, I was piloting a twin prop into remote aboriginal communities in northern Western Australia or staring down a microscope in a laboratory.

Now somewhat tamed, the microscope has morphed into a computer and I spend more time plotting dire situations for my protagonists than being in them myself.

I am the author of books that won't stay normal.

Also by Terina Adams

Ruinous Lies

Traitor in the Shadows

Labyrinth of Dreams

Thief of Hearts

Hells Gate series

Dark moon

Rising moon

White moon

Blue Moon

Dominus Trilogy

Dominus

Califax

Fated Chaos

Trial by Blood

Black Arcana

Sinner's Game

Deviant's Curse

Defiler's Soul

Manufactured by Amazon.com.au
Sydney, New South Wales, Australia

15087429R00406